365 Stories for Girls

PaRragon

Bath • New York • Singapore • Hong Kong • Cologne • Delhi
Melbourne • Amsterdam • Johannesburg • Shenzhen

Winnie the Pooh characters are based on the 'Winnie the Pooh' works by A. A. Milne and E. H. Shepard.
The movie THE PRINCESS AND THE FROG Copyright © 2009 Disney, story inspired in part by the book THE FROG PRINCESS
by E.D. Baker Copyright © 2002, published by Bloomsbury Publishing, Inc.
101 Dalmatians is based on the book *The Hundred and One Dalmatians* by Dodie Smith, published by The Viking Press.
The Aristocats is based on the book by Thomas Rowe.
The term 'Omnidroid' used by permission of Lucasfilm Ltd (The Incredibles).
Little Einsteins © The Baby Einstein Company, LLC. All Rights Reserved. Little Einsteins is a trademark of The Baby Einstein
Company, LLC. EINSTEIN is a trademark of The Hebrew University of Jerusalem.
The Great Mouse Detective is based on the *Basil of Baker Street* book series by Eve Titus and Paul Galdone.
The Rescuers and *The Rescuers Down Under* feature characters from the Disney film suggested by the books by Margery Sharp,
The Rescuers and Miss Bianca, published by Little, Brown and Company. Copyright © 2010 Disney/Pixar.
The Jungle Book is based on the Mowgli Stories in *The Jungle Book* and *The Second Jungle Book* by Rudyard Kipling.
Visit www.disneyfairies.com

This edition published by Parragon in 2012

Parragon
Queen Street House
4 Queen Street
Bath BA1 1HE, UK
www.parragon.com

Copyright © 2012 Disney Enterprises, Inc.
Copyright © 2012 Disney/Pixar

ISBN 978-1-4454-6479-4

Printed in China

101 DALMATIANS

New Year's Day

It was the first day of the new year, and Pongo and Perdita were out for a walk with their pets, Roger and Anita. The morning fog was beginning to part, and the air was clear and cold. "Oh, Pongo." Perdita sighed happily. "What a wonderful year we've just had – 15 puppies to be thankful for!"

"Yes, darling, and think of all we have to look forward to this year," said Pongo.

"Can you believe they all stayed up till midnight last night to ring in the new year?" Perdita cried. "And still awake when we left! I do hope they don't tire out dear, poor Nanny."

"Yes, that was quite a party we had at the flat last night," Pongo agreed. "And Lucky would have spent the whole night watching television if we had allowed him to."

"Perhaps we should be getting home now," said Perdita. "I am so afraid that Cruella De Vil may come around while we're out. I dread the way she looks at our puppies."

"I suppose we should," said Pongo. "But I'm sure Nanny has been taking good care of them." Pongo and Perdita gently pulled on their leads to let Roger and Anita know it was time to go home. The four of them walked towards home just as a new sprinkling of rain began to gently fall.

"Nanny! Puppies! We're home!" called Roger as he and Anita took off their muddy boots and Pongo and Perdy brushed off their paws on the mat in the hall. But no one answered.

"Pongo!" exclaimed Perdita, her panic rising. "Where are the puppies?"

Pongo raced up the stairs and began searching the rooms one by one. Perdita went to check the kitchen. Roger and Anita exchanged concerned looks, but tried to remain calm.

Pongo hurried into the sitting room to rejoin Perdita, who was on the brink of tears. "Oh, Pongo!" she cried. "Where can . . ."

"Hush, darling," said Pongo, his ears pricked intently. The two dogs fell silent. Then they both heard it: a tiny snore coming from the direction of the couch. There, nestled among the cushions, the puppies were sound asleep!

"I found Nanny!" Roger called. "She fell asleep in her chair!"

Perdita was busy counting the sleeping puppies. ". . . 12, 13, 14 . . . Oh, Pongo! One of the puppies isn't here!"

But Pongo had trotted into the next room. "Here he is, darling!" he called. "It's Lucky, of course. He's watching the New Year's Day celebration on television."

Three Cheesy Wishes

Long ago, before there was an Aladdin, a Jasmine, or even a Sultan, the magic lamp was making its way towards the Cave of Wonders, where Aladdin would one day find it. A travelling merchant had bought the lamp, along with some other 'junk.' Not knowing its value, he sold it to a cheese seller for some lunch.

Hassan the cheese seller looked at the lamp sceptically. He sighed, and began to shine it up. In a puff of smoke, the Genie appeared.

"Hello there! I'm the one and only magical Genie!" the big blue spirit announced.

"Excuse me?" said Hassan.

"Nice to meet you," said the Genie. "And what do you do here in Agrabah?"

"My name is Hassan, and I'm a – "

"Wait!" cried the Genie. "Let me guess! They say I'm a little psychic, you know!"

The Genie put his hand over his brow as he secretly looked around the man's shop. "You sell . . . cheese! Am I right or am I right?"

"You are right," said Hassan. "But that's an easy guess. Not very magical."

"You're very observant, Hassan," said the Genie. "So I'll give you three wishes."

"Three wishes, eh?" Hassan thought for a few minutes. Then he said, "It's hard to get enough good milk to make the best cheese. I wish I had many, many goats so I would always have enough milk."

Poof! In a flash, thousands of goats filled the streets of Agrabah. Goats were everywhere! They crowded the little shop, and knocked over the stalls in the market.

"Goodness!" Hassan cried. "I would have to wish for the biggest cheese shop in the world to sell the cheese from so many goats."

Poof! All of a sudden, Hassan's store began to grow and grow! His cheese shop was even taller than the highest sand dunes outside the city.

"This is terrible!" Hassan cried. Far below, the people looked like tiny ants. "I can't live and work in such a monstrosity. All I wanted was to make the finest cheese in Agrabah."

Hassan turned to the Genie. "I wish I'd never met you!" he cried.

Poof! Suddenly, the Genie was gone. Hassan found his shop back to normal. Outside, the marketplace was completely goat free.

Hassan searched high and low for the lamp, but it was already tucked into a little boy's pocket. Where would it end up next?

"It must have all been a crazy dream," said Hassan.

But, from that day, everyone said Hassan's cheese was the finest in all of Agrabah!

A Special Surprise

The underwater kingdom was quiet and peaceful. Every mermaid and merman was in bed fast asleep – everyone but Princess Ariel and her friend Flounder. "Hurry up, Flounder!" cried Ariel. "It's almost time. We can't be late!" Trying not to make a sound, Ariel and Flounder swam away from King Triton's palace. They began their journey towards the surface.

"B-b-but, Ariel," said Flounder, "are you sure we should go to the surface? Remember the last time? Your father got so angry."

"That's why this time, we can't get caught!" said Ariel, smiling.

She wasn't going to let anything ruin her plans for tonight. Prince Eric, the prince Ariel had saved in a shipwreck, was having a royal ball. Ariel had a very special surprise for him. "Swim faster, Flounder!" she cried. Flounder raced to keep up.

Just as Ariel and Flounder approached the surface, Ariel saw beautiful lights dance across the water. When they poked their heads out of the water, Ariel and Flounder saw colourful lights explode in the air above Prince Eric's castle.

"I've never seen anything so beautiful in all my life," said Ariel breathlessly. "The human world is a wonderful place!"

"It sure is pretty!" said Flounder.

Off in the distance, Prince Eric stood on the palace balcony. He just didn't feel like joining in the royal celebration. He couldn't stop thinking about the mysterious girl with the lovely voice who had saved his life in the shipwreck. *Why has she disappeared?* He wondered.

Flounder spotted the prince first. "Look, Ariel!" Ariel's heart leapt with joy when she saw Prince Eric.

"It's time for my surprise!" she said. They hid behind a nearby rock.

"R-r-ready?" asked Flounder. With a nod, Ariel closed her eyes, opened her mouth, and began to sing. Suddenly, the night was filled with the sweet sound of Ariel's voice. It was Ariel's special gift to him. Hearing her beautiful voice again, Eric's face lit up. "It can't be!" he said.

Eric remained on the balcony, enchanted by the beautiful song filling the night air. When the song was over, Eric looked out across the sea. He hoped to catch a glimpse of the wonderful girl who had saved him.

"Who are you?" he called out into the night. But all he heard was the echo of his own voice. "I'll be back soon," Ariel whispered as she and Flounder swam towards home. "Just wait and see..."

Cinderella
A Tiny New Friend

It had been a week since Cinderella's stepmother had forced her to move out of her bedroom and into the attic of the old house. But still Cinderella was not used to her new sleeping quarters. It was a cold, bare, lonely little room. The only other soul around to keep Cinderella company was a skittish little mouse who she had seen scurrying in and out of a hole in a corner of the room.

She had always been fond of animals, and mice were no exception. But how could she let the little fellow know that he shouldn't be afraid of her?

Well, thought Cinderella, he must be cold . . . and hungry.

So oneday, at suppertime, Cinderella slipped a piece of cheese into her apron pocket.

And that evening, when her work was finished, Cinderella hurried up to her room and pulled out her sewing basket. She used some scraps of fabric to make a mouse-sized suit of clothing: a red shirt and cap, a tiny orange coat, and two brown slippers.

"A tiny outfit for my tiny friend," she said.

Cinderella carried the clothes over to the mouse hole and knelt before it. She pulled the cheese out of her pocket and placed it, with the clothes, in the palm of her hand. Then she laid her open hand just in front of the mouse hole.

"Hello in there!" she called.

A mouse cautiously poked his head out of the hole and sniffed the air. Seeing the cheese, he inched out of the hole and over to Cinderella's hand. He paused and looked up at her questioningly.

"Go ahead," she said kindly. "They're a gift just for you."

Seeming to understand, but still skittish, the mouse scampered onto her palm, picked up the cheese and the clothes, and hurried back into the mouse hole.

Cinderella chuckled, then waited patiently for a few minutes, still kneeling in front of the hole.

"Well," she called after a short while, "let me see how they look on you!"

Timidly, the mouse came out in his new outfit. Cinderella clapped her hands.

"Perfect!" she said. "Do you like them?"

The mouse nodded. Then he jumped, as if an idea had just occurred to him. He scurried back into the mouse hole. Cinderella frowned. Had she frightened him?

But her worries vanished when the mouse reappeared – along with several other mice, who followed timidly behind him.

"More friends!" Cinderella cried. She hurried to get her sewing basket, delighted to have found the warmth of friendship in the cold attic room.

A Fairy Tale Kiss

Once upon a time in New Orleans, two young girls named Tiana and Charlotte were unlikely friends.

Charlotte believed in fairy tales and wishing on stars, but Tiana knew that wishing could only help her if she worked hard to make her dreams come true.

One night, Tiana was visiting with her mother, Eudora, who worked as a seamstress for Charlotte's family.

Tiana loved visiting Charlotte's big house and went there as often as she could.

That night, her mother was sewing a new dress while telling them a fairy tale about a prince who had been turned into a frog – Charlotte's favourite story.

"...And the beautiful princess was so moved by the poor frog's desperate pleas that she leaned forwards..."

"This is my favourite bit!" Charlotte whispered in Tiana's ear.

"...She drew closer, moving her lips to his, and then..."

"Yes, do it, princess!" whispered Charlotte under her breath.

No, don't do it! thought Tiana, looking disgusted.

"Smack! She kissed the slimy frog, which turned into a charming prince. They married and lived happily ever after!" said Eudora with a smile.

"Hurray!" exclaimed Charlotte. "Please tell us the story again!"

"Sorry, but it's late," said Eudora gently. "We must go home soon."

As Eudora was putting away her sewing things, Tiana said to Charlotte, "There is no way in this whole wide world I would ever, ever, ever – I mean never – kiss a frog!"

With that, Charlotte picked up a frog puppet and put it on the head of her kitten. The little animal tried to get away, but Charlotte held it up to Tiana saying, "Well, go on, kiss it, your prince charming!"

"Yuck! No way!" protested Tiana.

"Really?" asked Charlotte, surprised.

"I would kiss a hundred frogs if I could marry a prince and be a princess!" said Charlotte. She planted a big kiss on the nose of the kitten, who leapt away in horror!

"It's the frog who's disgusted by the princess!" cried Tiana, laughing. "You're going to have to brush up on your fairy tale kisses, Lottie!"

And the two girls rolled around on the floor laughing! They had know idea of the adventures the future would bring.

Disney PRINCESS

Beauty *and the* Beast

Just Desserts

Belle walked to the village, thinking about the wonderful book she had just finished reading. It was full of fire-breathing dragons, magical wizards and brave princesses. She sighed happily and turned her attention to more practical matters – whether she should get treacle or apple tart to enjoy with her father that night after dinner.

All of a sudden, Belle's thoughts were interrupted by a great crashing noise. Even before he spoke a word, Belle knew who was walking behind her. She could recognize that stomp anywhere.

"Gaston," Belle muttered.

"Belle, is it true?" Gaston said. "Have you come out from behind a book?"

"Bonjour, Gaston," Belle said. She was tempted to open her book again on the spot.

"Off to market, eh? I shall accompany you," Gaston announced.

Keeping up a steady stream of chatter about himself and his exploits, Gaston followed Belle into shop after shop.

"My, Gaston, you certainly do boast well," Belle said in a flattering tone.

"Yes! Thank you!" Gaston replied before realizing Belle was not complimenting him. His smile disappeared briefly as he opened the door to the bakery.

Belle stepped inside and quickly asked for an apple tart before Gaston could begin speaking again. When the tart was in her basket, she waved to Gaston and the shopkeeper. "Goodbye!" she called, walking quickly towards the forest path. She sighed in relief. It seemed she was rid of her annoying companion.

"Belle, wait." Gaston caught her arm.

"I really have no time to linger, Gaston," Belle replied. "I must get home to make dinner."

"I can walk you home," Gaston said, puffing out his massive chest. "I insist upon it. You need protection."

"Protection from what? These woods are my backyard!" Belle laughed.

"From predators. Monsters. Thieves," Gaston said dramatically.

Belle sighed and shook her head.

Then, suddenly, Belle and Gaston did hear something on the path ahead. Something large!

Quickly, Gaston pushed Belle out of harm's way. Belle tumbled to the ground. Her basket went flying.

"Look out!" Belle yelled. But it was too late. The 'predator' emerged. It was her father's horse, Phillipe! For the first time that she could remember, Belle smiled at the sight of Gaston. The apple tart had landed right on top of his head!

THE LITTLE MERMAID

Sebastian's Big Day

It was Sebastian's big day. As composer for the court of King Triton, he had been working very hard on a new piece of music, and that evening he was going to conduct the royal orchestra as they played his song before everyone for the first time. At last, thought Sebastian, his true genius would be fully appreciated!

That afternoon, in preparation for the concert, Sebastian went over every detail. He perfected the positioning of the musicians' chairs on stage. He prepared extra copies of the music in case any of the musicians forgot their own. He even had his bow tie washed and pressed.

Then, just before the curtain went up, the musicians began to gather backstage. Music filled the air as the trumpet fish and the conch shell players tuned their instruments.

Benny the octopus, the orchestra's drummer, was the last musician to arrive.

"Sebastian!" he exclaimed, rushing over to the conductor. "I – I can't play tonight!"

Sebastian stared at Benny in shock. "What do you mean? You *have* to play!"

"You don't understand," Benny replied. "I *can't*. I took a nap this afternoon and fell asleep on my tentacles, and now they're all tingly! I can't hold my drumsticks!"

The gravity of the situation hit Sebastian hard. "What am I going to do?" he exclaimed, looking around at the musicians. "My composition calls for eight drums. Benny has eight tentacles – one for each drum. Where will I find enough hands to take his place?"

Just then, Ariel and her six sisters swam backstage to wish Sebastian luck.

"Ariel!" Sebastian cried. "Am I glad to see you!" He explained his problem to Ariel and her sisters. "Could each of you help by playing a drum in the concert?" he asked.

"Of course!" the mermaid sisters replied.

Sebastian breathed a sigh of relief. "Okay, we have seven drummers. We just need one more!"

All the musicians stared at Sebastian.

"*Me?*" he said. "But I am the composer and conductor! This is the day my true genius will finally be appreciated. I cannot be hidden in the drum section. I must be front and centre!"

But, wouldn't you know it, when the curtain went up minutes later, there was Sebastian, drumming away. His day in the spotlight would have to come another time. As he played, he shrugged and smiled.

"Well, you know what they say," he whispered to Ariel, who drummed at his side.

"The show must go on?" Ariel guessed.

"No," Sebastian replied. "A true genius is never fully appreciated in his own lifetime."

POCAHONTAS

Listen With Your Heart

It was a clear, crisp day, and Pocahontas had decided to climb to the top of a high mountain with her friends Meeko the raccoon and Flit the hummingbird. She hadn't climbed this mountain since she was a little girl.

They came to a fork in the path. "Which direction should we take, Meeko?" asked Pocahontas. The raccoon pointed to the gentler, flatter path, which made Pocahontas laugh.

"Let's try this one!" she said, pointing to the narrower, steeper route. They climbed and climbed, and the path grew steeper and narrower. Meeko chattered away nervously, and even Flit seemed anxious. As Pocahontas sat down on a large tree stump to catch her breath, the winds suddenly picked up. Then the clouds moved in, and rain poured down on them.

"Uh-oh," said Pocahontas, jumping to her feet. "We can't stay here, and it's too slippery to climb back down. We need to keep moving!" Pocahontas didn't let on to Meeko and Flit but, as the water streamed down the steep path, she grew frightened. The footing was even more slippery, and she was getting colder and colder. Then she remembered something that her Grandmother Willow had told her.

"I need to listen," Pocahontas said to herself. "I must listen to the spirits all around us, and they will keep us safe." She tried to listen, but it was hard to hear anything over the pouring rain and rushing winds. Meeko chattered nervously and clung to Pocahontas.

"I must listen with my heart!" she said. And, suddenly, she heard them. The spirits spoke to her. They told her to climb a little higher, just a bit, and there she would find shelter.

"Come on, Meeko! Come on, Flit!" she called over the wind and rain. "We'll find shelter just a little way up!" Sure enough, they found an opening in the rocks just a bit higher up the path. Between the rocks was a small cave, and inside it was warm and dry. The three of them made their way into the cave and sat, listening to the rain and wind.

The storm soon passed, and the sun came out. "Come on!" Pocahontas cried to Meeko and Flit. "Let's go see what it looks like at the top!" They hurried the rest of the way up the trail until they came out on a wide, flat ledge. Far below, they could see the forest and, beyond it, the sparkling blue sea.

"You see, Meeko? See, Flit?" said Pocahontas. "We're seeing the world a different way. Isn't it beautiful? And just think," she said, more to herself than to the other two, "if I hadn't chosen that unexplored path, I would never have heard the spirits talk to me!"

Disney
Tangled

Once Upon a Flower

Once upon a time, in a land far away, a single drop of sunlight fell to the ground. It grew into a magical golden flower that possessed healing powers.

The only person who knew the location of the flower was a vain and selfish old woman named Mother Gothel.

Mother Gothel kept the flower secret. She used it to keep her looking young and beautiful.

As centuries passed, a glorious kingdom was built close to the cliff where the flower grew. The forever youthful Mother Gothel watched from the shadows – guarding her precious flower from the people of the kingdom.

One day the kingdom's beloved queen fell gravely ill. Everyone in the kingdom wanted to help. They had heard stories about a magical flower with healing powers.

The people of the kingdom searched far and wide – until, at last, they found the magical golden flower.

As Mother Gothel looked on in horror, a royal guard pulled up the flower and took it back to the palace.

The Queen drank a potion containing the flower, and instantly recovered! Soon after, she gave birth to a beautiful baby girl.

The King and Queen, and the whole kingdom, launched flying lanterns into the sky to celebrate the Princess' birth.

One night an aged and vengeful Mother Gothel crept into the nursery. While she stroked the baby's hair and sang softly, Mother Gothel became young again! The flower's magic lived in the baby's hair!

Mother Gothel greedily cut off a lock of the baby's hair – but the hair instantly lost its power and turned brown. The only way Mother Gothel could remain young was to keep the child with her, always. She snatched the baby and vanished into the night.

Everyone in the kingdom searched, but no one could find the Princess.

The King and Queen were heartbroken. But they remained hopeful that one day their daughter would return to them. Each year on the Princess's birthday, they released lanterns into the night sky.

They hoped their light would guide their daughter home…

But Mother Gothel was raising the Princess, who she named Rapunzel, in a soaring tower in a hidden valley. She loved the girl only for her hair and treated Rapunzel as a prized possession.

Would Rapunzel ever be able to return to the kingdom, where she belonged?

DUMBO

An Elephant Lullaby

Mrs Jumbo was very sad. More than anything else in the world, she had been longing for a baby elephant of her own. Many other animals in the circus had babies and, as she watched the mothers with their infants, she grew sadder and sadder. Then one day, a stork delivered a baby elephant to Mrs Jumbo! The tiny elephant was the most beautiful creature she had ever seen, and she was the happiest animal in the circus. But then it happened: her baby sneezed, causing his ears to unfold. They were extremely large ears, and the other elephants laughed at him in a way that was not nice at all.

"Instead of calling him Jumbo Junior," one elephant said drily, "he ought to be called Dumbo!" The others laughed loudly at this.

Mrs Jumbo ignored their taunts and curled her trunk around her beloved baby.

As the days went by, Mrs Jumbo grew to love her baby more and more. She played hide-and-seek with him, pretending to be surprised when he hid behind her legs. She played peeka-boo with him. She sang him lullabies at bedtime, and danced around with him when he woke up.

One evening, Mrs Jumbo found her precious baby looking terribly sad. She guessed that the other elephants had been taunting him again, and her eyes flashed with indignation.

But she tenderly put him to bed, tucking his large ears around him to keep him warm. "Don't mind what the others say," she whispered softly. "You are going to grow up to be a fine elephant! Shall I sing you a lullaby, darling?"

As Dumbo nodded, Mrs Jumbo heard the other elephants talking in low tones in the next stall. "Honestly!" one of them was saying. "You'd think he was the only elephant left on earth, the way she pampers him! She spoils him terribly, she does!"

But Mrs Jumbo ignored their whispers and began to sing:

Hush, little baby, don't you cry.
Mama's gonna sing you a lullaby.
And if someone should laugh at your ears,
Mama's gonna be here to dry your tears.
And if your tears can't be extinguished,
Mama thinks that large ears are really
*   distinguished.*

Then she continued to hum and rock her son until his eyelids grew heavier and heavier, and he fell asleep.

Mrs Jumbo hummed for a little while longer, then stood up. But wait – why was it so quiet?

All along the elephant stalls, soft snoring could be heard. Mrs Jumbo's lullaby had put all the elephants to sleep!

Disney · PIXAR
FINDING NEMO

Marlin's Story

"P. Sherman, 42 Wallaby Way, Sydney . . . P. Sherman, 42 Wallaby Way, Sydney." Dory kept muttering the address. She and Marlin were searching for Marlin's missing son, Nemo. They had just escaped an angry angler-fish, and now they were trying to find someone who could give them directions to Sydney. That's where Nemo probably was.

"P. Sherman, 42 Wallaby Way, Sydney . . . P. Sherman, 42 Wallaby Way, Sydney," Dory continued to chant.

Marlin had the address memorized and thought he would go crazy if he had to hear it again. "Dory!" he said with a sigh. "I know you just want to be helpful, but do you really need to keep talking?"

"I love to talk," said Dory. "I'm pretty good at it. Hmm . . . what were we talking about?"

"I just want to find Nemo," Marlin said.

"That's right, Chico," said Dory.

"One time, Nemo and I . . ." Marlin began.

"Go on," Dory said. "Is this going to be exciting?"

"Yes, it's an exciting story," said Marlin, relieved that he had got her to stop reciting the address. "Well," Marlin began, "one time, I took Nemo to the other side of the reef, to visit a relative of mine who was known as the fastest swimmer of all the clownfish, in his day. But

when we visited him, he was getting on in years."

Dory yawned. "When's the good part?"

Marlin sighed. "I was just about to get to it!" he said. "So, anyway, on the way back home, guess what we ran into?"

"What?" asked Dory, confused.

"A huge jellyfish! It was hovering in the water, blocking our way through two big tufts of sea grass."

"Uh-huh," said Dory. She seemed to be trying to remember something. "P. Sherman . . ." she muttered softly.

"For a moment there I thought we were goners," said Marlin. "But then . . . a huge sea turtle swam up and swallowed the jellyfish in one gulp!"

"Did you say thank you to the sea turtle?" asked Dory, who seemed back on track.

"Well, no," Marlin replied. "I was afraid he would eat us, too, so Nemo and I hurried on our way. But, ever since then, I have been fascinated with sea turtles. And I hope I never have to meet another jellyfish!"

"Say, I've got a story too!" said Dory excitedly. "It takes place at 42 Wallaby Way, Sydney. At P. Sherman. Now, at P. Sherman, 42 Wallaby Way, Sydney, there was this, um, fish . . . and . . . well . . ."

Marlin just groaned and kept swimming.

Ðɪsɴᴇʏ
THE
LION KING
Scaredy Cats

"Nala!" Simba whispered. "Are you awake?"

"Yes," Nala whispered back, stepping out of the dark cave where she slept with her mother. "Why are you here? You're gonna get us in trouble . . . again."

Earlier, Simba and Nala had gone to explore the forbidden Elephant's Graveyard, where they'd been trapped by hyenas. Simba's father, Mufasa, had rescued them.

"Come on," Simba hissed. "Follow me."

Soon the two cubs were on the dark savannah near the base of Pride Rock.

"What do you want, anyway?" Nala asked.

"I just wanted to make sure you weren't still scared," Simba said.

Nala scowled at him. "Scared?" she exclaimed. "*I'm* not the one who was scared!"

"What?" Simba cried. "You're not saying *I* was scared, are you? Because there's no way I'd be scared of a few stupid hyenas. I wouldn't have been scared even if we ran into *ten* hyenas."

"Well, I wouldn't have been scared even if we found *20* hyenas and an angry water buffalo," said Nala.

"Oh yeah?" Simba said. "Well, I wouldn't have been scared of *30* hyenas, an angry water buffalo and a – "

"FURIOUS HORNBILL?" a new voice squawked from the darkness.

"Ahhhhhh!" Simba and Nala cried, jumping straight up in the air.

Just then, a brightly coloured bird stepped out of the shadows. It was Zazu, Mufasa's most trusted adviser.

"Zazu!" Simba cried. "You scared us!"

"I wasn't scared," Nala put in indignantly.

"Me neither!" Simba added quickly.

Zazu glared at both of them over his long beak. "Not scared, were you?" he said drily. "That certainly explains the shrieking."

"You just startled us," Nala mumbled.

Zazu fluffed his feathers. "Listen up, you two," he said. "There's no shame in admitting you're scared. Even King Mufasa wouldn't deny that he was terrified when he found out you were missing. And, if it's good enough for him, it's good enough for a pair of scrawny cubs like you. Right?"

"I guess so," Simba said as Nala shrugged.

"Everyone gets scared," Zazu went on. "It's how you respond to it that counts. That's where *true* bravery lies. Get it?"

"Got it," Simba and Nala said.

"Good." Zazu marched towards Pride Rock. The sun was coming up and it was time for breakfast. "Now let's get you back home posthaste . . . or I'll *really* give you something to be scared of!"

Friends Forever

Experiment 626 was a blue creature from a distant planet, who was punished for being very naughty and destroying everything around him. One day, he escaped his planet in a police cruiser and headed straight for the tiny island of Kauai, on Earth!

On the island of Kauai was a little girl named Lilo. She found it hard to make friends and was very lonely. Lilo lived with her big sister, Nani, who was learning how to be a good parent. One night, the sisters had a big fight. Lilo went to her room and slammed the door shut. Out of her window, Lilo saw a falling star and made a wish. "I wish for someone to be my friend," she whispered.

The star that Lilo had seen was Experiment 626's ship crashing on the island. A truck driver found him and took him to an animal shelter. All the other animals were scared of 626, but he didn't care. He scrunched two of his four arms in towards his torso so he would look more like a dog. That way, he'd be adopted and have a place to hide from the aliens who were chasing him.

The next day, Nani decided to take Lilo to the shelter to pick a new pet.

"Hi!" Lilo said when she saw 626.

"Hi," the creature replied and then gave her a hug. Lilo went to the front room and told Nani she'd found the dog she wanted.

"He's good," she said. "I can tell. His name is . . . Stitch."

They took Stitch home even though Nani thought he looked strange. Nani was glad Lilo finally had a friend. When Nani left for work, Lilo and Stitch went for a ride on Lilo's bicycle. They rode all around the island, even stopping for ice cream along the way. Stitch was wild, but he and Lilo had fun.

At home, however, Stitch began to tear things apart and cause trouble for Nani.

"We have to take him back," Nani said.

"We adopted him!" Lilo cried. "What about 'ohana'? Dad said ohana means family! Family means –"

"Nobody gets left behind," Nani finished. "I know."

She remembered how welcoming her parents had been and how important family was to them. She changed her mind. She would give Stitch another chance – for Lilo's sake.

From then on, Lilo and Stitch stuck together through anything that came their way. Lilo helped Stitch learn how to behave, and Stitch became the friend that Lilo had wished for on a falling star.

Lady and the TRAMP

Spaghetti and Meatballs

Tramp had just escaped from the dogcatcher – again. He'd taught that dogcatcher who was boss!

Tramp could smell wood burning in fireplaces, dinner cooking . . . his stomach suddenly rumbled. Escaping from the dogcatcher always made him work up quite an appetite!

But where would he go for dinner tonight? He usually stopped by the Schultzes for some Wiener schnitzel on Monday, he had corned beef and cabbage with the O'Briens on Tuesday . . . but what he was really craving was some spaghetti and meatballs.

So, Tramp headed to Tony's Restaurant. He scratched at the back door, as was his custom.

"I'm coming! I'm coming!" Tony shouted. He appeared at the door wiping his hands on a towel. He pretended not to see Tramp, as he always did.

"Hey, nobody's here!" Tony shouted. "It must be April Fools' Day!" He pretended to think for a moment. "No, it's not the first! It's not even April! It's January!"

Tramp couldn't take it any more. He was so hungry! He barked.

"Oh, there you are, Butch my friend," said Tony. Tramp, aka Butch, jumped up and down. "I'll get your dinner," said Tony. "Relax, enjoy yourself."

Tramp sat down and looked around the cluttered alleyway. This was the life!

Just then Tony appeared with a plateful of pasta. He had given Tramp two, no make that three meatballs! This was quite a special night.

Tony stood and chatted with Tramp as he ate his meal, telling him about his day – the late delivery of fish, the customer who had complained that the tomato sauce was too garlicky, the trip that he and his wife were planning to take . . . .

Tramp finished eating and gave the plate one last lick. It was sparkling clean.

"That reminds me," said Tony. "There's something I've been meaning to talk to you about. It's time you settled down and got a wife of your own."

Tramp gave Tony a horrified look and began to back out of the alleyway.

Tony laughed so hard his sides shook. "Goodbye, Butch!" he called. "But mark my words, one of these days, you're going to meet the dog you can't resist! And, when you do, I have a good idea – you bring her to Tony's for a nice romantic dinner!"

Tramp barked his thanks to Tony. He walked down the block, shaking his head. He was footloose and collar free! Settle down? That was never going to happen!

A Never Land Story

It was a cold winter night, and John and Michael just couldn't get to sleep. They climbed onto the bed of their older sister, Wendy.

"Oh, tell us a story, Wendy!" said Michael.

"Yes, please. A Peter Pan story!" pleaded John.

"Certainly," said Wendy. "Have I told you about the time that Peter Pan outsmarted the evil Captain Hook?"

"Yes!" said Michael eagerly. "And we want to hear it again!"

Wendy laughed and began her story. "Well, one night, Captain Hook moored his ship in a secret cove close to the island of Never Land. He and his men rowed ashore quietly, for he was intent on discovering the hiding place of Peter and the Lost Boys. Captain Hook hated Peter Pan because the boy had cut off his hand in a duel and fed it to a large crocodile. And now that crocodile was determined to swallow up the rest of him. Luckily for Captain Hook, however, this crocodile had also swallowed a clock, so the pirate would always be alerted to the crocodile's presence by the sound of the ticking clock.

"Fortunately for Peter Pan," Wendy continued, "his dear friend Tinker Bell learned of Captain Hook's evil plan ahead of time.

She flew to Peter and warned him that the pirate was coming. 'Oh-ho!' laughed Peter. 'Well, we shall be ready for him then!' He found a clock just like the one the crocodile had swallowed. He whistled up into the trees, and a group of his monkey friends appeared. 'Here's a new toy for you!' Peter shouted, and tossed the clock up to them. 'Stay out of sight, now!' Peter told the monkeys, and then he and the Lost Boys hurried to their hiding places.

"When Hook came to the clearing, the first thing he heard was the ticking clock. The sound seemed to be coming at him from all sides! The monkeys were having a grand time, tossing the clock back and forth, and creeping up behind Hook. Seized with terror, Hook and his men raced to their boat and rowed madly back to their ship."

Just then, the Darling children's parents came in to check on them. "You're not telling more of these poppycock stories about Peter Pan, are you, Wendy?" their father asked.

"Peter Pan is real, Father!" cried the children. "We know he is!"

As the parents kissed their children good night, they didn't see that a boy in green was crouching just outside the nursery window. He had been listening to the story, and he would be back again – soon.

Snow White
and the Seven Dwarfs

A Bedtime Story

It was bedtime in the little cottage in the woods. Snow White kissed each Dwarf good night and tucked them into bed.

"Wait! Wait!" called out Happy before she blew out the candle. "Please tell us a story!"

"Very well," said Snow White, smiling. She settled down at the foot of the beds and began . . .

"Once upon a time, there lived a happy little princess – or rather, a mostly happy little princess, but for a single person: her stepmother, the Queen."

"Bah!" grumbled Grumpy with a sneer.

Snow White sighed. "You see, no matter what the Princess did – no matter how hard she worked or how good she tried to be – the Queen did everything in her power to make her sad."

"Poor Princess," murmured Bashful.

"Oh, but don't worry," Snow White assured him. "Mostly, the Princess was jolly! She found that if she whistled and sang while she worked, her work would fly by and her mood would be sunny. And then, there were always her daydreams – for she truly believed that if she wished for something hard enough, it surely would come true."

"What did sh . . . she . . . *ah-choo*! . . . wish for?" asked Sneezy.

"Well," began Snow White, "for one thing, she wished for a charming and dashing prince to find her and whisk her away. And then, one day, a prince did find her!"

"Really?" exclaimed the Dwarfs.

"Yes!" Snow White told them. "He rode right up to her castle and even scaled the wall to meet her. And, oh, was he ever charming! But here is the sad part. The very next day, the Queen's Huntsman took the Princess into the forest and told her to run far away and never return."

"So, did she?" Sleepy asked sleepily.

"Yes," Snow White replied. "She ran until she could run no farther. Only then did she realize she was terribly lost and lonely – with no friend in the world and no place to go."

"Poor Princess," whispered Bashful.

"That's what the Princess thought too," Snow White said. "For just a minute. But then she discovered she wasn't alone at all. There were chipmunks and squirrels and deer and rabbits and birds . . . all sorts of forest creatures there to help her. They took her to the sweetest little cottage you ever did see, and the most faithful friends a princess could ever have."

"And what happened next?" grumbled Grumpy.

"Well, they lived happily ever after, of course!" Snow White replied. "What did you think?"

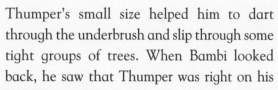

Bambi

The Race

"**G**ood morning, young Prince," Thumper greeted Bambi one bright winter day.

"Good morning, Thumper," Bambi said.

"I have a great idea, Bambi. Let's have a race," Thumper said. "We'll start from here." He drew a line in the dirt. "And whoever makes it to that big pine tree over there first, wins the race."

"But it would be silly for us to race," Bambi told his friend.

"Why's that?" Thumper asked, confused.

"Because I'll win," Bambi said.

"What makes you so sure?" Thumper challenged, puffing up his chest.

"Because I'm bigger and faster than you," Bambi explained.

"If you're so sure you'll win," Thumper said, "why are you afraid to race me?"

Bambi paused to think about this. He didn't want to hurt the little rabbit's feelings. "Fine," he said at last. "Let's race!"

"Great!" Thumper exclaimed. "Ready?"

"Ready!" Bambi said.

"Okay," Thumper said, crouching down. Bambi crouched down too. "On your mark. Get set. Go!" cried Thumper. They both took off as fast as they could.

Bambi, with his long legs and big, wide stride, immediately took the lead. But

Thumper's small size helped him to dart through the underbrush and slip through some tight groups of trees. When Bambi looked back, he saw that Thumper was right on his heels. Thumper took the opportunity to hop past Bambi. Bambi paused to jump over a tree that had been knocked down, blocking the path. Thumper was able to wriggle under it. He popped up in front of Bambi and took the lead.

Bambi took longer and longer strides, running faster and faster. Soon he had passed Thumper. But, in his hurry to go as fast as he could, he got tangled up in a bush. As Bambi struggled to free himself, Thumper hopped past him again.

They were quickly approaching the big pine tree. Bambi was running as fast as he could, jumping over logs and bushes. Thumper hopped as quickly as his bunny legs would carry him, ducking and weaving through whatever obstacles were in his way. As they crossed the finish line, they were in a neck-and-neck tie.

"See!" Thumper said, panting. "Little guys can keep up!"

"You are absolutely right!" Bambi said, also panting.

And the two friends, both winners, sat down together to catch their breath.

Sleepless Beauty

"Oh, there, there, little Aurora. There, there," cooed Flora, trying to calm the crying, fussy baby Princess. Flora and her fellow fairies, Fauna and Merryweather, stood huddled over the cradle of tiny Aurora and looked down anxiously and helplessly at their royal charge.

But Aurora's cries only grew louder. In fact, she had not stopped crying since the three fairies had arrived with the baby earlier that day at the secluded cottage in the woods.

"Oh, goodness!" cried Fauna. "What have we got ourselves into? We promised the King and Queen that we would hide Aurora out here in the woods, and raise her without magic. But we don't know the first thing about taking care of human babies!"

Flora gave Fauna a comforting pat on the back. "Now, now, don't panic, Fauna," Flora said. "It may be harder than we expected. But this is the only way to keep the Princess safe from Maleficent."

Merryweather and Fauna knew Flora was right. So, one after another, they tried different things to get the baby to stop crying and go to sleep.

"Well," said Flora, "fairy babies are soothed by a sprig of dandelion root placed in their cradle. Let's try that!" Flora hurried out of the cottage and returned minutes later with the sprig. She laid it at the baby's feet.

But the baby cried on. "Perhaps she needs to be entertained!" suggested Fauna.

So, Flora, Fauna and Merryweather locked arms and danced a little jig. They kept it up for quite a while, until they were out of breath and could barely stand up.

But baby Aurora took no notice – and carried on crying.

Now Fauna was getting desperate. "Come on," she said to the others, "let's use a little magic. Just to help her sleep. I can't bear to see her so upset!"

"No! It's much too dangerous!" cried Merryweather.

"Oh, fiddle-faddle!" shouted Fauna, who began to wave her wand over the sleeping child. Just then, she accidentally nudged Aurora's cradle, causing it to rock gently back and forth. Soothed by the rocking, the baby's cries slowly grew softer and softer.

"Fauna!" cried Flora. "You've done it!"

"Look how much she likes the rocking!" added Merryweather.

So, the three fairies continued to rock the cradle gently back and forth, and soon Aurora drifted off to sleep.

"Well," Fauna whispered to the others, once the baby was sleeping soundly, "that wasn't so hard, now, was it?"

January
19

Tinker Bell is Born

One winter's day in London, a baby laughed for the very first time. That laugh floated up and away to meet its destiny. It would become a fairy, just like all first laughs. It flew straight for the Second Star to the Right, and passed through it in a burst of light. On the other side was... Never Land!

The laugh floated towards a magical place in the heart of the island. This was Pixie Hollow, home of the fairies. Vidia, the fastest flying fairy of them all, guided the arrival into the Pixie Dust Tree. There, a dust-keeper named Terence sprinkled it with pixie dust, and it took the shape of a tiny fairy.

Clarion, queen of the fairies, helped the newcomer unfurl her two gossamer wings. The new fairy flapped her wings and realised she could fly!

Queen Clarion waved her hand, and several toadstools sprung up around the Pixie Dust Well. Fairies immediately fluttered forwards to place different objects on the pedestals. Rosetta, a garden fairy, brought a flower. Silvermist, a water fairy, carried a droplet of water. Iridessa, a light fairy, placed a lamp on her pedestal.

"They will help you find your talent," the queen explained to the new fairy.

The youngster timidly placed her hand on a beautiful flower. Its glow instantly faded. She reached for a water droplet, but that, too, faded. The fairy moved on without touching anything else – she was afraid to fail again – but then something amazing happened. As she passed by a hammer, it began to glow. Then it rose up off its pedestal and flew straight for her!

"I've never seen one glow that much before," said Silvermist.

Vidia glowered. She had one of the strongest and rarest talents in Pixie Hollow, and she wasn't looking for competition.

"Tinker fairies," called the queen. "Welcome the newest member of your talent guild – Tinker Bell!"

A large fairy named Clank and a bespectacled fairy named Bobble came forwards to greet Tink. Then they whisked her off for a flying tour of Pixie Hollow. It was almost time for the changing of the seasons, and they could see everyone getting ready.

Finally, the trio landed at Tinkers' Nook. Tink looked around and saw fairies fixing and fashioning all kinds of amazing, useful objects. She knew she would enjoy living here, and was excited about discovering her unique fairy talent.

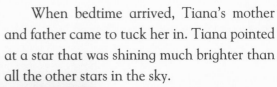

An Excellent Cook

After returning to her cozy home Tiana decided to help her father, James, cook dinner. Her father was an excellent cook, and just like James, the little girl loved to cook too.

"What are you going to make for us, sweetheart?" asked her mother.

"Gumbo!" replied Tiana. This was her father's speciality. He even had an enormous pot, which he kept especially for his Gumbo! So little Tiana sat perched on a stool stirring, seasoning and tasting! "I think it's done," Tiana announced and watched her father anxiously as he took a spoonful.

"Let's see," said James, as he put the spoon to his mouth. "Delicious sweetheart! This is the BEST gumbo I've ever tasted!" He then gave it to Tiana's mother to taste, who also thought it was delicious!

"You have a gift, Tiana! A gift this special just has to be shared!"

And with that, the family invited the neighbours to enjoy the Gumbo on the porch outside. The night air filled with the sounds of clinking spoons, conversation and laughter.

"You see," said Tiana's father, "food brings folks together from all walks of life. It warms them right up and puts smiles on their faces."

When bedtime arrived, Tiana's mother and father came to tuck her in. Tiana pointed at a star that was shining much brighter than all the other stars in the sky.

"I was told that if we wish hard enough, the Evening Star will make our dearest wishes come true."

Both parents encouraged the little girl to wish on the Evening Star. "But remember," added James, "you've got to help it along with some hard work of your own." Then, thinking of the night filled with good food, family and friends, he said, "Just never lose sight of what's really important."

Tiana looked at the picture that her father had once given her. It was of a beautiful restaurant. It was her father's dream to open a restaurant in the old sugar mill. Well, now it was Tiana's dream too, and she was ready to work hard to achieve their dream, with the help of the Evening Star.

"Our restaurant will be called 'Tiana's Place', and we will serve your gumbo to our customers," said James, giving Tiana a kiss goodnight.

I will make our dream come true! Tiana promised herself as she went to bed that night. She fell asleep peacefully, knowing she would have the courage to succeed.

The Sleigh Ride

Long ago, an enchantress cast a spell on a castle. She transformed the handsome young prince into a hideous beast and his servants into household objects.

"Just look at me," grumbled the Beast. "I've been so cruel, holding Belle captive in my castle. How will she ever see me as anything but a monster?"

"Come now," said Mrs Potts gently. "All you have to do is show her what is inside your heart."

"You must act like a gentleman!" Lumiere the candelabrum added. "Be romantic. Compliment her. And most of all, be kind, gentle and sincere!"

"And don't be so grumpy!" added Chip, Mrs Potts's young son.

"I have an idea!" said the Beast, smiling. "Why don't I invite Belle to go on a sleigh ride?"

"Perfect!" said Lumiere.

The Beast sent Lumiere to invite Belle on the sleigh ride.

"That sounds lovely!" said Belle. "I've been stuck in this castle far too long." Belle ran down the long staircase and stepped outside. Glimmering white snowflakes fell from the sky. Just then, the Beast pulled up in a gleaming horse-drawn sleigh.

"How beautiful!" exclaimed Belle.

The Beast smiled as he helped her into the sleigh. Once she was settled, he covered her with a blanket and they took off across the snow. Belle laughed happily as the Beast guided the sleigh through the forest to a clearing. Before them was a frozen pond.

"This is such a magical place," said Belle. "How did you find it?"

"I used to come here long ago," said the Beast. "It was one of my favourite places. I wanted to share it with you." Then the Beast asked Belle if she wanted to ice-skate.

"Oh, yes," she replied. "I love ice-skating!"

Soon Belle was spinning across the pond's smooth surface. The Beast was less graceful. Hitting a bump in the ice, he lost his balance and fell to the ground. He was angry, but then he saw Belle looking at him kindly. Remembering his friends' advice, he smiled as Belle helped him to his feet.

"Everyone falls sometimes," said Belle.

Before long, they were gliding across the ice, arm in arm.

Later, as they made their way home, Belle thought about the Beast. There was something different about him. He seemed kinder, softer. Perhaps they could be friends, after all...

Ariel's Peace

One day, as Ariel and Flounder were passing by, they heard King Triton speaking to his bravest soldiers.

"The humans are building boats! Humans use their boats to capture sea creatures," King Triton said. "For this reason, I am sending you to the coast to see how great a danger they pose to our people." Immediately, the soldiers headed for the coast.

"Come on!" Ariel told Flounder. "We're going with them!"

From a distance, Ariel saw some men were building a boat near the shore. Others were on land, gathering grain or fishing with big nets. Suddenly, Ariel saw that one of King Triton's soldiers was caught in a fishing net! Tridents in hand, the other mer-soldiers swam towards their friend to help.

The fisherman was dumbstruck when he heaved his net onto shore – and saw not fish, but a furious merman. He was even more shocked when a small army of mer-soldiers emerged from the sea. The fisherman called to his friends in the fields for help. Grabbing their pitchforks, the farmers raced to defend their comrade.

Where the land met the sea, humans met mer-soldiers, ready to fight. As Ariel watched, she knew she had to stop them.

"Wait!" she exclaimed. Ariel swam between them. She grabbed a trident from a soldier's hand. Before anyone could stop her, she swam up to the humans.

"We come as friends," she declared, offering up the trident. "These are gifts for you. They will last forever – just as the peace between our people should be everlasting."

The mer-soldiers watched the farmer lay down his pitchfork and smile as he gently took the trident from Ariel. Accepting Ariel's offer of peace, the mer-soldiers bowed to her respectfully. Then they too offered up their tridents.

The farmers and the fisherman quickly freed the mer-soldier from the fishing net. Then a farmer ran back to the fields. When he returned, his arms were full of wildflowers and stalks of grain.

"These are for you," he said, "and your people – from us, your new friends!"

Back at the palace, Ariel presented her father with the gifts from the surface world, and told him all about the peaceful encounter with the humans. At first, King Triton was angry with her for putting herself in danger. Then his soldiers told him how courageous Ariel had been, and he couldn't help but feel proud.

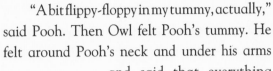

Say Ahhh, Pooh!

"Christopher Robin says it's time for my animal checkout," said Pooh.

"Checkout!" cried Piglet. "Oh p-p-poor P-P-Pooh – you're sick!"

"Sick?" asked Pooh. "No – I'm fine. Though I must say I am feeling a bit rumbly in my tumbly."

"Let's go together," said Piglet. "It's so much more friendly with two." So, Pooh and Piglet climbed the ladder up to Owl's house.

"Christopher Robin, why do I need an animal checkout, anyway?" asked Pooh once they had arrived at Owl's house.

"Silly old bear," said Christopher Robin. "Not an animal checkout – an annual checkup. We need to make sure you are healthy and strong. And this time, Owl will give you a special injection to help keep you well." Pooh's tummy flopped and flipped.

"It's okay," said Christopher Robin. "It will only hurt for a few seconds, and the medicine in the injection will keep you from getting mumps and measles and things like that."

Rabbit called for Pooh to go into Owl's room. Piglet wished him good luck. Once Pooh and Christopher Robin were inside, Owl entered with a flourish. "Well, if it isn't Winnie the Pooh!" he exclaimed. "Splendid day for a checkup, isn't it? I say, how are you feeling?"

"A bit flippy-floppy in my tummy, actually," said Pooh. Then Owl felt Pooh's tummy. He felt around Pooh's neck and under his arms and said that everything seemed to be right where it should be. Pooh was glad. Then Owl pulled a small rubber hammer from his bag. "Reflex-checking time!" he said grandly.

"What's a reflex?" asked Pooh. Owl tapped Pooh's knee – and his leg gave a little kick. "Oh do that again," said Pooh. "That was fun." So Owl tapped Pooh's other knee, and that leg gave a little kick, too. And it didn't bother Pooh in the least when Owl said… "Sit right here in Christopher Robin's lap. It is time for your injection."

"I know it will only hurt for a moment, and it will keep me from getting bumps and weasels," Pooh said bravely.

"That's mumps and measles, Pooh," said Owl.

Piglet came in and sat right next to Pooh while he had his injection. When Owl was done, Rabbit popped back in with a plaster.

"Wow," said Piglet. "You didn't even cry!"

"An annual checkup is no problem for a brave bear like Pooh," said Christopher Robin.

I'm just that sort of bear, thought Pooh with a smile.

101 DALMATIANS

Pongo Carries a Tune

"**I** don't know what we're going to do," Roger Radcliffe told his wife, Anita. "We have all these puppies to feed, and I don't have *one* song to sell!"

"Don't worry," Anita told him. "I'm sure you'll be inspired soon."

"I'm glad *you're* sure!" said Roger. "Because all I've got is a bunch of used paper." He pointed to the overflowing wastebasket.

"Don't give up," said Anita. "I know that you can do it."

After Anita left, Pongo watched his pet pace in front of his piano.

"Pongo, old boy, I must have written ten songs in ten days. But they're all terrible," said Roger, pointing to the wastebasket. "What am I going to do?"

Pongo wanted to help his pet, but he didn't know how.

That night, Pongo talked to Perdy about Roger's dilemma. They sat in the middle of the living room, surrounded by puppies.

"Roger has already written ten songs," explained Pongo. "He just doesn't think they're good enough to sell. But I know they are – I've heard him play them, and you don't have a songwriter for a pet without developing a good ear for hit songs. The songs are right upstairs, stuffed inside his wastebasket."

Perdy saw what he was thinking.

"Do you know the way to the music publisher?" she asked.

Pongo nodded. "I've taken Roger for walks there dozens of times."

"I think you should try it," said Perdy.

After Roger and Anita had gone to sleep, Pongo padded into the music room and gathered up the sheet music from the wastebasket. Then he sneaked out of the house, carrying the music to the publisher's office. Pongo pushed all the pages under the door, then trotted back home.

The next day, the phone rang. Roger answered.

"You what?" Roger said into the receiver. "You did . . . ? But how did you . . . ? Oh, I see . . . well, thank you. Thank you!"

Anita rushed over. "Who was that?"

"My music publisher," said Roger. "He's buying ten of my songs."

"Ten songs!" cried Anita. "I thought you didn't even have *one* to sell."

Roger scratched his head in confusion. "I didn't think I did."

"So, what happened?" asked Anita.

Perdy looked at Pongo and barked. Her husband could carry a tune too – all the way across town to Roger's publisher!

Mango Hunting

Once upon a time, long before Mowgli came to the jungle, Bagheera the panther met Baloo the bear for the first time.

This is how it happened.

Bagheera was younger then, but no less grave. He took himself very seriously indeed. When Bagheera hunted, he moved silently, with grace and speed. He never tripped, and he certainly never fell. When he slept, he kept one eye open. When he spoke, he chose his words carefully. And he never, ever laughed.

One day, Bagheera was edging along the branch of a mango tree leaning out over a river. There was one perfectly ripe mango right at the end of the branch, and Bagheera loved mangoes. The only problem was, the branch was slender, and, when Bagheera moved towards the end of it, it began to creak and bend alarmingly. The last thing Bagheera wanted was to break the branch and go for an unplanned swim in the river. His dignity would never allow such a thing.

So Bagheera, crouched on the middle of the branch, was just coming up with a clever plan, when he heard a "harrumph." He looked down and saw a great big grey bear. "It looks like you could use a hand," said the bear.

"No, thank you," said Bagheera politely. "I prefer to work on my own." But the bear paid him no heed, and began climbing up the tree.

"I'll tell you what," huffed the bear. "I'll just sit at the base of that branch and grab your tail. You can climb out and grab the mango, and I'll keep a hold of you in case the end of the branch breaks off. Then we can share the mango!"

"No, I don't think that's a very good idea," said Bagheera impatiently. "I doubt this branch can hold both of us any – "

Snap!

The bear had, of course, ignored Bagheera and climbed out onto the branch. And the branch had, of course, snapped under their combined weight. And now a very wet, very unhappy panther sat in the river next to a very wet, very amused bear.

"Oh, ha-ha-ha-ha!" hooted Baloo (for it was Baloo, of course). "Oh me, oh my, that was an adventure! Oh, come now," he said, seeing how angry Bagheera was, "it's not a total loss, you know." And Baloo held up the broken branch, with that perfect mango still hanging from the end of it.

"I'll tell you what," said the bear, "let's go climb onto that rock and dry off in the sun while we eat this mango. I'm Baloo. What's your name?"

"Bagheera," said the panther, as they climbed up onto the warm, flat rock. And then, almost despite himself, he smiled. And then, very much despite himself, he laughed. And Baloo laughed right along with him.

Show-and-tell

"Please?" pleaded Lilo.

"No way, Lilo!" Nani replied.

"He'll be good. I promise!" Lilo said.

"Oh, all right!" Nani said crossly.

Lilo had been pestering her big sister all morning, begging Nani to let her take their pet, Stitch, to dance class for "show-and-tell." Nani was worried it could cause a lot of trouble. The girls her age were not kind to Lilo, who had a lot of trouble fitting in. As a result, Lilo tended to lash out at them and get herself into trouble. And the problem was, her strange pet, Stitch, was just like her. Nani was convinced that the awful-looking creature they picked up at the pound wasn't even a real dog. Just like Lilo, Stitch didn't seem to fit in very well, either. The other dogs at the pound had certainly shunned him.

When they arrived at dance class, Nani gave her little sister a quick hug. "You behave yourselves!" she said.

"You'll behave yourself," Lilo said to Stitch. "I know you will."

Some of the girls sniggered as Lilo and Stitch walked in and sat down.

"All right," said the dance teacher. "What have you brought today, Lilo?"

Lilo stood up. "This is my dog. His name is Stitch. I got him at the pound."

"He sure is ugly!" said Myrtle.

"Now, Myrtle, be nice," the teacher said.

"Can he fetch?" Myrtle asked. She threw a water balloon that she had brought for show-and-tell right at Stitch!

Stitch caught the balloon neatly, then threw it back at Myrtle. "No!" yelled Lilo, and threw herself in front of Myrtle, accidentally knocking the other girl over. The water balloon hit Lilo and broke, sending water flying everywhere!

"Oh, Lilo," said the teacher, "I think it's time for your pet to go home." Lilo picked up Stitch and ran outside.

Lilo sat down at the kerb. Stitch sat down too. "You got us in trouble today," Lilo said to him. "Why did you hit Myrtle with that water balloon?"

Stitch growled.

"Oh, that's right," said Lilo, "you don't *do* fetch. How could I have forgotten?" She looked thoughtful. "How about we play catch, instead? That's almost the same thing as fetch, but there's an important difference. Fetch is something you play with a pet, and catch is something you play with a friend. I think you're more my friend than my pet, Stitch."

Stitch nodded eagerly and held up a ball. Lilo smiled, and the two friends spent a lovely afternoon together playing catch.

Geppetto's Gift

One day, Geppetto was in his workshop painting a clock, when he had an idea. "I know what I will do with that pine log I just found," he told his little cat, Figaro. "I will make a splendid puppet!"

He put down the clock and got to work. When he had finished making the puppet, he got out his jars of paint and some fabric. "Now," he said to Figaro, "should my puppet's eyes be blue or green? Should her hair be yellow or brown or black? Should her dress be red or purple?"

Suddenly, Geppetto heard a noise outside. He went to the window and looked out. He saw groups of children on their way home from school. Geppetto watched them skip past, laughing and shouting and swinging their schoolbooks. He sighed sadly. "How I wish I had a child of my own," he said.

Just then, he noticed a little girl walking quietly with her mother. Like the other girls, she carried a schoolbook under her arm. When a group of girls skipped by her, she looked at them shyly.

"That little girl must be new in town. She looks like she could use a friend," Geppetto said. Suddenly, he had an idea.

"Excuse me, young miss," he called from the window. "I wonder if you could lend me a hand?"

The girl hurried over, tugging her mother after her. Why, an invitation to Geppetto's workshop – how grand!

"As you can see, my friend here needs some eyes," Geppetto said, pointing to the puppet. "But I don't know what colour her eyes should be."

The girl thought hard. "Green," she decided.

Geppetto picked up his pot of green paint and painted two big green eyes onto the wooden face.

"Now, what colour do you suppose her hair should be?" Geppetto asked.

"Brown," the little girl said with a smile.

Carefully, Geppetto painted brown curls on the puppet's head. "She'll need a dress," he said next. "What do you think? Red? Green?"

The girl looked down at her own blue dress. "Blue," she told Geppetto.

So Geppetto made a little blue dress for the little puppet. Then he added a smiling red mouth to the puppet's face.

"Now there's just one last thing," Geppetto said. "I'm busy in my shop all day long, and I'm afraid this little lady might be lonely. Could you take care of her for me?"

The girl's face lit up with delight. "Thank you!" she cried. Hugging the puppet in her arms, she carried her out of the workshop.

"Thank you," the girl's mother said. "You know, you'd be a wonderful father."

Gepetto smiled. If only! he thought.

Dream Tales

One morning, Snow White got up early and prepared a special breakfast for the Dwarfs – fresh cinnamon porridge!

"Good morning!" Snow White greeted the Dwarfs. "Did everyone sleep well?"

"Bike a lady," Doc replied. "Er, I mean, like a baby. What about you, Princess?"

Snow White shook her head. "I had a bad dream," she said. "I dreamed my stepmother, the wicked Queen, was coming to get me."

"Oh, no!" Happy cried. "If she's coming, you'd better hide!"

"And quick!" Grumpy added. "That Queen is trouble, mark my words!"

The other Dwarfs nodded and looked nervous. Dopey even hid under the table.

Snow White laughed. "Why are you hiding?" she exclaimed. "Why, you should know that dreams aren't real! They can't hurt you one bit."

Snow White smiled at the Dwarfs. "What about all of you? Did you dream about anything last night?"

Happy laughed cheerfully. "I dreamed about the things that make me happy."

"Like what?" Snow White asked.

Happy paused for a moment. "Friends and work and sunny days... well, gosh, I guess all sorts of things," he replied. "Just about everything makes me smile."

Just then, a butterfly flew in the window and landed on Happy's nose. The Dwarf smiled widely.

"What about you, Sneezy? Do you remember your dream?" asked Snow White.

"Aaaa-choo!" Sneezy sneezed. "I dreamed I kept sneezing flowers. And every time I sneezed more flowers, they made me sneeze even more," Sneezy said.

"Dopey?" Snow White said. "Did you dream about anything last night?"

Dopey shook his head, looking sheepish.

Grumpy rolled his eyes. "Of course he did," he snapped. "He dreams he's the wisest ruler ever to sit upon a throne."

"That sounds like a marvellous dream, Dopey!" Snow White said, clapping her hands.

"But what about your dream, Princess?" Bashful asked quietly. "Aren't you scared?"

"Not a bit," Snow White replied. "Some dreams are scary. Some are funny. Some are nice." She smiled. "But remember, they're all just make-believe. They disappear as soon as you wake up!"

"I think it's time to make this breakfast disappear," grumbled Grumpy. And that's just what they did.

The Girl With The Magic Hair

Rapunzel's hair had magical powers. Upon a single touch it could cure an illness or make you young again. This is why Mother Gothel stole the little girl soon after she was born: she needed her hair so that she could stay young forever.

Mother Gothel didn't want Rapunzel to ever leave, so she locked the child away in a tall tower. Mother Gothel brought her up to believe that she was her mother and that the world outside was full of danger.

Rapunzel grew into a beautiful young woman, who loved to fill her time with activities. She played the guitar, brushed her long, long, long hair and did her chores… But what she liked to do best was paint. She covered the walls with paintings of the countryside and the stars, which she could see from her window.

On the day before her eighteenth birthday, Rapunzel wanted to break her usual routine. Throughout her life, Rapunzel had seen mysterious lights floating up into the night sky on her birthday. She felt they were meant for her. More than anything, she wanted Mother Gothel to take her to see them.

"Rapunzel! Let down your hair!" Mother Gothel called when she arrived at the tower.

"Right away!" The young girl leaned out of the window. She unwound her long hair until it touched the ground. Mother Gothel took hold of it and Rapunzel hoisted her up.

"Pull, pull harder!" It was very difficult, but Rapunzel never complained.

"Hi. Welcome home, Mother!" Rapunzel said as soon as she'd finished pulling her up.

"Oh! Rapunzel, how do you manage to do that every single day without fail?" Mother Gothel asked. "It looks absolutely exhausting, darling!"

"Oh it's nothing, Mother," the young girl replied politely.

"Then I don't know why it takes so long, Rapunzel!" Mother Gothel cried.

Rapunzel was confused. Was Mother Gothel joking? There was a moment's silence.

"Come now, dearest! I'm just teasing!" Mother Gothel finally said, laughing.

Phew! Rapunzel thought. *Because, if Mother Gothel hadn't been joking, it really would have been unfair!*

Sometimes, Rapunzel didn't understand Mother Gothel's jokes. But she loved her mother very much all the same.

Rapunzel took a deep breath, ready to ask Mother Gothel for the one thing she wanted more than anything…

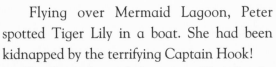

The Story of Peter Pan

One evening, Mr and Mrs Darling were getting ready to spend the evening in town. Before leaving, Mrs Darling popped into the bedroom of her children, Michael, John and Wendy, to wish them goodnight.

Soon after, Peter Pan and Tinker Bell landed on the roof. They'd come for Peter's shadow, which he'd left behind when he last visited!

Tinker Bell gave Peter a signal. He had barely opened the drawer when his shadow escaped. He chased it all over the room and the children were woken up by the noise.

"Peter! When are you going to take us to Never Land?" asked Wendy.

"I will," replied Peter Pan. "But first you must learn to fly. A little pixie dust should do the trick."

Tinker Bell sprinkled the children with pixie dust and soon, the children arrived in Never Land. Peter introduced Michael and John to his friends, the Lost Boys. They went off to play Indians in the forest. But all of a sudden, the real Indians came out from behind the trees and captured the children!

"My daughter Tiger Lily has been kidnapped!" shouted the Indian Chief. He thought the Lost Boys had done it, and wouldn't let them go.

Flying over Mermaid Lagoon, Peter spotted Tiger Lily in a boat. She had been kidnapped by the terrifying Captain Hook!

Peter confronted the pirate. They fought until the crocodile that ate the Captain's hand emerged from the water. The Captain ran away as fast as he could!

Back at the Indian village, the Chief held a banquet to celebrate the return of his daughter. All the children were set free!

But Captain Hook was not defeated yet. To get his revenge, he convinced Tinker Bell, who was jealous of Wendy, to tell him where Peter's hide-out was. Then he sent Peter a booby-trapped gift. It was a bomb! Then he kidnapped the Lost Boys and the Darling children!

Luckily, Tinker Bell, feeling very bad for betraying her friend, managed to warn Peter and save him from Hook's trap! In no time, Peter rushed to Hook's boat and freed his friends. After a mighty battle, the defeated Hook disappeared into the mouth of that waiting crocodile...

With a sprinkle of pixie dust, Hook's boat was transformed into a flying ship! Destination? The Darlings' home. The exciting journey to Never Land had taken barely any time at all... the equivalent of just one evening in the human world.

Leo's Baton

The Little Einsteins were inside their clubhouse. Suddenly Rocket's antenna lit up. "We have a mission!" exclaimed Leo. The team quickly headed to Rocket's Look-and-Listen Scope to discover their mission.

"I think it's a flower trying to push its way through the snow," guessed Quincy.

"Ooh, it's a crocus – the first sign of spring!" June exclaimed.

"Our mission must be to help spring arrive!" Leo said excitedly. "And to do that, we'll need to get the crocus to bloom."

Suddenly Leo realized something was wrong. "My baton is missing!" shouted Leo.

"Oh, dear!" exclaimed Annie. "You'll need it to conduct the crocus. We have to go back to the clubhouse and find it!"

Quincy was puzzled. "There has to be a clue around here somewhere."

"What do all these pictures mean?" asked Annie. Quincy looked intently at them, "Hmm, maybe it's a code we need to crack."

June had an idea. "Let's write down the first letter of each pictured word to see if it spells out a sentence."

"Let's see," said Leo. "If we write in an F for frog, an I for ice cream, an N for nail and a D for dog, we have the word FIND!"

"Awesome job, Leo!" said June. "Let's look at the next word: a Y for yo-yo, an O for owl, a U for umbrella and an R for rabbit – YOUR!"

"The final word is FOOTPRINTS!" shouted Quincy. "Find your footprints – that's the secret message!"

"Leo just needs to track down his footprints to find his baton," said June.

"Leo, didn't you have it on our last mission, in Vermont?" asked Annie.

"You're right, Annie!" exclaimed Leo. "And my footprints should be easy to find in the snow – let's go!"

Once they reached Vermont, the team quickly found Leo's footprints and followed them to a tree.

"Here it is!" June called, picking up Leo's baton.

"Following our footprints really worked!" exclaimed Quincy. "We found Leo's baton and now we're ready to wake up spring."

"Look!" exclaimed Annie. "The snow is melting, and leaves and flowers are popping up everywhere!"

"We followed our footprints, found Leo's baton and helped the crocus to spring into action," said Quincy.

"Great job, team!" exclaimed Leo. "Mission completion!"

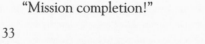

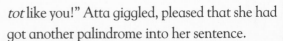

Palindrome-mania!

"**H**ey, Atta," Flik said. "Did you know that your name is a palindrome?"

Atta gave him a strange look. "What's a palindrome?" she asked.

"It's a word that reads the same forwards and backwards," Flik replied. "Spelled forwards, your name is A-T-T-A. Spelled backwards, your name is also A-T-T-A. See?"

"Oh," Atta said. "That's neat. I've never heard of palindromes before."

"Really?" said Flik. "I love them. There are other names that are palindromes, like *Bob*."

"Or *Lil*?" tried Atta.

"Right!" said Flik. "And *Otto*."

"And *Nan*!" added Atta. "This is fun!"

"What's fun?" said Dot, who had just run over to them.

"Thinking of palindromes," Atta replied.

"Huh?" said Dot.

"Exactly!" said Flik. "*Huh* is a palindrome!" Together, Flik and Atta explained to Dot what a palindrome was.

"Oh!" said Dot. "Wait! Let me see if I can think of another one." Dot looked around, hoping that something she saw would spark an idea. She spotted her mother, the Queen, off in the distance, lounging in the shade.

"*Mum!*" cried Dot. "That's one, isn't it?"

"Not bad," said Atta with a wink, "for a tot like you!" Atta giggled, pleased that she had got another palindrome into her sentence.

"Oh, yeah?" replied Dot with a mischievous grin. "Well, you ain't seen nothin' yet, *sis*!"

Taking turns, Dot and Atta challenged one another to think of more and more palindromes. Dot came up with *eye*, *pop* and *toot*. Atta countered with *gag*, *noon*, *did* and *redder*.

"Yes," Flik interjected, "*redder* is a nice, long one! It's harder to think of palindromes that have more than four letters. Believe me, I've spent hours on that. But there's always *Aidemedia* – that's a type of bird, you know. And *Allenella*, of course, which is a category of mollusc . . . ." Flik went on to list a longer palindrome for just about every letter of the alphabet – most of them sciencey words that Atta and Dot had never heard before. As he droned on and on and on, Dot and Atta looked at each other and rolled their eyes. Now they were both thinking of the same word, and it wasn't a palindrome: B-O-R-I-N-G.

When Flik had finally finished with his list, he looked up at Dot and Atta with a self-satisfied smile. Each of them had a palindrome ready.

"*Wow*," said Atta flatly, sounding more bored than impressed.

"*Zzz*," snored Dot, who had drifted off somewhere between *V* and *W*.

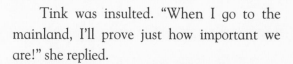

A Tinker's Talent

Tinker Bell had not long arrived in Pixie Hollow and was being shown around her new home. Two fairies named Clank and Bobble couldn't wait to show her all the handy things that tinker fairies made.

Soon Fairy Mary – the no-nonsense fairy who ran Tinkers' Nook – arrived. She noticed the new fairy's dainty hands. "Don't worry, dear, we'll build up those tinker muscles in no time," she exclaimed. Then, after reminding Clank and Bobble to make their deliveries, she was gone.

A little while later, they were on their way, with Cheese the mouse pulling the wagon. There were rainbow tubes for Iridessa – she explained she would roll up rainbows, put them in the tubes, and take them to the mainland.

"What's the mainland?" Tink asked.

"It's where we're going to go for spring, to change the seasons," replied Silvermist.

Next the tinkers stopped at the Flower Meadow, where Vidia was vacuuming the pollen out of flowers with her whirlwind.

"Hi! What's your talent?" Tink asked.

"I am a fast-flying fairy. Fairies of every talent depend on me," answered Vidia. She made it clear that she didn't think much of tinker fairies.

Tink was insulted. "When I go to the mainland, I'll prove just how important we are!" she replied.

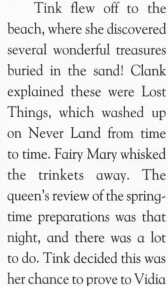

Tink flew off to the beach, where she discovered several wonderful treasures buried in the sand! Clank explained these were Lost Things, which washed up on Never Land from time to time. Fairy Mary whisked the trinkets away. The queen's review of the spring-time preparations was that night, and there was a lot to do. Tink decided this was her chance to prove to Vidia just how important a tinker's talent really was!

That evening, the Minister of Spring welcomed Queen Clarion to the review ceremony. Suddenly, Tinker Bell interrupted the proceedings. "I came up with some fantastic things for tinkers to use when we go to the mainland!" she told the queen excitedly.

Tink pulled a homemade paint sprayer out of the wagon and demonstrated it on a flower that needed colouring. But it exploded!

"Has no one explained?" Queen Clarion said gently. "Tinker fairies don't go to the mainland. The nature-talent fairies do all of those things. I'm sorry."

From this moment, Tinker Bell decided she would change her fairy talent for good.

Pesky Princes

Jasmine's father, the Sultan, was growing impatient. "My dearest daughter," he said pleadingly, "the law states that you should be married before your 16th birthday, and that is coming up soon. Must you be so picky? There are many princes who would love to marry you."

Jasmine sighed. "So far they've all been so . . . pompous," she said. "But I promise to try, Father."

The very next day, Prince Sultana arrived, carried on a litter and accompanied by a huge group of camels, trumpeters and servants. He bowed down low before Jasmine. "I know you will be pleased to hear that I have selected you as my bride," he said in a tone Jasmine didn't like one bit. "Shall we discuss our wedding?"

Jasmine tried to hide her dislike. "I was just about to take my pet for a little walk around the palace. He needs his exercise, you see. Why don't we discuss it while we walk him?"

The Prince readily agreed.

With a sly smile, Jasmine whistled. Out bounded her pet tiger, Rajah. When he gave a snarl of welcome, the Prince ran away.

"Well, he didn't last long," said Jasmine happily, as she gave Rajah a big hug. "Nice work, Rajah."

The next day, another suitor arrived, this time with an even bigger group of servants in tow. "Announcing . . . Prince Habibi!" the footman called out, as the procession arrived.

Jasmine poked her head out of her bedroom window and called down, "Hi! Sorry, I can't come down. The, uh, stairs are being polished. Do you mind taking my laundry to the royal cleaners? Catch!"

Prince Habibi stood below the tower, arms outstretched. *Boom!* A big laundry bag knocked him flat. "Harumph!" he cried, and off he went.

The next day, Prince Baklava arrived. "The Princess is at the royal pond, sire," the footman said. Prince Baklava headed there, with three servants holding up his cape so that it wouldn't get muddy. Upon arriving, he saw Jasmine, reading a book on a little island in the middle of the pond. All around her, huge alligators waited in the water, looking hungry.

"Hello!" Jasmine called to him. "Would you mind coming out to fetch me?"

Prince Baklava stared at Jasmine and then at the alligators. With a shriek of terror, he turned and ran as his servants jogged behind him, still holding up his cape.

Jasmine giggled and stood up. Then the Princess stepped daintily across the pond on the backs of the alligators. "Thanks, guys," she said with a wink as she headed back to the palace.

MULAN

Soup's On!

Mulan stood in the kitchen, moodily stirring a pot of soup for supper. Grandmother Fa sat at the table, sorting through grains of rice. Neither one of them spoke. They were both lost in thought at the recent news they had received: Mulan's father, Fa Zhou, had been ordered to join the Chinese army in order to help protect the Emperor from the invading Huns. One male out of every household was expected to report for duty. As Mulan had no brother, it was her father's duty to join. But though her father had been a great warrior in his day, Mulan knew that he was no longer young, and was not strong enough to withstand any more battles. Mulan was distraught, for she knew that if her father joined the army and went into battle, he would surely die.

"Why must my father fight?" Mulan asked her grandmother suddenly. "He is but one man, and the Emperor would never know the difference if he didn't join. Yet what a difference to our family it would be if he were to die!" She sighed heavily.

Her grandmother also sighed and continued to sort the rice silently for a few moments. Then she stopped and turned towards Mulan. "You are partly correct. One grain of rice, such as this one that I have in my hand, is small and insignificant." Then she held out her hand and tipped the grain into the large bowl of rice she had been sorting. "Yet together, you know, all the grains of rice in this bowl could feed many people. The Emperor needs an army of many, many people in order to defeat the invaders."

Mulan shook her head miserably, afraid that if she spoke she would cry. She was young and stubborn, and it was difficult for her to accept the sacrifice that her father was expected to make.

Grandmother Fa was just as unhappy as Mulan. But the older woman realized that it was useless to protest against some things. She stood up and walked silently out of the kitchen.

Mulan continued to stir the soup, even though it didn't need stirring. Next to the pot sat a small bowl, which contained a peppery red spice. She picked up the small bowl and looked at it thoughtfully. "One grain of rice is small and insignificant," she said to herself. "And yet, a tiny pinch of the spice from this little bowl could change the flavour of this whole pot of soup. Perhaps," she went on, "one person *can* make a difference, if she follows her heart."

Mulan dumped the whole bowl of spice into the pot, and smiled.

"Soup's on!" she cried.

Cinderella

Dear Sisters

"I had the strangest dream," Cinderella told her mouse friends one morning while she was getting ready for another day of drudgery. "My Fairy Godmother sprinkled happy dust over Anastasia and Drizella, and they were so nice to me."

"But that was only a dream," Jaq warned her.

"I know," Cinderella told him, "but it was so nice, that I think I'll try to pretend that it really happened. Whenever they're horrid to me, I'll pretend they actually said something sweet and kind."

"They don't seem so sweet and kind to me," Jaq told Gus as the three went downstairs. Gus nodded in agreement.

"Wash my dresses." Drizella threw her laundry at Cinderella.

"And polish my shoes." Anastasia opened her wardrobe door. "All of them."

"Do the dishes!"

"And mop the floor!"

"Draw the curtains!"

"And clean the rugs!"

"Right away, sisters!" Cinderella sang out, as sweet as you please. "Thank you!"

All day long, Drizella and Anastasia barked orders at Cinderella. But, no matter what they asked her to do, Cinderella always sang back, "Right away, sisters!" or "You're too kind!"

Finally, Anastasia pulled Drizella aside.

"No matter what we tell Cinderella to do, she stays happy," Anastasia said. "She acts like we're doing her a favour. It's making me nervous!"

"Do you think she's gone mad?" Drizella asked. Anastasia looked worried. "She could be! Who knows just what she's capable of!"

Just then, Cinderella walked in. She stopped, surprised to see her stepsisters looking at her as though she were crazy.

"Why, my dear sisters, whatever can be the matter? I do hope you're not ill," she said.

"*D-d-d-dear* sisters?" quavered Anastasia. "You called us your *dear* sisters?" She and Drizella edged towards the door.

"Of course," said Cinderella. "I adore you both. I'm the luckiest girl in the world to have such kind, caring siblings."

That did it. Convinced that Cinderella had lost her mind, the two stepsisters turned and ran. Cinderella listened as her sisters' doors slammed shut. Then she smiled at Gus and Jaq, who had been watching the whole time.

"They may not actually be caring or good-natured," Cinderella said to the mice, "but they'll be too frightened to come out of their rooms for at least a few hours. Who's up for a game of hide-and-seek while we've got the run of the house?"

The mice squeaked happily, and the friends spent a lovely afternoon together while Anastasia and Drizella cowered under their beds.

Beauty and the Beast

Snow Day

One cold February day, Belle sat on the windowsill in her room in the dreary castle, sad and homesick, watching the snowflakes swirl outside. She had agreed to remain in the Beast's enchanted castle in exchange for her father's freedom. How she missed her little home and her dear father! The Beast tried to be kind to her, but he was gruff and had such a terrible temper.

Suddenly, she jumped. The Beast had appeared, trudging through the snow beneath her window. She thought she saw him glance quickly up at her, but she wasn't certain. "What on earth is he doing?" she asked out loud. She watched him scoop up an armful of snow and try to form it into a ball, but it fell apart, spraying snow right in his face. Belle giggled to herself. "Why, I think he is trying to build a snowman!" she cried. "But he has no idea how to begin!"

Next, the Beast made a smaller snowball. This one managed to hold together, and he began pushing it around the courtyard. It grew bigger and bigger. Soon it was so big even the strong Beast could hardly move it. Belle watched him struggle to push it, and then suddenly fall headlong over the top of it, his enormous feet kicking vainly in the air. At this, Belle let out a peal of silvery laughter. It was the first time she had laughed since she had arrived in this dreary old castle.

A few of the servants heard Belle's laughter and ventured cautiously into the hallway outside her room. They, too, were under the enchantment and dearly wanted their master and this beautiful girl to fall in love, as that was the only way to break the spell.

"Do you suppose she is starting to like him?" Mrs Potts whispered to Lumiere.

"I don't know!" he whispered back. "I hardly dare to hope! But just in case, I must arrange for another romantic dinner for two this evening!" He hurried in the direction of the kitchen, already thinking about foie gras, flambé, soufflé and crème brûlée.

Belle watched the Beast slowly climb to his feet. Scowling, he began to roll another snowball. This time, he slipped on some ice and fell flat on his back.

With another laugh of delight, Belle jumped to her feet and threw on her cloak. She raced out of her room, and hurried outside to join the Beast in the snow. She even showed the snowy beast how to make a snow angel.

The servants all ran to the window to watch the two new friends play in the snow together. Maybe, just maybe, something good was about to happen!

7

Lady and the TRAMP

A Lady's Touch

Late one night, Lady's ears perked up and her eyes flew open with a start. The baby was crying! Lady had grown to love the new baby in the house, and she was very protective of him. If he was crying, she was going to find out why. She climbed out of her basket, pushed open the swinging door with her nose and tiptoed up the front stairs.

Meanwhile, Jim Dear and Darling were trying to calm the baby. "Oh, Jim, I just don't know what's the matter with him!" said Darling. She was holding the baby in her arms, trying to rock him and soothe him, but his little face was a deep red and covered with tears. Jim Dear sat groggily at the edge of the bed and looked at his wife helplessly.

"Well, we know he isn't hungry," said Jim Dear, "since we've just given him a bottle." He massaged his temples as though they hurt. Then he noticed Lady, who had walked tentatively into the bedroom. "Hello, Lady," he said to her.

Lady took a few steps closer to the cradle, where Darling was laying the baby down. His little fists were closed tight, and his shrieks had turned to loud sobs.

"We just don't know what's the matter with the little guy," Jim Dear said wearily to Lady. "We've fed him and changed him, and I've sung him every lullaby I know. Maybe you can figure out what's bothering him!"

That was all the invitation Lady needed. She jumped up onto the bed and peered into the cradle. The baby's eyes were squeezed shut and his cheeks were wet with tears. His little legs were kicking the covers. Lady reached in and tugged at the covers to smooth them out. The baby opened his eyes and looked at Lady. His cries dropped to a whimper, and he reached out to touch her. His tiny hand grabbed hold of her ear and tugged. Lady winced but held still. With her chin, she began to rock the cradle and, with her furry tail, she beat a rhythmic *thump, thump, thump* on the bedcover.

"Ga!" said the baby as he broke into a gummy smile, his big blue eyes looking like wet forget-me-nots. Still holding Lady's ear, the baby giggled.

"Oh, look, Jim Dear!" cried Darling delightedly. "Lady has got him to stop crying!"

"I just don't know what we'd do without you, Lady!" Jim Dear said gratefully.

Rock, rock, rock went the cradle. *Thump, thump, thump* went Lady's tail. Soon the baby's eyelids grew heavy, and then his eyes closed. Tears still streaking his little round cheeks, he relaxed his grip on Lady's ear, smiled and fell asleep.

Winnie the Pooh

Roo's New Baby-sitter

"I don't want to be baby-sitted!" cried Roo. Roo's mama, Kanga, was going shopping and Pooh was going to baby-sit.

"I want to go shopping!" cried Roo. He had a large bag and was filling it when Pooh arrived.

"Hello, Pooh," said Roo. "I'm shopping!" He put more tins in his bag, partly because he didn't want his mama to see how much he minded being left behind.

Roo and Pooh said goodbye to Kanga. Then Pooh gave Roo a hug and tried to feed him a nice smackerel of honey.

"I want to go shopping," squeaked Roo. "I don't want to eat."

"Hmmmm," said Pooh. "NOW what do I do?"

"You don't know how to baby-sit?" asked Roo. "I'm good at baby-sitting. I'll tell you how. The first thing a baby-sitter does is climb!"

Pooh, who was starting to think there was not much SITTING involved in baby-sitting, said, "Okay, let's find a good climbing tree."

They climbed the old apple tree in Roo's back garden. Roo hopped from branch to branch, and Pooh climbed up behind him.

"Mmmm," said Roo. "Look at those apples. Baby-sitters always pick apples for supper."

So Pooh climbed up to the highest branch, picked four bright red apples and then inched back down using one arm. They sat side by side and swung their feet and ate the sweet apples.

"This is the best supper ever!" cried Roo.

Next, Roo showed Pooh how babysitters pour a whole bottle of bubble bath into the bathwater. Roo disappeared under the bubbles. *Wfffffff.* Pooh blew on the bubbles but he couldn't see Roo!

"Look at me jumping," squeaked a little voice. Roo was jumping on his bed, all wet! Pooh dried Roo off, then helped put on his pyjamas.

"Time for your Strengthening Medicine," said Pooh, a little more sternly than when poohs usually say such things. But Roo didn't want it. He folded his arms across his chest.

"Oh well," said Pooh, slumping in a chair. "Why don't you give ME a spoonful? I think I could do with it!"

"Now, Pooh, dear, here's your medicine," said Roo in a cheerful, grown-up sort of voice.

"Ahhh!" said Pooh. "Thank you, Roo. You are a good baby-sitter."

Just then, Kanga opened the door and saw Roo and Pooh snuggled together in the chair.

"Mama!" cried Roo. "I'm babysitting Pooh!"

"Of course you are, dear," said Kanga.

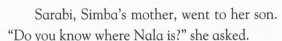

Simba's Secret

Simba and Nala were best friends. They liked to tell each other secrets.

"I'm scared of mice," Nala told Simba one day. "Don't tell anybody."

"Don't worry, I won't," Simba said.

One day, Simba and his father, Mufasa, were out for a walk. "Look at that mouse stuffing her cheeks with seeds," said Mufasa.

"That's so funny!" said Simba. "I don't know why Nala's scared of mice."

Nala had heard Simba talking with his dad, and she got really mad with Simba.

A few weeks later, Nala said, "I'm going to tell you a secret but it's a really big one. If you tell this time, I'll be so mad at you."

"I promise I won't say anything!" said Simba.

"Okay," said Nala. "Here's the secret: I found a huge cave yesterday, down in the red cliffs. I'm going back to explore it today."

Simba played all day without Nala. Before dinner he began to wonder when she was coming back. Nala's mother was worried. "Simba," she asked, "do you know where Nala is?"

"No," he answered. He'd made a promise to Nala, and he didn't want to break it. The sun went down and the moon shone in the sky.

Sarabi, Simba's mother, went to her son. "Do you know where Nala is?" she asked.

"I can't tell," said Simba. "It's a secret. I can't tell, no matter what!"

"Simba," said his mother, "you're a good friend to try not to tell Nala's secret. But there are some secrets that are good to keep and others that are important to tell."

Simba thought about what his mother had said. He decided that he had to tell everyone where Nala was.

The whole pride hurried to the red cliffs. At last, they heard a small voice. "M-mother?" It was Nala!

The lions rushed to the entrance of a cave, but it was almost completely blocked. A rock slide had trapped the little cub! The lions dug and dug, and finally they had cleared the rocks away. Nala rushed out of the cave and ran to her mother.

A few minutes later, Simba walked over and hung his head. "I'm sorry I told your secret, Nala," he said.

"If you hadn't said anything, I'd still be here. It was a stupid secret!" said Nala.

When they got home, it was time for bed. Nala and Simba snuggled together. "I'm happy you're home," said Simba. "And that's not a secret!"

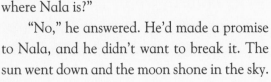

101
DALMATIANS

Rolly's Midnight Snack

"Time for bed!" called Pongo.

"Aw, Dad," complained Patch, "we're not tired!"

"No arguments," said Pongo. "Little puppies need their rest."

With a sigh, Patch joined the line of puppies climbing the staircase.

"I'm hungry," Rolly complained as the puppies settled down for the night.

"You're always hungry," said Patch.

"And you always want to stay awake and have adventures," said Rolly.

Patch sighed. "Too bad we never get what we want."

Hours later, Rolly felt a tap on his shoulder. "Is it morning?" he asked with a yawn.

"No," said Patch. "It's midnight. Wanna explore? I'll get you a snack."

"A snack!" cried Rolly excitedly.

"Shhhhh!" said Patch. "Come on."

Rolly followed Patch to the kitchen.

Patch nodded towards the table. "After dinner, I saw Nanny put some juicy bones up there. She's saving them for tomorrow's soup."

"Soup!" cried Rolly. "What a waste! Bones are for chewing on!"

So, Patch and Rolly came up with a plan.

First, Patch climbed onto Rolly's shoulders to reach the table.

Everything went fine until Patch threw down the first bone and it landed in the dustbin. Rolly took off after it and leaped inside!

Rolly was stuck. Patch tried hard not to panic. He thought and thought until he came up with another plan – a Rescue Rolly Plan!

Patch went upstairs and woke Lucky and Pepper. The two puppies followed Patch into the kitchen. Then Patch found his father's long lead and tossed one end into the dustbin.

"Take hold of the leash!" Patch told Rolly.

"Okay," said Rolly.

Patch turned to the other puppies and said, "Now, let's all pull on this end of the leash, on the count of three."

The three puppies pulled. The dustbin fell over and Rolly tumbled out onto the kitchen floor.

"Thanks!" said Rolly.

The puppies licked their brother, and they all returned to bed.

Before Rolly drifted off to sleep, he whispered to Patch, "Guess you finally got your adventure."

"Yeah," said Patch. "But I'm sorry you didn't get your snack."

"Sure, I did," said Rolly. "While I was waiting for you to rescue me, what do you think I was doing? I was eating that juicy bone. And, boy, was it good!"

DUMBO

Hide-and-seek

For quite a while, Dumbo was the newest baby in the circus. But then, one day, the stork arrived with a brand-new delivery – a baby girl giraffe.

"You know, Dumbo," said his friend, Timothy Q. Mouse, "I think we should ask that new baby to play with us."

Dumbo nodded. He loved making new friends!

So together, Timothy and Dumbo made their way to the giraffes' pen.

"Hello, Mrs Giraffe," Timothy said. "Can your lovely new baby come out and play?"

Dumbo gave Mrs Giraffe a big, hopeful smile. "Well . . . I suppose so," she said.

She gave her baby a kiss, and sent her off in the care of Timothy Mouse – and Dumbo.

"Okay, kids," said Timothy, standing before the two, "what do you feel like playing?"

Dumbo and the baby giraffe stared back at him blankly.

"Hmm . . . I see," said Timothy. "You don't know that many games. May I suggest hide-and-seek?"

Dumbo and the giraffe nodded happily, as Timothy closed his eyes and counted.

"Ready or not," he said finally, opening his eyes, "here I – hang on! Don't you guys know you're supposed to hide?"

No, actually, they did not.

"Okay," Timothy sighed. "Let's take it from the top. When I close my eyes, you guys hide. You find a place where you can't see me and I can't see you. Like this . . ." Timothy ducked behind a popcorn tub. "Get it?"

Dumbo and the giraffe slowly nodded.

"Okay then, let's try this again. One, two, three . . ." Timothy counted to 20, then opened his eyes. "No, no, no!" he groaned. "You can't hide behind the popcorn. You're too big. Let's try this one more time."

Again, he closed his eyes and counted. Then, very slowly, he opened them and looked around. "Much better!" he said, surprised. Of course, it didn't take him long to find Dumbo's wide body behind a narrow tent pole, or the giraffe's tall neck sticking up from behind the clowns' trunk. But they were getting closer!

"This time, guys, try to find a place for your whole body to hide," Timothy said.

So, Dumbo and the giraffe waited for Timothy to close his eyes once more, then they quietly sneaked behind the pole and trunk again. This time, the tall, skinny giraffe hid behind the tall, skinny pole. And short, wide Dumbo hid behind the short, wide trunk. And do you know what? They were hidden so well, Timothy Q. Mouse may still be looking for them to this very day!

Disney · PIXAR
FINDING
NEMO

The Induction

Nemo still had a satisfied smile on his face from the previous night's induction ceremony. I'm part of the club! he thought.

"So, Shark Bait, what did you think of that ceremony last night?" Gill asked.

"It was the best!" Nemo exclaimed.

"If only we could get Flo to be part of the ceremony," Deb mused. "But she never seems to want to come out at night."

"So, kid, what was your favourite part?" Jacques wanted to know.

"I think my favourite part was swimming to the top of Mount Wanna ... wannaha ... ha ..." Nemo tried unsuccessfully to pronounce it.

"Wannahockaloogie," Bloat said.

"Yeah," Peach reminisced. "I have a soft spot for my first climb too."

"I wonder," Nemo said. "Who came up with that name?"

Bubbles pointed at Gurgle, who pointed at Bloat, who pointed at Peach, who pointed at Deb, who pointed at Flo.

Deb shrugged. "I guess we came up with it together," she said.

"Why do they call it the Ring of Fire if there's no fire?" Nemo asked.

"Well, you see, it's like this – I don't know," Peach had to admit.

"But who made it up, then?" Nemo asked, confused. "Didn't you guys *invent* the ceremony?"

"I think Bubbles came up with the Ring of Fire," Gurgle offered.

"Aren't they beautiful?" Bubbles mused.

"I find it very unsanitary to swim through others' bubbles," Gurgle complained. "Which is why I came up with the chanting part of the ceremony. It's very cleansing both for the body and the mind, and circulates carbon dioxide through the gills."

"That makes sense," Nemo agreed, although it really didn't.

"Don't forget about the kelp fronds," Peach piped up.

"Oh, there's no big secret there," Deb confided. "I just like giving a good whack with the old kelp fronds every now and then." And she demonstrated by whacking Bloat, who immediately began to swell up.

"Was that really necessary?" Bloat asked as he floated away.

"What can I do in the next ceremony?" Nemo asked eagerly.

"Hopefully, we won't have another one. Not if we break out of here first, Shark Bait," Gill answered.

"Well, you never know," Deb said forlornly. "Maybe Flo will come around."

Everyone rolled their eyes, including Nemo.

THE LION KING

Tag!

Early one morning, Simba woke up ready to find Nala and continue their game of Tag. The night before, when their mothers had made them stop ("Time for bed, Simba!" "Time for bed, Nala!"), Simba had been It – which is a terrible way to go to bed! – and he was eager to tag Nala and make *her* It as soon as possible. But, when he arrived at the pride's meeting place, everyone, it seemed, was there except for Nala.

"Where's Nala?" he asked his mother.

"Oh, I heard her mother say she wasn't feeling well," she replied. "So they're staying in the cave and resting until she's better."

"But she has to come out," protested Simba. "I'm It and I have to tag somebody!"

His mother smiled. "I'm afraid you'll just have to wait, little Simba," she said.

"But that's so boring!" Simba groaned.

"You can play by yourself, Simba," she reminded him.

"Aw, all right." Simba sighed. First, he tried hunting grasshoppers. But they jumped so high and so far – and so fast! – he soon grew tired and frustrated.

Then he tried climbing trees. But the birds didn't much like a lion cub messing around among their branches and shooed him away.

Finally, he tried just lying down and finding pictures in the clouds. But that was Nala's favourite game, and it made him miss her.

He rolled over and swatted a bright wild-flower with his paw. "Tag, you're It," he said half-heartedly. Then, suddenly, an idea popped into his head. What if he picked some wildflowers and took them to his sick friend? It might even make her feel better!

With newfound energy, Simba picked as many flowers as he could carry in his mouth and made his way back to the pride's cave.

"Dees ah fur Nana," he said, dropping the flowers at Nala's mother's feet. "These are for Nala," he repeated. "I hope she feels better really soon."

"Oh, thank you, Simba," the lioness said. "But why don't you give them to her yourself? She seems to be feeling much better. Nala!" she called. And out came Simba's friend, smiling and looking very glad to see him.

She sniffed at the pretty flowers. "Are these for me? Gee, thanks, Simba." Then she turned to her mother. "Can I go out and play with Simba now, Mama?"

"I don't see why not," said her mother.

"Grrreat!" said Nala.

"Yeah, grrreat!" said Simba. Then he reached out and gently tapped her with his paw. "Tag! You're It!"

Mowgli Finds a Friend

Bagheera the panther found Mowgli in the jungle when he was just a baby, and decided to take the boy to a wolf family that lived nearby.

The mother wolf agreed to take care of him, and for ten years she raised him as one of her own. Mowgli was a very happy Man-cub.

One day, bad news arrived in the jungle. Shere Khan the tiger had returned after a long absence. The tiger was mean and hated everything. More than anything though, Shere Khan hated Man. This meant that it was no longer safe for Mowgli to live in the jungle. The wolves decided that he should go to a Man-village at once.

Bagheera had kept watch over Mowgli through the years and volunteered to take him. Later that night, the boy rode on the panther's back as they made their way through the jungle.

But Mowgli did not want to leave the jungle. It was his home. "I don't want to go to the Man-village!" he shouted. Then he added, "I can take care of myself."

Although Bagheera cared a lot for Mowgli, he eventually became tired of the Man-Cub's fighting, and he walked off into the jungle, leaving Mowgli alone.

Mowgli began to worry that maybe he couldn't take care of himself.

Before long, a bear named Baloo walked out of the jungle and spotted Mowgli. The bear tried to be friendly, but Mowgli told Baloo to go away and leave him alone. But Baloo did not listen. He decided the little Man-cub needed to have some fun.

"Hey, kid, Baloo's gonna learn you to fight like a bear," he said, jumping around. The bear's silly behaviour made Mowgli laugh and soon he was dancing and boxing just like Baloo. When they finished, Mowgli jumped up on his new friend's stomach and tickled him. "You're all right, kid," Baloo said gently.

Just then, Bagheera walked over to them. He had returned to make sure Mowgli was okay. The panther told Baloo that he thought Mowgli should go to the Man-village so he'd be safe from Shere Khan.

Baloo didn't want his little buddy to go to a Man-village. "They'll ruin him. They'll make a man out of him," the bear said.

Bagheera sighed. He knew it would be hard to persuade Mowgli to leave now that he had made friends with Baloo. The panther watched as the pair jumped into the river and floated lazily away.

Peter Pan's Visit

John and Michael Darling sat, silent and still, on Michael's bed, listening intently as their big sister, Wendy, told them yet another story about their favourite hero, Peter Pan.

Meanwhile, their dog and nursemaid, Nana, dozed peacefully under the open window of the Darling nursery.

"...And then," Wendy was saying, "with a quick slash of his sword, Peter Pan cut the evil Captain Hook's hand right off!"

Michael and John gasped. Nana started too, and jumped to her feet. But Nana wasn't alarmed by Wendy's story. She had heard a strange noise coming from just outside the window. Nana faced the window, listening carefully for the sound to repeat itself.

There it was again!

Unnoticed by the children, who were caught up in their story, Nana scurried over to the window and poked her head outside.

And there, just to one side of the window and crouched on a narrow ledge, was a red-headed boy dressed in green from head to toe.

Nana froze, then leaned towards the boy slowly, growling a low warning growl.

"There, there, Nana," the boy whispered softly. "Please, don't bark."

At the sound of her name, Nana froze again, then tilted her head to one side, as if trying to figure something out.

"You're wondering how I know your name," the boy whispered. "Well, I know a lot about you and Wendy and John and Michael. You see, I've been coming here, now and again, for quite a while to listen to Wendy's stories – stories about me!" He stood up straight and puffed his chest out proudly. "I'm Peter Pan, you know!"

Now, Nana was not a mean dog. But there was one thing – well, three things, really – that she was very protective of, and they were the three children inside that nursery. Nana knew it was up to her to make sure they were safe and sound. She also knew that strange boys crouching outside the nursery window – Peter Pan or not – were not to be tolerated.

And so, with another low growl, Nana suddenly lunged further out of the window and snapped her teeth at Peter Pan. The boy flew out of the way just in time, but his shadow was not quite so fast. It struggled to get loose, but it was held tight in Nana's mouth!

Startled, Peter Pan flew off into the darkness and began his journey home to Never Land. But he knew he had to get his shadow back. He would have to return to the Darling nursery – and soon! And *this* time, he would need to go inside....

48

THE JUNGLE BOOK

Go Fish!

"Okay, small fry," said Baloo the bear. "Today I'm going to teach you to fish like a bear!"

Mowgli was delighted. He loved his new friend Baloo. Unlike Bagheera the panther, who kept insisting that Mowgli should live in the Man-village for his own protection, Baloo made no such demands on Mowgli. Baloo was much more interested in having a good time living in the jungle, and so was Mowgli.

"Now, watch this, kid," said Baloo as they arrived at the riverbank. "All ya gotta do is wait for a fish to swim by and then . . ."

Whoosh! Quick as a flash, Baloo held a wriggling silver fish in his paw. "Now you try it!" he said to Mowgli.

Mowgli sat very still, waiting for a fish to swim by. Then – *splash*! – he toppled headfirst into the water.

"Hmm," said Baloo after he had fished Mowgli out and set him down, dripping. "Now I'll show you my second technique."

Baloo and Mowgli walked towards another part of the river. This time, the fish could be seen occasionally leaping out of the water as they swam down a little waterfall. Baloo waded a few steps into the water, waited for a fish to jump, then – *whoosh*! – he swiped a fish right out of the air. "Now you try, buddy."

Mowgli waded in just as Baloo had done. He waited for the fish to jump and then leaped for it. *Splash*!

"Okay, plan C," said Baloo, after he had fished Mowgli out a second time. "I'll take you to the big waterfall. The fish literally fall into your paws. All ya gotta do is reach out and catch one!"

Mowgli followed Baloo to the big waterfall. Sure enough, silvery fish were jumping all the way down the fall. Catching one would be easy!

In the blink of an eye Baloo held up a fish for Mowgli to admire.

"I'm going to do it this time, you watch me, Baloo!" said Mowgli excitedly. He scrunched up his face with concentration. Then – *flash*! – for an instant, Mowgli actually had a silvery fish in his hands. But, a second later, the fish shot out of his grasp and jumped into the water again. Mowgli looked down at his empty hands with a sigh.

"You know what, kid?" said Baloo, clapping a huge paw on Mowgli's skinny shoulders. "I think you're working too hard. That's not how life in the jungle should be! It should be fun, happy and carefree. So, come on. Let's go shake a banana tree instead!"

And Mowgli cheerfully agreed.

Happy Valentine's Day

"Whatcha doin', Doc?" Happy asked.

Doc was hard at work carving a heart out of a piece of wood. "I'm making a present for Snow White," he replied.

"A present for Snow White?" Happy exclaimed. "Oh, dear! Did I miss her birthday?"

"No, silly," Doc said. "It's Valentine's Day."

"Valentine's Day?" Happy turned to Dopey. "Have you ever heard of Valentine's Day?"

Dopey shook his head.

Doc cleared his throat. "Valentine's Day," he began, "is a very special tradition that gives people the opportunity to let loved ones know how important they are."

"I'm giving Snow White these handker-chiefs," Sneezy said as he sneezed into one of them. "Well, maybe not *this* one."

"That's very thoughtful," Doc answered. "I'm sure she'll be able to use them."

"If he has any left," Grumpy moaned.

Then Bashful shyly held out a paper flower he had made.

"Wonderful! And you?" Doc asked Dopey.

Dopey held up a paper aeroplane he'd just made for Snow White.

"You know what I'm going to do? I'm going to juggle for Snow White for Valentine's Day," Happy offered.

"She'll love that!" Doc said.

Sleepy yawned as he held up a pretty card he made.

"And you?" Doc asked Grumpy.

"Well, all right," Grumpy confessed. "I wrote Snow White a poem."

"A poem! Really? Can we hear it?" Doc asked.

"Don't push your luck!" Grumpy snapped.

Just then, the cottage door opened. Snow White had arrived!

"Happy Valentine's Day!" the Seven Dwarfs sang, each holding up his gift for Snow White to see.

"What a wonderful surprise!" Snow White exclaimed. She was holding a bundle of valentines – pretty red and pink hearts on lacy doilies – and handed them out to the Seven Dwarfs, placing a kiss on each of their cheeks. The Seven Dwarfs all thought they were the most beautiful valentines they had ever seen. Even Grumpy was pleased. Bashful blushed an especially bright shade of red as Snow White kissed him on the cheek, and Sleepy started yawning before Snow White could hand him his card. Then Sneezy sneezed, blowing his card into the air. Happy laughed, and Dopey smiled too.

If you asked any of them, he'd tell you it was the best Valentine's Day ever!

Making Dreams Come True

Tiana lived in New Orleans in the 1920s. She was a very pretty and intelligent young girl. She hadn't had the good fortune to be born as rich as her best friend Charlotte, but she had inherited her father's gift for cooking. Even though her father had passed away, she still wanted to make their dream come true for both of them – Tiana was determined to open the restaurant they had always dreamed of owning.

But Tiana didn't have much time for fun. She worked hard as a waitress, trying to earn as much money as she could. She hoped to one day buy the building she'd found that would house the restaurant of her dreams.

One morning, Tiana was serving breakfast at Duke's Diner when Charlotte's father, Big Daddy, came in for a bite to eat.

"Good morning Mr La Bouff!" Tiana greeted him. "And congratulations – I hear you were voted king of the Mardi Gras parade!"

"Caught me completely by surprise . . . for the fifth year in a row!" chuckled Charlotte's father. "Now, how about I celebrate with –"

"Some beignets?" guessed Tiana, with a full plate already perched on her arm. "They've just come out of the oven!"

Just then, Charlotte burst into the restaurant. "Oh, Tia! Have you heard the news? Prince Naveen of Maldonia is coming to New Orleans!"

Charlotte showed Tiana a picture of the attractive young man, adding, "And Big Daddy invited him to our masquerade ball tonight!"

Charlotte's eyes shone with excitement. She would do anything to become a princess... including marrying the first prince that came along!

"That's wonderful, Charlotte," said Tiana. "I've got a little word of advice – my Mother always says that the quickest way to a man's heart is through his stomach!"

The girl turned to her father who was busy feasting on doughnuts. He looked as if he were in heaven. Her friend was right!

"You're a true genius, Tiana! I am going to order five hundred of your man-catching beignets for this evening!"

Charlotte handed her a bundle of notes, and Tiana almost exploded with happiness. This was enough to finally allow her to make the first payment on her restaurant!

It just shows, she thought. *Charlotte and I have very different dreams . . . but they might each help the other to come true!*

Fish-in-the-box

"Ariel?" Flounder called out timidly, poking his head inside Ariel's secret grotto. Ariel had told Flounder to meet her there, but she hadn't arrived yet. "I guess I'll wait for her inside," Flounder said to himself. He swam around slowly, gazing at Ariel's collection of things from the human world. The rock ledges were filled with various objects the Little Mermaid had found in sunken ships and up at the surface – everything from a clock to a music box to a knight's helmet. It was Ariel's favourite place.

But, without Ariel there, Flounder found the place lonely . . . and quiet . . . and . . . creepy.

"Yikes!" Flounder screamed, startled by the sudden appearance of another fish as he swam past a piece of a broken mirror. When he realized it was just his own reflection, Flounder breathed a sigh of relief. "Oh, Flounder, don't be such a guppy," he told himself, repeating the line Ariel always used on him.

Flounder swam past one object that he had never noticed before – a square metal box with a handle on one side.

"I wonder what that thing does," said Flounder, staring at the handle. After a few moments' hesitation, Flounder summoned his courage. By flapping his tail fin and pushing the handle with his nose, he managed to turn

it around once . . . twice . . . three times. Nothing happened. Flounder was halfway into the fourth turn when –

Boing!

The latch to the top of the jack-in-the-box released and the spring-loaded jester inside popped out of the box and lunged at Flounder.

"Ahhhhhhhhhhhh!" Flounder screamed as he raced backwards away from the jack-in-the-box and collided with the lid of an open treasure chest. The force of the collision caused the lid of the chest to slam shut, trapping Flounder inside.

Moments later, Ariel swam through the door of the secret grotto.

"Flounder?" she called. "Are you here yet?"

From inside the chest, Flounder yelled to Ariel. *"Mm-nn-eer!"* came the muffled cry.

Ariel followed the sound of his voice and swam over to the chest. Lifting the lid, she found her friend inside. "What are you doing in there?" Ariel asked with a giggle.

Thinking quickly, Flounder replied, "I'm about to do my imitation of that thing." He pointed at the jack-in-the-box. Then Flounder sprang suddenly out of the chest, raced out of the door . . . and kept on swimming.

He'd had enough of Ariel's secret grotto for one day!

Bambi

Practice Doesn't Always Make Perfect

One day, Bambi and Thumper were playing in the meadow.

"Look, Bambi!" exclaimed Thumper.

A herd of stags was thundering towards them.

"I wish I could be a stag!" Bambi exclaimed.

"Well, you know what my father always says," said Thumper.

"I know," said Bambi. "'Eating greens is a special treat. It makes long ears and great big feet.'"

"No, not that!" said Thumper. "I mean, he does say that, but he also says, 'If you want to hop well, but your hop is all wrong, then you have to practise all day long!'"

"I have to hop all day long?" asked Bambi.

"No!" cried Thumper. "If you want to become a stag, you have to practise!"

Bambi glanced back at two big deer. They suddenly ran towards each other, locking horns to test their strength. They looked so powerful and majestic. Bambi wanted to be just like them!

"Okay," Bambi told Thumper.

"Okay," said Thumper. "Follow me."

Thumper hopped to the edge of the meadow. He stopped by a big oak tree. "Lower your head," he told Bambi.

Bambi lowered his head. "Now what?" he asked, staring at the ground.

"Run straight ahead," said Thumper.

Bambi ran straight ahead – towards the trunk of the old oak tree! But, before he got there, a voice cried, "Stop!" Bambi did, skidding to a halt only a few inches from the tree trunk.

Thumper and Bambi looked up. Friend Owl looked down at them with big curious eyes. "Bambi, why were you going to butt my tree trunk with your head?" asked Friend Owl.

"I'm practising to become a big stag," said Bambi. "Stags butt heads to show their strength."

Friend Owl laughed and said, "Bambi, the stags have antlers to protect their heads! And becoming a stag is not something you can practise. It's something that will happen to you with the passing of time."

"It will?" said Bambi.

"Of course!" Friend Owl assured him. "Next summer, you'll see. You'll be bigger and stronger. You'll also have antlers – and, I hope, enough sense not to butt heads with an oak tree!"

"Yes, sir," said Bambi.

"Now go on, you two," said Friend Owl. "And don't be in too much of a hurry to grow up. You'll get there soon enough, I promise you!"

"Okay," said Bambi and Thumper. Then the two friends returned to the snowy meadow to play.

Chaos in the Kitchen

"Now, now, dearie," said Aunt Flora to little Aurora, "it's time for your nap." Flora had just given the baby (who was now named Briar Rose) her bottle and settled her in her cradle.

"Time to make supper!" Flora said to Fauna and Merryweather, turning away from the snoozing baby Princess and clapping her hands together purposefully.

Flora, Fauna, and Merryweather gave each other uneasy grins. It was the first meal the three fairies had to prepare in the little cottage in the woods, where they would live until Aurora's 16th birthday. The King and Queen had sent their beloved daughter into hiding to try to protect her from a curse laid on the Princess by the evil fairy Maleficent. In order to be sure to keep Aurora well hidden, the three fairies had vowed to give up their magic wands and live as ordinary humans. None of them had ever cooked, cleaned or cared for a baby before. This was going to be quite an adventure!

"Now, remember, dearies," said Flora firmly, "we're to use no magic when preparing this meal!"

The three fairies sighed. This was not going to be easy! "I shall cook a stew," announced Merryweather. The others thought that was a wonderful idea. What a cosy meal for their first night in the cottage! Stew sounded hearty and delicious!

"I'll bake some blueberry biscuits and mash the potatoes!" said Flora.

"Are you sure you know how?" asked Fauna.

"How hard could it be?" said Flora. "Fauna, why don't you make a salad?"

"I'll try!" said Fauna brightly. So Merryweather chopped meat and vegetables, Flora mixed flour and water for the biscuits, and Fauna shredded, chopped and diced the salad vegetables.

But, an hour later, dinner still wasn't ready. Merryweather's stew smelled like old boots. Flora opened the oven and pulled out her biscuits, which were not only blackened, but also as flat as pancakes. The mashed potato was terribly lumpy. And somehow most of the salad greens had ended up on the floor.

The three fairies looked at each other in dismay. "Back to the drawing board, girls," said Flora. "But let's not be too hard on ourselves – after all, we've got 16 years to learn how to cook without magic!"

"And that's how long it's going to take!" replied Fauna.

Merryweather laughed. Fauna was obviously joking – wasn't she?

Stitch Upon a Time

"Once upon a time," read Lilo.

"Wait," said Stitch.

"Wait for what?" asked Lilo.

"Snacks," said Stitch. He climbed off the bed and scampered to the bedroom door.

"You better not let Nani hear you," warned Lilo. "She thinks we went to bed."

Stitch crept into the hall, lifted his big ears and listened.

"No Nani," he whispered. Then he dashed downstairs and into the kitchen.

"Soda, pineapple, pickles, coleslaw," recited Stitch, peering into the fridge. "Hmm . . . pineapple-pickle-coleslaw sandwich . . ."

Lilo tiptoed up behind him. "You can't put all that in a sandwich," she whispered.

"*Yaaaaahhhhh!*" shouted Stitch.

"Sorry," whispered Lilo. "I didn't mean to startle you."

"*What* is going on in here?" demanded Nani, storming into the kitchen.

"Stitch wants a snack," Lilo explained.

"It's not time for snacks," Nani said. She shut the refrigerator door and marched them both back up the stairs. "It's time for bed."

"*Story,*" said Stitch as he climbed into bed and held up the book. "Time for story."

"Please?" Lilo asked. She and Stitch both blinked their big dark eyes at Nani.

Nani sighed and said, "Oh, all right. But it had better be a short one."

"Goody!" cried Stitch as Nani climbed into bed too.

After Nani settled in between Lilo and Stitch, Lilo opened the book and began to read, "Once upon a time, there was a sad little puppy named – "

"Stitch!" cried Stitch.

Lilo continued, "There was a sad little puppy named . . . *Stitch*. He was sad because he was lost."

"Lost," repeated Stitch.

Lilo passed the book to Nani and said, "Your turn."

Then Nani began to read, "But one day, he met a little girl named – "

"Lilo," whispered Lilo.

Nani smiled. "He met a little girl named . . . Lilo."

Then Nani continued reading the story, until she reached the very end.

". . . and they lived happily ever after," Nani finished, shutting the book.

"Ever after," murmured Stitch, closing his eyes.

"Ever after," echoed Lilo, closing her eyes.

Nani waited until they were both sound asleep, then headed downstairs for a snack. Maybe she'd have a pineapple-pickle-coleslaw sandwich!

Follow Your Star

Jiminy Cricket was a wanderer. He loved the independence, the excitement and the simplicity of his way of life. For many a season, he had roamed the countryside, stopping to rest in towns along the way, and moving on when he grew restless.

But lately, Jiminy Cricket had noticed that there was one thing missing from his vagabond lifestyle: a purpose. Camping one night by the side of the road, he sat on his sleeping bag and gazed into his campfire.

"I wonder what it would feel like to be really helpful to someone," he said.

Jiminy lay on his sleeping bag and tried to get comfortable on the hard ground as he gazed up into the starry night sky. As his eyes scanned the many tiny points of light, one star to the south jumped out at him and seemed to shine brighter than all the rest.

"Say, is that a Wishing Star?" he wondered aloud. Since he couldn't know for certain, he decided it would be best to make a wish on it, just in case. "Wishing Star," he said, "I wish to find a place where I can make a difference and do a bit of good."

Then, his wish made, Jiminy Cricket suddenly felt a strange impulse: an urge to get up, gather his things and follow that star – the Wishing Star. He couldn't quite explain the feeling, but he felt it just the same.

So do you know what Jiminy Cricket did?

He put out the campfire. He gathered his things. And he took to the road. He followed that star all through the night. He walked for miles along highways and byways, across fields and over hills. He walked until the sun came up and he could no longer see the star to follow it. Then he made camp and he slept.

He did the same thing for several more nights and several more days.

Then, one night, he came to a village. Looking up at the Wishing Star, Jiminy Cricket noticed that it seemed to hang directly overhead.

It was very late at night as Jiminy Cricket walked into the village and looked around. Every window of every house was dark – except for one window in a shop at the end of a street. So Jiminy Cricket hopped over to the window. Peering inside, he saw that it was a woodcarver's workshop, dimly lit by the embers of a fire dying in the fireplace. It seemed a warm and pleasant place to stop for the night.

Little did Jiminy Cricket know that it was the home of Geppetto, a kind old woodcarver who had just finished work on a puppet he called Pinocchio.

And little did he know that he had just found a place where he would do more than just a bit of good.

Minnie's Rainbow

Minnie has just finished reading a book. She's asked all her friends to come take a look....

She learned about something you see in the sky. A colourful arc that the birds fly right by.

But what makes a rainbow that follows the rain?

Let's find out as Minnie explains . . .

Minnie pictures the rainbow in her head, and remembers the first colour is red.

Red makes a rainbow so fiery bright – it's for strawberries, stop signs and Mickey's night-light.

Next there is orange. It's cheerful and cute – the colour of tigers and sunsets and fruit.

Now look again at the pretty rainbow; you might find the third colour is one that you know!

Yellow gives rainbows their light, happy rays; a reminder of ducklings and warm, sunny days.

There's a garden of green in each rainbow you see. It's for pickles and peas and the leaves of a tree.

Look at the rainbow, you'll see what I mean, can you name the fourth colour?

That's right, it is green!

Inside every rainbow is cool, calming blue, for blue skies and bluebells and blue dungarees, too.

Now look at the rainbow beside Donald's hand . . .

It's clear now that blue is the rainbow's fifth band.

Violet you'll find at the end of the line.

It's the colour of lilacs and grapes on a vine.

Red, orange and yellow are one, two and three.

Green is four. Blue is five. Violet's six, as you can see.

But there's more to each rainbow you see in the sky.

There's a whole spectrum of colours, so let's find out why!

A rainbow is made of the colours of light. When we look at it whole, we can see only white.

But when white light is split, then more colours appear.

If you tried counting them, it might take a whole year!

There are not only colours like red, green and blue.

There are some you can't see with your eyes. Yes, it's true!

So what makes a rainbow? What is it we see?

All the coloured waves that are part of light, naturally!

Winnie the Pooh

The Mysterious Backson

One morning, Winnie the Pooh woke up to his tummy rumbling. He was certain a walk in the Hundred-Acre Wood would turn up some honey.

On his journey, Pooh passed by Eeyore and noticed that his tail was missing! The friends decided to hold a contest to find a new tail.

"It's okay," said Eeyore sadly. "I'll learn to live without it."

Pooh then stopped by Christopher Robin's house and he found a note.

Pooh brought it to Owl. "It says, 'gone out, busy Backson.'" Owl looked horrified. "Christopher Robin has been captured by a creature called the Backson!" Luckily, Rabbit came up with a clever plan to capture the Backson. Pooh and Piglet got straight to work digging a pit. Tigger decided to track the Backson on his own.

Meanwhile Pooh's tummy craved honey. He started having strange dreams. Pooh woke from his daydream in a puddle of mud!

The rest of Pooh's friends were looking everywhere for Pooh. Suddenly, they heard a loud THUD! "The plan worked!" Rabbit exclaimed. "We caught the Backson!" The friends peered into the pit, only to discover that it was Pooh! The friends tried to throw the anchor in so Pooh could climb up, but instead they all fell in – apart from Piglet! Now Piglet had to save everyone. A terrified Piglet made his way through the Wood – until he saw a red-eyed monster glaring down at him! He realized the monster was only B'loon stuck in a tree and tugged him free.

Suddenly, an enormous shadow fell over him! "B-B-B-BACKSON!" he shouted. Holding on tight to B'loon, he ran off. But it was only Tigger dressed as a Backson. B'loon lifted Piglet up and away. As he floated down nearer the pit, he crashed into Tigger. Everyone in the pit was relieved to see Piglet and Tigger, and not the Backson. Luckily the friends were finally able to climb out. Back above ground, Christopher Robin had appeared. Pooh handed him the note. Christopher Robin explained he had written that he would be "back soon"– not "Backson"!

Relieved, the friends went on their way. Pooh was hungry for honey still. He got to Owl's front door and pulled the bell rope... and realized that it was Eeyore's tail! Pooh decided that returning Eeyore's tail was more important than satisfying his tummy.

Pooh was declared the winner of the tail contest and was presented with a big pot of honey. All his honey dreams had come true, after all!

Grumpy Rajah

It wasn't always so easy being the daughter of a sultan. Sometimes Jasmine thought she would be the loneliest girl in Agrabah – if it weren't for Rajah, her tiger (and best friend).

But, apparently, it was not always so easy being a tiger either. Rajah was having a bad day.

"Grrr," Rajah growled.

"What's got into you?" Jasmine asked him.

Rajah looked at her with a 'none of your business' glare and growled again.

"Hmm," Jasmine said thoughtfully. She was determined to cheer up the tiger. For one thing, he was her only friend, and life gets pretty unpleasant when your only friend is in a bad mood. And, for another, Jasmine just wasn't allowed to do much, being a princess, so she was always glad to have a project. Right now, her project was to make Rajah purr.

"You know what you need?" Jasmine asked.

Rajah paced back and forth.

"You need to try to relax!" Jasmine told him.

Rajah looked at her with a raised eyebrow.

"You know," Jasmine explained, "loosen up, have a good time."

Rajah began a low-grade growl again.

"All right, all right!" Jasmine surrendered. "I'll stop."

But she just couldn't let it go. She really wanted Rajah to be happy!

"Rajah, don't be mad." Jasmine patted him on the back. "I wouldn't be saying this if I didn't care about you."

Rajah walked away to take a rest, but Jasmine kept talking. "You have to enjoy life, not growl at it! Look at me – I spend all my time talking to the brainless, unpleasant princes my father brings around. But I still try to have fun whenever I can!"

Rajah lay down and put his paws over his ears.

"Oh, I get it." Jasmine caught on. "You're jealous of all those princes!"

Rajah looked up. Jasmine was right. He *was* sick and tired of all those princes coming around.

Jasmine lovingly scratched Rajah behind the ear. "Jealousy isn't becoming," she teased him, "even in tigers. I know I haven't been spending much time with you lately, Rajah. But it's not like I have a choice. The law says I have to find a prince to marry."

Princes, Rajah thought. Yuck!

"But you know," Jasmine continued, hugging her tiger around his big furry neck, "I like you better than any prince."

Rajah began to purr. Jasmine smiled. Mission accomplished!

"Princes!" Jasmine said. "Yuck!"

The Perfect Birthday

Mother Gothel was a wicked old woman, who stole a princess when she was just a baby. Though she pretended to love the girl, Rapunzel, she truly only loved Rapunzel's magical hair, which kept the old woman forever young.

Mother Gothel had convinced Rapunzel that she needed to protect her magical hair by never leaving the tower.

But being stuck in a tower didn't change Rapunzel's bright spirit.

She and her friend Pascal, the chameleon, stayed busy every day, doing lots of activities, including her favourite – painting! But Rapunzel had one dream that she longed to make come true.

Throughout her life in the tall tower, Rapunzel had seen strange lights floating up into the night sky on her birthday. She felt they were especially for her. More than anything, she wanted Mother Gothel to take her to see them.

On the day before her eighteenth birthday, with Pascal urging her on, Rapunzel decided to tell Mother Gothel what she really wanted on her birthday.

"I want to see the floating lights!" she blurted out, revealing a painting she had done of them.

"Oh, you mean the stars," Mother Gothel lied. She wanted Rapunzel to forget her wish.

"That's the thing," countered Rapunzel, "I've charted the stars and they're always constant. But these? They appear every year on my birthday – only on my birthday. I have to know what they are."

"Go outside?" asked Mother Gothel in shock.

Mother Gothel insisted that the world outside was far too scary for a weak girl. There were ruffians, quicksand and snakes!

"Rapunzel, I'm only thinking of you. If you want a perfect birthday, don't ever ask to leave this tower again!" Mother Gothel insisted.

Rapunzel fell silent. She put her arms around Mother Gothel's neck. She understood why her mother wanted to protect her.

Unseen by Rapunzel, the wicked woman gave a sly smile. "Let's put this silliness behind us," Mother Gothel said, patting Rapunzel on her head.

Rapunzel sighed and smiled weakly. *After all. What more could I want?* Rapunzel wondered. *I have everything I could dream of right here.*

Rapunzel knew that she should have been happy with what she had. But she just couldn't give up on her dream.

Cinderella

Chore de Force

Cinderella watched as a blue-and-pink-tinted bubble floated up from her bucket. "Isn't that pretty?" she said as she watched the bubble float higher and higher and finally pop into nothingness. Gus and Jaq and all the rest of Cinderella's mouse friends nodded in agreement.

"I bet it would be fun to float around in a bubble all day! I could see whole cities at a time, bounce on clouds and soar with the birds," Cinderella said dreamily. Her bird friends chirped happily. They liked the idea of sharing the skies with her.

"What am I doing?" Cinderella suddenly said. "I should stay focused on my chores." She finished cleaning the windows and prepared to mop the floor.

Cinderella plunged the mop into a bucket of soapy water, then dragged it across the floor. At first, she felt worn out. Then it occurred to her, as the mop slid across the slippery floor, "This is like dancing! How I love to dance!" Gus and Jaq copied Cinderella as she twirled around the room with the mop. "What fun!" she cried happily.

"Oh, my," Cinderella caught herself. "Did I say that aloud?" Maybe I just need to get away from all these bubbles, she thought. Ironing should do the trick!

She was ironing away and humming merrily to herself when she realized how dark the sky had grown.

"Look at the time!" Cinderella exclaimed. "I've been daydreaming the day away and haven't even started dinner."

Cinderella hurried to the kitchen where she chopped and minced and grated and stirred. "I don't know where this day has gone," she fretted as she added ingredients to her stepsisters' favourite soup. "I've got absolutely nothing done!" And, just then, Cinderella's stepsisters, Anastasia and Drizella, barged into the kitchen.

"Where's my laundry?" barked Anastasia. "Done," Cinderella said.

"And my ironing?" Drizella added.

"Done," Cinderella replied again.

"Did you mop the floors?"

"Wash the windows?"

"Make our dinner?"

"Done, done, done!" Cinderella said gaily.

The sisters marched out of the kitchen muttering with displeasure.

And there Cinderella stood, all alone in the kitchen once more. As she stirred the pot of soup, she thought, I guess I did get a lot done, after all! She twirled across the room in celebration – and Jaq and Gus and the rest of her mouse friends joined her.

MICKEY MOUSE
Leaping Leap Year

It was a sunny morning, and Mickey and Pluto were outside playing catch. Mickey threw Pluto a ball. Pluto took a deep breath, did a fancy spin and leaped into the air to catch it.

"Nice job," Mickey said, cheering him on. "Great catch! Great leap!"

Great leap? Mickey's words echoed in his head. "Oh, my goodness, do you know what today is?" he asked Pluto.

Pluto leaped into the air again and again. He wanted Mickey to take the ball from him and toss it again.

"I almost forgot. Today is leap year!" Mickey exclaimed.

Pluto dropped the ball at Mickey's feet.

"I mean, today's not actually a year – it's a day," Mickey continued, talking to himself.

Pluto wasn't sure Mickey understood him. He wanted to play! So he leaped into the air again and again.

Leap! Leap! Leap!

Leap! Leap! Leap!

"That's the spirit!" Mickey encouraged him. "Leap year is something to be excited about! After all, it happens only once every four years. Well, almost every four years."

Mickey took a pad and pencil out of his back pocket and started working out figures. "There's a mathematical equation to figure this out if you really want to be exact." He scribbled some notes. "That's zero divided by . . . hmm, let me see here . . . carry the . . ." Mickey started blushing. "Maths is not really my thing." He put the pad back in his pocket. "Let's just say once every four years! Imagine if your birthday were on 29 February – 29 February only comes once every four years. So instead of being 12, you'd be three!" He laughed. "Just kidding . . . I think!"

Pluto sat down, panting with exhaustion, as Mickey continued explaining it to him. "Every four years, there's an extra day in the calendar – 29 February – and that's today!

"Do you know why we have leap year?" Mickey asked. "Because we have 365 days in a year, but it actually takes the earth a little longer to orbit the sun. So we have to make up for lost time!"

The excitement in Mickey's voice got Pluto excited again. He was back on his feet, tail wagging, ball in his mouth, leaping up and down.

"That's right," Mickey agreed, and joined Pluto in his leaping.

Leap! Leap! Leap!

Leap! Leap! Leap!

"Hooray!" shouted Mickey. "It's leap year!"

Winnie the Pooh

March Comes in Like a Lion

"Oh dear," said Pooh as the wind whipped around him. "It's very windy. Are you sure this is a good idea, Tigger?" He and Tigger were carrying Pooh's kite out into a clearing in the middle of the Hundred-Acre Wood.

"Don't be silly, Pooh Boy," Tigger responded. "Today is the perfect day to fly your kite. After all, what else is wind for?"

"Yes," Pooh replied. "I suppose you're right." He leaned into a particularly strong gust to keep it from blowing him over as they walked on. Winter was on its way out of the Wood, and spring was on its way in – and it seemed the wind was rushing in to fill the space in between, for it was one of the blusteriest days Pooh could remember.

At last, struggling against the wind, Pooh and Tigger reached the middle of the clearing and got ready to launch the kite. Pooh unrolled some kite string while Tigger held the kite.

"Okay, Pooh," said Tigger. "Get ready! You hold on to the string, and I'll toss the kite up into the wind. One . . . two . . . THREE!"

With that, Tigger tossed the kite and it was immediately seized by the strong wind and carried high into the air where it danced and darted this way and that.

Meanwhile, Pooh struggled to hold on to the roll of kite string.

"Let out some more string, Pooh!" Tigger suggested. "Let's see how high we can fly it!"

So Pooh let out some more string. The kite sailed higher into the air and, blown around by stronger and stronger gusts, it tugged harder and harder on Pooh's end of the line.

"Fly it higher, Pooh!" exclaimed Tigger.

So Pooh let out more and more string until he had let it all out. He clung tightly to the end of the line as the kite soared, seeming almost to touch the low clouds.

Then, all of a sudden, a tremendous gust of wind blew through the clearing. At the end of the kite string, Pooh felt his feet leave the ground as the wind grabbed hold of the kite and carried it sharply upward.

"My goodness!" said Pooh, realizing that he was being lifted up. Then, before he could be carried too high, he let go of the kite string and tumbled gently to the ground.

But the kite sailed on – up and away, dancing on the breeze for what seemed like forever, until it came to rest at last in the high branches of a very tall tree at the edge of the clearing. Pooh wondered how he would ever get it down.

"Oh well," said Tigger, patting his friend sympathetically on the back. "Guess you flew it just a little too high there, Pooh Boy."

Tink's Trinkets

Tinker Bell had decided she wanted to change her unique fairy talent, so she could visit the mainland. Tinker-talent fairies were not allowed to go. Reluctantly, the other fairies agreed to help. No fairy had ever changed his or her talent before!

Fawn, one of the animal fairies, tried to show Tink how to teach baby birds to fly. Unfortunately, Tink's baby bird seemed terrified. Tink then saw a majestic bird soaring in the sky. She decided she would ask it to help her. But the bird was a hawk!

Tink quickly escaped and flew straight into a fairy called Vidia. They jumped down a tunnel inside a tree. When Vidia reached the end of the chute, she stopped in the nick of time – but Tink accidentally slammed into her and sent Vidia shooting out of the tree. The hawk opened its beak, ready to strike. Luckily, the other fairies were able to chase the bird off, but Vidia was furious, and Tink felt awful.

Tink soon realised her friends didn't want her to change her talent. Desperate, she went to visit the only fairy she thought might be able to help – Vidia.

But Vidia was in a bad mood, and had an idea to get Tink in trouble! She suggested that Tinker Bell prove she was a garden fairy by capturing the unruly Sprinting Thistles.

Tink knew this was her last chance to get to go to the mainland. She tried hard to herd the thistles, but Vidia cheated by blowing open the corral gate. All of the Thistles ran right out. It was a stampede! The Thistles trampled over the carefully organised springtime supplies, and Tink was devastated.

Queen Clarion soon appeared and scolded Tinker Bell. Tink decided she must leave Pixie Hollow forever, but she couldn't go without one last visit to the workshop – she had to admit that she did love to tinker.

At the workshop, Tink noticed some trinkets she had found on her first day in Pixie Hollow. Then, she had an idea . . .

That night, clever Tink showed the Queen how she had designed speedy machines using the trinkets, to fix what the Thistles had trampled. Vidia was furious!

Queen Clarion looked sharply at Vidia and sent her to capture the Thistles. The other fairies worked all night using Tink's machines. By morning, the fairies had more springtime supplies than they had ever seen! The fairies cheered.

"You did it, Tinker Bell," congratulated Queen Clarion.

A Beastly Makeover

One evening, the Beast was heading towards the dining room when Lumiere suddenly stopped him.

"You can't go to dinner looking like *that*!" Lumiere said.

"Why not?" the Beast demanded. "I'm wearing my best outfit!"

"Clothes aren't enough," Cogsworth chimed in. "You have to make a good impression."

"You always told me looks don't matter, anyway," the Beast growled.

"There's a difference between looks and style," Lumiere told him.

"And you may have no control over your looks," Cogsworth added, "but you certainly can do something about your style!"

"What's wrong with my style?" the Beast said, looking a bit hurt.

"Okay," Cogsworth began, "let's talk hair."

"What's wrong with my hair?" the Beast cried, offended.

"Women like hair long, but neat – not straggly," Cogsworth explained. "When was the last time you combed it?"

"I–" the Beast began.

"You've got it all wrong," Lumiere interrupted. "Women like hair short, closely cropped." He brandished a pair of scissors.

"I don't *want* a haircut!" the Beast said.

"We could always try ringlets," Cogsworth offered, nodding wisely.

"Or braids," Lumiere suggested. At this, the Beast climbed onto a table and, from there, onto a bookcase that swayed dangerously under his weight.

"How about a French twist?" Cogsworth said.

A low growl began in the Beast's throat.

Just then, Belle hurried into the room, interrupting the stand-off, and this is what she saw: the candelabrum and mantel clock brandishing combs and ribbons at the snarling, cornered Beast – who was scrabbling to stay on top of the bookcase. Belle burst into laughter.

"What's going on?" she asked.

"We were just trying to fix his hair," said Lumiere. "It's a dreadful mess!"

"Actually," Belle said, "I happen to like it just the way it is. Beast, are you going to stay up there all night?"

And at that, the Beast leaped off the bookcase and strode towards her.

"Do you really like my hair?" he asked.

"It looks just fine," Belle reassured him. "Now, would you escort me to dinner?"

"I would be honoured," the Beast replied.

Cogsworth and Lumiere looked baffled as the two headed off to the dining room.

"Kids these days," Cogsworth said.

Lumiere just shook his head.

Lady *and the* TRAMP

Don't Mock Jock

Aunt Sarah had only just arrived to look after the baby while Jim Dear and Darling were away, but already her Siamese cats, Si and Am, had caused nothing but trouble. When they made a huge mess in the living room, Lady had been blamed for it, and Aunt Sarah had taken Lady to be fitted with a muzzle!

Meanwhile, left alone in the house, Si and Am had discovered the doggy door that led out to the garden.

"What works for doggies, works for kitties, too," hissed Si.

They slunk out to the garden. They dug in the flower beds, scared the birds at the bird-bath and chased a squirrel up a tree.

Then they found a small hole in the garden fence. They poked their heads through the hole and spied Jock snoozing by his kennel.

"Time for a wake-up call?" said Am.

Si smiled and nodded. They squirmed through the hole and stole silently across the yard until they were sitting on either side of the sleeping Jock. Then, at the same moment, they let loose a shrill, ear-splitting yowl.

Jock awoke with a start. By the time he had identified the culprits, Si and Am were halfway across the lawn, heading for the fence.

Jock tore after them, barking. But, in a flash, the cats squirmed through the small hole and were out of Jock's reach. The opening was too small for Jock. He had to be content with sticking his head through and barking at the cats as they strolled casually up the back steps of Lady's house and through the doggy door. Then they collapsed in a laughing fit on the kitchen floor.

"Dogs are so dim-witted." Si cackled.

They waited a while, then crept out through the doggy door again, itching to try their trick once more. Peeking through the hole in the fence, they spied Jock, eyes closed, lying in front of his kennel. They squirmed through the hole and crept towards him.

But, this time, Jock was ready for them. When the cats got within five feet of him, the feisty Scottie leaped to his feet and growled. The cats gave a start, wheeled around and raced for the fence, only to find the way blocked by Jock's friend, Trusty the bloodhound, who stood, growling, between the cats and the hole.

Jock and Trusty chased Si and Am around Jock's garden until Jock was confident they had learned their lesson. Then they allowed the cats to retreat through the hole in the fence.

This time, they didn't stop running until they were up the back steps, through the doggy door, and safely inside.

And inside is where they stayed.

The Little MERMAID

The Wrong Gift

"Wow, Flounder, everyone's here!" cried Ariel. Mermaids and mermen had come from all over the ocean to wish Ariel's sister Aquata a happy birthday.

Unfortunately, Ariel still needed to pick out a gift for her sister. So, Ariel and Flounder left the party and swam to her secret cave.

Together they looked over Ariel's vast collection of bells, clocks, jewellery and other human knick-knacks she'd scavenged from shipwrecks.

"How about this?" asked Flounder, swimming around a ship's wheel.

"Too big," said Ariel.

"Or this?" suggested Flounder, nudging a single gold earring.

"Too small," said Ariel.

Suddenly, Ariel noticed a music box.

"This is it!" she cried. "The perfect gift! I've listened to this one again and again, and it plays a really beautiful song."

Ariel swam back to the celebration. Beside King Triton, Aquata sat on a clamshell, and, one by one, the guests presented her with their birthday gifts.

While Ariel waited her turn in line, Sebastian the crab swam by. "Hello, Ariel," he said. "What gift do you have for Aquata?"

When Ariel proudly told Sebastian, his jaw nearly dropped to the ocean floor. "Are you out of your mind?" he cried.

Ariel's eyes widened. Sebastian was right! King Triton hated humans. And Ariel was not supposed to have anything from their world. That's exactly why she'd kept her cave a secret!

Just then, King Triton's deep voice bellowed, "Ariel, you're next."

Ariel hid the present behind her back.

"What gift do you have for your eldest sister?" asked Triton.

"Uh . . . um . . ." Ariel stammered.

"A song!" Sebastian announced.

Ariel racked her brain for a song to sing, and then she hit on it! She opened her mouth, and sang the melody from the music box.

When she finished, Flounder swam behind her, replacing the gift in her hand with a beautiful starfish for Aquata's hair.

"It's beautiful!" said Aquata. "And so was your song!"

King Triton smiled approvingly, and Ariel sighed with relief. How she wished her father would change his mind about humans!

"I'd give almost anything to see what the human world is like," she told Flounder. "Do you think my father will ever understand?"

"Maybe when he finally sees what it means to you," said Flounder, "someday he will."

Bambi

Spring Has Sprung!

Spring had come at last to the forest. *Sniff, sniff* – Bambi could smell the change in the air. The days were growing longer. The nights were getting shorter. The ice and snow were quickly melting away. Crocuses and daffodils were pushing new green shoots out of the ground.

And the forest didn't feel quite as lonely as it had during the cold weather. In just the last few days, Bambi had noticed that there were more animals peeking their heads out of their holes and burrows and dens.

As he took a walk through the forest very early one morning on the first day of spring, Bambi came upon Mrs Possum and her children hanging upside down by their tails from a tree branch. She and Bambi had not seen one another in a long while. But Mrs Possum recognized him just the same.

"Well, hello, Bambi," said Mrs Possum.

"Hello, Mrs Possum," Bambi replied. "I haven't seen you since autumn. Where have you and your family been all winter long?"

"Oh, we like to spend most of our winter indoors," Mrs Possum replied. "But now that spring is here, it's so nice to be out in the fresh air again." Then Mrs Possum and the rest of her family closed their eyes and dozed off, because they liked to spend most of their days sleeping, you know.

Walking on through the forest, Bambi stopped by a tree filled with twittering birds.

"Hello, Bambi," said one of the birds.

"Hello," Bambi replied. "And where have you birds been all winter long?"

"Oh, we fly south for the winter, to warmer places where we can find more food," the bird explained. "But we are so happy it is spring once more. It is lovely to be back in the forest."

Then the bird joined her voice with her friends' twittering tunes. After so many months without it, the chirps and tweets were sweet music to Bambi's ears.

Bambi walked further, meeting old friends at every turn. He came upon mice moving from their winter quarters back into their spring and summer homes. He noticed the squirrels and chipmunks snacking leisurely on nuts, no longer storing them away in their winter stockpiles. He heard a woodpecker rapping at a pine tree. And he spotted the ducks out for a swim on the pond.

Yes, thought Bambi, it had been a long, cold, difficult winter. But somehow the arrival of spring made him feel that everything would be all right. Everywhere he looked there was life, there were new beginnings . . . and, most importantly, there was hope.

Transformation of a Prince

Prince Naveen was completely unaware of it, but New Orleans was a city of magic, good and evil. Bad experiences might be waiting just around the corner – particularly if you were a carefree young prince! On top of that, Naveen's parents had cut off his income. They wanted him to take responsibility for himself.

But this didn't bother Naveen. His only thought was to enjoy himself and have fun!

When he disembarked from his ship, he put on his crown and began to sing, dance and play the ukulele all round the town. Lawrence, his faithful valet, tried to make him see sense...

"We must go to this masked ball, my Prince! Your hosts are waiting for you!"

"But first, Lawrence, it's my round of drinks!" Prince Naveen declared.

"That's all very well, but you've got nothing to pay with!"

However, Naveen refused to look for work. There was just one solution: to marry a rich young girl. But marrying would deprive him of his freedom, and he didn't much like the idea of that either!

Just then, a sinister character passed by the Prince in the street...

"What an excellent stroke of luck for me!" he laughed. This was Dr Facilier, a fearsome sorcerer who had his sights set on taking Naveen's place and seizing his wealth.

"Delighted to meet you, your Highness!" Dr Facilier greeted Naveen as he went by. "Let me introduce myself: Dr Facilier. I can tell your fortune, read your future... and make your dearest wishes come true!"

Careless of any danger, Naveen followed him into his den, at the end of a dark alleyway. Terrifying whispers haunted the place. Scary masks grimaced grotesquely. Shadows danced on the walls.

The sorcerer said, "Trust me! I know how to solve your money problems!"

Naveen was hearing exactly what he wanted to hear! He was fascinated. Facilier took advantage of his opportunity. He waved a magic talisman, pricked Naveen's finger with it and filled the vial with his blood! Naveen began to shrink and shrink, and was transformed into a frog!

"Welcome Prince Frog!" Dr Facilier cruelly roared with laughter.

Poor Naveen! It was true, money wouldn't be a problem for him from now on, but what would happen to him? He had no idea what life as a frog would bring.

THE JUNGLE Book

The Den of Doom

"Where are we going, Baloo?" Mowgli asked. He and Baloo had been travelling through the jungle for a while now.

"Have you ever heard of the Den of Doom, Man-cub?" replied Baloo in a hushed voice.

Mowgli gasped. "The Den of Doom? They say that the Den of Doom is a giant cave filled with bears who will eat anything – or anyone! They say that those bears can hear for miles and see in the dark! They say that even Shere Khan is afraid of them!" he exclaimed.

"Mmm-hmm," said Baloo. "They do say that. They *also* say that all of the bears in the Den of Doom are over eight feet tall, that their teeth are green and razor-sharp, and that their battle cry is so loud that the whales in the ocean hear it and shake with fright. They say all that, and much, much more."

"And we're *going* there?" Mowgli squeaked. "We can't! Baloo, those bears aren't like you! They're dangerous!"

"Too late, Man-cub," Baloo said with a grin. "We're already there!" He picked up Mowgli, whose knees were knocking together so hard he could barely stand, and strode right into a thicket. The bear ducked under a huge palm frond and emerged into a large, sunlit clearing in front of an enormous cave. Baloo put Mowgli down. The boy looked around in complete and utter surprise.

Mowgli had expected to see hundreds of fierce, angry bears. Instead, he saw hundreds of relaxed, happy bears having a really good time. Bears were swimming in a small pond, splashing and laughing. Bears were resting in the cool shadows of the cave. Bears were playing tag out in the clearing and chomping on piles of ripe, delicious fruit. It was, in short, a bear party.

"I don't understand," Mowgli said to Baloo. "This is the Den of Doom?"

"Yep," Baloo said happily, grabbing a palm frond and fanning himself with it. "It used to be called the Den of Delights, but we had to change the name. See, everyone in the jungle knew that the Den of Delights was the most fun place around. We bears never turned anyone away from our party. But then it got so crowded that it just wasn't any fun any more. So we spread a few rumours, changed the name, and *presto* – it's the Den of Doom! Now no one bothers us bears any more."

"But what about me?" Mowgli said anxiously. "I'm not a bear."

"You're an honorary bear, Mowgli," Baloo replied with a smile. "You sure have enough fun to be one!"

DISNEY

DUMBO

Float Like a Butterfly

One day, Dumbo's best friend, Timothy Q. Mouse, found Dumbo looking sad. "What's the matter, little guy?" the mouse asked the elephant. "Have people been teasing you about your ears again?"

Dumbo nodded. The little elephant looked totally miserable.

Timothy shook his head. The two were very good friends and did everything together. He didn't mind one bit that Dumbo had large ears. In fact, he thought they were great.

Timothy was trying to think of a way to cheer up his dear friend. And then he saw something. "Look, Dumbo!" he cried, racing over to a nearby fence post. Hanging from the fence was a large cocoon. "It's a butterfly cocoon!" Timothy said excitedly.

Dumbo came over to examine it.

"And look – it's about to hatch into a butterfly," said Timothy. He looked thoughtful for a moment, and then he turned to Dumbo. "You know what? You are a lot like the little caterpillar that made this cocoon."

Dumbo looked at Timothy quizzically.

"Yep, it's true. You see, a caterpillar is something nobody really wants around much. They think it's kind of plain looking, and it can't really do anything very interesting. But then one day, the caterpillar turns into a beautiful butterfly, and everyone loves it. And you

know what? I think you're going to be that way, too. When you get older, everyone is going to admire you rather than tease you!"

Dumbo smiled gratefully at his friend, and wiped away a tear with one of his long ears.

Suddenly, it started to rain. "Oh no!" cried Timothy. "The butterfly is going to get its new wings all wet. It won't be able to fly if it gets rained on. What'll we do? We need an umbrella!"

As Timothy looked this way and that for an umbrella, Dumbo smiled and unfurled his long ears. He draped them over the fence post so that they made a lovely roof for the insect, protecting it from the falling droplets of rain.

"Great idea!" said Timothy admiringly. The two friends stood there during the downpour, which didn't last very long. While they waited, they watched the beautiful new butterfly emerge from its cocoon and unfurl its colourful wings. When the rain stopped, the butterfly spread its wings (which were quite dry, thanks to Dumbo) and flew away.

"You know, my friend," said Timothy as they watched it fly away, "I think someday you're going to be a big success. You'll be like that butterfly – happy, carefree and floating along. Well, not floating for real, that's impossible. Imagine that, a flying elephant!"

March

10

Homesick

Nemo still couldn't believe everything that had happened to him. First, he'd been snatched up by a scuba diver in the ocean. Then, he'd travelled a long way in a big water cooler. Finally, he'd been dumped in a fish tank in a dentist's office. The other fish in the tank seemed nice, but Nemo missed his dad and his old home. He couldn't think about anything except getting back to the ocean. But would their plan to escape really work? It seemed hopeless . . . .

"Hey, kid," Bloat the blowfish swam over to him. "Are you okay? You look a little down in the gills."

"I'll say," said Nigel the seagull.

Peach the starfish glanced over from her spot on the tank wall. "He's just upset," she said. "It's only natural." She smiled kindly at Nemo. "It's okay, hon. We know how you feel."

"How could you know?" he muttered, feeling sorry for himself. "You weren't grabbed out of the ocean, away from your dad."

"Well, no," a fish named Gurgle admitted. "But we all had families back where we came from. We all miss them."

"Really?" Nemo blinked in surprise. He hadn't thought about that.

"Sure," Peach said. "The lady who sold me over the Internet kept lots of us starfish in her basement." She sighed sadly. "I still wonder where all my brothers and sisters ended up. I'd give two or three of my arms to see them again."

"I hear you," Bloat agreed. "I was hatched in somebody's garage. They sold me and a whole school of my brothers and sisters and cousins to Bob's Fish Mart. Just when we made friends with the other fish there, he came in and bought me." He waved a fin towards the dentist in the office outside the tank. "It could be worse, though," Bloat continued. "You guys are the best friends I've ever had."

A fish named Deb nodded. "I'm lucky he bought me and my sister together. Right, Flo?" She smiled at her own reflection in the glass of the tank. When the reflection didn't answer, Deb shrugged. "I guess Flo is too choked up to talk right now. But I can tell by her smile that she agrees. We don't know what we'd do without each other. But we still miss the rest of our family."

"Wow," Nemo said, looking around at his new tankmates. "I guess you guys *do* know how I feel."

Even though he was sad that the other fish had been taken from their families, it made Nemo feel a little less alone. At least they understood how much he wanted to find his way back to his father. Now, a little braver and more determined than ever, Nemo was ready to escape from the tank – no matter what.

THE LION KING

Just Like Dad

"Dad, when I grow up, I want to be just like you," Simba said to his father.

Mufasa nuzzled his son's head gently. "All in good time, son," he said.

Just then, Simba's friend Nala bounded up to them. "Come on, Simba!" she called. "Let's go play by the river!"

On their way, Simba stopped abruptly. "Listen to this," he said. He threw back his head and roared as loudly as he could. Then he looked at her expectantly. "Do I sound like my dad?"

Nala tried unsuccessfully to suppress a giggle. "Not quite," she said.

Soon they reached the river. The waters were high as a result of the recent rains. Simba found a quiet pool at the side and stared down at his reflection. "Do you think my mane is starting to grow?" he asked Nala.

Nala sighed. "Maybe a little," she replied. "But, Simba, what's the big rush? Let's just have fun being young!"

Simba was eyeing a tree branch that extended over the raging river. "Well, I may not be as big as my dad yet, but at least I'm as brave as he is!" he shouted, and raced up to the tree. Climbing its gnarled trunk, he began walking along the branch over the water.

Nala hurried over. She heard a loud crack. "Simba!" she yelled. "Come back here! The branch is going to break!"

But Simba couldn't hear her over the loud waters. Nala bounded away to get help.

Simba felt the branch begin to sag. "Uh-oh," he said to himself. Suddenly the whole thing broke off and Simba tumbled into the water. The current was strong, and he struggled to swim towards the shore. He was running out of strength, and he realized he might not make it.

Then he felt himself being lifted out of the water and tossed onto the bank. Dripping and coughing, he looked up – right into the angry eyes of his father.

"Simba!" thundered Mufasa. "There's a big difference between being brave and being foolish! The sooner you learn that, the better chance you will have of growing old!"

Simba hung his head. Out of the corner of his eye, he saw Nala, pretending not to overhear. "I'm . . . sorry, Dad," he said softly. "I just wanted to be brave like you."

His father's gaze softened. "Well," he said. "As long as we're soaking wet, why don't we go to a quieter part of the river and do some swimming?" He looked over to where Nala was sitting. "Come on, Nala!" he called. "Come with us!"

"Yippee!" cried the cubs, and they all went off together.

Peter Pan

Pixie Play

"What do you say, Tink? Can you get it?" asked Peter Pan.

Peter and Tinker Bell were floating high above the streets of London, right outside a large open window. Inside, three children were sleeping soundly.

Tinker Bell made a confident, jingling sound.

"All right, then. In you go!" said Peter.

Tink darted through the window. Then, leaving behind a trail of pixie dust, she flitted around the nursery searching for Peter's missing shadow.

When Peter had last visited this house, the children's nurse, Nana, had spied him outside the nursery window. She tried to grab him, but all she got was his shadow. Tonight, Peter had come to get his shadow back. He knew it wouldn't be easy, because Nana was a Saint Bernard dog. And Peter knew it was easy to fool children but hard to fool a dog. So, for this job, he needed a fairy's help.

Peter watched as Tinker Bell flew around the nursery. First, she flew over the eldest child, Wendy Darling, and then her two younger brothers, John and Michael. All three kept right on sleeping.

But, when Tinker Bell flew over Nana, the dog awoke with a sneeze! Tinker Bell's pixie dust had tickled Nana's nose.

"Woof! Woof!" barked Nana, trying to grab the fairy. All of a sudden the poor dog's feet couldn't find the floor. The pixie-dust magic had lifted her up. Now Nana was floating around the room!

When Peter heard Nana bark, he raced inside. Then he saw Nana floating and started to laugh.

Suddenly, the pixie dust wore off, and Nana's paws hit the floor again. With an angry growl, the dog charged at Peter Pan!

"Yikes!" Peter cried, darting through the window with Tinker Bell right behind him.

"Back to Never Land, Tink!" said Peter. "We'll get my shadow back tomorrow night."

On a twinkling trail of light, Peter and Tinker Bell soared into the sky and vanished.

Back inside the nursery, Wendy suddenly woke up. "What's this!" she cried, touching the window. Her hand sparkled with pixie dust.

"Peter Pan must have come back, looking for his shadow. I'm sorry I missed him," Wendy told Nana with a frown of disappointment.

"Woof! Woof!" said Nana.

"Yes, I know," Wendy replied. "Time for me to go back to bed."

But, as Nana licked Wendy's cheek good night, Wendy promised herself that she would be ready to meet the remarkable Peter Pan the next time he paid her a visit!

Bagheera Bears Up

Mowgli danced around, humming happily to himself.

"What are you doing, Mowgli?" Bagheera asked from his perch in a nearby tree.

"Practising being a bear," Mowgli told him. "You should try it."

"Me?" Bagheera said, stunned. "I couldn't possibly do such a thing."

"Why not?" Mowgli wanted to know.

"Well, I'm a panther and I happen to like being one," Bagheera replied. "Why on earth would I want to be a bear?"

"Are you kidding?" Mowgli exclaimed. "Bears have the life! They hang out all day long, and they eat ants!"

"Eat ants?" Bagheera asked. "And that's a good thing?"

"Sure!" Mowgli said. "Well, truthfully, they tickle your throat at first. But you get used to it soon enough."

"Have you?" Bagheera asked.

"Not yet," Mowgli confessed. "But I will!"

"Whatever you say, Mowgli," said Bagheera.

Mowgli thought for a moment. "And if you were a bear, you would eat fruit and drink coconut juice, and you would relax, just like us!"

"If you ask me," Bagheera said. "I don't see anything so bad about being a panther. In fact, I like it very much."

"I think you're scared," Mowgli told him.

"Absolutely not!" Bagheera protested. "What on earth would I have to be scared of?" He stood up, stretched and gracefully jumped out of the tree and onto the ground.

"Exactly," Mowgli said. "So, why not try it?"

"You've got to be kidding me!" Bagheera said.

"You know what your problem is?" Mowgli said.

"I'm afraid to ask," Bagheera said.

"You're like a beehive," Mowgli told him. "You work too hard." He stared at Bagheera. "Come on, dance with me!" he cried, grabbing Bagheera's paw and prancing around the panther. After a bit, Bagheera began to dance too, moving his feet and twitching his tail.

"That's it!" Mowgli cheered.

"You know what?" Bagheera admitted. "This isn't so bad after all."

"Now you're getting it!" Mowgli exclaimed. "Now you see why being a bear is so great!" The Man-cub stopped dancing and threw himself on a soft patch of moss. "It's not so bad, is it?"

"Actually," Bagheera said, scratching his back against a rock, "it's sort of fun!"

"One more time!" Mowgli cheered, and they began dancing again.

Disney Princess
Cinderella
Bedtime for Gus

Cinderella looked out of her bedroom window as the sun was setting. The clock in the tower of the castle struck eight o'clock. Cinderella tapped gently on the walls of her attic room.

"Bedtime, everyone!" she called. Jaq, Suzy, Gus and the other mice hurried out of their mouse hole.

"Buh-bedtime?" Gus asked. Gus was Cinderella's newest mouse friend. She had just rescued him from a trap that morning, while she was cleaning.

"Close eyes and... fall asleep!" Suzy explained. Gus looked confused. He closed his eyes and started to tip over. Jaq caught him. "Not fall, Gus-Gus," he said. "Fall asleep. Like this." He put his head on his hands and pretended to snore.

Cinderella laughed. "Gus has never lived in a house before. We'll have to teach him about getting ready for bed." Cinderella said, "First, you have to put on your pyjamas." She went to her dresser and pulled out a tiny pair of striped pyjamas for Gus.

"Now sleep, Cinderella?" Gus asked. Cinderella smiled. "Not quite yet," she said. "Now you need to wash your face and brush your teeth. Then, I'll kiss you good night, and Suzy will tuck everyone in."

Gus began to brush his teeth. "Mmm-mmm," he said, tasting the minty toothpaste. Gus watched as the other mice washed their faces with tiny cloths and patted themselves dry. Gus did the same.

When the mice were all neat and clean, Cinderella kissed each of them good night. "It's time for everyone to go to sleep," she said sweetly.

"Follow me," Jaq told Gus. He ran over to his little bed and hopped in. Then he pointed to the bed next to him. "That's your bed," he said. Gus grinned and got under the covers. Suzy tucked in each of the mice.

"Story, Cinderella!" someone cried.

Cinderella smiled. "All right," she said. "Once upon a time, there was a young prince who lived in a castle..." She continued the story for a long time. Each time she tried to stop, the mice begged for more. After a while, they couldn't keep their eyes open anymore.

When the last mouse had fallen asleep, Cinderella tiptoed to her own bed and climbed in. Gus began to snore. Cinderella giggled and pulled up her covers. She glanced once more at the clock on the castle tower.

"Oh, my," she murmured sleepily. "It's nearly midnight!" She snuggled against her pillow and yawned. "If only some of my stories would come true...."

Snow White
and the Seven Dwarfs

Home Sweet Home

As the sun rose above the Seven Dwarfs' cottage, Snow White was already thinking about what to make for supper that evening. She had arrived at the cottage just the day before, after her evil stepmother, the Queen, had driven Snow White from the palace and the Queen's huntsman had left her alone in the forest. Luckily, a group of helpful woodland creatures had befriended Snow White and led her to the Dwarfs' little cottage. Now, for the first time in a long time, she felt safe and happy.

She was so grateful to the Dwarfs for sharing their cosy home with her, she wanted to give them a special treat.

"Perhaps we'll have gooseberry pie for supper tonight!" she said to her furry woodland friends after the Dwarfs had gone to work. The little animals nodded in agreement. Together they left the cottage and headed to the forest to pick berries. With all her friends helping, Snow White quickly filled her berry basket. Then she sat down among the sweet-smelling flowers with a sigh.

"How different life has become," she said to her friends. "I don't miss the grand castle at all. I love living in this funny little cottage. A home does not need to be grand to be a happy one! Remember that!"

The animals exchanged looks with one another. They began tugging at her skirt to pull her to her feet.

"What is it, dears?" she asked them. "Oh! Do you want to show me where all of *you* live? I would love to see!" she said delightedly.

Two bluebirds were first. Twittering excitedly, they fluttered around their nest, which had been built in a cosy nook of a nearby tree.

"What a lovely nest!" cried Snow White. The birds looked pleased.

The fawns were next. Pulling at her skirt, they brought Snow White to a sun-dappled clearing in a warm glade.

"How cosy!" exclaimed Snow White. The fawns flicked their tails happily.

Next, the chipmunks and squirrels showed her the hollow in an old tree where they lived. Then the rabbits proudly showed her the entrance to their burrows.

"You all have such pretty little homes," said Snow White, as they made their way back to the Dwarfs' cottage. "Thank you for showing them to me. We are all lucky to live where we do, aren't we?" she said with a smile.

And with that, she skipped the rest of the way back to the cottage to start preparing her pie. She could hardly wait until the Dwarfs got home!

Berry Picking

Once upon a time, in a forest far away, there lived a lovely princess who did not know she was a princess, and three good fairies who pretended to be mortal. (Of course, you know exactly to whom we are referring . . . so let's get right to the story of Briar Rose and her three 'aunts.')

One morning, Flora called the group together to suggest they go out to search the forest for berries.

"What a wonderful idea," said Briar Rose.

"Yes, indeed," said Merryweather. "If we pick enough, we can make a berry pie."

"If we pick enough," declared Fauna, "we can make enough jam to last us through the whole year."

"Well, we'll never have enough if we don't get started now," said Flora. And so they gathered their berry baskets and set out.

They followed a shady path through the forest until they came upon a thicket bursting with berry bushes. And, without delay, the four berry-pickers got to work. But, as you will see, just because they got to work, doesn't mean their baskets actually got full.

Merryweather, for one, had a terrible time keeping her basket upright. Every time she bent to pick another berry, her basket tipped and out spilled all but two or three.

Fauna, on the other hand, had an entirely different problem keeping her berries in her basket – somehow they kept finding their way into her mouth!

And as for Briar Rose, her heart and her mind were miles away from her berry basket . . . dancing instead in the arms of a handsome stranger.

"All right, dearies," Flora called as the sun began to sink. "It's time to start back to the cottage. Let's see what you've got."

"Um, well . . ." said Merryweather. "I don't seem to have many berries in my basket."

Flora rolled her eyes and moved on to Fauna. "Let me guess . . ." she said as she looked from Fauna's empty basket to her purple mouth.

"Ah, yes . . ." Fauna said as she guiltily dabbed at a drop of juice on her lips. "Berries . . . delicious!"

Flora sighed. "And you, Briar Rose?" she asked hopefully.

But Briar Rose just looked down sheepishly at the empty basket in her hands. "I'm sorry, Aunt Flora," she said. "I guess I got a little bit distracted."

"Well," said Flora, shaking her head, "no berry pie for us this week, I guess." Then she shrugged. "But we can always have chocolate cake instead!"

MICKEY MOUSE
St Patrick's Day Switcheroo!

Huey, Dewey and Louie were getting dressed one morning when Louie had an idea.

"Hey," he said to his brothers, "are you two wearing green for St Patrick's Day?"

"Yes, of course," said Dewey.

"Me too," said Huey.

"Well," replied Louie, gesturing at the green shirt and hat that he wore every day, "then I bet we could really confuse our Unca Donald!"

Huey and Dewey both smiled as they contemplated Louie's sneaky idea.

"He's so used to seeing me wearing red . . ." said Huey.

"And me wearing blue . . ." said Dewey.

"That if he doesn't look closely," said Louie, "he'll be totally confused!"

The three of them chuckled as they headed towards the kitchen. Then, while Huey and Dewey hid in the hallway, Louie walked in and sat down next to Donald Duck, who was reading the newspaper at the breakfast table.

"Morning, Unca Donald," said Louie.

"Morning, Louie," Donald replied. "Will you go get your brothers? Breakfast is ready."

"Okay," Louie replied, leaving the room.

Next, Dewey walked into the kitchen and sat down. "Morning, Unca Donald," he said.

Donald looked up only briefly from his paper. "I thought I told you to go get your brothers, Louie," he said.

"No, you didn't," Dewey replied. "And I'm not Louie."

Donald looked up and scrutinized Dewey's face. "Oh," he said. "I'm sorry, Dewey. Go get your brothers, would you?"

"Okay," Dewey replied.

A few minutes later, Huey walked into the kitchen and sat down at the table.

Donald glanced up from the newspaper. "Well, where are they?" he asked Huey impatiently.

"Where are who?" said Huey.

"Your brothers," Donald replied. "I asked you to go get them."

"No, you didn't," said Huey.

"Yes, I – " Donald looked up from the paper and stared at Huey hard. "Oh . . . Huey," he said, realizing his mistake. "I thought you were . . . hey!" Donald looked at Huey suspiciously. "Are you three trying to confuse me? Is that why you're all wearing the same thing?"

Huey looked up at Donald with a blank stare. "Whatever do you mean, Unca Donald?"

"It's St Patrick's Day," said Louie, coming in from the hallway.

"Yeah," said Dewey, following Louie into the kitchen. "That's why we're all wearing green. Happy St Patrick's Day, Unca Donald!"

Winnie the Pooh

Happy Mother's Day!

One fine May day, Roo hopped over to Winnie the Pooh's house.

"I have a problem," Roo told Pooh. "Mother's Day is almost here, and I don't know what to give my mama. Do you have any ideas?"

"Let me think," said Pooh. He thought very hard (or at least as hard as a bear of very little brain can think). "Think, think, think. A gift for Mother's Day . . . ."

Luckily, Pooh spotted a big pot of honey sitting in his cupboard. "That's it!" he cried. "Mothers like *honey*!"

"They do?" asked Roo.

"Doesn't everybody?" Pooh asked.

So Pooh gave Roo a small pot of honey. Roo bounced over to Rabbit's house next.

As usual, Rabbit was working in his garden. "Hello, Roo," he said. "What's in the pot?"

"It's honey," Roo explained. "To give to my mama on Mother's Day."

Rabbit frowned. "No, no, no," he said. "Mothers don't like honey. If there's one thing a mother wants to get on Mother's Day, it's a big bunch of fresh carrots."

"They do?" Roo said doubtfully.

"Oh, yes," said Rabbit. He reached into his wheelbarrow and pulled out a bunch of freshly picked carrots.

"Thanks, Rabbit," said Roo. Then he hopped to Eeyore's house of sticks.

"What do you have there, Roo?" Eeyore asked.

"Some gifts for my mama for Mother's Day," said Roo.

"I suppose some mothers might like carrots," Eeyore said. "And maybe others might like honey. But, in my opinion, you can't go wrong with prickly thistles."

"Prickly thistles?" asked Roo.

"Yes," replied Eeyore. "Here, take these. Then Kanga will be sure to have a happy Mother's Day. If that's what she wants."

"Well, thank you," said Roo, tucking the prickly thistles into his pocket and heading for home. He thought about his gifts as he ate his dinner. He wondered which gift to give his mother as he put on his pajamas and brushed his teeth.

The next morning, bright and early, Roo bounded into the living room. "Happy Mother's Day, Mama!" he shouted.

"Why, thank you, dear," said Kanga.

"I thought and thought about what to give you," Roo explained. "Pooh said honey. Rabbit said carrots. And Eeyore said thistles. But I decided to give you this," he said, throwing his arms around his mama.

Kanga smiled. "Thank you, Roo. That's the best Mother's Day gift of all."

Meeko's Wild Ride

"What a perfect day for a canoe ride," Pocahontas said to her friend Meeko the raccoon, who lounged in the bow of the canoe as Pocahontas paddled down the river. Flit the hummingbird was flying alongside them.

It was a warm, sunny, early spring day. The chunks of ice on the river had melted away, and there were only small patches of snow here and there along the riverbank. In fact, all of the melted ice and snow had added several feet to the water level. The river was high and moving fast, but Pocahontas confidently guided the canoe downstream.

Soon, they came to a fork in the river. To the left, the river flowed swiftly but calmly as far as Pocahontas could see. But gazing down the other arm of the river, Pocahontas caught a glimpse of white water.

"Ooh," she said, "rapids!" She steered the canoe to the right and headed straight for them, eager for a challenge.

But Meeko, who had been reclining lazily, sat bolt upright. He knew that he was in for a wild ride! He scurried to hide behind Pocahontas, then clung to her as the canoe took a sudden dip and plunged into the rapids.

"Meeko, relax," said Pocahontas with a chuckle. "These are baby rapids."

A small wave sprayed water lightly into Meeko's face. He shrieked, scurried onto Pocahontas's shoulder, and buried his face in the back of her neck.

The canoe bobbed along on the white water. Pocahontas laughed gleefully. But poor Meeko climbed onto the top of her head, trying to get as far from the water as possible.

Then, spying a mini-waterfall up ahead, Meeko closed his eyes and wrapped his arms tightly around Pocahontas's head.

"Hey!" Pocahontas said with a laugh. "I can't see a thing!"

Nonetheless, she piloted the canoe gently and easily down the waterfall and into a calm pool of water on the other side.

Meeko was still clinging to Pocahontas's head with his eyes shut tight, when Pocahontas ran the canoe aground on the riverbank.

"Okay, brave Meeko," she said, teasing him. "It's safe now."

Opening his eyes and spying dry land, Meeko clambered down and raced along the canoe's gunwale toward the riverbank. But, in his haste, he lost his footing. He slipped and landed with a splash in the shallow water.

Pocahontas couldn't help laughing. "Let your guard down too soon, eh?" she said.

Meeko just scowled and decided to keep his paws on land for a while.

ALICE *in* **WONDERLAND**

The Silent Treatment

The Queen of Hearts loved to shout orders at her royal subjects. She shouted so much, in fact, that it wasn't surprising when she came down with a terrible case of laryngitis.

"There, there," said her husband, the diminutive King. "Rest your voice and let me do the ruling for you, my dear." The Queen hardly let the King get a word in edgeways, so he was looking forward to being in charge for a change.

As they strolled through the royal garden, the Queen noticed that the fence was painted pink instead of the required red. "Off! Off!" the Queen croaked. She wanted the King to punish the royal gardeners with her favourite order, "Off with their heads!"

Instead, the King said, "The Queen decrees that you may have the day off!" The gardeners cheered as steam escaped from the Queen's ears. "You must relax, sweetheart," the King warned her, "or you simply won't get well."

Soon the couple paused to play a game of croquet. The Queen hit the hedgehog ball with the flamingo mallet, and the hedgehog rolled willy-nilly across the lawn. The playing-card wickets knew better than to let the Queen make a bad shot. They jumped all over the grass, making sure the ball passed underneath them. "I'm undefeated!" the Queen rasped triumphantly.

"What's that, dear?" asked the King. He couldn't understand exactly what his wife was saying. "The Queen says she cheated!" he finally announced.

The entire royal staff gasped. Those nearby ducked as the Queen swung a flamingo at the King's head.

"That's enough croquet for today," crooned the King soothingly. "You don't want to tire yourself out."

He led his wife to a bench in the shade. The Queen sat down, pointed to the servants hovering nearby and acted out drinking a cup of tea.

The King stood up and announced, "You're all invited to have tea with the Queen!" Of course, this was not what the Queen had in mind at all.

A table was laid with tea, fancy cakes and sandwiches. Everyone ate, laughed and had a wonderful time. The Queen, ignored by everyone, seethed with anger.

She grabbed one of the flamingo mallets, then charged the table. Unfortunately, she didn't see the croquet ball in her path. As she tripped, the flamingo's beak plunged into the ground, causing the Queen to pole-vault up and over the table of guests and through her open bedroom window.

"A splendid idea, my dear!" called the King. "A nap will do you good!"

Tangled

Flynn Rider

While Rapunzel was getting ready to celebrate her eighteenth birthday, hidden away in her tower, a thief called Flynn Rider was escaping into the forest with his latest stolen prize, a royal crown, and his two partners in crime, the Stabbington brothers. Suddenly, Flynn stopped in front of a WANTED poster. He frowned.

"Heh! It doesn't look a bit like me! Have you seen the nose they've given me? It's outrageous! I'm much better looking in real life!"

"We couldn't care less, Flynn!" the Stabbingtons grumbled. "We've got to get out of here!"

Too late – the royal guards appeared at the top of the hill. The thieves ran off as fast as they could but soon found themselves trapped in a dead end, up against a stone wall! There was only one way out – to climb over the top! Flynn turned to his accomplices.

"Give me a leg up chaps. Once I'm up there I'll pull you up."

But the Stabbingtons didn't trust him. Flynn had a reputation for being a bit of a rogue – sly as a fox, crafty as a monkey! They shook their heads.

"If you want us to give you a leg up, first of all give us the satchel with the crown, just in case you decide to run off without sharing it!"

"Oh, great! Nice to know you trust me!" said Flynn, pretending to get cross. "When I think of everything we've been through together and now this. Here's the satchel! Will you help me now?"

The Stabbingtons brothers agreed, and with their help Flynn was over the wall in a flash. They then asked Flynn to help them climb it, but he refused and burst out laughing.

"Sorry chaps, I've got my hands full!" He waved the satchel that contained the crown in the air.

The Stabbingtons were furious. Flynn had managed to get hold of the crown without them seeing!

"You're right. I had no intention of sharing it with you!" added Flynn as he made off. "Good luck in prison!"

He was glad to be rid of them – they were too ruthless and dangerous to be trusted.

Flynn tore off into the woods but the royal guards were already hot on his heels.

Suddenly, Flynn realized that Maximus, horse to the captain of the guard, was even more determined to catch him than the guards were. How was he going to escape capture now?

a bug's life

Bird Trouble

It was the height of the rainy season, and the roof of the ant colony had sprung a leak. "Bucket brigade!" shouted Princess Atta. The ants obediently lined up and began catching the water in cupped leaves, passing them along the length of the line and dumping them into the stream. It was exhausting, but the ants were used to hard work.

"There's got to be an easier way," Flik said. "Tomorrow I'm going to invent a way to fix the roof!"

"What are you doing, Flik?" Dot asked the next morning. The rain had let up for a moment, and the two were outside. Flik had arranged dozens of torn pieces of leaves along one side of the sloping roof.

"I'm fixing the leak," he said cheerfully. "See, these leaves act as rain deflectors. Then the water will run into these hollowed-out flower stems that will act as gutters."

"Wow," said Dot. She was the only ant who thought Flik's inventions were worthwhile.

"The only thing I'm missing is some sort of deflection device for the ant hole itself," he said. "Aha!" he shouted a moment later. He had spotted a buttercup. "That flower should work perfectly. Come on, Dot. Give me a hand. Boy, oh, boy, is this invention ever going to impress the Princess!"

Together, the two ants dragged the buttercup to the top of the anthill.

"What on earth are you two doing?" It was Princess Atta.

"Flik figured out a way to fix the leak!" shouted Dot triumphantly.

Flik shrugged modestly. "It's very simple, really. See, what I did was . . ."

Suddenly, the ant lookout began shouting, "Bird! Bird! Bird coming!"

Flik, Atta and Dot ran for cover. Sure enough, a hummingbird was hovering just above the anthill.

"It's going for the flower!" shouted an ant. The hummingbird pressed its long beak into the buttercup Flik had dragged over the anthill.

"Avalanche!" shouted the ants. The delicately built anthill began to collapse. Ants scrambled to get out of the way. The bird flew off.

"Nice work, Flik," said Princess Atta. "This is going to take weeks to rebuild."

Flik sighed and hung his head.

"Don't worry, Flik," whispered Dot. "Someday you'll do great things."

"Oh, you're sweet, Dot," Flik said sadly. "If only it hadn't been for that bird. I should have known it would like the flower. Birds are so predictable." Now Flik looked thoughtful. "Maybe someday I could use that to my advantage."

Flik smiled at Dot. "Imagine that," he said. "An ant using a bird in his plan!"

Aladdin

Monkey See, Monkey Do

"Come on, Abu!" Aladdin called across the busy Agrabah marketplace.

From his perch on top of the basket-seller's cart, Abu barely heard the call. He was captivated by the monkey he had just spotted peeking out at him from behind the fruit-seller's cart. Abu jumped off the basket cart and darted over to say hello.

But the other monkey scurried away and hid behind a wheel. From his new hiding place, he peeked out at Abu.

Abu looked around, trying to think of a way to draw out the monkey. The fruit seller was distracted, talking to a customer, so Abu hopped up onto the cart and picked up an apple. He balanced it on top of his head. Then he scurried over to the edge of the cart and peered down, hoping to attract the monkey's attention.

But he was gone.

Abu heard monkey chatter behind him. He turned around to find the monkey standing at the other end of the fruit cart, balancing an apple on *his* head, just like Abu.

Abu laughed and picked up a pear and an orange. He began juggling them in the air, hoping to amuse the other monkey.

But the other monkey didn't look amused. He looked annoyed! He thought Abu was trying to show him up. Not to be outdone, the monkey also picked up a pear and an orange and began to juggle them, just like Abu.

Abu put the fruit down. He did a handstand on the cart railing.

The other monkey did a handstand too.

Abu grabbed hold of the cart awning, then flipped over and swung from the awning by his tail.

The other monkey did the same.

Abu laughed again. He thought this game was fun. But now he wanted to find a stunt that the other monkey couldn't copy. Abu looked around. He spotted Aladdin coming his way.

Abu had an idea. He jumped off the fruit cart, darted over to Aladdin and scrambled up the length of his friend's body until he was lounging comfortably on top of Aladdin's head.

The other monkey stared in amazement. He didn't know that Aladdin was Abu's friend. How could he copy that stunt? He looked around. The closest human was the fruit seller. Throwing caution to the wind, the other monkey scurried over to him – but he'd only climbed as high as the fruit-seller's shoulder before the man chased him away.

Then, from behind the basket cart, the other monkey crossed his arms, pouted and watched that sneaky Abu laugh and wave good-bye as he was carried away on top of Aladdin's head.

MULAN

Good Luck Charm

In ancient China, it was believed that crickets were good luck. But, on one particular night, long, long ago, Mulan's Grandmother Fa was having trouble remembering that. It was very late. There was a cricket loose somewhere in her bedroom, and every time she was about to drop off to sleep . . .

Cri-cket! Cri-cket! the cricket chirped loudly.

"This cricket will bring good fortune to our home," Grandmother Fa said, looking on the bright side.

All was quiet for a few minutes. Grandmother Fa slowly relaxed, wondering if perhaps the cricket itself had finally dropped off to sleep, when –

Cri-cket! Cri-cket!

"Ugh!" exclaimed Grandmother Fa, throwing off the covers and getting out of bed. Now she was determined to find that cricket.

She lit a candle and began her search. She looked under the bed. She peeked behind the chest of drawers. She looked everywhere.

But there was no sign of the cricket.

Grandmother Fa blew out the candle. She got back into bed and tried to sleep.

Cri-cket! Cri-cket!

Grandmother Fa got out of bed again and relit her candle. She searched in her wardrobe. She looked inside her slippers. She checked under her pillow. But she didn't find the cricket.

One more time, Grandmother Fa climbed into bed and tried to sleep.

Cri-cket! Cri-cket!

Grandmother Fa sighed and dragged herself out of bed. She relit the candle. Was there anywhere that she hadn't yet looked?

Just then, a slight movement on the windowsill caught Grandmother Fa's eye. There, sitting on the windowsill, was a tiny cricket. She scooped it up gently and cradled it in her hand.

That's when Grandmother Fa noticed that the window was open. And it looked as if a rainstorm was brewing outside.

"Well, little cricket," said Grandmother Fa, "is that why you were trying to get my attention?" Had the cricket been trying to save Grandmother Fa from waking up to a puddle beneath her open window? "Maybe you're good luck, after all," she said.

She decided that she would hold on to the cricket and see if it brought her more luck. So Grandmother Fa pulled out a bamboo cricket cage, gently placed the cricket inside, and put the cage on her bedside table.

Then, she climbed into bed, blew out the candle and closed her eyes. At last, she thought, she'd be able to get some sleep.

Cri-cket! Cri-cket!

Or would she?

Winnie
the
Pooh

Piglet's Pink Eggs

Winnie the Pooh had dropped in to visit Piglet, who was busy dyeing Easter eggs. "Easter is coming up, you know," Piglet explained.

On Piglet's kitchen table were six little cups. Pooh peered inside them. Each one held a different-coloured dye: blue, green, red, yellow, orange and pink.

Then Pooh noticed a basket filled with some eggs Piglet had already dyed. Every one of them was pink.

"Would you like to dye the last egg, Pooh?" Piglet asked.

"Oh yes," Pooh replied. "I would like that very much."

So Piglet showed him how to place his egg in the wire dipper, and how to use the dipper to dip the egg into the cups of dye.

"What colour should I dye my egg?" Pooh asked.

Piglet smiled. "That's the fun of it, Pooh," he said. "You can choose any colour you want!"

Pooh looked over at Piglet's basket of pink eggs. Then he looked back at the cups of dye.

"You don't seem to have a yellow egg yet," said Pooh. "So I think I will dye mine yellow."

"Good idea!" Piglet exclaimed.

Pooh dipped his egg into the cup filled with yellow dye. He let it sit in the dye for a few minutes, then lifted it out again.

"It worked!" cried Pooh. "Piglet, look! What do you think of my yellow egg?"

"Oh Pooh, it's great," Piglet said. "It's b-bright . . . a-and it's sunny . . . and i-it's very, very yellow, isn't it?"

Piglet was quiet for a moment. Then he cleared his throat.

"D-do you think . . . I don't know for sure, mind you. But do you think it could maybe use a little bit of, say, pink?" Piglet said.

Pooh took another look at his egg. "I think you're right," Pooh said. So he dipped his egg into the cup filled with pink dye. He let it sit there for just a few seconds before lifting it out. The little bit of pink dye on top of the yellow dye made the egg look pinkish-yellow.

"Hmm," said Piglet. "That's very pretty. But – if you don't mind my saying so, Pooh – I think it could use just a little more pink."

"Okay," said Pooh. So he dipped the egg back into the pink dye. This time he let it sit for five whole minutes before lifting it out. More pink dye on top of the yellow-and-pink colour made the egg look as pink as pink could be.

"Well, what do you think?" asked Pooh.

"Perfect!" Piglet exclaimed.

They let Pooh's egg dry. Then Piglet put it in the basket with all the other pink eggs.

"Well, what do you know," said Piglet. "It fits in so nicely!"

Annie's Solo Mission

Leo was giving Annie flying lessons!

"Today you'll learn the three most important tricks for flying Rocket," said Leo. "Are you ready?"

"Ready!" Annie said excitedly.

"Okay, here's the first lesson – the Up-and-Down Trick," said Leo. "If you want to make Rocket jump over something, you need to reach your arms up really high and then bring them down really fast."

"I think I've got it!" exclaimed Annie.

"Great job, Pilot Annie!" Leo said, beaming. "Next, you'll need to know the Squeeze Trick," explained Leo. "It comes in handy when you need to fly Rocket through a really tight space."

"That sounds hard!" said Annie.

"It's actually easy," said Leo. "Just cross your arms and pat your shoulders."

"This is fun!" Annie shouted.

"Okay, this next one is a bit difficult," cautioned Leo. "To make Rocket do big roller-coaster loops in the air, you need to clap your hands in a circle." Annie joined in and made big clapping circles in the air with him.

After Annie's flying lesson, the team decided to blow some superbubbles. The Little Einsteins blew their superbubbles into some pretty wild shapes! Annie ran to find her camera. She wanted to take pictures before they all popped.

June, Quincy and Leo blew a superbubble so big that it carried all three of them away!

Annie raced back, but her friends were nowhere to be found.

"Hey, where did they go?" Annie wondered aloud. "I wanted to take a picture!"

"Up here, Annie!" shouted Quincy.

"We need you to rescue us," said June. "If you fly Rocket up here, you can catch our bubble in his Bubble Wand."

Annie was nervous. "Me? But I've never flown Rocket by myself before!"

"You can do it, Annie," Leo assured her.

Inside Rocket, Annie prepared for her solo mission.

"According to this flight plan, I need to do the Up-and-Down Trick over the mountains, then perform the Squeeze Trick to fly through a small opening between two rocky cliffs and finally do a Loop-de-Loop Manoeuvre to get to the superbubble."

Annie was nervous but she knew the others were counting on her. She took off and followed the flight plan perfectly. "We're so proud of you, Pilot Annie!" exclaimed June.

"Way to go, sis!" Leo beamed. "I'm bubbling over with pride!"

Disney Princess
Cinderella
Of Mice and Rice

"Cinderella! Help!" shrieked Drizella. "And hurry!" yelled Anastasia.

Cinderella dropped the broom she was holding and rushed down the hallway. "What is it, stepsisters?" she called.

"We're stuck!" yelled Anastasia.

Cinderella hurried to the parlour. She barely managed to suppress a giggle at what she saw. Her two stepsisters were stuck in the doorway, so hasty had they both been to leave the room first. Their grand hoop skirts were wedged tightly in the doorway! With a bit of tugging and pulling, Cinderella managed to get the sisters unwedged. Smiling to herself, she headed back to the kitchen.

"*Meeeeeowww!*" came a cry.

"What on earth . . . ?" said Cinderella. She hurried into the kitchen. Lucifer the cat was howling at the top of his lungs. "What is the matter, Lucifer?" she said, running over to the fat feline. "Oh! You silly thing! You've got yourself stuck too!" Cinderella laughed and tugged him out of the mouse hole he had wedged his paw into. With a haughty look at Cinderella, the cat strode away.

"Oh, that naughty cat!" she said. "He got himself stuck chasing after you poor little defenceless mice, didn't he?" She peeked into the tiny mouse hole.

The mice crept cautiously out of their hole. "You little dears," Cinderella said softly. "Why, you're all shaken up! Well, do you know what I do when I feel sad or afraid? I find happiness in my dreams." She picked up her broom. "You see this broom? I like to pretend that it is a handsome prince, and the two of us are dancing together!" She and the broom began gliding around the room.

The mice squeaked with delight. Then suddenly they dashed for their hole. Someone was coming!

It was Cinderella's stepsisters. "What on earth are you doing, Cinderella?" said Drizella.

"I was just, uh, sweeping," Cinderella replied quietly, blushing.

"Well, you looked as though you were having too much fun doing it!" snapped Anastasia. Then a nasty smile appeared on her face. Picking up a bowl of rice from the table, she dumped it onto the floor. "Perhaps you need something else to sweep!" she said with a mean laugh. The two sisters left.

Cinderella's mouse friends rushed out and began to pick up the grains of rice. That gave Cinderella an idea. "Why don't you take the rice for yourselves?" she said. The mice squeaked happily, and Cinderella smiled. "You know," she said, "I think we'll be just fine if we all look out for each other."

Wendy's Music Box

Tinker Bell had been trying to learn a new fairy-talent since she arrived at Pixie Hollow. She wanted to visit the mainland and tinker-fairies could not. Tink tried to be an animal fairy, a light fairy, a water fairy and a nature fairy. But she was not good at any other talent.

Tinker Bell sat on the beach. "Great," she muttered. "At this rate, I should get to the mainland right about, oh, never!"

She angrily threw a pebble and heard a *CLUNK!* Tink went to investigate and found a broken porcelain box. By the time her friends found her, Tinker Bell was putting her discovery back together. The final touch was a porcelain ballerina that fit into the lid. Tinker Bell gave the dancer a spin, and to her delight, the box played music!

"Do you even realise what you're doing?" asked Rosetta. "Fixing stuff like this – that's what tinkering is!"

"Who cares about going to the mainland anyway?" Silvermist added.

Later that day, Tink saved the fairies' springtime supplies by tinkering and making wonderful new tools. Tink realised that her talent was very important after all. The fairies were very pleased with Tink and wanted to help her.

"Queen Clarion," said Silvermist. "Can't Tink come with us to the mainland?"

"It's okay," Tink protested. "My work is here."

Fairy Mary – the no-nonsense fairy who ran Tinkers' Nook – flew over, looking sternly at Tink. "I don't think so, missy!" she said. She gave a little whistle, and Clank and Bobble led in the wagon. Tink's music box was inside, all polished and shiny.

"I'd imagine there's someone out there who's missing this. Perhaps a certain tinker fairy has a job to do after all… on the mainland," said Fairy Mary.

So the nature fairies and Tink went to London to deliver their springtime magic. Tinker Bell found the home where the music box belonged, and tapped on the windowpane. A little girl named Wendy Darling poked her head out of the window. Tink watched from her hiding place as Wendy's face filled with happiness at the discovery of her long-lost treasure. The girl took a small key from a chain around her neck and turned it in a slot. The music box began to play!

Soon the fairies' work was done and it was time for them all to return to Never Land. Tink couldn't wait to get home – she had lots of tinkering to do!

PRINCESS FROG

The Masked Ball

The masked ball was in full swing at Charlotte's house. All of the important people from New Orleans were there! All apart from Prince Naveen.

"It's just not fair! I never get anything I wish for!" Charlotte complained to Tiana.

"There are still some late-comers due to arrive," Tiana tried to console her.

"No, he's not coming!" sobbed Charlotte. "It's my fault, I didn't wish hard enough on the Evening Star!" Charlotte gazed up and pleaded, "Please, please, please –".

Tiana let out a sigh – her friend still believed in fairy tales.

Suddenly the doorman announced the arrival of the Prince, and Charlotte hurried to welcome him. Tiana was amazed. She was just wondering if the star really had granted her friend's wish, when she spotted the estate agents from whom she was supposed to be buying the old mill, to turn into her restaurant.

"Have you brought me the contract to sign?" she greeted them cheerily.

"No, our agreement has been revoked, madam. Someone has just offered us a better price."

Tiana was so disappointed that she fell against the food and ruined her costume!

Charlotte arrived to help. "Oh, my dear Tia!" she consoled her friend. "Come with me, I'll lend you one of my princess gowns!"

She led her to her room and Tiana quickly changed. She looked beautiful, but she was too upset to return to the ballroom with her friend. Tiana went out onto the balcony alone to watch the night sky.

"My dream of opening my own restaurant will never come true," she whispered to herself. "Unless... I cannot believe I'm doing this," she said. And she started to wish on the Evening Star! She closed her eyes and concentrated.

When Tiana opened her eyes again, a frog had appeared on the balcony!

"Great," said Tiana ironically. "So I'm supposed to kiss you, I assume?"

"Kissing would be nice, yes!" exclaimed the frog, smiling.

"A talking frog?!" Tiana shrieked and ran back into Charlotte's bedroom. Really, what a ridiculous evening. First, she had wished on a star and now she was seeing things!

"I'm going to end up believing in the impossible!" she panicked.

Tiana thought she was starting to believe in fairy tales, just like Charlotte did, and she couldn't think of anything more terrifying!

Dance, Daddy-o!

Deep in the jungle at the temple ruins, the monkeys and their ruler, King Louie, were always looking to have a swingin' time.

"Let's have a dance-off!" King Louie suggested to the monkeys one evening.

"Hooray!" the monkeys cheered.

"What's a dance-off?" one monkey asked.

"You know, a contest," said King Louie. "An opportunity for everyone to get down, strut their stuff, cut a rug! And whoever lays down the smoothest moves is the winner!"

"Hooray!" cheered the monkeys.

King Louie rubbed his chin. "The first thing we need is some music," he said, pointing at the monkey musicians. "Hit it, fellas!"

The musicians blasted out a jazzy tune, blowing through their hands like horns, knocking out a beat on some coconuts and drumming on a hollow log. Soon, all the monkeys were gathered around the musicians, tapping their toes and shaking their tails.

"Now," said King Louie, "who will dance?"

All the monkeys raised their hands. King Louie looked around. "Let's see," he said scratching his head, "I choose . . . me!"

"Hooray!" the monkeys cheered. They were disappointed not to be chosen. But, after all, King Louie *was* their King.

So King Louie moved his hips from side to side. He waved his arms in the air. He closed his eyes so he could really feel the beat.

"Dance, Daddy-o!" one monkey cried.

King Louie boogied and bopped like he had never boogied and bopped before. Then, when the song was over, King Louie stopped dancing and scrambled onto his throne. "Now it's time to choose the winner!" he said.

"But King Louie . . ." one monkey began to object. All the other monkeys were thinking the same thing: didn't you need more than one dancer to have a dance-off?

"Oh, silly me," said King Louie with a chuckle. The monkeys looked at each other and smiled, expecting that the King had realized his mistake. But, King Louie said, "Of course, we need a judge! Who will judge?"

Everyone raised their hands. King Louie looked around, then said, "I choose . . . me!"

"Hooray!" the monkeys cheered.

"And as the judge, I will now choose the winner of the dance-off," King Louie continued. He looked around at all the monkeys. "Now, let's see. I choose . . . me! Let's hear it for the winner!"

"Hooray!" the monkeys cheered, because, after all, King Louie was their King – and a pretty swingin' dancer, too!

Disney
Pinocchio

A Helping Hand

"Oh, Pinocchio!" cried Geppetto. "I can hardly believe that my little puppet is alive!" It was the morning after the Blue Fairy had visited Geppetto's house and brought Pinocchio to life. "You must get ready for school, my boy," said Geppetto.

Pinocchio was full of curiosity. "Why must I go to school, Father?" he asked.

"Why, so that you can learn!" Geppetto replied. "Now be a good boy and go make the bed while I clear away these dishes."

Ever eager to help, Pinocchio sprang up from the breakfast table and ran over to Geppetto's workbench. He found a hammer, a nail and a piece of wood, and began to pound loudly with the hammer.

"Pinocchio! Whatever are you doing?" cried Geppetto.

"Well, you asked me to make the bed," said Pinocchio. "So I was starting to make one."

With a little smile, Geppetto patted him on the head and said, "Perhaps it would be better for you to put the cat out."

As Geppetto turned back to the breakfast table, Pinocchio jumped up and grabbed a pitcher of water. Hurrying over to Figaro, Pinocchio threw the water onto the cat.

"*YEEEEOOWWWW!*" shrieked Figaro.

"Pinocchio!" shouted Geppetto. "Why did you do that?"

"You . . . you told me to put the cat out. I thought he had caught fire," said Pinocchio in a small voice.

"Oh, my dear boy, you have much to learn!" Geppetto sighed as he dried off Figaro. "Okay, you can be a helpful boy by helping me to pick up the house a bit before you leave for school."

"All right, Father!" said Pinocchio, and he raced out the front door.

"Where in the world is he going?" Geppetto wondered aloud, as he followed Pinocchio outside.

Pinocchio was crouching at the base of the house, trying with all his might to lift it.

"What are you doing, son?" asked Geppetto with a twinkle in his eye.

"Trying to pick up the house, Father," said Pinocchio, his voice straining with effort.

Geppetto chuckled and gently guided Pinocchio back inside. "My boy, the sooner you go to school and learn about the world, the better for us both," he said. He collected Pinocchio's hat, his schoolbook and an apple for the teacher, and sent him on his way.

As Geppetto watched his new son walk off to school, he shook his head worriedly. "I hope he manages to stay out of trouble today," he said to himself. "My little boy has much to learn about the world."

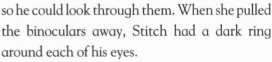

Who's Fooling Whom?

Lilo had only had her new dog, Stitch, for a little while. Already he had managed to break just about everything he touched, and got Lilo's sister Nani dismissed from her new job.

Then April Fools' Day rolled around, and Lilo decided that, for one day, she was allowed to be a pain in the neck *back*.

Lilo got started first thing in the morning. She left a whoopee cushion on Stitch's chair at the breakfast table. When he came in to eat and sat down, a very loud and very rude noise reverberated around the kitchen.

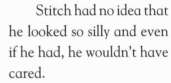

Lilo laughed and shouted, "April Fools'!"

Stitch shrugged. He made rude noises all the time, so he wasn't embarrassed one bit.

After lunch that day, Lilo handed Stitch a cream-filled cookie. She had replaced the filling with toothpaste mixed with pickle juice.

Stitch took a bite.

"April Fools'!" cried Lilo.

Stitch took another bite . . . and another . . . and another, until he finished the cookie. Then he licked his lips. Ugh! thought Lilo. Stitch would eat anything!

Later that day Lilo smeared some of Nani's eyeliner around the eyepieces of her binoculars. She pretended to see something interesting out on the water. "Check out that huge wave," she said. Lilo held the binoculars up to Stitch's eyes

so he could look through them. When she pulled the binoculars away, Stitch had a dark ring around each of his eyes.

"April Fools'!" cried Lilo.

Stitch had no idea that he looked so silly and even if he had, he wouldn't have cared.

Stitch also didn't seem to notice the fake blood dripping from Lilo's mouth before dinner, the ping-pong balls that rained down when he opened the bedroom door, or the arrow-through-the-head hat Lilo put on at bedtime.

"You're no fun to fool, Stitch," said Lilo.

Then she pulled back the covers on her bed and climbed in. But, for some reason, she couldn't extend her legs all the way.

"Hey!" Lilo exclaimed. "Someone short-sheeted my bed! Nani!"

Nani poked her head into Lilo's room.

"Very funny," Lilo said to her.

Nani looked at Lilo with a blank stare. "What's very funny?"

Nani looked as if she didn't know what Lilo was talking about. But that only left . . .

No way, thought Lilo. Stitch was just a dog. Lilo looked at him, sitting at the foot of her bed, wagging his tail. There was no way he could have short-sheeted her bed.

Was there?

The Good Thing About Rain

"Rise and shine!" cried Pongo. One by one, he nudged each of his 15 Dalmatian puppies with his nose.

The puppies yawned and stretched.

But Rolly just rolled over and slept on.

"Aw, come on, Rolly," Pongo whispered in the pup's ear. "It's morning! Don't you want to go out?"

At the mention of the word 'out,' Rolly was instantly wide awake!

Rolly was not alone. As if by magic, the sleepy group had become a pack of jumping, barking puppies. They raced together through the kitchen to the back door, where they jumped up and down, waiting for Nanny to let them out into the garden.

"Okay, here I come," said Nanny, as she made her way across the kitchen. Then she flung the door open wide and stepped out of the way to let the puppies race past.

But they didn't move. It was raining!

"Oh, go on," said Perdita, trying to nudge the pups out the door. "It's only a little water."

But they wouldn't budge.

The next morning, Patch awoke with a start. With a few sharp barks, he helped Pongo wake the other puppies. Within seconds, all 15 were crowding around the back door.

Nanny rushed to open the door again.

And once again, the puppies were very disappointed to see raindrops falling.

"Well," said Pongo with a sigh, "April showers bring May flowers!"

The next morning, the puppies weren't in any hurry to go outside. After all, it was probably still raining. They thought that all they had to look forward to was another whole day spent inside.

So, when Nanny opened the door on a sunny morning, the puppies were so surprised that they didn't know what to do.

Then, springing into action, they tumbled over one another in their rush to get out the door. They raced off in different directions, ready to sniff, dig, roll and explore.

But then, almost at once, all 15 puppies froze in their tracks. They looked around at each other, then down at themselves. What was this stuff getting all over their spotted white coats? It was brown. It was wet. It was squishy. It was mud! And it was FUN!

From the doorway, Pongo and Perdita looked out at their muddy puppies and laughed.

"You know what this means, don't you?" Pongo asked Perdita.

Perdy nodded. "Baths."

Pongo smiled, watching the frolicking puppies. "Let's not tell them – just yet," he said.

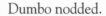

DUMBO

You're Gonna Be Huge!

Dumbo sat in the corner with a big frown on his face.

"What's the matter, kid?" Timothy asked.

Dumbo just shook his head.

"You've got nothing to be sad about," Timothy continued.

Dumbo didn't say anything.

"Well, if you're not going to tell me what's bugging ya, I guess I'll just have to figure it out for myself," Timothy said. "I know!" he exclaimed. "You're hungry?"

Dumbo shook his head.

"Thirsty?" Timothy asked.

Dumbo shook his head again.

"Concerned about the June-bug population in Saskatchewan?" Timothy suggested.

Dumbo shook his head doubly hard.

"Well, then," Timothy concluded. "It can only be one thing. It pains me to say it, but I think you have a case of 'feeling sorry for myself-itis'."

Dumbo's large ears pricked up.

"Yes," Timothy continued. "It's a dangerous disease that has affected many of us. Even the strongest cannot avoid it."

Dumbo looked to his left and to his right, then pointed to himself.

"Yes, that's right – you!" Timothy said. "I bet I know what's got you down – your above-average ear size."

Dumbo nodded.

"And the fact that people make fun of you," Timothy continued.

Dumbo nodded even more.

"And, on top of all that," Timothy said, "you've been separated from your mother."

A tear started to form in Dumbo's eye.

"Don't feel sorry for yourself!" Timothy ordered.

Dumbo looked up, surprised.

"You know why?" Timothy asked. "Because one day you're gonna be huge!"

Dumbo blinked in disbelief.

"We're talking autographs, your name in lights. They're gonna eat their hats for the way they treated you," Timothy predicted.

Dumbo looked nervous.

"I don't mean eat their hats for real," Timothy explained. "It's just a figure of speech. Not that some of them wouldn't deserve having to eat their hats. But that's not what we're talking about. They're gonna be really sorry they treated you so bad, understand?"

Dumbo nodded his head.

"All right then," Timothy said. "Feeling better?"

And Dumbo nodded doubly hard as visions of success, happiness – and being with his mother again – filled his head.

A Change of Scenery

Dr Sherman had left for the day when Gill called everyone together for a Tank Gang meeting.

"We need to make some changes around here," Gill began. "We've all been living in this glass box for how long now? And every day we stare at the same scenery – the same volcano, the same sunken ship, the same treasure chest and tiki hut. Well, seeing as how we can't change what's in our tank, I propose we rearrange things a little. Who's with me?"

"Great idea!" cried Peach the starfish.

"I'm with you," said Deb. "And Flo is too," she added, pointing at her reflection.

Everyone agreed it sounded like a good idea. "We can completely transform the place," said Bloat.

"All right!" said Gill. "Then how about we start with the tiki hut? Bloat, you hoist it up. Gurgle and I will help you move it. The rest of you guys tell us where you think it should go."

Gill, Bloat and Gurgle swam over to the tiki hut. Bloat wriggled his body underneath it and blew himself up, hoisting the hut a few inches off the gravel. Meanwhile, Gill and Gurgle stationed themselves on either side of the hut and prepared to push.

"Let's try it over there," said Peach, pointing to a far corner of the tank.

With blown-up Bloat acting as a cart underneath the hut, Gill and Gurgle pushed the tiki hut into the corner.

"Oh, no," said Deb, "that's all wrong. Can we see what it looks like over there?" She pointed to the opposite corner of the tank.

So Gill, Gurgle and Bloat worked together to move the tiki hut again.

"That's a disaster!" exclaimed Jacques.

"Yeah, he's right," said Nemo.

Gill, Gurgle and Bloat were getting worn out by all the moving. "Can we all just agree on where it should go?" said Gill. "And quickly?"

"Ooh! I know!" said Deb. "Bring it over this way." She led Gill, Gurgle and Bloat over to a shady spot next to some plastic plants. "Put it down here," she said. So they did.

"I like it!" exclaimed Peach.

"The perfect spot," said Jacques.

"Mmm-hmm," said Bubbles.

Gill stepped back and looked around. "Guys, this is where it was in the first place!"

"Is it?" asked Peach.

Deb giggled. "Well, no wonder it just seems to fit here!"

The other fish nodded – except for Gill, who sighed in frustration.

And that was the end of the tank redecoration for the evening.

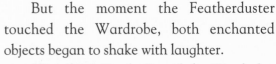

Beauty and the Beast

Castle Cleaning

It was a particularly warm and sunny April morning, and Belle and Chip the teacup were gazing out of a castle window at the blue sky and the budding trees and plants.

"Well, Chip," Belle said, "it is definitely spring at last. And you know what that means, don't you?"

Chip hopped up and down in excitement. "It means we get to play outside?" he asked.

Belle laughed. "Well, yes, that too," she replied. "But first it's time to do some spring cleaning."

So Belle got together a few cleaning supplies. "I think I'll start in the dining room," she said. Belle pulled the silverware out of the silver cabinet and began polishing a fork.

"Ooh!" exclaimed the enchanted fork. "Careful! Ouch! Not so hard around the tines!"

"Oh, dear!" said Belle. "I'm sorry." She gently polished the rest of the utensils.

Next, Belle gathered all the dishes. But when she dipped the first enchanted dish into the soapy water in the sink, it cried out, "Ahh! Too cold! Too cold!"

Belle gasped . . . and hurried to add more warm water to the sink.

After finishing the dishes, Belle moved to her bedroom, where she began dusting the Wardrobe with the Featherduster.

But the moment the Featherduster touched the Wardrobe, both enchanted objects began to shake with laughter.

"Hee, hee! Ha, ha!" said the Wardrobe. "That tickles!"

"You've got that right!" the Featherduster said.

Belle went to the library to take a break from her cleaning. Chip hopped in. "Oh, Chip," she said wearily, "spring cleaning in this castle is a challenge. I'm not used to cleaning enchanted objects!"

Chip giggled. "And I guess we're not used to it either. We always just clean ourselves!"

"Clean yourselves?" said Belle.

That gave her an idea. If the enchanted objects could clean themselves, they could clean other objects too!

Belle called the enchanted objects together. "I wonder if I could ask your help with a little project," Belle began.

Soon Belle had a small army of enchanted objects cleaning everything else in the castle. In a few short hours, the entire castle had been cleaned, and Belle and Chip were relaxing in the library.

"Well," Belle said as she sank into a comfortable chair, "you know what they say: 'Many hands make light work.' And a little enchantment never hurt either!"

Disney
Lady and the TRAMP

Tony and the Tramp

Tramp licked the last of the tomato sauce from his chin. "So, what do you think, Pidge?" he asked Lady.

"That was the most wonderful meal I've ever had," Lady gushed.

"What did I tell ya?" Tramp boasted. "There's no one in the world who can cook up a meal like Tony!"

"I couldn't agree with you more," Lady said. "Can I ask you a question?"

"Sure thing," Tramp said. "Ask away!"

"I was just wondering," Lady began, "how you and Tony met."

"How I met Tony?" Tramp laughed. "Now that's a story!"

"I bet!" Lady said.

"Well, see, it goes like this," Tramp began. "It was a cold and snowy night. I don't think it had ever been that cold before, and I know it hasn't been since. I had been walking uphill for miles. Icicles were hanging from the tip of my nose."

"Wait a minute!" Lady interrupted. "You were walking for miles – uphill? In this town?"

"That's right!" Tramp said. "You've never seen the likes of it."

"Exactly!" Lady told him. "You know why?" Tramp shook his head.

"Because it isn't possible! There are no big hills around here!" Lady said.

"Not possible?" Tramp said. "Okay, you're right," he confessed.

"So, then, what's the truth?" Lady asked.

"The truth is," Tramp began, "I wasn't always the slick, handsome devil you see before you."

"Is that right?" Lady was amused.

"And this one afternoon I was being harassed by a group of mangy mutts who outnumbered me ten to one. So, I took off as fast as my paws could carry me. And as they were chasing me, along came this dogcatcher!"

"Oh, no!" Lady exclaimed.

"Exactly!" Tramp continued. "The mutts scattered out of sight, so I didn't have *them* to worry about any more. But now the dogcatcher was closing in! I thought I was a goner!"

"What happened?" Lady asked.

"Then Tony came running out with a bowl of steaming hot pasta," Tramp explained. "He told the dogcatcher I was his dog. The dogcatcher didn't believe him. But, when Tony put the bowl of pasta down in front of me, he had no choice. Let me tell you, I thought I'd died and gone to heaven."

"I can relate to that," Lady said, recalling the meal.

"And the rest," Tramp said, "as they say, is history!"

"And a tasty one at that!" Lady concluded.

Ariel Changes the Tune

Sebastian rapped his claw on a piece of coral and cleared his throat. But the mermaids kept talking as if the little crustacean were not even there. With a heavy sigh, Sebastian grabbed a huge conch shell. After a lot of effort he managed to hoist it to his mouth and blow.

The shell sounded like a giant horn. The mermaid princesses looked startled, and, to Sebastian's relief, they stopped talking.

"Shall we begin?" the small crab asked calmly. He was anxious to start rehearsing. King Triton's daughters had amazing singing voices, but they still had not decided on the right song to sing for their father's birthday. And there were just a few days left before the celebration!

Sebastian raised his claw and was about to bring it down to start the vocal warm-up when Aquata interrupted him.

"Ariel's not here," she said.

"Oh, Ariel!" Sebastian cried. Ariel was constantly swimming off on her own and holding things up.

"Do you want us to find her?" Arista asked.

"No." Sebastian sighed dramatically. "Then you will all be lost, and I don't know what I would tell your father."

"We wouldn't get lost," Attina protested.

"We *always* show up on time," Adella added. The other sisters nodded their heads in agreement.

"Why do we have to sit around and wait for her?" Alana grumbled. The rest of her sisters nodded angrily.

"Girls, girls!" Sebastian said, trying to calm them. He wished they could go ahead without Ariel, but her voice was by far the most beautiful.

Suddenly, Ariel swam up with Flounder.

"I hope you weren't waiting for me," she said sweetly.

"Ariel!" Sebastian didn't know whether he should be angry or relieved.

"Where have you been?" Aquata put her hands on her scaly hips.

"We still don't have a song for father!" Attina added.

"We do now!" Ariel said cheerfully. She couldn't tell them, but she had been to the surface. It was forbidden. But she had got something very special from her seagull friend Scuttle today. A new song! Ariel began singing the human tune. After only a moment, Ariel's sisters began to sing along.

Sebastian closed his eyes and listened. The song was perfect! "Where did you learn it?" he asked when they were done.

Ariel looked at Flounder. "A little bird told me," she said with a wink.

Easter Egg Hunt!

The Easter holiday was quickly approaching, which meant one thing: the annual Pelekai Easter egg hunt! Lilo couldn't wait to begin painting eggs. First she asked Nani to help make some hard-boiled eggs. Then Lilo found Stitch, Jumba and Pleakley, and everyone took turns painting the eggs.

"This is my favourite part," Lilo said. "I'm going to paint one pink with purple polka dots!"

"I'm going to draw mosquitoes on mine," said Pleakley, grabbing a crayon.

"Blue!" cried Stitch, dunking his egg violently in the cup of blue dye.

While everyone cleared up, Nani went down to the beach to hide the eggs. When everyone got to the beach, Nani announced the rules. "There are twenty-five eggs hidden on this beach. Whoever finds the most eggs will win the prize."

"What's the prize?" Lilo asked.

"Oh, you'll see," Nani replied with a smile. "On your mark . . . get set . . . go!"

The sun shone on the brilliant white sand as Lilo, Stitch, Jumba and Pleakley searched high and low for the eggs. They found one buried under a sand castle, another hidden under a beach blanket, and even one atop the belly of a man snoring on the beach!

As the afternoon sun began to sink, everyone gathered to count the eggs. Jumba had six one gathered to count the eggs. Jumba had six eggs, and so did Pleakley. Stitch had six too. Then they finished counting Lilo's eggs, ". . . four, five and six!" But that added up to only 24. There must be one more egg hidden somewhere on the beach.

So they split up and went looking for the last egg. Finally, Lilo spotted something under a palm tree. "Everybody, come quick!" she cried. "I think I've found the last egg!"

Nani, Jumba and Pleakley came running. "Look," said Lilo, "it's a huge foil egg. The biggest chocolate egg I've ever seen!"

"It sure is," said Nani. "This is the prize, Lilo, and since you all found the same number of eggs, it looks like you all get to share it!"

"But where's Stitch?" said Lilo. Just then, the huge chocolate egg began to twitch. It rattled and shook, and then –

Stitch popped out of it, yelling, "Ta-daaa!" Bits of chocolate scattered everywhere.

"Wow!" cried Lilo. "Did you guys plan that?"

"No, Lilo," said Nani, looking completely confused and a little disturbed. "I have *no idea* how Stitch got in there without breaking the foil."

"My secret!" said Stitch cheerfully. He began munching on a piece of the chocolate egg.

Nani and Lilo smiled and shrugged, and then they all sat down and ate bits of chocolate egg while they watched the sun set over the water.

Disney

Tangled

A Big Girl Now

Flynn Rider, the thief, was escaping from the palace guards through the forest. In his bag was his precious stolen prize – the royal crown! Guards and bowmen were following him, and even Maximus, horse to the captain of the guard, was determined to catch him.

But Flynn was cunning. The thief swung on a vine, knocked the Captain off the horse, and landed in the saddle himself. Flynn clung to the satchel as Maximus snorted furiously, twirling until he finally sunk his teeth into the bag.

"Give me that!" yelled Flynn. As he yanked the satchel free, it went flying into the air.

The satchel snagged on a tree branch that extended over a cliff's edge. But that didn't stop Flynn or Maximus. They both made their way out onto the branch. Flynn reached the bag just ahead of Maximus. "Ha-ha!" the thief crowed triumphantly. CRACK! The tree branch splintered and they both toppled into the canyon below.

Flynn instantly took off. As he felt his way along a rock face, he was thrilled to discover a hidden entrance to a cave and soon emerged to an astonishing sight. There, in the centre of a hidden valley, stood an enormous tower.

It was the perfect hiding place! "There's not even a door!" he remarked.

Using two arrows, Flynn climbed the tower and into the open window at the top. Finally, he breathed a sigh of relief. He had his satchel and he was safe from that manic horse.

CLANG! Suddenly, everything went black.

Rapunzel had seen the ruffian climbing the tower and hit him with a frying pan! He was out cold.

Using the frying pan, she opened his lips. His teeth weren't pointy. In fact, nothing about this man seemed ugly and scary, as Mother Gothel had warned. He was actually very pleasant looking.

Quickly, she stuffed him in a closet and propped a chair against it. Then she stopped to consider her situation. She had just defended herself from an outsider. Rapunzel felt exhilarated! Surely this act of bravery would prove to Mother Gothel that she could handle herself in the outside world.

"Too weak to handle myself out there, huh, Mother? Well..." she laughed, "Tell that to my frying pan!" Rapunzel boldly brandished the frying pan above her head and *WHAM!* she accidently hit her own head!

"Oh no!" she moaned, upset. It was a good thing Mother Gothel hadn't seen that.

The Prettiest Flower

One morning, Bashful went out to pick the prettiest flower he could find. Suddenly, he heard a noise just over the hill.

"*Ah-choo!*"

Bashful climbed the hill and saw his friend on the other side.

"These darn flowers are making me sneeze," said Sneezy. "But it's worth it – because I've picked the prettiest flower for Snow White's hair." He showed Bashful the white orchid he'd picked.

"That sure is pretty," said Bashful. "But I've got a flower for her too. It's even prettier."

Bashful showed Sneezy the rosebud he'd picked. Then he blushed pinker than its petals.

"*Ah-choo!* Yours is pretty too," said Sneezy. "Let's go home and see which one Snow White likes best."

On the path back to their little cottage, Sneezy and Bashful came upon Doc, Happy and Sleepy. They were all arguing about something.

"Snow White bikes liolets," insisted Doc. "I mean she likes violets!"

Happy laughed. "No. She likes daisies!"

"I think she likes muuuuuums," said Sleepy with a yawn.

"You *would* think that!" grumbled a voice behind them. It was Grumpy. He held a long stem with small pastel blossoms.

"That's the perfect flower for you, Grumpy," said Doc. "Snapdragons!"

"Very funny!" Grumpy snapped.

When they all arrived at their house, they saw Dopey.

"Dopey, what do you have behind your back?" Doc asked.

Dopey showed them a single yellow tulip.

"*Another* flower!" cried Happy.

When the Seven Dwarfs went inside, they found Snow White in the kitchen.

"We all wanted to thank you for being so good to us," said Doc. "So we each picked a flower for your hair."

"Now it's *your* turn to pick the flower you like best," said Grumpy.

Snow White felt terrible. She loved all the Dwarfs and she didn't want to hurt any of their feelings by choosing one flower over another.

"I have an idea," she told them. "Put all of your flowers down on the table, and go outside for five minutes. When you come back in, I'll be wearing the flower I think is the prettiest."

The Dwarfs went outside. When they came back in, they gasped in surprise. Snow White had made a flower crown.

She'd found a way to wear all their flowers!

"I love every one of your flowers!" she told them. "Just like I love each and every one of you!"

Bambi

First Impressions

Bambi was just discovering the wonders of the forest. His mother had brought him to a little clearing in the woods. The sudden sunshine and bright green grass surprised and pleased him, and he bounded around on his still-wobbly legs, feeling the warm sun on his back and the soft grass under his hooves. While his mother grazed nearby, Bambi began to explore.

He found a patch of green grass and clover, and he bent down to eat. This was not an easy feat, as his long legs made it difficult for his little neck to reach the ground. When his nose was just a few inches from the tips of the grass, he suddenly leaped backwards in alarm. A leaf had just sprung up from the patch of grass and had landed a few feet away. A hopping leaf? he wondered. He followed it and, as soon as he drew close, the leaf hopped away from him again! Bambi looked around at where his mother stood, still grazing. She seemed to think they were in no great danger. So, he followed the leaf all the way to the edge of the clearing, where a wide brook babbled over craggy rocks.

Bambi's fascination with the hopping leaf faded as he approached the brook. Water cascaded smoothly over the rocks, bubbling and frothing in shallow pools. He took a step closer and felt his foot touch a rock at the edge of the water. Suddenly, the rock moved! It shuffled towards the water and then – *plop*! – jumped right in and swam away. Bambi was dumbfounded as he watched it dive beneath the surface and vanish. He stared at the spot where the rock had been for a moment, and then stooped down to have a drink, widening his stance in order to do so.

Suddenly, he jumped back in alarm. There in the water, staring right back up at him, was a little deer! Cautiously he approached again, and there it was!

Bambi turned and bounded back across the clearing to his mother. "Mama! Mama!" he cried breathlessly. "You will never guess what I have seen!"

His mother lifted her head and gazed at him with her clear, bright eyes.

"First," he said, "first I saw a jumping leaf. Then, I saw a rock with legs that walked right into the water and swam away! And then," he he continued in amazement, "and then I saw a little deer who lives right in the water! He's right over there, Mama!"

His mother nuzzled her son, thinking over what he had said. Then she laughed gently. "Darling," she said. "I think you have just seen your first grasshopper, your first turtle and your very own reflection!"

Fairy Medicine

Deep in the forest, in a humble cottage, the three good fairies had been secretly raising Briar Rose for many years. One morning, the girl woke up with a terrible cold.

"We must nurse her back to health," said Flora.

Fauna and Merryweather agreed. So, while Briar Rose stayed in bed, Flora brought her a bowl of soup. Fauna fetched her a cup of tea. And Merryweather gave her a dose of medicine.

"Ooooh!" said Briar Rose, wrinkling her nose. "That tastes awful!"

"Most medicine tastes awful, dear," said Merryweather. "Just drink it down."

"Would you like anything else?" Flora asked.

The princess blew her nose and gazed out her window at the beautiful spring day.

"What I really want is to get out of bed," she said. "*Ah-choo!*"

"Oh, no, dear," said Flora. "You're far too sick."

Then the fairies left Briar Rose and went downstairs.

"I feel bad for the sweet girl," said Fauna. "Staying in bed all day is boring."

"What can we do?" asked Merryweather.

"I know!" cried Flora. "We'll entertain her!"

"Splendid!" said Merryweather. "I'll fetch my wand and conjure up some fireworks, a puppet show, and – "

"And perhaps that clever dog who jumps through hoops!" added Fauna.

"No!" Flora cried. "We all agreed to give up our fairy magic until Briar Rose turns 16 and she's safe from Maleficent's curse."

"Not even a little magic?" asked Fauna. "Just a few fireworks?"

"No!" Flora said again, stomping her foot.

"Well," said Fauna, "how do mortals entertain themselves when they're sick in bed?"

"I know!" cried Flora. She brought out a deck of cards. "We'll play card games! That will be fun!"

The three fairies then went up to Briar Rose's room and played card games with her all afternoon. Briar Rose won almost every game, too, which really cheered her up.

After a while, Briar Rose yawned and said she was ready to have a sleep. So the fairies went back downstairs.

When Flora went outside to do some gardening, Fauna approached Merryweather. "Tell me the truth," she whispered. "Did you use magic to let the princess win?"

"I just used mortal magic," confessed Merryweather. "No harm in a little sleight of hand. After all, you must admit, if you're feeling down, winning is the best medicine!"

Tinker Bell and the Moonstone

Pixie Hollow was abuzz with excitement! The fairies were preparing to celebrate the arrival of autumn, and Tinker Bell had been asked to make the sceptre that would hold the precious moonstone – which helped to make blue pixie dust and restore the Pixie Dust Tree.

Bursting with joy, Tinker Bell rushed to tell Terence the good news. He offered to help, but before long the little fairy began to get irritated with him getting in the way. Eventually, Tink lost her temper and accidentally broke the moonstone! Tinker Bell was in despair; she didn't know what to do.

That night, at the theatre, a fairy named Lyria told a story of lost treasure. Far away, on a forgotten island, there was a mirror, hidden in a boat, with the power to grant one wish. Tinker Bell decided to go in search of the mirror to put right her silly mistake. She set to work building a hot-air balloon and gathering her supplies.

Along the way, Tinker Bell met Blaze, a little firefly. One morning, the two new friends were surprised by a violent storm! When the fog cleared, they realized the balloon was stuck in a tree. Tink flew down to the ground, and the balloon drifted away and was carried far beyond their reach.

Tinker Bell was sad, but luckily Blaze and some new little bug friends were there to help her. Tink realized how much she missed Terence, her best friend who always did his best to be there for her.

Tink finally caught sight of the lost boat and discovered, at the bottom of the wreck, the magic mirror!

But, annoyed by Blaze's buzzing, Tinker Bell hastily asked for silence – instead of a new moonstone. And her wish was granted! Tinker Bell had just thrown away her last chance!

Tinker Bell started to think about Terence again, and she started to feel very bad about getting angry with him.

Then, as if by magic, Terence appeared behind her! He had flown all night long and had even found her balloon.

Back in Pixie Hollow, the Autumn Revelry was about to begin. They had no time to waste!

During the journey home, Terence helped Tinker Bell to make a new sceptre out of the shattered fragments of moonstone. They arrived for the ceremony just in time.

The blue harvest moon lit up the strangely beautiful sceptre, and blue pixie dust started to fall from the sky. Hurray! Tinker Bell had succeeded – with a little help from her friends!

Abracadabra!

Manny was not at his best. Gypsy could tell. Already that day, he had lost two magic wands and stepped on his turban.

And with the matinee show at P.T. Flea's World's Greatest Circus about to begin, Gypsy knew she had to be on her toes. Manny was going to debut his new trick: the Levitating, Flaming and Disappearing Water Torture Chamber of Death.

"Ladies and gentlemen," Manny announced, "prepare to be stunned and amazed by the Levitating, Flaming and Disappearing Water Torture Chamber of Death. You will watch as my lovely and talented assistant, Gypsy, climbs inside this chamber" – Manny motioned towards the empty sardine can at his side – "where I will bind her hands and feet. Then I will fill the chamber with water, seal it, levitate it five inches off the ground and set it ablaze. And, finally, you will watch in awe as the chamber disappears before your very eyes!"

Manny and Gypsy had rehearsed the act thoroughly. Everything was planned down to the last detail. But, if one little thing went wrong with the trick, Gypsy could be in big trouble.

As it turned out, one little thing didn't go wrong – three big things went wrong!

Manny made his first mistake when he tied Gypsy's hands and feet together. He was supposed to leave the strings loose so that Gypsy could wriggle out of them once she was inside. But Manny accidentally tied them too tight!

Then Manny filled the chamber too high with water. In rehearsals, he had left a bit of space at the top so that Gypsy had some air inside. But, this time, he forgot!

Manny's third mistake was locking the trapdoor. Together, he and Gypsy had rigged an escape hatch in the back side of the sardine can. Once Manny sealed her inside, Gypsy wriggled out of her bonds, opened the trapdoor, and, unseen by the audience, escaped from the chamber before Manny levitated it, set it on fire and made it disappear. But, this time, Manny accidentally nudged the latch that secured the trapdoor from the outside. Gypsy was locked inside.

Luckily, Gypsy hadn't left anything to chance: she had stowed a sharp shard of glass inside the sardine can. She had learned to hold her breath for ten minutes. And she had put a release latch on the inside of the trapdoor.

She was safely out of the chamber in one minute flat.

At the end of the trick, Manny called Gypsy in front of the audience. "How did you do it, my dear?" he asked dramatically.

"It was magic!" she replied, with a smile and a sigh of relief.

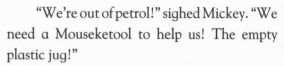

Let's Get Goofy

Everyone was gathered at the Clubhouse, ready for a day of fun! Everyone except Goofy. "Where is he?" asked Minnie.

"Maybe he's inside already," said Mickey. "Let's go see!"

"Goofy?" everyone called. The Clubhouse was quiet.

"Let's go up to the roof top and see if we can spot him!" said Mickey.

But there was no sign of Goofy. Then Mickey looked through the Mousekespotter towards the west and chuckled. "I know where Goofy is!" he said.

"Where?" asked Daisy.

"He's at home!" said Mickey. "He's still asleep! Come on, let's get him!"

But first, they needed some Mouseketools; a compass, an empty plastic jug, the Mystery Mouseketool and a yellow feather. Then everyone got into the Toon Car and Mickey drove off.

When they reached a crossroads, they were unsure which way to go.

"It's time for a Mouseketool," said Mickey. He held out the compass and the arrow pointed north. Now Mickey knew which way was west!

As they continued, the car moved slower and slower until, finally, it stopped.

"We're out of petrol!" sighed Mickey. "We need a Mouseketool to help us! The empty plastic jug!"

He and Minnie took the jug and went to the petrol station. They filled the car with petrol and were on their way again.

But up ahead, in the middle of the road, was a large hog. The hog wouldn't move out of the way. "It's time for the Mystery Mouseketool," Mickey said.

"What is it?" Minnie asked.

"Two ears of corn!" said Mickey.

Donald took the corn, then laid them on the grass. The hog walked onto the grass and started munching it.

"Enjoy the corn!" said Minnie.

They finally arrived at Goofy's house, but he was still asleep. Goofy wouldn't wake up!

"Let's try the feather Mouseketool!" said Mickey.

Mickey tickled Goofy's foot with the feather. Goofy opened his eyes and sat up.

"Hiya, Goofy!" said Mickey.

Goofy removed ear plugs from his ears.

"But, Goofy," said Minnie, "how could you hear your alarm if you were wearing ear plugs?"

"My new alarm clock kept going off every hour. If I hadn't worn the ear plugs, I wouldn't have got any sleep!"

Snow White
and the Seven Dwarfs

A Friend in Need

Whatever could be keeping the Seven Dwarfs?" said Snow White. "They should have been home from work by now!"

Just then, Happy came through the front door looking upset. "Come quickly! A young deer is hurt in the woods."

Snow White followed Happy, and they soon reached a small clearing. Everyone stood in a circle around the deer.

"Thank goodness you're here, Snow White!" said Doc. "This little fella's in trouble!"

"He must be cold," said Snow White, covering him with her long cape.

"Maybe he's just tired," said Sleepy. "A nice long rest should do the trick!"

"Why, you could be right, Sleepy," said Snow White. "But he's not closing his eyes, so I think it might be something else."

"Maybe he has a... aahhh... aaaahhhh... choooooooo... a cold," said Sneezy.

"Well, that's possible, but then he probably would have stayed in his thicket until he was feeling better," said Snow White.

"I know!" said Happy. "Maybe he's feeling sad and needs a little cheering up!"

"I'm sure that would help, Happy," said Snow White. "But he looks like he may need something more than a merry story or a song."

"I, uh, don't know for sure," said Bashful softly. "But perhaps he's too shy to let us know what's the matter."

"We all feel shy sometimes, don't we, Bashful?" said Snow White.

Then Dopey started pacing back and forth and pointing over his shoulder.

"Maybe you're right, he could be lost," said Snow White.

"I'll bet I know what happened," said Grumpy. "The wicked Queen probably cast a spell on him! She's always up to no good!"

Suddenly, Doc walked up to the deer. "May I lake a took – er, I mean, take a look?" he asked. Doc knelt down beside the deer.

"Well, would you look at that!" cried Doc, pointing at the animal's foot. "The poor deer must have stepped on a thorn. "

Doc gently removed the sharp thorn. The deer jumped up and licked him.

"Oh, how relieved you must be!" cried Snow White.

The deer licked Snow White's hand and ran off into the forest. Snow White and the Seven Dwarfs went home to their little cottage.

"I am so proud of each and every one of you," said Snow White, smiling at her friends. "You each did your best to help a friend in need!"

THE LITTLE MERMAID

A History Lesson

"Ariel, what am I going to do with you?" King Triton asked with a sigh. He looked wearily at his daughter. "You know you're not allowed to visit the surface. None of us are – it's just too dangerous!"

Ariel hung her head. She had been caught going to visit the surface – again – to visit her seagull friend, Scuttle. King Triton just couldn't understand the Little Mermaid's interest in the human world. It made him sad that most of his conversations with his favourite daughter involved him yelling and her storming off. Suddenly, the King had an idea.

"You know, Ariel," he said thoughtfully, "you're so interested in learning more about the human world, but I bet you don't know that much about the world you live in!"

Ariel looked up. "What do you mean, Daddy?" she asked, looking confused. "What's there to know?"

"Well," said Triton, "for starters, do you know about the first Queen of the Merfolk?"

"I guess not," Ariel replied.

Ten minutes later, Ariel and her father were swimming slowly through the Royal Merseum (that's a merfolk museum, you know), and Ariel was discovering that merfolk history was much more exciting than she had ever imagined.

"This is a portrait of Queen Fluidia, the first Queen of the Merfolk. She was my Great-great-great-great-great-great-great-great-great-great-great-great-great-grandmother," said King Triton. He gestured at a sandpainting of a regal mermaid holding a pearl sceptre. "That would make her your Great-great-great – well, you get the idea. Anyway, Fluidia united all the merfolk into one kingdom many years ago, to fight an invasion of sharks. The Shark Army was the greatest, fiercest army the ocean had ever seen, but Fluidia was more than a match for them! She used that pearl sceptre as a club – she was so strong that she could start whirlpools just by swinging it around."

"Wow," said Ariel. "She sounds pretty fierce."

"She was. She drove those sharks off almost single-handedly, and in gratitude the merfolk made her Queen," King Triton said.

"You know, you come from a pretty interesting family," he continued. "And you remind me a lot of Fluidia, Ariel. You have her strength of will. I think you'll do great things – even if you and I won't always agree on *how* you'll do them."

"Thank you, Daddy," said Ariel, giving her father a hug. She decided not to mention to her father how much his trident looked like a dinglehopper. Maybe she would tell him some other time!

Disney
THE
LION KING

Pictures in the Stars

Ever since Mufasa had died and Simba had left the Pride Lands, Timon and Pumbaa had been Simba's only friends – but what fun the three of them had together. One of their favourite things to do after their evening meal was to lie on their backs in the tall grass and gaze up at the night sky, looking for shapes in the stars.

"Okay, okay, I got one," said Pumbaa, lifting a foreleg to point to one area of the sky. "See, over there, that long, thin, curving outline? It's a big, juicy, delicious slug!" Pumbaa licked and smacked his lips, imagining the taste of a slug snack. "Mmm-mmm!"

Simba chuckled. "Pumbaa, how can you still be hungry? We just ate!"

Pumbaa shrugged. "It's a gift," he said.

Timon cleared his throat. "I hate to disagree with you, Pumbaa my friend, but that's no slug you see up there. That's an elephant's trunk. If you follow that curving line of stars, you see it connects with the elephant's head at one end. And there are the ears," Timon said, tracing it all out with his finger, "and there are the tusks."

Simba chuckled again. "Somebody still has his mind on that elephant stampede we almost got flattened by this afternoon," he said.

"Hey . . ." Timon said defensively, "what's that supposed to mean?"

"Oh, no offence, Timon," Simba replied. "I just think it's funny that the things you and Pumbaa see in the stars just happen to be the same things that are on your mind at the time."

"Ooh! Ooh! I've got another one!" Pumbaa interrupted. "A big bunch of tasty berries right over there," he said, pointing at a grouping of stars. "Don't they look good?"

"See what I mean?" Simba said to Timon, gesturing at Pumbaa.

"All right, all right, Mr Smarty-Pants," Timon replied. "So what do you see in the stars?"

"Well, now, let's see," said Simba, gazing intently at the tons of tiny points of light twinkling down at them. There were so many that you could see practically any shape in them that you wanted to. It all depended on how you looked at them. But just to get Timon's goat, Simba wanted to find something really bright – something really clear. Something Timon couldn't deny that he saw too.

Just at that moment, a shooting star streaked the entire length of the night sky.

"I see a bright streak of light rocketing across the sky!" exclaimed Simba.

"Ooh! Me, too!" said Pumbaa. "Timon, do you see it?"

Timon had to admit that he did. "Yeah, yeah, I see it," he muttered grudgingly. "Ha-ha. Very funny, Simba."

Should I Stay or Should I Go?

Wendy sat watching Michael and John play with Peter Pan and the rest of the Lost Boys.

"John and Michael seem so happy," Wendy said to herself. "And why wouldn't they? Never Land is such a beautiful place, and the flying is so much fun!

"Still," she had to admit, "it is also dangerous. Who knows what sort of trouble we could get into, especially with Captain Hook running about?

"And," Wendy continued, "I don't think that Tinker Bell likes me very much."

Wendy considered this, then burst out, "What am I talking about? I'm making it sound like it's an awful place, but the truth is, Never Land is the most wonderful place on earth!

"Perhaps that explains it!" Wendy suddenly realized. "Maybe I really want to stay in Never Land, but in my heart of hearts I know I shouldn't. After all, Mother and Father must miss us terribly. And we miss them too! Oh, and what about Nana?" Wendy began to fret. "She must worry about us endlessly!

"That settles it!" Wendy stood up abruptly. "We must leave for home immediately.

"But if I stay –" Wendy stopped herself. "I'll never have to grow up!"

Wendy thought about the pros and cons of never getting old. "Then again, I always wanted to be an adult someday," she concluded.

Just then, Peter Pan swooped down beside her. "What are you doing, Wendy?" Peter asked.

"Oh, nothing," Wendy told him.

"Then why don't you come join us?" he suggested.

"I will," Wendy told him. "In a minute."

"All right! But last one there is a rotten – " Peter took off before he could finish his sentence.

"How can I ever leave Peter and the Lost Boys?" Wendy wondered. "They need me so much.

"But so do our parents," she quickly reminded herself.

"Should I stay?" she wondered aloud. "Or should I go?"

Wendy's eyes fell upon a daisy. She bent over and pulled it out of the ground. "Should I stay?" she asked as she pulled a petal from the daisy. "Or should I go?" she asked as she pulled a second petal from the daisy.

Wendy did this over and over again until there was only one petal remaining on the daisy. "Well," she said, "this flower says we should go back home. And I suppose it's right. We'll go back . . . but maybe not just this minute."

Wendy stood up. "Hey, Peter, wait up!" And with that, she flew off after Peter, her mind at ease at last.

Cinderella

A Birthday Surprise

"Get up, Jaq! Get up!" Gus cried.

"Go away, Gus," Jaq mumbled sleepily and rolled over.

"No, no, Jaq. Get up. It's a special day." Gus pulled on his tail. "It's Cinderelly's birthday."

Jaq sat up. "Today?" he asked, wide-eyed. "Today is her birthday?"

Gus smiled and nodded vigorously.

"Well, come on! We haven't got much time!" Jaq cried. "We have a lot to do if we're throwing a surprise party!"

Soon the birds and mice were gathered on the windowsill for a meeting.

"We can make a cake!" Suzy and Perla volunteered.

"Watch out for L-L-Lucifer," Gus stuttered. Baking would mean stealing eggs and butter from the kitchen!

"We'll take care of that cat," Mert and Bert said, crossing their arms.

The birds whistled that they would decorate the room.

"But we still need a present," Jaq said.

"Something pretty!" Gus cried.

"I've got it!" Jaq sat up straight. "I saw some slippers in the garbage last night when I was looking for food. There's a hole in one toe, but the bottoms were okay."

"We can fix them," the mice chorused.

"And I have a bit of ribbon I've been saving. We can use it on the slippers to pretty them up." Jaq pulled a rose-coloured silk ribbon from his small bag. "Now, let's get to work. We have lots to do!"

It took the mice all day to get ready, but everything turned out beautifully. The sun was setting when the mice and birds heard Cinderella's soft steps coming up the stairs.

"Here she comes!" Gus whispered.

Jaq took a match and lit the candle stump that was stuck in the iced cake. Beside it the slippers were mended and wrapped. The ribbon was twirled into two pink roses, one at each ankle.

The door opened slowly.

"Surprise!" the mice squeaked. The birds twittered and dropped confetti.

"Oh, my!" Cinderella gasped. "This *is* a surprise!"

"Happy birthday," Gus said shyly.

"It's all so lovely," Cinderella said. "But I'm afraid it's not my birthday."

"It's not?" Jaq's smile vanished. The rest of the mice and birds were silent.

"I'm afraid not, but that's what makes this such a special surprise." Cinderella beamed. The animals laughed and they all sat down to share the delicious cake together.

Beauty and the Beast

A Little Help

"This is bad," fretted Cogsworth the clock, pacing at the bottom of the castle's staircase. "Bad, bad, bad!"

"What is wrong, my friend?" asked Lumiere the candelabrum.

"The Beast hurt Belle's feelings," said Cogsworth. "Then Belle hurt the Beast's feelings. Now they're sulking in their rooms."

"Ah, that *is* bad," said Lumiere. "We will never be human again unless the spell on the Beast is broken. And the spell won't break until Belle falls in love with him."

"Well, there's no chance of that happening now!" cried Cogsworth.

"Nonsense," said Lumiere. "Sometimes love just needs a little help."

After Lumiere told Cogsworth his plan, they got to work. When everything was ready, Lumiere knocked on Belle's bedroom door.

"*Mademoiselle*," he called sweetly. "I am here to tell you that the Beast is very sorry about what happened."

"He is?" asked Belle.

"Oh, yes," said Lumiere. "Now do you wish to see your surprise?"

The door slowly opened. "My surprise?" asked Belle.

"*Oui, mademoiselle*," said Lumiere. "Just follow me."

At that very moment, Cogsworth was standing outside the Beast's bedroom door, his gears quaking with fear. "Darn that Lumiere," muttered Cogsworth. "Why do *I* get the Beast?"

Gathering his courage, Cogsworth finally knocked.

"Go away!" roared the Beast.

Cogsworth wanted to! But, instead, he called, "Master, I am only here to tell you that Belle is very sorry about what happened!"

After a long pause, the Beast said, "She is?"

"Oh, yes indeed," said Cogsworth. "Now follow me to see your surprise."

The door slowly opened. "My surprise?" asked the Beast.

"Yes, Master," said Cogsworth.

Both Belle and the Beast were led into the large drawing room. The room had been filled with fresh flowers from the greenhouse. And there stood Plucky the golden harp.

"Ohhhhh," said Belle and the Beast when they heard the beautiful harp music.

"You're sorry?" asked Belle.

"I am," the Beast admitted.

"I am too," said Belle.

They smiled at each other.

Lumiere and Cogsworth sighed. "You see, my friend," whispered Lumiere, "in their hearts, each really was sorry. They just needed a little help to admit it!"

Lady and the TRAMP

Howling at the Moon

Lady had been having a really bad day. First, she'd had a run-in with two nasty cats. Then, she'd been put in a horrible muzzle. But, because of Tramp, everything had changed.

"It's amazing how a day can start off terribly but end wonderfully," Lady told Tramp as they trotted through the moonlit park. "Thank you for helping me escape that terrible muzzle – and for dinner at Tony's."

"Aw, shucks, don't mention it!" said Tramp. "Hey, you wanna have some real fun?"

"I don't know," Lady said cautiously.

While she was very fond of Tramp, she also knew they were very different dogs. Tramp was used to life on the streets. So his idea of 'fun' might be very different from hers.

"Don't worry," Tramp teased. "This is something I think you'll enjoy."

"What is it?" asked Lady.

"Well, for starters, you have to look up," said Tramp.

Lady did. The sky was filled with stars and a big, bright moon.

"What am I looking for?" she asked.

"The moon, of course!" cried Tramp. "Haven't you ever howled at the moon?"

Lady laughed at Tramp's suggestion.

"What's so funny?" asked Tramp.

"I'm a practical dog," explained Lady. "I bark politely when the situation calls for it, but I don't see any point in howling at the moon."

"Why not?" asked Tramp.

"Well," said Lady, "what's the use of it?"

"You know, Lady," said Tramp, "a thing doesn't have to be useful to be fun. You like to chase a ball, right?"

"Right," said Lady.

"So, there you go," said Tramp. "Sometimes it's good to chase a ball. And sometimes it's good to just let go and howl at the moon, even for no reason."

Lady thought it over. "Okay," she said. "What do I do?"

"First, sit up real straight," said Tramp. "Then, look up at the moon, take a deep breath, and just let all the troubles of your day disappear in one gigantic howl!" He demonstrated: "Ow-ow-OWWWWWWW!"

Lady joined Tramp and howled as loudly as she could.

"You're right!" she cried. "It does feel good to howl at the moon!"

"Stick with me, kid," said Tramp. "I know what's what."

Lady suspected Tramp did know what was what, but there was an even better reason for her to stick with him. He'd become the very best friend she'd ever had.

WET CEMENT

THE PRINCESS AND THE FROG

Two Frogs Instead of One

Tiana had just discovered a frog on the balcony of her friend Charlotte's room. The frog had started to talk! Tiana ran back into the room in terror – she couldn't believe it. It was a lot of nonsense, like something from a made-up fairy tale!

"I didn't mean to frighten you," apologized the frog. It jumped onto a piece of furniture to take a closer look at Tiana, who was dressed in Charlotte's clothes and looked like a princess.

"Please allow me to introduce myself," he said. "I am Prince Naveen of Maldonia. I was very handsome and very charming, until I was transformed by an evil sorcerer!"

Terrified, Tiana grabbed a large book from a shelf. "If you're the prince, then who was that waltzing with Lottie on the dance floor?" She had seen Prince Naveen dancing at the ball downstairs. She got ready to throw the book at the frog.

"Wait! I know that story!" the frog interrupted, looking at the cover of the book. "It's the story of the Frog Prince!"

Naveen leafed through the pages of the book, and turned from a picture of a frog to one of a prince. "Don't you see?" he asked. "It's just like the fairytales. If you kiss me, I'm bound to turn back into a prince!"

Tiana grimaced in disgust, but the frog Naveen insisted.

"I don't kiss frogs," refused Tiana.

"You might like to know that as well as being fabulously attractive, I have a fabulously wealthy family! Help me to regain my appearance and, in exchange, I will give you whatever you want..."

Tiana thought. This might be her only chance of finally being able own the restaurant she and her father had dreamed of.

"Just a kiss, then?" she murmured.

"Several if you wish, my dear!" smiled the frog.

Tiana closed her eyes. She took a deep breath and – *smack!* – she planted a quick kiss on the frog's pursed lips.

When she opened her eyes again, nothing had happened. Apart from one thing – she had turned into a frog too! "Aaaaaah!" she screamed when she caught sight of her reflection in the mirror.

"Don't panic!" begged Naveen. "I know, getting two frogs instead of one wasn't exactly what we had in mind. But at least we've got company!"

Tiana, mad with rage, did not reply. She tried one of her new talents, and leapt – *boing!* – at Naveen's throat!

Dinglehoppers and Jibbermutts

Ariel sat on a rock, talking with her friends, Scuttle the seagull and Flounder the fish. She loved visiting the surface, although she knew it was dangerous for mermaids to venture there. Her father would definitely not approve, but then, these days, he seemed to disapprove of so much of what she liked to do.

"What's it like on land, Scuttle?" she asked.

"Land?" echoed Scuttle. "Oh! Land! Yeah, well, it's great on land. I know all about humans."

"Like what?" Ariel asked eagerly.

"Well! For instance . . . you know all about the dinglehoppers they use to comb their hair, right? And the snarfblatts that they make music with?"

"Yes," said Ariel.

"Well, did you know that they also have these strange rectangular objects with sheets of paper inside? They're called jibbermutts. Humans like to throw them to one another," Scuttle explained.

"Oh, Scuttle," said Ariel breathlessly. "Would you fly up to Eric's window and come back and tell me what you have seen?" Eric was the young prince whom Ariel had rescued after he was shipwrecked during a terrible storm. Even though she had seen him only once, she had fallen head over fin in love with him.

Scuttle flew off. While he was gone, Ariel lay back on the rock in the warm sunshine, dreaming of what life must be like on land. Scuttle wasn't gone long.

"Did you see him?" asked Ariel eagerly. "What was he doing?"

"Yep, I saw him!" Scuttle replied importantly. "He was trying to eat with a dinglehopper! And he had a jibbermutt, but it almost looked like he was trying to read it, instead of throwing it like he's supposed to. Ariel, I don't think your prince is too bright . . . ."

Ariel sighed dreamily, imagining her handsome love. She did wonder why he would try to use a dinglehopper to eat, though. Maybe he was so distracted by thoughts of her, he didn't know what he was doing, the Little Mermaid thought hopefully.

"Don't suppose you'd want his dinglehopper for your treasure chest, would you?" asked Scuttle with a mischievous glint in his eye.

"Oh, Scuttle! You didn't!" shouted Ariel.

"Yup. Just as soon as he set it down, I flew in through the window and grabbed it. Boy, was he surprised!"

Ariel clutched the dinglehopper to her chest. "I'll probably never know what it's like to live on land, but no matter what happens, Scuttle, I will treasure this forever!"

Snow White
and the Seven Dwarfs

Good Housekeeping

Snow White and the Prince were going to be married. Her dear friends, the Seven Dwarfs, were filled with joy to see Snow White so happy. But they knew they were going to miss her – not to mention her wonderful cooking and how she kept their cottage so clean and tidy.

Snow White was also worried about how the little men were going to get along without her. She decided it was time they learned how to cook and clean for themselves.

"First, let's see you sweep out the cottage," she said. "Remember to push the dirt out the door and not just move it around the floor." The men all grabbed brooms and set to work.

"*Ah-chooooo!*" boomed Sneezy as a huge cloud of dust rose into the air.

"Don't forget to open the door *first*," Snow White added. She moved on to the next task. "Now we'll wash the dishes. First you dunk the plate, then you scrub it, then you rinse and dry it," she said, demonstrating as she went.

Doc stood, holding a dirty plate. "Let's see," he mumbled. "Scrub, dunk, dry, rinse? Or is it dunk, rinse, dry, scrub? Or . . . oh, dear!"

Snow White chuckled good-naturedly. "Never mind," she said. "On to the laundry! First you heat the water over the fire, then you scrub the clothes with a bar of soap, rinse them

and then hang them on the line to dry."

Dopey was first in line. He jumped into the tub and rubbed the bar of soap all over the clothes he was wearing.

"Dopey," said Snow White, "it's easier if you wash the clothes *after* you've taken them off."

A bit later, the Dwarfs trooped into the kitchen for a cooking lesson.

"Today we're going to make stew," said Snow White. "You take a little of everything you have on hand, throw it into a pot, and let it simmer for a long time."

As Snow White was leaving, Doc said, "Don't worry, Snow White. We're going to be fust jine . . . I mean, just fine."

The next night, the Dwarfs made dinner. When their guests arrived, Dopey led Snow White and the Prince over to the large pot simmering over the fire and grandly lifted the lid. An old boot, some socks, a bunch of flowers, and a cake of soap were floating on the top. "We made it with a little of everything we had on hand, just like you said," Sleepy said.

"Perhaps we should go over that recipe again," Snow White said gently. Then she brought out four gooseberry pies from her basket. Ordinarily, Snow White didn't believe in eating dessert before dinner, but this time she would make an exception!

Who's Tricking Whom?

Rapunzel was feeling very pleased with herself. A stranger had climbed in through the tower window and she had managed to knock him out and lock him in her wardrobe! Now Rapunzel noticed the satchel Flynn had dropped when he fell.

She reached inside and pulled out a gold crown encrusted with jewels.

Pascal looked on curiously as Rapunzel inspected the strange object – she had never seen such a thing before. She tried slipping it over her wrist, but it fell right off. Then she placed it on top of her head. It fit perfectly!

Rapunzel gazed into the mirror. Something seemed familiar –

"Rapunzel! Let down your hair!" Mother Gothel called out.

Quickly Rapunzel hid the crown. Then she threw her endless locks of magic hair out of the window so that Mother Gothel could climb up into the tower.

"I've got a surprise for you!" the wicked woman exclaimed. "This evening I'm going to make you your favourite soup!"

"I've got a surprise for you too," mumbled Rapunzel staring at the wardrobe.

Then Rapunzel turned to Mother Gothel and spoke confidently, "You know you said I mustn't leave the tower because I would never be able to manage on my own outside? Against all the dangers, Mother? Well, don't worry any more – I've just –"

"That's enough!" Mother Gothel suddenly roared angrily. "You're not leaving this tower! EVER!"

Rapunzel was shocked. Realizing she would never get out of the tower unless she took matters into her own hands, Rapunzel quickly asked for another birthday present.

"Oh, of course." Rapunzel said. "I just wanted to tell you that instead of leaving the tower I would much rather have some mother-of-pearl paint for my birthday."

Mother Gothel frowned. To make this paint she would have to collect shells from a shore far away, three days' walk.

"Yes, I think I'd rather stay here in safety and get the paint I need to finish my pictures," the young girl insisted.

"It's a deal," Mother Gothel agreed and sighed with relief. "I'll be back in three day's time." She went off smiling – she had tricked Rapunzel!

From the top of her tower, Rapunzel watched her heading off into the distance. She was smiling too... because, in her own way, she had managed to trick Mother Gothel.

Donald Takes Flight

"Daisy, I have a surprise for you," said Donald Duck one clear spring day. "I've been taking flying lessons."

"That *is* a surprise," said Daisy Duck.

Donald took Daisy to a nearby airport. On the runway sat an old-fashioned plane with open-air seats. Together they climbed into the small plane. Then Donald started the engine.

"Up, up and away!" he cried as they took off.

"Can you do any tricks?" shouted Daisy.

"Sure!" called Donald. He steered the plane into a loop-the-loop.

"You're a very good pilot, Donald!" Daisy cried, clapping her hands.

Donald was so proud of himself, he told Daisy he would fly wherever she wanted to go.

Daisy thought it over. "Let's go to Paris, France!" she said. Donald was so eager to impress Daisy that he didn't think twice. "Paris, here we come!" he cried. Before long, however, the plane's engine began to cough and choke.

"Uh-oh," Donald said to himself as the plane began to drift towards the water.

"Is anything wrong?" asked Daisy.

Donald knew they were running out of fuel. But he didn't want Daisy to find out.

"Everything is fine, Daisy," Donald said nervously.

Just then, he saw something floating below them. It looked like an airport runway. But what would a runway be doing in the middle of the ocean?

As the plane drifted closer to the water, Donald realized he had no choice. He'd have to land his plane on the floating runway.

Just before he landed, Donald's eyes nearly popped out of his head. It wasn't a runway at all. It was the top deck of a huge ocean liner!

"Duck!" yelled one of the ship's passengers, and a dozen people scattered.

Donald zoomed over their heads and carefully landed the plane on the long, wide deck.

"Hey, it really *is* a duck!" cried one of the passengers.

Just then an announcement came over the ship's speakers. "Good evening, ladies and gentleman. Dinner is served!"

Donald helped Daisy out of the plane. He was sure she would be upset. But she wasn't. "Dinner on a cruise ship!" she cried. "Donald, you're just full of surprises, aren't you!"

"Yes, indeed," said Donald with a huge sigh of relief. "And here's one more surprise: I think this ship's on its way to France!"

"Oh, Donald, you're the best," said Daisy.

No, I'm not, thought Donald, as Daisy hugged him. What I really am is one lucky duck!

Snake Eyes

"I'm ssstarved," hissed Kaa the python as he slithered across the jungle treetops. "I need a sssnack . . . ."

Suddenly, Kaa noticed a small figure relaxing on the ground below. It was Mowgli. Kaa slithered over to him.

"Are you feeling ssssleeepy?" hissed Kaa. "You look sssleeepy; jussst look into my eyesss . . ."

Mowgli tried not to look into the snake's eyes, but it wasn't easy. When he turned one way, Kaa was there. When he turned another, Kaa was there too!

"Sssslip into ssssilent ssslumber," Kaa hissed. "And sssleep . . . sssleeep . . . sssleep . . ."

Before Mowgli knew it, his body went completely limp. Kaa had hypnotized him!

Thank goodness Mowgli's friends walked by at that very moment.

"Look!" cried Bagheera the panther. "Kaa's after Mowgli again."

"Get over there and do something," Baloo told Bagheera.

"The last time I interfered with Kaa, he hypnotized me," said Bagheera. "You do something."

Kaa's fangs watered as he coiled his long body around Mowgli. Then Kaa opened his giant python mouth above Mowgli's head and – hey! Someone had jammed a stick into his jaws, propping them wide open!

"Hello there, Kaa," said Baloo, leaning one big paw against the tree.

The python's powerful jaws snapped the stick. "You sssshould not insssert yourssself between a sssnake and his sssnack," he hissed.

"Oh! Sorry!" said Baloo. "I was just admiring how very talented you are."

"Talented?" Kaa said. "Me?"

"Sure!" said Baloo. "I'm very impressed how you hypnotized Mowgli there. I bet you could hypnotize almost anything in the jungle. Almost . . ."

"What do you mean *almost*?" said Kaa.

Baloo coolly polished his claws against his fur. "Well, let's see," he said. "I bet you can't hypnotize . . . a fish." Baloo pointed to the pond.

"Jusssst you watch me," Kaa told Baloo as he slithered towards the pond.

Hanging his head over the water, Kaa hissed, "Jussst look into my eyesss. You feel ssssleeepy . . . ssssleeepy . . . ssssleeepy. . . ."

Suddenly, Kaa stopped hissing. Or moving. He just stared into the water.

Bagheera stepped up to Baloo and whispered, "What's the matter with him?"

Baloo just laughed. "Kaa was so determined to prove me wrong, he didn't even notice the water was reflecting back his image. That crazy snake hypnotized himself!"

Winnie the Pooh

Pooh's Neighbourhood

"I say, it's a splendid day in the neighbourhood!" cried Owl.

"Which neighbour wood are we talking about?" asked Pooh.

"Neighbour*hood*," said Owl. "The place where we live and where all our neighbours live and are neighbourly."

"Oh," said Pooh, "it is a splendid day in it, isn't it?"

"Now I'm off for an owl's-eye view!" said Owl. He flew up and circled once around Pooh's house. "I can see the Hundred-Acre Wood spread out below me, and it's a fine place indeed."

As Owl flew off, Pooh began to think about what it means to live in a neighbourhood, and he thought perhaps he would bring a neighbourly present to his closest neighbour, Piglet. Pooh went inside his house and took a honeypot out of his cupboard. He tied a nice blue ribbon round it.

When he reached his Thoughtful Spot, Pooh suddenly had a thought: I could take the path straight to Piglet's house. Or – I could go up the path and around the whole neighbourhood. And sooner or later the path would take me to Piglet's house, anyway. So that's what he did.

As he walked the long way to Piglet's house, Pooh came across each of his neighbours in turn. He joined Kanga and Roo for a snack at the picnic spot, and collected some carrots from Rabbit. After lunch and a longish snooze at Christopher Robin's house, he soon reached Eeyore's Gloomy Place, which was where Eeyore lived.

Eeyore was feeling sad, so Pooh offered him a nice lick of honey. Pooh put the jar down, and Eeyore peered in. The honey pot was empty! Pooh walked away glumly and, before long, Owl flew over.

"I've seen our whole neighbourhood today," Pooh told him. "But now I have no neighbourly present left for Piglet."

"The bees have been quite busy at the old bee tree lately," said Owl. "Perhaps you can get a fill-up there."

So they walked together until they came to the old bee tree. Up, up, up Pooh climbed. Owl had a thought, and told Pooh to go to the very top of the tree and look around.

"Our neighbourhood!" cried Pooh. "Our beautiful home!" The Hundred-Acre Wood was spread out below him.

"That's the owl's-eye view," said Owl grandly.

Then, Pooh filled the honeypot once more, and he and Owl went to Piglet's house for supper.

Disney
Pinocchio

Look Sharp, Jiminy!

"Gosh." Jiminy Cricket scratched his head between his antennae and yawned a big yawn. Climbing into his tiny matchbox bed, he gazed again at the wooden boy, who was fast asleep.

Jiminy still could not believe his eyes – or his luck. It had been a miraculous night. Not every cricket got to witness a wish granted by the Blue Fairy and see a puppet come to life. And not every cricket was chosen to be somebody's conscience!

Jiminy hopped out of bed. It was pointless to try to sleep. He already felt like he was dreaming. Being a conscience was a big job, but he was just the bug to do it. "Right and wrong." Jiminy looked from one of his hands to the other. "Sure, I know the difference. All I have to do is tell Pinoke. It'll be a snap." Jiminy snapped his fingers. "And I'll even look good doing it."

Jiminy ran his hands down the new jacket hanging by his bed. He picked up the hat and twirled it. "My, my," he said, shaking his head. Then he could not resist any longer. He put on his new shirt, coat, hat and shoes. Then he hopped over to Cleo's fishbowl to see his reflection.

Jiminy whistled low. "Don't you look smart," he told his reflection. "Smart enough to help that wooden boy. Except for that smudge." Jiminy leaned down to inspect a dull spot on his shoe.

He breathed on it and rubbed it with his sleeve. Soon it was shining like new. He looked like a million dollars!

Suddenly Geppetto snored loudly. Jiminy jumped and looked up. Outside the sky was starting to lighten.

"Would you look at that?" Jiminy knew he had to get to bed. A conscience needed to be alert! He hurried out of his new clothes, hung them up carefully, and tucked himself back in bed. "Big day tomorrow." He yawned. "Very big day." A moment later the little cricket was chirping in his sleep.

Jiminy woke to the sound of hundreds of cuckoo clocks. He sat up and rubbed his eyes. He barely remembered where he was. Then the events of the evening before flooded back. Why, he had work to do!

"Get up, Pinoke!" Jiminy called towards the big bed. But Pinocchio was already gone. The bed was made and Geppetto and Figaro were gone too!

Cleo swished nervously in her bowl and pointed towards the door.

"I must have overslept!" Jiminy pulled his new clothes on quickly. "I can't let Pinoke start school without me. You don't have to be a conscience to know that's wrong!" And, quick as a flash, Jiminy hopped out of the door.

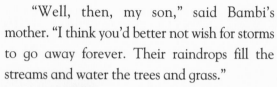

Bambi

Rain, Rain, Go Away

Rrrrumble, rrrrumble, BOOM! The loud clap of thunder startled Bambi and his friends.

"I don't like thunderstorms!" cried Thumper, looking a little scared.

"I don't like them either!" exclaimed Flower.

"Bambi!" called his mother as the clouds grew dark and the rain began to fall. Bambi followed his mother out of the open meadow and into the woods. From their warm, dry thicket, Bambi watched sheets of rain pour down.

"I don't like thunderstorms," he told his mother, echoing Thumper's words. "I wish the storm would go away and never come back again."

"Oh, my," said his mother. "Do you mean you never again want to drink the cool, fresh water from the forest stream?"

"Well, no," said Bambi.

"Then, do you want the big trees to go thirsty? Their leaves to wither and branches to become brittle?" asked his mother.

"No! Of course not!" cried Bambi. "The trees give us shelter, and their branches give the birds a place to make their nests."

"Then, do you want the sweet grass to turn brown?" asked his mother.

"No," said Bambi. "We eat the grass. We'd go hungry if that happened!"

"Well, then, my son," said Bambi's mother. "I think you'd better not wish for storms to go away forever. Their raindrops fill the streams and water the trees and grass."

"But storms are so scary," Bambi said.

Just then, the rain began to let up, and Bambi's friends scampered through the underbrush and into Bambi's thicket.

"Look at the pond!" cried Flower.

Bambi peered through the thicket. The pond was alive with activity. The frogs were leaping and playing. And a family of ducks was shaking their feathers and waddling into the water.

"Uh-oh," said Thumper. "That old bullfrog's gonna get a surprise."

Bambi watched the lily pad with the big bullfrog drift closer and closer to the line of ducklings. The last duckling wasn't paying attention. The sudden collision sent the frog toppling off its lily pad with a startled croak! and surprised the duckling so much it did an underwater somersault!

Bambi, Thumper and Flower laughed.

"I guess I like thunderstorms after all," Bambi told his mother.

"You didn't like thunderstorms?" said Thumper. "That's silly! Why would you ever say a thing like that?"

How Rose Dozed

The moon hung high in the sky, and the stars twinkled around it. It was late at night, and Briar Rose was supposed to be sleeping. But, with all those owls hooting and the frogs in a nearby pond croaking, who could sleep? So, after tossing and turning for hours on end, Briar Rose woke up her three trusted aunties, Flora, Fauna and Merryweather, to see if they could help.

"I've got the solution!" Fauna exclaimed. "You need to count sheep."

"Lie down now, dear," Flora joined in, "and picture a fence. Then imagine sheep jumping over it one by one, and don't lose count!"

Briar Rose lay back and did as they said. But, when she got to sheep 544, she knew it wasn't working. Briar Rose went back to her aunts. "No luck," she said.

"Oh, dear," said Flora. "We'll have to think of something else instead."

"Sleep, schmeep!" Merryweather chimed in. "The night has its own brightness, twinkle and shine. It's such a shame to sleep through it all of the time!"

"You really think so?" Briar Rose asked.

"Absolutely!" Merryweather exclaimed. "Look at the stars burning bright and the moon sending down its own special light."

"That's all well and fine," Flora interrupted.

"But if Briar Rose doesn't sleep at night, she'll be tired during the day."

"Good point," Briar Rose agreed.

"Well, then, try reading a book! Reading always puts me to sleep," Merryweather said with a yawn.

"But I *like* reading," Briar Rose protested. "I'll never fall asleep."

There was a pause, as each of the aunts thought and thought about how to help Briar Rose.

"I know a way to help you sleep!" Fauna said suddenly. "All you have to do," she explained, "is think good thoughts about the day that's passed, and hope for the happy things that tomorrow may bring."

"Is that true?" Briar Rose asked.

"Absolutely!" Flora agreed.

"Now, close your eyes," Merryweather instructed, "and we'll see you in your dreams."

Briar Rose wasn't sure at first, but Flora, Fauna, and Merryweather had never let her down before. So she lay back down and closed her eyes. She remembered her favourite things from that very day, then thought about the wonder tomorrow would bring. Just as she was drifting off, she thought, I hope that never happens to me again. I need my beauty sleep! And wouldn't you know, pretty soon, she was lost in her dreams.

Disney
ALICE
in
WONDERLAND

"R U Slee-P?"

As Alice wandered around Wonderland, she encountered a blue Caterpillar sitting on a mushroom. He was smoking an exotic-looking pipe, and every puff of smoke formed a different letter.

"R U slee-P?" asked the Caterpillar's smoke.

"Am I sleepy?" Alice scratched her head. "I hadn't thought about it – I'm so worried about getting home, it's hard to think about anything else. I don't know, I suppose."

"U kn-O," said the Caterpillar, puffing out a U and an O in red-and-orange smoke.

"I do?" asked Alice.

"Ye-S, U do," said the Caterpillar. "For instance, have U O-pened your mouth without speaking?"

"Oh! You mean a *yawn*?" asked Alice. "No, I haven't yawned."

Then the Caterpillar yawned himself and asked, "Have U felt your I-lids gr-O-ing heav-E?"

"My eyelids growing *heavy*?" repeated Alice. She blinked, trying to determine if her eyelids had gained any weight since the morning.

"No," she told the Caterpillar, "my eyelids are no heavier than usual."

"I C," said the Caterpillar, puffing out a yellow *I* and a lime green *C*. Then his own eyelids began to flutter, and his head began to nod.

"Perhaps *you're* the one who's sleepy,"

Alice observed, watching the Caterpillar.

"Y?" asked the Caterpillar.

"You yawned, then your eyelids drooped, and you began nodding off," Alice explained.

"I cannot B slee-P," the Caterpillar replied, "because n-O one has sung m-E a lul-lab-I."

"I can sing you a lullaby if you like," said Alice.

"Pro-C-d," said the Caterpillar.

"Hmm . . . let's see . . . ." murmured Alice. Ever since she'd entered the world of Wonderland, none of the poems and songs she knew came out quite right.

"I'll just try an easy one," she said with a shrug. Then she sang:

"Tow, tow, tow your rope
Slowly up the wall.
Merrily, merrily, merrily, merrily,
Life is a round ball . . . .

"Blow, blow, blow your soap
Bubbles in the tub.
Merrily, merrily, merrily, merrily,
Rub-a-dub-a-dub . . . ."

After she finished, Alice asked the Caterpillar, "How did you like it?"

"Come back l-A-ter," said the Caterpillar. "U may B right. I am the slee-P one."

And, with that, the Caterpillar fell fast asleep.

Chief Mischief-maker

Like all raccoons, Meeko was curious – and that often got him into trouble. And though Pocahontas had a lot of patience when it came to her small furry friend, other members of the tribe were not as understanding.

"Pocahontas, you must teach that animal how to behave!" Chief Powhatan exclaimed when he caught Meeko playing with the tribe's peace pipe.

"Not him again!" cried the women when Meeko upset the baskets of grain they had spent the entire morning threshing.

"Don't worry," Pocahontas told her friend. "They can't stay mad at you for long. Tomorrow is your birthday, after all!"

Meeko chattered excitedly. He loved birthdays – especially opening presents!

"Now stay out of trouble," Pocahontas warned. "I'll be back soon."

Meeko sat outside the hut Pocahontas shared with her father. He wondered what gift his friend had chosen for him this year. Soon, unable to resist temptation any longer, he slipped inside and spied a parcel. He wasted no time unwrapping it and discovered . . . a feather headdress just his size!

Meeko couldn't wait to try it on. He didn't want to be discovered, so he grabbed his gift and scampered off towards the river. There, he put on the headdress and gazed at his reflection. As he was admiring himself, the headdress fell into the water.

The raccoon fished it out, dragging it through the mud as he pulled it ashore.

Meeko's heart was pounding. He rinsed the feathers as best he could and headed back to the village. On the way, the headdress caught on the bushes. By the time he reached the village, all the feathers except one had fallen out.

Meeko knew what he had to do. He found Pocahontas and showed her what was left of the present. Pocahontas looked at Meeko sternly, but after a moment her face softened. "Meeko, I am proud of you. You had the courage to admit what you have done," she said. "But you must try to do better. No more getting into places where you shouldn't!"

All day on his birthday, Meeko behaved perfectly. That night, Pocahontas presented him with a gift. It was the headdress, but now it had two feathers instead of one. "For every day that you are able to stay out of other people's belongings, we will add another feather," she said.

Meeko was grateful to Pocahontas for being so understanding, and he was determined to make her proud. He would do his best to fill the headdress – but he knew it would probably take him until his *next* birthday!

A Special Song

King Triton's birthday was in a couple of days, and Sebastian was planning a special performance. Triton's daughter, Ariel, would sing while the orchestra played a brand-new tune. But they still had a lot of work to do.

During rehearsals, a young mermaid named Coral kept accidentally dropping her cymbals. Sebastian threw down his baton. "Rehearsal is over!" he yelled, and stormed off.

Ariel comforted Coral and invited her to see all her treasures in her grotto. Ariel told Coral the grotto could be her secret place too.

A few days later, Ariel heard someone singing in the grotto. The voice was strong and sweet. When Ariel arrived, she saw her new friend.

"Coral! You have such a lovely voice! You should be singing in the concert, not playing the cymbals."

The little blond mermaid shrugged. "I just like singing to myself," she explained. "I've never actually performed."

The next day at rehearsal, Sebastian made Ariel and the orchestra practise over and over.

"The big day is tomorrow!" the crab said, fretting. "Let's try it again." By the end of the afternoon, everyone was tired.

"See you tomorrow," Ariel said. Her voice was raspy.

On the day of the concert, Ariel had lost her voice! Luckily, she knew who could take her place.

"Me?" Coral said when the princess asked her. "But I can't!"

"You must!" Sebastian insisted, "Or King Triton's birthday celebration will be ruined!"

Coral knew her new friend was counting on her. "All right," she said. "I'll do it."

That night, when Coral peeked out from backstage, she nearly fainted. The entire kingdom was there! She took a deep breath, swam onstage and started to sing. Before she knew it, the concert was over and the audience began to cheer!

"Coral," said Sebastian, smiling, "from now on, you're going to be a court singer!"

After the show, Ariel found Coral with her family.

"I didn't know you could sing!" one of Coral's sisters exclaimed.

"No one ever would have known if it wasn't for Ariel," replied Coral. "She believed in me."

Ariel still couldn't speak, but she gave Coral a big hug. It had been a wonderful evening.

Flik Wings It

Flik knew that Hopper and his gang of hungry grasshoppers would soon come to steal all the food from the peaceful ants of Ant Island. So Flik headed off to the big city to find warrior bugs to help fight the grasshoppers.

On his way, Flik saw a shiny dragonfly flutter across the sky.

"Wow, I wish I could fly like that!" he exclaimed.

Suddenly, Flik had an idea. "I built a harvester that harvests pretty well. I wonder if I could invent a flying machine?"

Flik got to work. He gathered sticks and vines and leaves. He found a mushroom cap to use for a seat, and a long red feather for a tail.

When he had gathered all the parts, Flik began to strap the pieces together.

After lots of hard work, Flik took a step back and studied his invention.

"Well, it certainly *looks* like it could fly," Flik said finally. "It has wings that flap and a long red tail."

The frame of Flik's flier was made of twigs, and the wings were made of leaves. The whole machine was tied together with strong vines.

"Time for a test flight," Flik decided.

He climbed onto the mushroom cap seat and used a vine as a safety belt. Then he put his feet on the little pedals and started to pump.

Faster and faster, the green wings began to flap. Soon, Flik's flier began to rock; then it leaped into the sky!

"It's working!" Flik cried. He was flying!

With the air racing between his antennae, Flik watched the world flash under his feet. He saw frogs and turtles and other creatures that ate ants.

"Flying is so much safer than walking," said Flik.

But he spoke too soon, for high in the sky above Flik a mother bird was teaching her three little hatchlings how to fly. She spied Flik's strange-looking contraption and thought one thing – dinner!

Flik looked up and saw the mother bird and her babies coming down on him like dive bombers!

"Test flight over!" Flik cried.

Pedalling faster, Flik steered his flier through the limbs of a tall tree. The mother bird and two of her babies were blocked by the branches. But the third baby bird raced between the leaves and caught up with Flik.

Pecking wildly, the little bird ripped a wing from Flik's flier. Spinning out of control, the machine crashed to the ground.

Luckily for Flik, he had also invented a parachute out of a spider's web, and he made a soft landing in the middle of a daisy.

"Another failed invention," Flik said with a sigh. "Maybe someday I'll have a chance to make a flying machine that really works!"

Patch and the Panther

One dark night, 15 Dalmatian puppies sat huddled around a black-and-white television set. They watched as Thunderbolt, the canine hero, crept through a deep, dark jungle.

Suddenly Thunderbolt pricked up his ears. The puppies held their breath. Two yellow eyes peered out of the bushes. It was a panther!

"Thunderbolt, look out behind you!" Penny barked at the television.

"How will Thunderbolt escape the hungry panther?" the TV announcer asked. "Don't miss next week's exciting episode!"

"Aww!" the puppies groaned, disappointed that their favourite show was over.

"I'll bet Thunderbolt tears that ol' panther to pieces," said Patch.

"I'd be scared to fight a panther," said his brother Lucky.

"Not me!" cried Patch.

"All right, kids. Time for bed," Pongo said, shutting off the television with his nose. He watched as the puppies padded upstairs and settled down in their baskets.

"Good night, pups," Pongo said.

"Good night, Dad," the puppies replied.

Pongo switched off the light. Moments later, the sound of soft snores filled the room. The puppies were fast asleep.

All except for one. Patch was wide awake.

He was still thinking about Thunderbolt and the panther.

"I wish some ol' panther would come around here," Patch said to himself. "I'd teach him a thing or two."

Just then a floorboard creaked. Patch pricked up his ears. Then he crawled out of his basket to investigate.

The floorboard creaked again. What if it's a panther? Patch thought with a shiver. But I'm not scared of any ol' panther, he reminded himself.

Suddenly Patch saw a shadow flicker across the doorway. The shadow had a long tail. Panthers have long tails, Patch remembered. Just then two yellow eyes peered out of the darkness.

"Aroooo!" Patch yelped. He turned to run, but he tripped on the rug. In a flash, the panther was on top of him. Patch could feel its hot breath on his neck. He shut his eyes . . . .

"Patch, what are you doing out of bed?" the panther asked.

Patch opened his eyes. It was Pongo!

"I – I was just keeping an eye out for panthers," Patch explained.

Pongo smiled. "Why don't you get some sleep now," he suggested. "I can keep an eye out for panthers for a while."

"Okay, Dad," Patch said with a yawn.

Pongo carried Patch back to his basket. And in no time at all, the puppy was fast asleep.

Disney

POCAHONTAS

Follow Your Heart

Pocahontas was an Indian princess. She was exploring the forest, high on a cliff with her friend Meeko, a raccoon, when her friend Nakoma called to her from the river. "Your father's back!" she shouted. "Come down here."

When they arrived at the village, Chief Powhatan was happy to see Pocahontas. "Kocoum has asked to seek your hand in marriage," he told his daughter.

"But he's so serious," Pocahontas replied unhappily. The young woman was troubled. She went to see the ancient tree spirit, Grandmother Willow, to ask for her advice. Pocahontas told her about a spinning arrow she kept seeing in a dream. "It is pointing you down your path," the wise spirit told her.

Soon, a ship filled with English settlers seeking gold arrived. Before long, Pocahontas met one of the settlers, John Smith, face to face. As they got to know each other, she showed him how the land and water, the people and animals, were all connected to one another.

Smith then learned that the settlers wanted to attack the Indians. He told Pocahontas and together they tried to figure out how to keep the peace. They had realised how much the settlers and the Indians could teach each other.

Pocahontas and Smith set off to talk to Chief Powhatan to see if peace could be reached.

They never made it, though. Along the way, an Indian warrior attacked Smith. Then, another settler shot the warrior, but Smith took the blame. He was taken prisoner. The Indians decided Smith would die the next morning.

"I'm so sorry!" Pocahontas cried. "It would have been better if we'd never met. None of this would have happened."

"Pocahontas, I'd rather die tomorrow than live a hundred years without knowing you," John Smith told her.

Pocahontas was heartbroken. Then Meeko handed her John Smith's compass. Looking at it, Pocahontas saw the spinning arrow that she had dreamed about. Now she knew what path to follow.

Quickly, she ran to the village and stepped in front of John Smith, willing to give up her life to protect him. Chief Powhatan laid down his weapon, but the settlers had arrived. Governor Ratcliffe fired his gun. "No!" yelled Smith. He jumped in front of the Indian chief, taking the bullet himself.

John Smith had to return to London to have his wounds treated. Pocahontas watched the settlers and Indians begin to share food, and she knew she must stay. She told John Smith, "No matter what happens, I'll always be with you." Then she kissed him goodbye – forever.

Peter Pan to the Rescue

One day, John and Michael disguised themselves as pirates and took a small boat towards Captain Hook's ship.

John and Michael had just climbed over the side of the ship when they found a telescope.

Suddenly Smee walked by. "Do you see anything mateys?" he asked, mistaking them for members of the crew.

"Uh, a storm!" John blurted out.

"I should go and tell the captain," Smee said.

John and Michael followed Smee and saw him enter a cabin. John peered through the porthole and saw Captain Hook. Unfortunately, the Captain also saw him!

"Spies!" thundered Hook. Smee led the boys inside. "What's the meaning of this?" Captain Hook demanded. Smee explained that they weren't spies.

"Yes," Hook agreed. "My mistake, but our attack on Peter Pan's hideout is only days away, security's very important."

When the boys were outside, John whispered, "We have to warn Peter!" Quickly, they climbed overboard and began rowing towards shore. Captain Hook laughed as he watched through his telescope. "They'll lead us straight to Pan!" he said.

When John and Michael reached the shore they realized they'd been followed and scrambled up a hill, with John leading the way. At the top, he called, "This way, Michael!" But there was no answer.

Captain Hook stood at the bottom of the hill holding Michael. "Keep going, John!" cried Michael.

A few minutes later, John burst into Peter's hideout and told them what had happened. Peter shook his head. "It was a trick."

John groaned. "I've made a terrible mess of things. Will you help?"

"Sure," Peter replied.

On the pirate ship, Smee tied Michael to a chair. Just then, they heard a girl's voice say, "Captain Hook?" It was Wendy, standing on the plank. Hook had captured her too!

"Watch the boy, Smee," Hook said. "I'll be right back!" As soon as Hook was gone, John looked into the porthole.

"Not you again!" Smee exclaimed and chased after John. The Lost Boys hurried inside to untie Michael, then climbed into a boat waiting below. Then John opened his umbrella, leapt over the side of the ship and floated down to join them. Meanwhile, on the ship's plank, Captain Hook reached out to grab Wendy. Suddenly, a green blur scooped her up. It was Peter Pan!

"Blast you, Pan!" Hook cried.

Dressed to Scare

Cinderella worked from morning until night doing the bidding of her stepmother and stepsisters. In return, they treated her unkindly and dressed her in tattered old clothes. It wasn't a very fair deal.

Luckily, Cinderella had the friendship of the animals in the manor, including two mice named Jaq and Mary.

"Poor Cinderelly," said Jaq as he and Mary watched their dear friend scrubbing the floor. "She needs a present."

"Hmm," Mary replied. She led Jaq out to the barnyard so that Cinderella wouldn't hear them planning. "Let's make a new dress!" she suggested.

"Good idea!" Jaq replied. But he wondered what they could use for cloth. Jaq looked around, then scurried over to a sack of feed and gnawed it open with his teeth.

"Jaq, no!" Mary scolded. "You can eat later."

"No-no," Jaq explained. "This cloth is for Cinderelly's new dress. See?" He gestured toward the sack.

The other mice joined to help. They cut out the dress in no time, sewing it together with some thread they had borrowed from Cinderella's sewing kit. They stepped back to admire their work. "Too plain!" Gus announced.

"Yes," Jaq agreed in a disappointed voice.

"What should we do to fix it?"

The birds in the barn twittered excitedly. They had just the thing! In no time, they strung berries and kernels of corn, then helped the mice stitch them along the hem, sleeves and neck of the dress.

"There!" said Perla. "Much better!"

With the birds' help, the mice hung the dress on a post in the garden where Cinderella kept her straw hat. "Cinderelly's gonna love it!" Jaq proclaimed.

The mice went inside, got Cinderella, then told her to close her eyes as she walked out into the garden. "Open your eyes now, Cinderelly!" Jaq instructed.

"Surprise!" the mice shouted.

Cinderella gazed at the sackcloth dress on the post with her hat perched on top. "Oh, thank you!" she exclaimed. "I've been needing a scarecrow for the garden!"

Jaq opened his mouth wide to explain, but Mary clamped her paw over it.

"You're welcome, Cinderelly," Mary said.

After Cinderella had gone, Jaq frowned. "We sewed a bad dress."

"But we made a good scarecrow," Mary told him, trying to look on the bright side.

"Yes! And Cinderelly's happy!" Jaq agreed. And to the mice, that was the most important thing of all.

A Good Team

"Go, Khan," Mulan whispered to the horse. "Faster!"

The horse flicked an ear towards her. But his pace didn't change.

Mulan shrugged. She was happy to have company, even if Khan didn't seem too crazy about her. She could hardly believe she was riding through the woods on her way to join the Emperor's army. But what else could she do? If she didn't take his place, her elderly father would be forced to fight.

"It will be all right," she told Khan. "This is the right thing to do."

The horse snorted. For a second Mulan thought he was answering her. Then he stopped short, almost sending Mulan tumbling.

"Hey," she said. "What are you doing?"

She kicked at his sides. But, instead of moving forward, the mighty warhorse backed up a few steps, his massive body shaking fearfully.

Mulan looked ahead. Just a few yards away, a deep, shadowy ditch crossed the path.

"Is that what you're afraid of?" Mulan asked the horse. "Don't be silly. It's just a small ditch – step over it, you big chicken."

She kicked again. Still the horse refused to go. Instead he danced nervously on the spot.

"Come on!" Mulan shouted impatiently. "You're being ridiculous!"

She kicked him. She slapped him on the neck with her hands. She even grabbed a thin branch from a nearby tree and smacked him on his hindquarters.

But the horse wouldn't take even one step forward.

Finally, Mulan didn't know what else to try. She collapsed onto Khan's neck, feeling hopeless.

"Now what?" she said.

But she didn't seem to have much choice. Sliding down from the horse's back, she walked towards the ditch. To her surprise, she heard Khan following her.

Mulan gasped. Could it be? Could the big, bold, strong warhorse really be trusting her to lead him over the scary ditch?

"Come on," she said, reaching for his bridle.

The horse allowed her to lead him forward. A few more steps, and he was standing at the edge of the ditch.

"The last step is the big one," Mulan warned.

Holding the reins, she hopped over the ditch. For a moment, she was afraid he wouldn't follow. Then he jumped. Mulan was yanked forward as Khan landed ten feet past the ditch.

"Good boy." Mulan patted the horse. "I think we might just make a good team, after all."

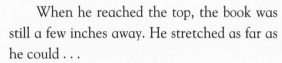

Beauty and the Beast

The Mysterious Book

"What are you looking at, Belle?" Chip asked. Belle smiled at the little teacup. "Oh, you caught me daydreaming, Chip," she said. "I was just looking up there."

She pointed to the highest shelf in the Beast's library. The only thing on the shelf was a single book.

Belle had wondered about that book almost since the day the Beast had first shown her the library. The trouble was, none of the ladders quite reached the shelf. So the book had remained a mystery.

Belle's curiosity had grown until she could hardly stop thinking about the book. What could it be about? Surely it had to be the most magical, unusual, wonderful book in the world!

She explained the problem to Chip. He went straight to his mother, Mrs Potts.

Mrs Potts called a meeting of all the enchanted objects. As soon as she told them about the book, they wanted to help Belle.

"What we need is a plan," Cogsworth said.

"Yes!" Lumiere cried. "And I've got one!"

That evening the enchanted objects gathered in the library. First the Wardrobe stood at the base of the shelves. The Stove climbed on top of her, then the Coatrack climbed up next. Soon a whole tower of enchanted objects stretched almost to the top shelf. Finally Lumiere started to climb.

When he reached the top, the book was still a few inches away. He stretched as far as he could . . .

"What are you doing?" Belle exclaimed from the doorway.

"Oh, *mademoiselle!*" Lumiere cried. "You're just in time – *voilà!*"

With that, he finally managed to reach the book, knocking it off the shelf into Belle's hands. A moment later the tower collapsed in a heap.

As soon as Belle made certain that everyone was all right, she opened the book. She couldn't wait to see what new wonders lay within its covers . . . .

"Oh!" she said when she saw the first page.

"What is it?" Chip asked breathlessly.

Belle smiled sheepishly. "I can't believe it! I've already read this one."

The enchanted objects sighed with disappointment. Had their plan been for nothing?

"But thank you anyway!" Belle said quickly. "It's so nice of you to get it for me." She hugged the book to her. "Even though I've read it before, it's one of my favourites – it's full of far-off places, magic spells . . . well, let me show you . . . ."

Soon all the enchanted objects were gathered around as Belle read the book to them. And, wouldn't you know, it became one of their favourite books too!

A Question Of Charm

Rapunzel had been kept in a hidden tower her whole life by a woman she thought was her mother – Mother Gothel. Rapunzel had managed to make Mother Gothel leave the tower for a few days, and she decided to ask the stranger she had locked in her wardrobe if he would do her a big favour. She held up a frying pan, ready to hit him if he turned dangerous. Then she opened the wardrobe.

Wham! The intruder fell out onto the floor. Rapunzel tied him to a chair with her enormously long hair. Then her pet chameleon, Pascal, licked his ear to awaken him.

"Huh?!" the stranger said, astonished. "Is this real hair?"

"What do you want with my hair? To cut it? Sell it?" Rapunzel exclaimed.

"No!" shouted the stranger, "Listen, the only thing I want to do with your hair is to get out of it lit-er-a-lly!"

Rapunzel looked at him suspiciously. "Who are you, and how did you find me?" The young man suddenly smiled. His most attractive smile. "I know not who you are, nor how I came to find you, but may I just say... Hi. How ya doin'?"

Rapunzel didn't react. The intruder finally answered. "My name's Flynn Rider, blondie!"

"I'm Rapunzel, not blondie."

"Hey! Where's my satchel?" asked Flynn, noticed his bag containing a stolen crown was missing.

"I've hidden it!" Rapunzel said. "Something brought you here, Flynn Rider. So I've got a deal to offer you."

Rapunzel showed him the picture she had painted. It was of the floating lanterns in the sky that appeared on each of her birthdays.

"Tomorrow evening, these lanterns will appear in the sky. I want to know where they come from. If you take me there and then bring me back, I will give you back your satchel!"

Flynn shook his head. "I can't be seen hanging around the castle right now."

"In that case, bad luck: you'll never see your satchel again!"

Not knowing what to do, he tried to charm Rapunzel once again. "All right, listen! I didn't want to have to do this, but you leave me no choice. Here comes the smoulder." Rapunzel just stared at him and, before long, it was Flynn who gave in. "OK, blondie. I'll take you to see the lanterns."

Rapunzel was delighted. Finally, after all these years, she was going to leave the tower. Her birthday wish had come true. She was going to see the floating lanterns!

A Visit in the Night

It's not easy to read with a broken arm! Alone in his room, young Carl was trying to turn a page without letting go of his flashlight.

Suddenly, he heard a gentle rubbing noise. Then a blue balloon forced its way through his bedroom curtains!

"Ouch!" cried Carl, as he knocked his plaster cast against the bedside table.

A merry little face, framed by a mop of red hair, appeared at the window and Carl let out a second cry.

"It's me! I thought you might need a little cheering up!" whispered Ellie, his new friend, before she leapt down onto the floor.

She slipped quickly under the cover that Carl had made into a tent.

"Look!" she said, showing him a small notebook. "I'm going to show you something I've never shown to anyone else. Swear you won't tell anyone; cross your heart!"

Carl promised and Ellie opened up the book. A photo of the explorer Charles Muntz had been stuck on the first page.

"It's my adventure book! When I grow up I'm going to be an explorer too. And I'll go to South America, to Paradise Falls!"

Carl looked admiringly at the beautiful waterfalls, next to which Ellie had drawn the little house where they'd met each other that same afternoon.

"Obviously it'll be tricky to move the clubhouse all that way!" said Ellie, who had noticed Carl's look of astonishment.

The boy didn't say a word, but couldn't stop his eyes from looking up to the shelf where his collection of miniature airships stood lined up, including a model of Muntz's Spirit of Adventure.

Ellie followed his gaze and immediately understood.

"But of course!" she cried out. "You can take us there in an airship! Promise me you'll do it! Promise!"

Carl promised. He could see no reason not to. Ellie was a true adventuress!

"See you tomorrow, right?" she said, getting up. "You're one hell of a chatterbox, you know?" she added, laughing, before straddling the window and disappearing into the night.

"Wow!" murmured Carl, totally bowled over by his new friend. Just ten minutes in Ellie's company was one of the biggest adventures of his life!

That night, as he slept, he dreamt of a colourful little house perched at the top of Paradise Falls.

Disney
Lady and the **TRAMP**

In the Doghouse

"Good morning, Tramp," said Lady, with a yawn and a stretch. She rolled over on her silk cushion. "Wasn't that just the most wonderful night's sleep?"

But Tramp's night's sleep had been far from wonderful. In fact, he hadn't had much sleep at all. The past night had been Tramp's first sleeping in Lady's house . . . or in any house, come to think of it.

"How do you do it?" he grumbled. "That bed is so soft, I feel like I'm sinking in a feather pool. And between Jim Dear's snoring and the baby's crying, I could barely hear the crickets chirping."

"Oh, dear," Lady said, feeling truly sorry for her mate. "I know!" she exclaimed. "Jim Dear and Darling love you so – I'm sure they'd let you sleep up on their bed tonight. There's nothing in the world better than that!"

But Tramp shook his head. "I'm afraid it's the outdoors I need," he explained. "I mean, I know you grew up this way and all . . . but it's just so much fun to sleep under the stars. And the moon too. There's nothing to howl at in this bedroom."

"You can see the moon out the window," Lady told him.

But Tramp shook his head. "It's not the same. You know," he went on, "we've still got that fine doghouse in the yard. What do you say we go back out there tonight? It'll be like a honeymoon!"

"Well . . ." Lady looked at Tramp's tired eyes. "Okay."

And so that night, as soon as the sun set and the moon began to rise, Lady and Tramp went out to the garden.

Happy at last, Tramp turned three times and then plopped down. "Oh, how I love the feel of cool dirt on my belly!" he said with a dreamy smile . . . while Lady gingerly peeked into the dark and slightly damp kennel. The stars were not even out, and already she missed the comforts of Jim Dear's and Darling's room.

Tramp watched as Lady stretched out on the kennel floor, then got up and moved outside, then back in once again. It was plain to see: try as she might, Lady just could not relax on the cold, hard ground.

"Don't worry," Tramp announced, "I have an idea."

And with that, he ran into the house . . . and in seconds reappeared with Lady's cushion in his teeth. Carefully, he swept the kennel with his tail, and laid the cushion down just the way Lady liked it.

Lady smiled and lay down. And, do you know what? That night, they both had the sweetest dreams either one had ever had.

THE PRINCESS AND THE FROG

A Deal is a Deal

Tiana had just had a big shock! She had kissed a talking frog, who was once Prince Naveen, in order to turn him back into a prince. But it hadn't worked. Instead, she had turned into a frog too!

"What did you do to me? I - I'm green and I'm - slimy!" Tiana hurled herself at Prince Naveen, mad with rage. As they were tussling with each other, they landed in the middle of Charlotte's masked ball. The appearance of the two frogs obviously caused great panic amongst the guests. Fortunately, Naveen managed to grab a bunch of balloons, and with Tiana clinging to his neck they made an airbourne escape. Now they were drifting through the darkness above the bayous, the swamps of Louisiana, which were filled with all manner of dangers.

"Who was the fake Prince Naveen dancing with Charlotte?" asked Tiana.

"My valet! He is hoping to make his fortune by obeying the sorcerer!" he replied.

"Voodoo? You mean to tell me all this happened because you were messing with the Shadow Man? It serves me right for wishing on stars. The ONLY way to get what you want in this world is through hard work," she muttered.

"Hard work?" retorted Naveen surprised. "A princess doesn't work!"

"I'm not a princess. I'm a waitress."

At these words, Naveen uttered a cry, ""Well, no wonder the kiss didn't work," said Naveen indignantly. "You lied to me! You were wearing a crown!"

"It was a costume party!" Tiana shouted.

Realizing his mistake, Naveen decided to get revenge on Tiana.

"Well, the egg is on your face, because I don't have any riches! I am completely broke!" He started to laugh.

At that moment, the balloons burst on the branches of a tree, and the frogs tumbled into the mud.

"And you call *me* a liar?" fumed Tiana.

"I didn't really lie," protested Naveen. "I intend to be rich again! Once I marry Miss Charlotte La Bouff if she will have me!"

Suddenly, hungry alligators surrounded them! Quickly, Tiana took refuge in a hollow log by the water's edge. Naveen begged her to save him.

"A deal is a deal," replied Tiana. "Tell me you'll keep your promise or I won't save you!"

"It's a deal," relented the Prince. "But you have to keep your side of the deal – to turn me back into a prince."

Tiana sighed. She had just been caught in her own trap!

Tink Takes Charge

It was a perfect sort of day in Pixie Hollow, but Tinker Bell was not in high spirits. Something was bothering her. What I need is a problem to solve! Tink thought. At that moment, there was a loud thud. Tink rushed off to see what it was.

In the middle of the courtyard was a huge, black ball! The sight of the destroyed courtyard made Tink's heart ache. Incredibly, every fairy had escaped harm.

Tink marched bravely up to the ball and gave it a hard smack. "Hold on!" she said. "I see a mark that looks like a hook! And you know what that means."

"Captain Hook!" cried several fairies.

"Of course. It's a cannon ball!" Tink declared.

Just then, Tink's friend Terence arrived with a grim look on his face. Tink's bedroom had been destroyed by the ball! Tink took a deep breath. "We'll just rebuild it," she said. "And it will be even better than before. In the mean time, we're going to get rid of that horrid cannon ball."

The fairies set about trying to push the cannon ball. They used all their strength, but the ball simply refused to budge. Well, Tink, you wanted a challenge, she said to herself. And now you've got one. But am I up to it?

Then, Tink had an idea. "We can float it away with a giant balloon carrier!" Tink asked the fairies to use their talents to make the balloon. It slowly lifted the cannon ball as high as a fairy's knee.

But suddenly, the cannon ball fell from the balloon carrier and began rolling away! It splashed into Havendish Stream. "Oh, no!" Tink said. "The stream is blocked!"

The other fairies looked at Tink and waited for another good idea. The others believed that she could solve the problem.

"I've got it!" Tink hollered. "The cannon ball was much to heavy for us to move. But we can move lots of little things. We need to break the ball into tiny pieces!"

Before long, the fairies were able to carry away tiny pieces of the ball. They flew together towards Captain Hook's boat and used fairy dust to bring the pieces back together. Then the cannon ball fell through the bottom of Hook's boat! The sun was setting as the fairies flew home, glad to finally be rid of the cannon ball.

The next day, one of the fairies asked Tink to fix a baking sheet. "I know it's not much of a challenge…" she said.

"Believe me," said Tink, "that is just fine with me."

Ariel's Love Poem

"Ahhh," Ariel sighed as she stared dreamily into space.

"Oh, no," Sebastian fretted. "A sigh like that can only mean one thing."

"What?" said Flounder.

"She's obviously writing love poetry for that human she's so obsessed with," Sebastian said.

"Oh," said Flounder.

Ariel was hard at work writing in her seaweed notebook. "How do I love thee . . ." she said out loud.

"Oh, yuck!" Flounder exclaimed.

"You're telling me," Sebastian agreed. "Terribly trite and overused."

"What would you write?" Ariel asked.

"Me? Well, this is just off the top of my head." Sebastian ceremoniously cleared his throat. "But I would write something like, 'Oh, crabby crab/ Oh, crab of my heart/ My crabbiest crab/ May our claws never part!' "

"Double yuck!" Flounder exclaimed again.

"What do you know?" Sebastian snapped.

"But he's a total stranger!" Flounder cried, turning back to Ariel.

"What's that supposed to mean?" Now Ariel looked offended.

"How can you be in love with someone you don't even know?" Sebastian said, joining in.

"I know him," Ariel protested. "Besides, haven't you ever heard of love at first sight?"

"Oh, please!" Flounder moaned.

"You're such a guppy!" cried Ariel.

"Who's being a guppy?" Flounder said defensively.

"Flounder is right," Sebastian interrupted. "This human doesn't even know you exist!"

"You don't know that!" Ariel exclaimed and went back to work on her poem.

She wrote, and wrote, and wrote some more.

Finally, when she had finished, she cleared her throat dramatically.

"How's this sound?" she asked Sebastian and Flounder, and began reading:

"I'm always thinking of you,
It sets my heart a-twitter.
But I'm also easily distracted – ooh!
By things that shine and glitter.
Do you remember me?
Of me have you thunk?
Sorry, I've just got to go see
This boat that has just sunk.
(Now I'm back)
I love you more than anything,
Even more than my snarfblatt.
I wish this was a song to sing.
I'm really much better at that."

"Wow – " Sebastian exclaimed.

" – that's pretty bad!" Flounder finished.

"True love, indeed!" Sebastian concluded.

Survival of the Smallest

It was the first day of summer, and Dot and the other Blueberries were getting ready for a big adventure. They were heading out for the First Annual Blueberry Wilderness Expedition. Their journey would take them to the thicket of tall grasses next to the ant colony. It was only a few yards from home – but, to a little ant, it seemed like an awfully long way.

As the group prepared to leave, some boy ants arrived to tease them.

"How do you expect to go on an expedition without supplies?" asked Jordy.

Dot put her hands on her hips. "For your information," she said in a superior tone, "the whole point is to survive using our smarts. Whatever we need, we'll make when we get there."

The Blueberries hiked a few yards from the ant colony, then Dot consulted her survival manual. "Okay," she said, "the first thing we need to do is build a shelter from the sun."

"I know!" Daisy volunteered. "We could make a hut. All we have to do is stick twigs into the dirt side by side to make the walls, then lay leaves over the top for the roof."

The rest of the Blueberries decided this was a great idea. With a lot of teamwork and determination, they completed a shelter to comfortably hold the troop.

"Now," said Dot, looking at the manual again, "it says here we need to protect our campsite."

So the girls dug a narrow trench in front of the hut, just as the manual instructed.

The girls gathered some seeds and went into their homemade hut to have some lunch. A short while later, they heard a scream. When they went to investigate, they discovered Reed, Grub and Jordy at the bottom of the trench.

It was clear to the Blueberries that the boys had been up to no good.

"Girls," said Dot, pointing to the boys, "observe one of the Blueberries' most common natural enemies – though certainly not one of the smartest."

When it was time for the Blueberries to pack up and hike home, the boys were still stuck in the trench. "Say the magic words and I'll get you out of there," said Dot.

"Okay, okay!" Reed, Grub and Jordy agreed.

"Well?" demanded Dot.

"Blueberries rock," the boys admitted.

Dot lowered down a ladder she had expertly made of sticks. "You bet we do!" she said. "'Cause if we can survive you, we can survive anything!"

Snow White
and the Seven Dwarfs

A Dance with the Bride

No one could remember a more glorious wedding day. The sun was shining, the church bells were ringing, and the bride was unquestionably the fairest one of all. Nearly everyone in the land had come to see the Prince take Snow White's hand in marriage, including seven rather short men sitting in the front row, soaking their handkerchiefs with tears of joy.

After the ceremony, a great ball and banquet were held at the castle. As the guests arrived in the ballroom, each was announced. "Doc, Happy, Sneezy, Bashful, Grumpy, Dopey and Sleepy!" the page cried into the great room as the Seven Dwarfs tripped over one another, dazzled by the splendour.

"Gawrsh," Bashful said, hiding behind Doc, overawed by the marble and chandeliers.

With a blast of trumpets, the bride and groom arrived. Then, as the orchestra began to play, the Prince took Snow White in his arms and they waltzed across the dance floor.

The Dwarfs sighed. They could not take their eyes off Snow White.

"Wouldn't it be wonderful to dance with Snow White?" Happy asked. That gave Doc an idea. He led the other Dwarfs into the cloakroom and borrowed a few things.

"Sneezy, stand here. Bashful, you stand on his shoulders. Dopey, do you think you can make it to the top?"

When Dopey was balanced on Bashful's shoulders, Doc wrapped a cloak around the tower of Dwarfs and buttoned it around Dopey's neck.

Wobbling, the Dwarf prince tottered towards the dance floor and Snow White.

"May we have this dance?" Bashful asked, muffled from within the cloak.

"Of course." Snow White giggled when she saw the familiar faces peeking up at her from beneath the cloak.

As the song began, Snow White and the Dwarf prince lurched and swayed precariously into the middle of the room.

"Yikes!" Sneezy squeaked. "This cloak is tickling my nose!"

Above them all, Dopey was having the time of his life, when suddenly the Dwarfs heard a sound that made their blood go cold.

"*Ah . . . ah . . . ah . . .*"

"Hang on, men!" Doc shouted.

"*. . . CHOOO!*"

The cloak billowed. The Dwarf prince was knocked off balance and veered towards the banquet table.

"I got you!" The Prince caught the Dwarfs just in time. After steadying them, he turned to his bride and held out his hand. "May I cut in?" he asked.

Finding Ne-who?

"The coral reef is falling down, falling down, falling down."

Nemo was home, brushing up against the anemone, when the most awful singing he ever heard in his life made him cringe. He swam deeper into the anemone, but it didn't help. The song went on.

"My fair octopus."

And there was something familiar about it . . . . Still cringing, Nemo poked his head out of the golden tentacles to see who was making the awful racket.

"Dory!" Nemo should have known. How could he have forgotten that voice? Nemo swam as fast as he could toward the regal blue tang fish. "Dory! Where have you been?" It seemed like a whale's age since Nemo had seen the fish that helped his dad rescue him from the dentist's fish tank. And he couldn't wait to give her a big hug!

When Nemo got closer Dory stopped singing. That was good. But when she looked at him her face was blank. That wasn't so good.

"Did you say something, kid?" she asked.

"Dory, it's me. Nemo," he replied.

"Ne-*who*?" She looked at Nemo blankly. "Sorry, kid, don't know you. I was just swimming by, minding my own business, singing a song. Hey, why was I singing? Am I famous? Maybe that's how you know me."

"Dory! We're friends, remember?" Nemo had been missing Dory a lot. She just *had* to remember who he was.

"Friends? I just made friends with a hermit crab . . . I think." Dory swam in a circle looking for the crab, but got distracted and started chasing her tail.

"Please try to remember, Dory," Nemo asked again. "You helped save me. You helped me find my dad. You know my dad. Big orange guy? Three white stripes? Looks kind of like me?"

"My dad? Looks like you? Sorry, kid, you don't look anything like my dad." Dory looked at Nemo like he was crazy and began to swim away.

Nemo swam after her. "Just think about it for a second," he pleaded. She *had* to remember something. "I'm Nemo!"

Dory did not turn around but she slowed down. Swimming in a wide circle, she came back. She looked at Nemo sideways, and then started laughing so hard bubbles came out of her nose.

"Had you going, huh?" Dory gave Nemo a big hug and smiled at him slyly. "That was just my little joke. You know I could never forget you!"

Nemo giggled and swam circles around his friend. "Good one, Dory!" He grinned.

Dory smiled back. "Good one, *who*?"

Nemo groaned. That Dory!

Bambi

Sweeter than Clover

"Hi, Bambi," said a soft voice.

Bambi looked up from the grass he was eating, and his friend Flower stopped searching for berries. Standing there was the pretty young fawn Bambi had met that spring.

"Hi, Faline," Bambi said. "It's nice to see you!"

"It's nice to see you too," Faline said shyly.

"Faline!" a young male deer called across the meadow. "Come over and play with me!"

Bambi's eyes narrowed. He didn't like the idea of Faline going off to play with someone else.

Faline blinked in confusion. "Do you want me to go?" she asked Bambi.

"No, don't go," said Bambi. But what could he say to make her stay? he wondered. Suddenly, Bambi had an idea.

"I want to show you something special," he told her.

"Something special?" asked Faline.

"I know where to find the sweetest clover you'll ever taste," Bambi bragged. Thumper had shown him exactly where to find it.

"Where?" asked Faline.

"Just follow me!" exclaimed Bambi.

He led Faline across the meadow to the babbling brook. Then he followed the brook all the way up a steep grassy hill. Finally they came to a big waterfall.

"The sweet clover is right here by this weeping willow tree," said Bambi.

Bambi couldn't wait to share it with Faline. But, when he got to the tree, there wasn't one single clover blossom left.

"Oh, that Thumper!" complained Bambi.

"What's the matter?" asked Faline.

Bambi shook his head. He felt very silly. He'd brought Faline all this way, and now he had nothing special to share with her!

But, just then, Bambi looked up.

"Look," he whispered. "Up in the sky."

Faline looked up and gasped.

Shimmering bands of colour had formed an arc over the waterfall.

"It's so beautiful," whispered Faline. "I've never seen anything like it."

"Neither have I," said Bambi. "But I remember hearing my mother talk about it. I think it's called a rain . . . bow."

"It's wonderful!" cried Faline.

"I'm glad you think so," said Bambi, a little relieved. "But I'm sorry you came all this way for no clover."

"Oh, Bambi," said Faline. "I came because I wanted to be with you. And, besides, a rainbow is a much sweeter surprise than some silly old clover, anyway!"

Beauty and the Beast
Belle's Special Treat

"And from that moment on, the princess had flowers every day of her life. The End," Belle read and closed the book.

"What a treat!" she said to the Beast, as she gazed out of his library window at the cold, snowy hills. "The winter is lovely, of course but to have flowers every day, I'd give anything. Wouldn't you?"

The Beast looked surprised. He had no idea Belle loved flowers that much. That evening, after Belle had gone to sleep, the Beast made his way to a part of his castle he hadn't visited in years – the royal greenhouse.

"Are we really going where I think we're going?" Lumiere the candelabrum asked with delight, as he lit the Beast's way.

But his master only nodded. When the Beast walked to the greenhouse, he was pleased to see that his beloved flowers were still alive.

"There's still a lot of work to be done," he told Lumiere excitedly as he rolled up his sleeves.

One morning when Belle woke up, the first thing she saw was a big bouquet of daffodils – the earliest flowers of spring. "But it's still snowing outside," she said, utterly bewildered. "Wherever did these come from?"

Throughout the day, Belle discovered flowers all over the castle. There were tulips in the dining room, lilies in the library and six different colours of roses in the ballroom! Finally, just as the sun was setting, Belle heard a knock on her door. It was the Beast.

"Where have you been?" Belle asked. "I've missed you."

"Really?" The Beast looked surprised.

"Really," Belle assured him. "And you've missed the most –"

Just then, Belle noticed there were leaves caught in the Beast's thick fur.

"Why, the flowers are from you!" she cried.

"Oh, um..." the Beast answered gruffly. Then he added, "There's something I'd like to show you... that is, if you're willing."

"Of course," Belle said with a smile.

Eagerly, the Beast led Belle to the greenhouse. She gasped as she entered the room. The mountains of colourful blooms nearly took her breath away.

"I'd almost forgotten about this place," the Beast confessed. "That is, until you reminded me. Then I realized there was a way to have flowers every day."

"I really don't know how to thank you," Belle said, still amazed.

"Just enjoy them," the Beast told her. "That's what friends – and flowers – are for."

A Salty Surprise

Briar Rose picked up a large basket and stepped out of the door. It was a beautiful afternoon, and she couldn't help but sing a little song as she headed into the forest.

Rose had spent many afternoons in the forest and knew exactly where the cherry trees grew. She put her basket down by her favourite tree and began to fill it with juicy cherries. A pair of bluebirds came and landed on her shoulder while she picked. Soon the basket was heavy with fruit.

"That should be more than enough for a pie," she told the bluebirds. She was going to bake her aunts a surprise pudding. Still humming to herself, Rose carried the cherries back to the cottage.

Rose put down the basket and looked around the cozy kitchen. She felt nervous. She had never baked a pie by herself! She wasn't even sure where to find all the ingredients.

"It can't be that hard to find the butter, flour and sugar," she assured herself.

Taking a deep breath, Rose searched the cupboards. Then she set to work cutting the butter into the flour for the crust. After adding cold water, she gently patted the dough into a ball.

"And now for the tricky part," she said to the bluebirds, who had followed her home.

Rose put the dough on the worktop and began to roll it out. Soon it was a large, flat circle.

"Here we go," Rose said as she folded it in half and lifted it into the pie tin. After unfolding it, she crimped the edges. It looked perfect.

"And now for the filling," Rose said. She washed the cherries and pitted them. Then she mixed in some spice and sprinkled on spoonfuls of the coarse, white sugar.

The pie was just coming out of the oven when her aunts tumbled through the door.

"What is that delicious smell, dear?" Flora asked as she took off her pointed hat.

Rose beamed. "It's a cherry pie," she said. "I baked it myself!"

Fauna clapped her hands together. "How wonderful!"

After dinner, Rose cut four nice-sized pieces of pie. Smiling, everyone dug in. But their smiles soon turned to severe puckers.

Then Rose burst into tears. "Salt!" she cried. "I used salt instead of sugar!"

"There, there, dear," Flora consoled her. "I once made the same mistake with an entire batch of fruitcake – 20 cakes! – and it took a while before anyone would touch my cooking again! But they got over it eventually."

Rose wiped her tears as Merryweather began to giggle. "I remember that!" she said.

Rose smiled, then giggled too. After all, she had ruined only *one* pie!

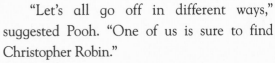

A Misunderstanding

One fine autumn morning, Winnie the Pooh found a lovely pot of honey outside his door with a note. "Whoever could have given it to me?" he wondered.

Pooh, Piglet, Rabbit, Eeyore and Tigger decided to ask Owl to read the note.

"This letter has been written by Christopher Robin," declared Owl. "He's gone far away to s-c-h-o-o-l. Skull! You must rescue him!"

To help them find the little boy, Owl came up with a plan. The friends set off with a map and came to a strange forest with scary plants and an enormous boulder towered up in front of them!

The travellers found an opening in the boulder, they looked inside and saw it was filled with a tangle of thorny branches. Then they all thought they heard a growling Skullasaurus and Piglet ran as fast as he could out of the forest – leaving his friends behind.

Piglet found himself in a valley full of butterflies. As his friends arrived, the butterflies lifted Piglet off the ground! "Are you doing parachuting, Piglet?" asked Pooh.

Pooh jumped up to rescue him. Once Piglet was back on the ground, the hikers went off in search of Christopher Robin once more, and soon arrived at a cave. Inside, there were lots of crossing paths.

"Let's all go off in different ways," suggested Pooh. "One of us is sure to find Christopher Robin."

While the others were having their own adventures, Pooh found some ice crystals that made him look big and scary. He cast a scary shadow over his friends, and they heard more growling noises that grew louder and louder.

Tigger yelled, "It's the terriblest Skullasaurus ever!"

They all ran away – including Pooh, who slipped and fell into a deep hole with an icy floor!

"Hey! Hey! Can anybody hear me?" Pooh called.

Luckily, the other friends were found by Christopher Robin and they lowered a big honey pot down to Pooh to rescue him!

"You misunderstood my message!" Christopher Robin said. "It said I was going to school."

"But what about the Skullasaurus?" squeaked Piglet. "We heard him growling!"

"That's no Skullasaurus," Christopher Robin said with a chuckle. "That's the sound of the rumbly tummy of a hungry-for-honey bear."

Christopher Robin gave Pooh the pot of honey. "Now we're all together, let's enjoy the afternoon!"

Tangled

Leaving the Tower

Thief Flynn Rider wanted his satchel back – the crown he had stolen was inside! But Rapunzel refused to give it to him unless he took her to see the floating lanterns. She had been kept hidden in a tall tower her whole life, and she wanted to know why there were floating lights in the sky every year on her birthday.

"Are you coming blondie?" Flynn slipped down the wall using his arrows as steps.

Leaning from her window, Rapunzel hesitated... but with one glance back at her painting of the floating lights, Rapunzel overcame her fear.

With Pascal on her shoulder, and clasping on to her long hair, she made her way down the outside of the tower. She was so quick that she soon overtook Flynn, who stopped in astonishment. Once at the bottom, she put one foot on the soft grass, then the other.

"Oooh! The grass is exactly as I imagined it would be! It's wonderful! I can run, dance and jump without stopping! I'm free!"

Overcome with excitement, Rapunzel began to roll around on the ground.

"I can't believe I did this! I can't believe I did this!" she shouted.

Rapunzel began to explore. But she also felt guilty for betraying Mother Gothel,

who she believed was her mother. She didn't know Mother Gothel only wanted Rapunzel's magical hair, which kept the old woman forever young.

One moment Rapunzel was jumping excitedly, and the next she was sobbing facedown in a field of flowers. "I am a despicable human being," she cried.

Flynn saw the chance to get hold of his satchel without fulfilling his part of the bargain. He murmured, "Don't worry too much about your mother. When we grow up, we always argue with our parents – it's normal. Your mother will be broken-hearted. Her heart will be in so many tiny pieces that it can never be mended. But she'll get over it."

"Do you think so? Her heart is broken?"

"In smithereens!"

Rapunzel looked sad. Flynn accompanied her back to the tower, adding, "I'm letting you out of the deal, let's go back to the tower. I get back my satchel, and you get back a mother-daughter relationship."

Rapunzel suddenly froze.

"I'm seeing those lanterns," she insisted, and she turned around and stormed off away from the tower.

Flynn was amazed at Rapunzel's strength. He couldn't help but give in.

Ariel's Big Rescue

The news was travelling throughout the undersea world – a human ship had been spotted not too far away.

"Flounder," Ariel said excitedly to her best friend. "Come on! Maybe we'll see some humans!"

Ariel was thrilled as she swam to the surface. A captain stood at the bow and there was a girl, who looked just like a princess.

Suddenly, the ship lurched, causing everyone aboard to stumble and fall. The sailors began scrambling about and shouting. A few minutes later, the captain approached the girl.

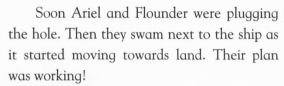

"Princess, I'm afraid I have some bad news," Ariel heard him say. "Our ship has hit a reef and sprung a leak. We're close enough to shore that we can make it. But I'm afraid we will have to toss items overboard to lighten the load."

Ariel and Flounder quickly ducked below the surface. "Maybe we can help," Ariel said.

As the two friends went under the ship, they noticed that there was a large hole, and water was rushing into the ship! The captain must have been trying to protect the princess by not telling her how serious it was.

"Quick, Flounder!" Ariel said. "Gather all the seaweed you can! We'll stuff it into the hole. It may give them time to get to shore!"

Soon Ariel and Flounder were plugging the hole. Then they swam next to the ship as it started moving towards land. Their plan was working!

"Woo-hoo!" cried Flounder when the ship finally reached the shore. "We did it!"

Relieved, Ariel took one last look at the ship. Then as she swam towards home she saw a trunk on the ocean floor, overflowing with human clothes. "Flounder, this must be the princess's trunk!" she exclaimed. Ariel pulled a long, blue gown out. "I've never seen anything so beautiful!" she exclaimed. Carefully, she held it up and smiled.

"Gee, Ariel, you look almost... human," Flounder said.

"I know." Ariel sighed. "It's wonderful!" Then she stopped. "I should really return them to the princess," Ariel said.

"Oh, no!" Flounder replied. "We're not going anywhere near those humans."

But that night, with Flounder by her side, Ariel took the trunk close enough to shore so that the tide could wash it up on the beach.

"Maybe someday I'll be able to walk onshore and wear dresses just like hers," Ariel said dreamily. "I'll be a human princess, too."

Lady and the TRAMP

Lost and Found

Lady stretched and rolled over. It was so cosy up on the window seat. Sunlight shone through the glass and glinted on her diamond-shaped name tag. Lady sighed contentedly. The tag was her most prized possession. Besides her owners, of course. Jim Dear and Darling were very good to her. Just last night, they had given her and Tramp steak bones to munch on. There were so many, they had not been able to eat them all.

The bones! Lady had almost forgotten them. Leaping off the window seat, she hurried to the kitchen. Luckily, they were still right next to her food bowl.

Lady began to carry the bones into the garden. It took three trips, but soon the bones were lying in a heap on the grass. Then she got to work.

Dig, dig, dig. The soil piled up behind her as Lady dug yet another hole. She carefully nosed the last bone into the hole and covered it with soil. After prancing delicately on top to pat down the soil, she collapsed in an exhausted heap. Burying bones was hard work!

Rolling over, Lady let the sun warm her belly. The garden was the perfect place for a late-afternoon nap. She was just dozing off when, suddenly, her neck itched. Sitting up, Lady gave it a scratch. But something was missing.

Lady stopped scratching and gingerly felt her neck. Her collar! It was gone!

Panicked, Lady searched the garden for the collar. It was nowhere to be found.

I must have buried it with one of my bones! Lady realized with a jolt. She looked at all the freshly dug holes. It would take her all night to dig up the bones. But she just had to find her collar!

Tramp will help, Lady thought. She ran inside to get him. He was playing with the puppies, but ran outside as soon as he heard what was wrong. Soon the two dogs were busy undoing all of Lady's hard work.

"I see something shiny!" Tramp called. Lady was by his side in an instant, but it wasn't the collar. It was just an old bottle cap. Lady dropped her head sadly.

Lady and Tramp got right back to digging. And, just as dusk was falling, Tramp unearthed a thick blue band with a golden, diamond-shaped tag. Lady's collar!

Lady let out a happy bark. Then she carried the collar into the house and sat down at Jim Dear's feet.

"Your collar came off, Lady?" Jim asked as he fastened the collar around Lady's neck. "It's a good thing you didn't accidentally bury it with your bones!"

The Flying Blueberries

Everyone in the ant colony was in a good mood. The grasshoppers had been driven off once and for all, and none of the ants had even been hurt. But Flik's amazing fake bird had taken quite a beating, and the Blueberries were determined to mend it.

"Fixing that bird is a big job," said Mr Soil, Dot's teacher, "but I know the Blueberries can do it."

The Blueberries stared at the fake bird. It was a big mess!

"I'll be back in a little while to see how you're doing," said Mr Soil before he left.

"How can we ever fix this thing?" one of the Blueberries cried.

"We can do it!" said Dot. "I bet we can make it even better this time!"

With a cheer, the Blueberries went to work. Some picked new leaves to cover the frame. Others glued those leaves into place with sticky honey.

After hours of hard work, the bird was mended.

"Let's sit in it!" Dot said.

But, just as the Blueberries crawled inside the bird, the wind began to blow. Suddenly, the breeze caught the wings. The bird took off!

It was up to Dot to save the day. She hopped into the pilot seat and took control. The Blueberries flew around Ant Island once, then twice. Soon they weren't afraid any more.

"Look!" screamed Rose. "Real birds are attacking the worker ants!" Dot jiggled the controls. The fake bird dived out of the sky and frightened the real birds away.

"Hooray!" yelled the Blueberries.

"Don't cheer yet!" Dot cried. "This contraption is out of control!"

With a bump and a crash, the bird hit the ground and skidded to a halt.

"Everybody get out!" Princess Dot commanded. One by one, the Blueberries escaped.

"It's wrecked again!" said Rose. "And here comes Mr Soil! He's going to be so mad!"

But, surprisingly, Mr Soil was smiling.

"You're heroes!" he told them. "You saved the worker ants."

"But the bird is wrecked again," said Rose.

"And you can fix it again too," Mr Soil replied.

"Yeah," said Dot, "and when it's fixed again we'll go up for another flight."

"Hooray!" the Blueberries cried.

"And here is a merit badge for you, Princess, in honour of your first flight," said Mr Soil.

Dot was confused. "I've already made my first flight," she said, fluttering her tiny wings.

"Ah, but this is a special badge," Mr Soil replied. "It is for making your first flight not using your wings, but using your head!"

Curses, Jafar!

"If I am to become Sultan, I must make Princess Jasmine my bride," said Jafar, pacing the Sultan's throne room.

"Well," said Iago, "you know what they say about evil magic. Use it or lose it!"

Jafar agreed. With his cobra staff in hand, he went looking for Jasmine. He found her in the palace gardens, playing with Rajah.

"Good afternoon, Princess," said Jafar.

"Go away," Jasmine told him. "You're no different from my father and Prince Ali. You all treat me like some kind of prize to be won."

Rajah growled in agreement.

"All right, I'll go," said Jafar. "I just wanted to let you know that I do understand you. You feel trapped here," he cooed. "What you really want is to see the world."

"That's true," she told him. "But I make no secret of wanting freedom, or wanting to travel. You'll have to do better than that."

"I could show you the world," promised Jafar, "*after* you marry me and I become Sultan."

Jasmine still didn't trust Jafar, and neither did her tiger. Rajah growled again.

"Don't you wish to see the world's wonders?" asked Jafar.

"Like what?" she asked.

"The ocean," said Jafar. "You've only seen the desert. But I will show you a place where blue waves stretch forever."

"Really?" said Jasmine, her eyes widening, impressed despite herself. "What else?"

"The mountains," said Jafar. "The land around Agrabah is flat and brown. But I'll show you mountains that touch the clouds."

Jasmine's eyes widened further.

"Aacch! What are you waiting for?" Iago whispered to Jafar, from his shoulder. "Her eyes can't get any wider!"

"I . . . I . . ." Jasmine said, looking into the spinning eyes of the wizard's cobra staff. She didn't realize Jafar was hypnotizing her!

With a huge growl, Rajah leaped between Jasmine and the wizard's staff. Jafar jerked back, and the eyes on the staff stopped spinning.

Jasmine shook her head and said, "I think you should go."

When Rajah growled again, the parrot cried, "Aacch! You heard the lady!"

Outraged, Jafar left.

"Don't take it too hard," Iago told his master on the way out. "There's a very good reason your trick didn't work – a 400-pound reason with long, razor-sharp teeth!"

Fit for a Princess

Cinderella hummed to herself as she slipped the silver needle through the colourful fabric. She had been working hard on her new quilt for weeks, and it was finally almost finished!

Though it was made of scraps of fabric from her stepsisters' old gowns and other rags, Cinderella knew the quilt would be fit for a princess. The worn fabrics were colourful and soft, and with the cotton wadding she'd found in the attic, the quilt would be wonderfully cosy. No more shivering under her threadbare blanket!

Gus agreed. He couldn't help but climb between the sewn-together quilt fabric and snuggle into the cotton filling.

"This is very cosy, Cinderelly," he called from deep inside the quilt. "I think I'd better see how it is for sleeping . . . ."

Suzy and Perla, the mice who were helping Cinderella with the sewing, giggled.

"Go and get us some more thread, sleepyhead," they called. But Gus was already dozing off. The sound of his snores drifted out from between the layers of quilt.

"Gus!" Jaq called. But the snores only got louder. "That mouse hasn't helped with this quilt one bit!" Jaq sighed and went to get the spools of thread himself.

Cinderella, the mice and the birds worked all evening. They were just sewing together the last edge when loud footsteps echoed on the attic stairs.

"Cinderella!" called an angry voice. It was Anastasia, her stepsister. A moment later she stormed into the room, carrying a fancy blue gown. "My dress was not ironed properly!" she shouted. "Can't you do anything right?" Then she spotted the quilt.

"It's beautiful!" she cried. "And it will look wonderful on my bed!"

Cinderella looked at Anastasia in shock. Would her stepsister really steal her quilt? Cinderella knew Anastasia and Drizella could be mean, but that would be very cruel!

Suddenly the quilt began to move. A moment later Gus's quivering nose poked out from between the unsewn pieces of fabric.

"A rodent!" Anastasia screamed. She dropped her dress in fright and leaped onto a small wooden chair. "Why, that quilt isn't fit for use in the stable!" she cried.

Cinderella tried not to laugh as her stepsister leaped off the chair and fled down the stairs.

Yawning, Gus climbed the rest of the way out of the quilt.

"Well, Gus," Jaq said admiringly, "I guess you did end up helping with the quilt, after all!"

A Royal Visit

Snow White was very happy. She had married her true love and she lived in a beautiful castle. But she missed her good friends from the forest, the Seven Dwarfs, very much.

"Well, why don't we go for a visit?" the Prince said.

"That would be lovely!" Snow White cried.

Snow White wrote a note to tell her friends that she was coming, and asked a bluebird to deliver it.

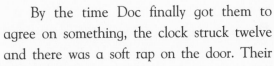

At the Dwarfs' cottage, Doc read the note then ran downstairs to tell the others. "Hooray!" Happy cheered. "Snow White is coming!" But the other six Dwarfs looked around their messy cottage. "We have a lot to do, men!"

"She'll want lunch." Grumpy huffed. "Someone's gonna have to cook!"

"Why don't you and Happy fix somethin' suitable for Snow White to eat?" Doc suggested. The Dwarfs started to work on their chores right away. It didn't go very well. Sleepy got tired and lay down. Sneezy kept sneezing as he dusted. And Dopey knocked furniture over as he swept. Meanwhile, Happy and Grumpy couldn't agree on what kind of sandwiches to make.

"Snow White likes peanut butter and jelly, I know," Happy declared.

"She likes ham and cheese," Grumpy grumbled. "Everyone knows that."

By the time Doc finally got them to agree on something, the clock struck twelve and there was a soft rap on the door. Their beloved princess was here! They smiled as Snow White hugged each of them and kissed their foreheads. "How I've missed you all!" she cried.

"Please forgive the mess, Princess," Bashful whispered to her. "We didn't quite get it cleaned up."

"Oh, please," Snow White said with a laugh, "forgive me for giving you such short notice! Besides, I've come to see you – not your cottage."

"Would you care for a ham-and-jelly sandwich?" Doc offered, holding up a platter. "Or peanut butter and cheese?"

"Oh, how sweet," Snow White kindly replied. "If I had known you'd go to all this trouble, I wouldn't have brought a picnic with me."

"Picnic?!" the Dwarfs exclaimed.

"Well, yes. I remembered how much you liked it when I cooked, so I brought some of your favourites. But let's eat your sandwiches first."

The Dwarfs looked at one another and Doc cleared his throat.

"We can have ham and jelly any time," he said. "Let's enjoy your picnic and have a great visit." And that's exactly what they did.

Beauty and the Beast

Together Is Better

The Beast paced up and down his castle's long hallway. *Click, click, click* went his claws against the marble floor.

"It's been hours," he grumbled. "What do you suppose she's doing in there?" the Beast asked Lumiere.

"Reading," Lumiere replied. "After all, *monsieur,* it *is* the library."

"I know it's the library!" bellowed the Beast. "I know my own castle!"

Suddenly, the library doors burst open. Belle stormed out. She looked around the hallway.

"What is going on?" she asked. "There's a terrible ruckus out here."

"It's the servants," complained the Beast. "They make too much noise."

"Don't blame them," said Belle. "*You're* the one who's been clicking your claws for hours."

"I have not," said the Beast, embarrassed.

"You have so!" insisted Belle. "It's been driving me crazy!"

"You were hearing things," said the Beast.

"And then you started bellowing," said Belle.

"So what if I was?" roared the Beast. "It's my castle!"

Suddenly, Mrs Potts rolled up on a serving cart. "Anyone care for tea?" she asked.

"Not me," huffed Belle.

"Me, neither," huffed the Beast.

"Oh, come now. Just a spot?" asked Mrs Potts, pouring two cups anyway. Humming merrily, she rolled her cart into the library.

Belle and the Beast followed her in and sat down.

"So why were you so angry?" asked Belle, sipping her tea.

"I was bored," said the Beast. "I guess I . . . missed you."

"Why didn't you just say so?" Belle wondered.

"Because . . . I didn't think you missed me," said the Beast.

"I've been reading," said Belle. "I just love to read."

"I know," said the Beast.

Belle thought for a moment. "I have an idea," she said. "How about we read together?"

Belle picked out a book about a princess and a dragon. First Belle read aloud to the Beast. And then the Beast read aloud to Belle.

"That was fun," said the Beast.

"Yes," said Belle. "Let's do it again tomorrow night."

"Tomorrow," he said, "and every night after."

In the hallway, Lumiere sighed with relief.

"Maybe now we'll get some peace!" he said to himself.

Lady *and the* TRAMP

A Tramp Tale

It was a warm, spring evening, just about the time the first star comes out to shine, and *long* past the time for Lady's and Tramp's puppies to go to sleep.

"Just one more story, Dad," begged Scamp.

Tramp rolled his eyes.

"Well . . ." he said, "okay, but just one."

Happily, the puppies snuggled down onto their cushion. Tramp stretched out beside them.

"Did I ever tell you kids about the time I stole my very first sausage?" he asked.

"*Tramp!*" Lady warned him from her seat across the parlour. "That hardly sounds like a proper story for the children."

"Oh, tell it, Dad!" Scamp urged him.

"Well, maybe 'stole' isn't exactly the right word," Tramp reassured his wife. "And besides, it's got a great moral!" And with that, he began his tale:

"Now this all happened way back when I was just a little pup, already living on my own in the big city. I hope you puppies know just how good you have it living here in this nice house, with Junior and Jim Dear and Darling. Your old dad, though, was not so lucky. Oh, I had a lot of friends. And I had a lot of fun. But I'd be lying if I said I wasn't hungry – just a little – nearly every day.

"Well, one day I was especially hungry, and my nose was picking up all sorts of savoury scents. If there was bacon frying a mile away, I could have told you how many strips. So you can imagine the interest I developed in a certain, spicy smell coming from the butcher shop. Well, I followed my trusty nose, which has still never let me down and, sure enough, there was a heaping tray of steaming sausages. Can you believe it?"

"So you jumped up and gobbled them all up! Right?" Scamp broke in.

"That's my boy!" Tramp laughed. "But no. Don't forget, I was just a little guy. Couldn't reach the tray. All I could do was think about how to get that sausage . . . when up walked a lady with a kid in a carriage. Well, at first I was irate. Competition! But then I noticed the crumbs all over the carriage. Hey! I thought to myself. This might be the ticket – this kid obviously can't hang on to anything. Sure enough, when the lady handed the kid a piece of sausage, the kid dropped it, and down it fell into my waiting mouth! Delicious!

"See, Lady," Tramp added with a grin, "no stealing!"

"And what exactly is the moral of that story?" Lady asked.

Tramp laughed. "Why, good things come to those who wait, of course!"

WET
CEMENT

Simba's Thank-you Present

Simba lounged in the jungle, feeling happier than he'd felt in ages. After the terrible stampede near Pride Rock, he didn't think he'd ever be happy again. But his new friends Timon and Pumbaa had helped him feel better.

"I should do something to thank them," Simba told himself as he watched his friends splash in the river nearby. "Something really special!"

He decided to make them a present. When he saw a large piece of bark lying on the ground, he had an idea.

"Ta-da!" he exclaimed a while later, leading his friends to the gift.

Pumbaa blinked. "Thanks," he said. "Er, what is it?"

"A scratching spot," Simba said, flexing his claws. He'd used vines to attach it to a thick tree trunk at shoulder height.

"Gee," Timon said. "Nice thought and all, Simba. But it's a little high for me." He stretched to his full height but could barely reach it.

Pumbaa nodded. "And I don't scratch." He held up one foot. "Hooves, you know."

"Oh." Simba hadn't thought of that.

"Thanks anyway, kid," Pumbaa said.

Simba decided to try again by building them a nice, soft bed to sleep in. He dug a cosy hole in the ground, then filled it with soft things – feathers, sand and bits of fur.

"Ta-da!" he cried when he showed his friends.

Timon sighed. "What are you trying to do, kill us? Prey animals here, remember? If we sleep on the ground, we become somebody's midnight snack!"

Simba sighed as they left again. Why couldn't he come up with a present they would like?

"I would've loved that scratching spot," he mumbled. "The bed, too."

Suddenly he sat up straight, realizing what he'd just said. All this time he'd been thinking of presents HE would like – but the presents weren't for him.

"I've got to think like they think," he whispered. Slowly, a smile spread across his face . . . .

A little while later he called them over. "I've got something for you." He pointed to a pile of palm fronds. "I think you're really going to like it. Ta-da!"

He pulled back the leaves. Underneath was a mass of wriggling, squirming, creeping, crawling creatures – bugs and grubs and worms of every shape and size . . . and flavour.

Timon and Pumbaa gasped with delight. "Simba!" Timon cried. "You're a prince! It's just what we always wanted!"

"Yeah, thanks," Pumbaa mumbled through a mouthful of grubs. "You're a real pal!"

Simba smiled. "No," he said. "Thank *you*. Both of you. *Hakuna matata!*"

Disney **Peter Pan**

The Lost Boys Get Lost

The Lost Boys were walking single file through the woods of Never Land, on their way home after an afternoon of adventure-seeking, when Slightly, who led the way, stopped in his tracks on the bank of Mermaid Lagoon.

The others – Rabbit, the Raccoon Twins, Cubby and Tootles – came to an abrupt halt behind him.

"Wait a minute," said Slightly. "We already passed Mermaid Lagoon. What are we doing here again?"

Behind a bush, Tinker Bell giggled as she watched the Lost Boys looking around in confusion.

Tink had spotted them on their march and had not been able to resist playing a joke. So, she had flown ahead of them and used her fairy magic to enchant various landmarks on their route home. She had made Bald Rock look like Spiky Rock, causing the Lost Boys to make a right turn where they should have turned left. Then she had enlisted the help of the sparrows, convincing them to move from their usual perch in the Sparrow Bird Grove to another group of trees, thus tricking the Lost Boys into making another right turn too soon. And finally, she had enchanted the Towering Elm Tree to look exactly like the Weeping Willow, and the Lost Boys had made yet another wrong turn, thinking they were nearly home.

But now, here they were, walking past Mermaid Lagoon, when Slightly remembered passing the same spot a good while back.

"I think we're walking in circles!" Slightly proclaimed. "Lost Boys, I think we're . . . lost!"

Tinker Bell overheard and tried desperately to stifle her laughter. But, before she could contain it, one giggle exploded into a full-fledged laugh and –

"Hey!" said Cubby. "Did you hear that?"

He darted over to a bush growing alongside the path and moved a branch to one side. There was Tinker Bell, hovering in mid-air, holding her stomach and shaking with laughter.

"Tinker Bell!" cried Tootles.

It didn't take them long to work out that Tinker Bell was laughing at *them* – and that she was the cause of their confusion.

Still laughing, Tinker Bell flitted away, taking her normal route home to the fairy glade: left at the Weeping Willow Tree, right just before Sparrow Bird Grove, right again at Spiky Rock, and on towards the Sparkling Stream, which led to Moon Falls and the fairy glade entrance.

But – wait a minute! After turning right at Spiky Rock, Tinker Bell saw no sign of the Sparkling Stream anywhere. Where was she? She had got completely lost.

Do you know how?

A Hair-raising Experience

Ariel looked at her hair in the mirror and sighed. *Ugh*! It was so straight . . . and red . . . and boring! Ordinarily, it wasn't such a big deal. She'd run a dinglehopper through it, and that would be that. She had more important things to think about, you know. But today, for some reason, she felt like a change.

Ariel was still staring in the mirror when her six mermaid sisters arrived.

"Hi, Ariel, what are you doing?" the oldest, Aquata, asked.

"Oh, nothing," said Ariel. "Just trying to figure out something new to do with my hair."

"Just parting it on the other side can make a big difference," said Aquata. "Shall I try?"

"Sure!" said Ariel.

But, when Aquata had done it, Ariel's sister Andrina shook her head. "Not enough," she declared. "What you need, Ariel, are some curls."

"Okay." Ariel shrugged. She sat patiently as Andrina rolled her hair in curlers and took them out a half hour later.

"Oh, my," said Ariel, gazing into the mirror.

"Still not enough," said another sister, Arista. "Imagine how great your hair would look if we coloured it black with squid ink!" And, just to prove her point, that's exactly what she did.

"Well it certainly is different," said Ariel, looking at her new inky-black hair.

"Different, yes," said her sister Attina, "but if you want *better*, you should really put your hair up. You know, a ponytail or two . . . no! I know, three!" And soon Ariel's new hair was in not one, not two, but three curly black ponytails – all sticking straight up from her head.

"You know what you need?" said her sister Adella, looking at the finished product. "Braids! Definitely braids! Girls, come and help me." And, before she knew it, Ariel's ponytails had been divided into 99 tight, twisty plaits.

Ariel looked in the mirror . . . and then looked away twice as fast!

"What if we just cut it all off?" said her sister Alana.

"Hold it!" said Ariel, suddenly jumping up. "You're *not* cutting off my hair! I wanted a change – not a total reconstruction!" She reached up and began to unbraid her hair.

"Suit yourself," said her sisters. They helped her undo their hard work. Soon Ariel was back to normal, to her great relief. Still, she thought, it had been an interesting experiment. Changing her hair hadn't worked out so well, but what about changing something else? She shook her head and sighed. She was a red-headed mermaid princess, and that was that.

Or was it?

Snow White
and the Seven Dwarfs

A Relaxing Picnic

"What a lovely day for a picnic!" Snow White cried as she arrived at the Dwarfs' cottage for a visit one spring morning.

"We can't have a picnic," Grumpy said. "We have to work."

"But we've been working so hard in the diamond mine." Sleepy yawned. "Can't we take a day off?"

The other Dwarfs cheered – all except for Grumpy. He just folded his arms and frowned.

"Please don't worry, Grumpy," said Snow White. "A relaxing picnic will cheer you up."

"I doubt it," he grumbled.

"Now, what shall we rake – I mean take – on our picnic?" Doc asked.

"How about some porridge?" suggested Sleepy with a yawn.

"That is not a very good picnic food," said Snow White. "It's much more fun to pack food you can eat without spoons or forks."

"Gosh, like s-s-sandwiches?" stammered Bashful shyly.

"Exactly!" cried Snow White.

"How about fruit?" asked Doc.

"And cookies!" suggested Happy.

"And hard-boiled eggs," added Sneezy.

"Wonderful!" exclaimed Snow White. The Dwarfs helped Snow White pack.

"After lunch, we'll want to play," said Snow White. "So you should pack up some things to play with."

They did, and then they were off, hiking through the forest. When they came to a clearing with a babbling brook, Snow White spread a blanket on the grass, and they all sat down to eat.

After lunch, Doc and Happy played draughts, Bashful and Sneezy tossed a ball back and forth, Sleepy took a nap and Dopey launched an enormous blue kite.

Snow White watched Dopey as he ran through the meadow. She clapped when the wind took the kite up in the air. Then the kite lifted Dopey off the ground too!

"Oh, my!" cried Snow White. "Someone help! Dopey is flying away!"

Grumpy, who had been pouting by the brook, jumped to his feet. He raced after Dopey. Huffing and puffing, he followed the kite up one hill and down another.

Finally, Grumpy climbed all the way up a tall oak tree and grabbed Dopey as he flew by. Snow White cheered.

Still huffing and puffing, Grumpy collapsed on the blanket.

"Jiminy Crickets!" he cried. "I can't wait to get back to the diamond mine tomorrow. Relaxing picnics are way too much work!"

Cinderella

The Dance Lesson

"Just imagine," said Cinderella excitedly. "There's a ball at the palace tonight in honour of the Prince, and every maiden in the land is invited. That means me, too!"

All of Cinderella's animal friends clapped and chirped. They loved their 'Cinderelly'.

"Oh, dear," said Cinderella with a sigh. "There is so much to do! I can only go if I finish my chores. There is washing, mending, cooking and –"

Suddenly, three loud shrieks came from downstairs somewhere.

"Cinderellllllaaaa! Come down here immediately, and help us get ready for the ball!" her stepsisters cried together.

"Mend my dress!" screeched Anastasia.

"Polish my shoes!" whined Drizella.

"Iron my cloak!" cried her stepmother.

Hours later, Cinderella began her other chores. Suddenly Jaq had an idea. "I know!" he said to the other mice. "We help-a, Cinderelly!" The mice nodded in agreement.

"What would I do without you!" said Cinderella, "You are so good to me."

Everyone joined in the cleaning, singing happily. As she worked, Cinderella began to imagine the evening ahead. Cinderella would wear her mother's beautiful gown. The ballroom would come alive with music

and dancing. The handsome young Prince would bow before Cinderella and ask her to dance...

Suddenly Cinderella stopped dreaming. "Oh, no!" she cried. "I don't even know how to dance!"

"Don't you worry, Cinderelly!" Jaq smiled reassuringly. "Us show you! Easy pie!"

With that, Jaq bowed before Perla and extended his hand.

"Dance, please, missy?" he asked.

Perla blushed as she took Jaq's hand. Gus was the conductor. He got all the birds to sing. Jaq and Perla spun around and around, gliding across the floor.

"See?" said Perla. "Not so scary."

Using her broom as an imaginary partner, Cinderella danced and twirled gracefully around the room. She led everyone across the floor, sweeping and cleaning as they went.

"Good-good, Cinderelly!" said Jaq, beaming. "Lucky Prince gets to dance with Cinderelly."

The mice collapsed on the floor, laughing.

"Thank you all so much," Cinderella told her friends. "With your help, tonight might be the night that all my dreams come true!"

Disney
POCAHONTAS
Fishing Hole

"Come on, slowpoke," Pocahontas teased. "It's just ahead."

John Smith followed her across a grassy meadow and up a hill. Pocahontas moved as quickly and quietly as a deer. Sometimes it was difficult for John to keep up.

Pocahontas waited at the top of the hill. Below, a river wound its way through a wide canyon.

She pointed. "The fishing hole is down there."

She raced down the other side of the hill towards the water. John hurried after her. Soon they were at the water's edge.

Pocahontas leaned forwards slowly and peered into the water. Then she raised her spear and – *splash*! – thrust it into the water. But, when she lifted it out, the spear was empty.

"We prefer to use fishing rods," John said with a laugh. He baited his hook, cast it into the water and waited. But the water was moving so quickly, the line was soon unwinding with remarkable speed.

"I see," Pocahontas said.

John reeled his line in and got ready to cast again. But then a low growl startled him.

"Hold still," Pocahontas instructed.

John turned his head slowly and saw a large grizzly bear above them on the boulders.

"Grrrr!" The great animal rose up on its hind legs.

In an instant, John had dropped his fishing rod and was raising his rifle.

"No, John," Pocahontas said. "Follow me." Keeping her eyes on the bear she began to move, very slowly and carefully, away from it.

"Grrrr!" the bear growled. John's hand instinctively lifted his rifle a second time.

"He's just telling us that this is his territory," Pocahontas whispered calmly. "He doesn't want to hurt us. He just wants to fish."

John wasn't so sure, but he knew that he didn't want to shoot the grizzly. They were very big and hard to kill. And a wounded grizzly would be dangerous.

Pocahontas kept moving along the river's edge, away from the bear. When they were about 100 feet away, the grizzly leaped off the boulder, landing in the exact spot where John and Pocahontas had been fishing a few minutes before.

"Grrrr!" the bear rumbled a third time, before beginning to fish.

While Pocahontas and John watched, the grizzly caught salmon after salmon with its giant claws.

Pocahontas laughed. "I guess the bear's method is best!"

John had to agree.

Bambi

A Manner of Speaking

Bambi and his mother were out for a summer's walk. As always, they stopped by the rabbit den where Thumper lived.

"And how are you today, Thumper?" asked Bambi's mother.

"I'd be better if my mum didn't just give me a dumb old bath," he said.

"Thumper! Mind your manners!" his mother scolded.

"I'm sorry, Mama," Thumper said. He looked back at the doe. "I'm fine, thank you," he replied.

Bambi and Thumper were given permission to play, and they headed off into the woods. "So, what do you want to play?" the fawn asked his friend.

"How about hide-and-seek?" Thumper suggested. "I'll hide first, okay?"

Bambi turned his back to Thumper, closed his eyes, and started to count. "One . . . two . . . three . . . four . . . five . . ."

"Save me! Help! Bambi, save me!" Thumper cried. Bambi whirled around to see Thumper hopping towards him with a terrified look on his face. A moment later, a mother bear emerged from a nearby cave with three small cubs toddling behind her.

Though he was terrified, Thumper *still* managed to make a rude comment. "That's the ugliest, meanest-looking creature I ever saw!"

"I beg your pardon?" the mother bear said.

"First, you come into my home and disturb my children while they're sleeping. And then you have the nerve to call me ugly and mean? I think you owe me an apology!"

"Do it!" whispered Bambi. "Apologize."

"I'm s-s-sorry you're ugly and mean," Thumper stammered.

"Thumper!" Bambi cried. "That isn't funny."

Thumper looked confused. "I wasn't trying to be funny," he said.

"Try again!" the bear boomed.

"Um, ma'am," Thumper tried again. "I'm, um, sorry I disturbed your cubs . . . and, um, you look just like a bear mum should look . . . which is big. And nice. Yup, you sure look nice."

Before the mother bear let Thumper and Bambi go, she said, "Like I always tell my children: manners are important. Today, young man, they saved your life!"

Bambi and Thumper ran home as quickly as they could. When they arrived at Thumper's, his mother said, "Just in time for a nice lunch of greens." Thumper was about to tell his mum how awful he thought the greens tasted, then changed his mind. "Thank you, Mama. That sounds wonderful," he said.

Thumper's mother beamed. "What lovely manners! I guess you have been listening to me, after all!" she said, pleased as could be.

Woodland Washing

"La, la, la, la, la," Briar Rose sang as she hung the sheets on the washing line. She could feel the sunshine on her back and it felt good. It had been raining for days, and the change in the weather was a welcome surprise. She could catch up on the washing and spend some time outdoors.

"Doesn't the sunshine make you want to sing?" she asked a bluebird who was chirping along with her. The bird chirped a new song in response, and Briar Rose laughed as she pulled her Aunt Flora's red dress out of the basket of clean laundry. Once she was finished, she could take a nice walk through the forest.

Aunt Merryweather's blue dress was next. Briar Rose was just pegging the shoulder to the washing line when suddenly a pair of cheeky chipmunks leaped onto the line from a tree branch and raced down the length of it, covering the dresses and the sheets with muddy footprints.

"Look what you've done, you naughty chipmunks!" Briar Rose scolded, shaking a finger at the wayward creatures. "It took me two hours to get those dresses and sheets clean!"

The chipmunks leaped up to a tree branch and twittered guiltily at her in response. Then they turned and scampered off into the forest, their striped tails waggling.

Sighing with frustration, Briar Rose unpegged the sheets from the line and pulled a fresh bucket of water up from the well. Then, taking the washboard and the bar of laundry soap, she began to scrub out the muddy prints. It looked as if she wouldn't get a walk in today after all.

Suddenly, a chattering noise caught her attention. Looking up, she saw the chipmunks hurrying out of the forest with several other forest animals at their heels! There were two rabbits, four chipmunks, three bluebirds, a deer, a skunk and an owl.

Briar Rose laughed. "Why, you've brought all your friends!"

The chipmunks chattered excitedly while everyone got to work. The bluebirds lifted the sheet into the air so the edges wouldn't get dirty while Briar Rose scrubbed. The deer, the skunk and the rabbits brought fresh water from the well. And the chipmunks scampered across the laundry soap to get their feet all soapy, then walked across the muddy parts of the sheets until they were clean. Then everyone helped hang the newly washed laundry on the line for a second time.

Briar Rose smiled at her animal friends and gave the chipmunks a little pat. "Finished at last," she said. "Now we can all take a walk in the forest . . . together!"

Rabbit's Frightful Garden

Rabbit woke up bright and early. He had a lot of work to do in his garden. There were weeds to be pulled up. There were vines to be trimmed. And there were lots of delicious, ripe vegetables just waiting to be picked. The only problem was that Rabbit had lent all his tools to his friends – and they hadn't returned them.

In the meantime, Pooh and Piglet were enjoying breakfast at Kanga's and Roo's house when Roo bounced in with a bunch of wildflowers for his mother.

"Thank you, Roo!" Kanga exclaimed, giving him a kiss. "Let me just trim these and put them in some water." She rummaged around in a kitchen drawer, where she came across Rabbit's gardening shears. "Oh, no," Kanga said. "I never returned these to Rabbit after I borrowed them."

"That reminds me," said Piglet. "I still have Rabbit's rake. And, Pooh, I'll bet you still have Rabbit's shovel."

The friends decided the neighbourly thing to do would be to return Rabbit's tools right away. When they arrived at Rabbit's house, though, their friend was not at home. He was on his way to *their* houses to get his tools back.

"Rabbit's garden could use some work," Kanga said. "Why don't we take care of it for him as a way of saying that we're sorry for keeping his tools for so long?"

Everyone agreed that this was a splendid plan. Pooh set about weeding while Piglet raked. Kanga snipped ripe tomatoes, peppers and cucumbers off the vines. Roo gathered them into big baskets.

When they had finished, they spotted some birds hungrily eyeing the harvest.

"This garden needs a scarecrow!" cried Roo.

The work crew sprang into action, and soon a towering scarecrow was planted right in the middle of the garden. They propped the tools against the scarecrow, placed the baskets of food in front of it, and started for home. "Won't Rabbit be surprised!" Piglet said proudly.

When Rabbit returned home a few minutes later, he couldn't quite believe his eyes. First he looked at the vegetables, all neatly picked. Then he looked at his garden tools, which had mysteriously reappeared. Finally, he looked at the strange scarecrow, which seemed to be looking right back at him! "D-d-d-did you do this?" he stammered to the straw man. Just then, a gust of wind knocked over the rake resting on the scarecrow's arm.

Convinced his garden was haunted, Rabbit turned and ran for his life. "Ahhhhhhhhh!" he screamed as he rushed past his friends.

"I *told* you he'd be surprised," said Piglet.

Disney
The **Fox** and the **Hound**

The Chase

"**W**hoopee!" Tod cried as he tumbled head over tail towards the water. He hit the surface with a splash. A second later, his friend Copper landed right next to him.

"It certainly is a beautiful day," Copper said.

"Yeah, it sure is," Tod agreed. The two friends swam to the edge and climbed up on the bank. As they sat in the warm sun, a great big blue butterfly landed on Copper's tail.

"Looks like you've made a friend," said Tod.

But the butterfly was frightened away by a booming voice.

"Copper!" the voice rumbled. It was Amos, Copper's master. Amos was usually grumpy, and right now he sounded angry too. "Where are you, mutt?" he shouted.

Tod silently climbed out of the water. He could tell that Amos was nearby, and that his other dog, Chief, was with him.

Copper crept up beside Tod. "I'd better go," he said. "Amos sounds awfully mad."

"Why don't you sneak back to your barrel so you're there when he gets back," Tod suggested. "He can't be mad if you're already home when he finds you."

Copper scratched behind his ear. "But he's right in my path, and Chief is with him. Chief will hear me or smell me for sure."

Tod grinned. "You just leave that to me."

He winked at his friend and dashed up the hill, right past Amos and Chief.

"There's that varmint fox!" Amos cried as Chief took off after Tod, barking like mad.

Amos gave chase, running as fast as he could on his long, skinny legs.

Tod leaped over branches and darted around trees. More than once, Chief got close, his hot breath on Tod's tail. But Tod was smart. He led Chief towards a rocky outcrop and dashed into a small cave. Chief stuck his snout into the opening, growling away. But he was too big to fit.

"Never mind, Chief," Amos said when he finally caught up. "We'll get him later."

Chief gave a final growl into the cave, but Tod had already escaped at the other end and was dashing home.

Exhausted, Amos and Chief started home, too. And, by the time they got there, Tod was napping next door in front of the Widow Tweed's fireplace, and Copper was sitting in his barrel. Next to him, his supper bowl was empty.

"There you are," Amos grumbled. He shook his head. "And I suppose you've been sitting here almost the whole time. We could have used your help catching that dang fox – it's almost as if you're trying to avoid hunting him!"

Tangled

A Three-Star Pub

Rapunzel had finally left the tower that she had lived in her whole life. But there was no point in trying to hide it – being outside was terrifying. Mother Gothel – an old woman that Rapunzel thought was her mother – had told Rapunzel terrible stories about the outside world! Rapunzel didn't know Mother Gothel was just trying to keep her hidden.

Rapunzel had made a deal with a thief called Flynn Rider. She would give him back his satchel – which contained a stolen royal crown – as long as he took her to see the lights that appeared in the sky every year on her birthday.

Suddenly, There was a noise in the bushes and Rapunzel jumped, terrified. "Is it ruffians? Have they come for me?"

Just then a little rabbit hopped out from the bushes. Rapunzel blushed. If she carried on like this, Flynn would guess that she had never been out of her tower before!

But Flynn had realized what Rapunzel was scared of, and that gave him an idea. He decided that a little pub called the Snuggly Duckling was the perfect place to take her for lunch. "I know a pub, in the forest. Shall we go there?" he suggested.

"Oh, yes please!" Rapunzel agreed quickly.

Meanwhile, Mother Gothel was returning to the tower and saw Maximus, a horse that had been chasing Flynn. She thought the guards might have come for Rapunzel – who was actually the Princess.

Mother Gothel ran to the tower. "Rapunzel!" she called. But there was no reply. She tore open a hidden entrance and soon realized the awful truth: Rapunzel was gone. That's when she saw something glimmering beneath the staircase. It was the crown in Flynn's satchel! Then she found Flynn's WANTED poster too. Now she knew who had taken Rapunzel – and nothing would stop her from finding him!

Meanwhile, Flynn and Rapunzel had arrived at the pub. Rapunzel was horrified! The place was full of ruffians and they were loud and scary – one of them even touched her long, golden hair!

"You look very pale, blondie," said Flynn, delighted at his idea of bringing the delicate Rapunzel to the disgusting pub, so she would want to go back to the tower. "Don't you like it here then?"

Flynn escorted her to the door, thinking it was about time one of his plans had finally worked! But, little did he know, he wasn't going to trick Rapunzel that easily! She was stronger than he thought...

A Frog's Appetite

Tiana and Naveen, now transformed into frogs, found themselves lost in the bayou. They had to get back to New Orleans quickly, so they could find out how to undo the sorcerer's evil curse. Tiana, working hard as usual, had just finished building a raft to cross the swamp. As for Naveen, he was happy to sing while she manoeuvred their makeshift boat.

"I could do with a little help!" she grumbled.

"I'll sing louder then!" replied Naveen without moving.

Suddenly, an enormous alligator emerged from the muddy waters! The frogs froze in terror. But he wasn't dangerous. This was Louis, who was mad about music! He loved the jazz pieces that Naveen was singing.

"I am Naveen, Prince of Maldonia, and she is Tiana, the waitress," introduced Naveen. Then he leaned closer to Louis, "Do not kiss her."

"Delighted to make your acquaintance, Louis," Tiana intervened, ignoring Naveen. "And thank you for not eating us... but we're in a hurry!"

"Where are you going?" asked Louis.

"To find someone who will be able to turn us back into humans," explained Naveen. "An evil sorcerer changed us into frogs!"

"We'll have to ask Mama Odie!" exclaimed Louis. "Queen of the bayou! She's a real voodoo priestess...but one who does good magic!"

Louis was frightened about going to find Mama Odie, who lived in one of the most remote and dangerous swamps. But in the end he agreed to guide Tiana and Naveen, his new friends.

They sang and entertained themselves along the way, until Naveen started to get hungry. Very hungry. So hungry that his frog's tongue suddenly shot out all by itself – *doing!* – into the path of a cloud of mosquitoes! Then, a big firefly landed on a nearby dandelion... and this time, Tiana's tongue shot out without warning!

"Oh no, no, no!" she panicked as she slapped a leg over her mouth. "There is no way I'm kissing a frog and eating a bug in the same day!"

But Tiana couldn't fight it. Her tongue shot out in the direction of the chubby firefly at the same time as Naveen's. And *splosh!* they missed the firefly, but got their tongues tangled up!

"What an embarrassing situation!" laughed the firefly, fluttering around them. "I've always said: there is nothing worse in the whole bayou than a frog's appetite!"

Ariel and the Seahorse Race

"Ariel!" King Triton's voice thundered. "How could you sign up for the Annual Sea-Horse Race? No mermaid has ever competed in this race."

Ariel raised her chin defiantly. "Mermaids ride sea horses, too, Daddy," she said. "And Stormy may be small, but he's fast."

"No, Ariel. I forbid you to enter the race!" he said.

Ariel moped around the racecourse all week long. Her best friend, Flounder, tried to cheer her up but it was no use.

"That's it!" cried Ariel. "I'll be a merman – Arrol, the merman!"

Ariel swam around the palace, looking for a racing uniform and helmet. When suddenly she swam smack into Sebastian the crab.

"Sorry, Sebastian," said Ariel. "I guess I just had racing on my mind."

"You and your father both," Sebastian said. "He keeps going to the closet to look at his old racing uniform."

"Thanks, Sebastian!" said Ariel. Now she knew where to find a racing uniform!

On the morning of the competition, Ariel hid with Stormy near the starting line, her tail swishing back and forth nervously.

A spark shot out of the tip of Triton's trident. The racers steered their sea horses through the water at breakneck speed. When they reached the coral reef, many of the more powerful sea horses could not fit through and had to swim around. But Stormy was small and Ariel was brave. They zipped in and out of the spiky coral. It was not long before they were in the lead.

"YAHOO!" Ariel shouted with joy. Her cry gave Stormy a burst of energy. The sea horse whipped around the next turn. But this time he was too fast! Ariel's helmet hit the coral and popped off. Her long red hair streamed out behind her.

All of Atlantica could see them now. The crowd gasped as everyone recognized King Triton's daughter.

Ariel and Stormy crossed the finish line first. Ariel smiled broadly and waved. Then she caught sight of her father. He looked stern.

Nervously, Ariel steered Stormy towards the royal box. There stood King Triton, holding the gleaming trophy.

"Daddy, I..." Ariel began, but she didn't finish because King Triton hugged her tightly.

"Oh, Ariel, I'm sorry," he said. "I had forgotten how much fun racing could be. Will you forgive me?"

Ariel nodded and kissed his cheek. Then, proudly, King Triton handed his daughter – the first mermaid ever to win the Annual Sea-Horse Race – her trophy.

Carl and Ellie's House

After their first meeting, Carl and Ellie became best friends. Every day they would meet at Ellie's clubhouse to play and dream together about exploring the world.

One sunny morning, they decided there was no two ways about it – one day, they would go to South America and live next to Paradise Falls.

The years passed and Ellie grew up to be a cheerful and rather talkative young woman. Carl grew into a dependable and quiet young man.

Their friendship grew into love, and they got married when they were both aged 19. They bought the little empty house they had played in as children and set up home there.

Of course, the old house needed doing up! Ellie busied herself filling in the holes in the roof and Carl fixed a new weather vane.

They also patched up the walls, the windows and the floors. Finally, they painted the whole house in bright colours, exactly as it looked in Ellie's adventure book.

One morning, the only thing left was the letterbox. Ellie decided to take care of it. But she had hardly given the metal its first lick of paint when Carl leant carelessly against it!

Ellie burst out laughing at the big mark left by his hand. She then pressed her own hand to the side of the box. When she lifted it off, the two prints seemed to be joining as if to hold hands....

To earn enough money for their journey to South America, the couple found jobs at the town zoo. Ellie looked after the animals and Carl sold balloons to the children.

When they returned home in the evening, they were pleased to get back to their pretty house.

Ellie painted a superb picture of Paradise Falls, which she stuck above the fireplace. In front of it she placed a fragment of pottery and a small statue of a tropical bird.

Carl added a pair of binoculars and his Spirit of Adventure model. Then he put a jar on a table in which, every month, they put aside some money for their trip.

Unfortunately, whatever they managed to save steadily disappeared! They had to buy new tyres for the car, pay for a plaster cast for Carl and then replace the roof of the house.

But over the years they continued to dream, enjoy themselves and, in the evenings, dance together in their lounge.

Neither of them was worried. They knew that one day they'd leave and live out their big adventure.

ALICE in WONDERLAND

Alice's Mad Manners

"**C**lean cup! Clean cup! Move down!" the Mad Hatter shoved Alice aside, nearly spilling her tea. Poor Alice had been at the tea party for some time and had not even had a sip. It was a most unusual tea party.

Alice took a new spot and waited patiently while the Hatter and the March Hare poured a fresh round of tea. Folding her hands in her lap, Alice tried to recall what her mother and sister usually did at tea parties. It seemed to her that they just sat around and chatted. Perhaps, thought Alice, that is what I ought to do too.

"Pardon me," Alice addressed the March Hare because the Mad Hatter seemed quite busy buttering his saucer. "Our neighbours got a new dog. He's a – "

"A dog? *A dog?*" the March Hare shouted. "Where?" He hopped up onto the table, upsetting a plate of toast.

"Oh, I'm terribly sorry." Alice stood and tried to calm the poor hare. "I should have known you wouldn't like dogs. Dinah hates them too, you know." The March Hare was hopping all around the table and Alice had to jog in circles beside him to keep up the conversation. "When Dinah sees a dog, she practically climbs the curtains."

"Very sensible!" the Hatter said, waving his butter knife. "Just who is this clever 'Dinah'?"

"Oh, she's my – " Alice stopped herself. She had got into trouble for mentioning her cat before. The Dormouse had run off in a panic, and the Hatter and March Hare had given chase. She would not make that mistake again. She whispered in the Hatter's ear. "She's my kitten."

"But that's a baby cat!" the Hatter cried.

Just as Alice feared, the Dormouse bolted. The March Hare started hopping about just as soon as the word 'cat' was out of the Hatter's mouth. The Hatter chased the Dormouse round and round the garden. Finally, the Hatter tossed his hat over the little creature. Alice caught him in the teapot and closed the lid.

"Really, my dear. It is most rude to threaten us on our unbirthdays!" the Hatter cried.

"I'm really very sorry," Alice sighed, sinking back into a chair. She was only trying to be polite. Perhaps, Alice thought to herself, in this place it is better to say what you think you oughtn't instead of what you think you ought.

Turning to the Hatter, she said, "This party isn't very fun, and you aren't very nice!"

The Hatter grinned. "Thank you ever so much, my dear young lady. Tea?" he asked.

"Thank *you* ever so much," said Alice. She was beginning to get the hang of this!

Disney · PIXAR
FINDING
NEMO

Dory's Surprise Party

One day, Nemo was telling his dad Marlin that Dory's birthday was coming up. Nemo wanted to throw a surprise birthday party for her!

Nemo asked his friends, Pearl the octopus, Tad the butterfly fish and Sheldon the sea horse to help plan the party.

"What kind of food should we have?" asked Nemo.

"Kelp cake and algae ice cream," Sheldon replied.

"What about sea-plant pizza?" asked Tad.

"I'm getting hungry already," said Nemo. "What about music?"

"We could be the band," said Pearl. "I'm great on the mussel tambourines."

"Yeah, and I play the clamshell drums," said Sheldon.

"Great!" cried Nemo. "Let's meet here tomorrow after school to practise."

The next day, Nemo and his friends were carrying their musical instruments when they bumped into Dory.

"Hi Mimo! Hi kids!" Dory exclaimed. She had trouble remembering Nemo's name. "What are you up to?"

"Music-class homework," Tad piped up.

The friends smiled and began to practise.

Soon, it was the day of the party! Nemo and his friends got up early and started decorating.

Then Nemo suggested they practise singing "Happy Birthday." Just as they finished the line "Happy Birthday, dear Dory," Dory appeared! "How did you know it was my birthday?" she exclaimed.

"You told me," said Nemo.

"Really, Pluto?" asked Dory, "I don't remember."

"Now the surprise is ruined," said Nemo, sadly.

"What surprise?" said Dory. It sure was helpful that Dory's memory wasn't very good!

"Another close call," said Nemo to his friends.

A few hours later, the guests arrived. They all hid and waited. When Dory and Nemo swam in, everyone shouted, "Surprise!"

"Look, Pluto, it's a party for you!" Dory cried.

"No, Dory, it's for you," Nemo said. "It's your birthday."

"Oh, yeah. Cool, a party for me!"

Later, she swam over to Marlin and Nemo. "I sure am glad your dad and I found you, Nemo. This is the best birthday I've ever had."

"Hey, Dory," said Nemo. "You remembered my name."

"What's that, Flipper?" asked Dory.

"Oh, nothing," Nemo said with a sigh. "Happy birthday!"

The Trouble With Tink

One sunny afternoon in Pixie Hollow, Tinker Bell was taking a break from tinkering. All the fairies were playing tag in the meadow. Once the game was over, Tink reached for her hammer hanging on her belt, but it wasn't there! She checked everywhere, but the hammer was nowhere to be found.

As Tink flew home, tears of frustration rolled down her cheeks. What will I do without my hammer? she wondered. Tink was also upset because she had a spare hammer, but she had left it in Peter Pan's hideout. She was terribly scared about going to get it. When Tink thought about Peter, her heart ached. Since he had brought Wendy to Never Land, Tink and Peter had hardly spoken.

"I'll make do without it," Tink told herself. She tried to continue fixing pots and pans. She fashioned a hammer from a pebble, but it was no use. The fairies started to think that Tinker Bell had lost her talent. Tink was too ashamed to tell the others the truth.

Soon, Tink heard that Queen Clarion's beautiful bath had sprung a leak! It was expected the Queen would ask Tink to fix it. All she had to do was find a new hammer.

Later, in the tearoom, Tink joined the other tinker fairies at their table. Everyone was talking about how they were going to fix the queen's bath. Suddenly, Tink realised that the queen had not asked her to fix it. She rushed out of the tearoom, with her friend Terence close behind.

"What's really going on?" he asked.

"I lost my hammer!" Tink blurted at last. She explained to Terence that she had left her spare at Peter Pan's hideout.

"I could go with you," Terence said. "To Peter Pan's, I mean."

"You would do that?" Tink asked.

"I'm your friend," said Terence. "You don't even need to ask."

The next morning, the two friends left Pixie Hollow. Tink felt a flutter of nervousness. How would it be to see Peter? They soon arrived at the hideout.

"Tink!" Peter cried. "It's awful great to see you!"

The grin on Peter's face was so wide it was impossible not to like him. He found Tink's spare hammer, and Tink smiled. She had discovered that it wasn't so hard to see Peter, after all!

Back in Pixie Hollow, Tink flew straight to Queen Clarion's quarters. "I've come to fix your bath," she announced.

"Good luck," Terence said.

"I don't need it!" Tink replied.

Looks Can Be Deceiving

Yao, Ling and Chien-Po missed Mulan. They had become friends in the army – even though when they had first met her, Mulan was disguised as a young man. They forgave her for tricking them, because Mulan went on to bravely save China from Shan-Yu and the rest of the Huns. Mulan was famous; even the Emperor himself had bowed to her!

Now, her three friends decided they would journey to her village and follow Mulan in whatever adventure she might embark on next.

"But what if Shan-Yu is seeking revenge?" Ling said. "He might be looking for us. After all, we did help Mulan defeat him."

Yao thought they should disguise themselves. So the friends donned kimonos, wigs and makeup, and set out for Mulan's village, looking like a trio of women.

When they arrived, the Matchmaker instantly approached them. "And who would you lovely ladies be?" she asked. The Matchmaker was desperate. There weren't many single women in the village, and she had a list of bachelors a mile long to marry off!

"Visitors from far away," said Chien-Po, speaking in a high voice.

"And are you unmarried ladies?" the Matchmaker asked.

Ling said, "We're unmarried, all right!"

"Well, let me be the first to welcome you to our village," the Matchmaker said, ushering them into her house. "Would you like some tea?"

The three men were hungry and thirsty after their long journey. They didn't realize the Matchmaker wanted to see if they would make suitable wives.

"Perhaps you would like to pour?" she asked Yao. He tried to remember the way his mother served tea at home. Yao set out the cups and poured as daintily as he could.

"Cookie?" the pleased Matchmaker asked Chien-Po, holding out a plate.

Chien-Po resisted the urge to grab a fistful of cookies. Instead, he chose one, stuck out his little finger, and took small bites.

Perfect! The Matchmaker was delighted.

Next she asked Ling what his favourite pastime was. "Wrestling," he answered.

Then, seeing the shocked look on the Matchmaker's face, he added quickly, "Yes, I find that *resting* keeps my complexion lovely." He batted his eyelashes.

The Matchmaker led the three back outside, just as Mulan was riding into the village. "Stop! You can't marry them off!" Mulan cried, seeing her friends with the woman.

"I certainly can," said the Matchmaker. "Unlike you, Mulan, these three are real ladies!"

Lucifer's Bath

Cinderella's stepsisters didn't like the idea of Cinderella going to the Prince's ball.

"But Stepmother told me I could," said Cinderella.

"*Only* if you finish your chores," pointed out Drizella. "Which includes giving our cat, Lucifer, his bath."

"And that reminds me," said Anastasia. "I'll be needing a bath myself."

"Me, too," said Drizella.

"You heard my girls, Cinderella," her stepmother said. "Get their baths ready at once!"

Cinderella already had far too many jobs to do. But she didn't argue.

Once Anastasia and Drizella were soaking in their bubble baths, all Cinderella had to do was mend their clothes, clean the house, wash the curtains and give Lucifer his bath – then she could get ready for the ball.

Unfortunately, her stepsisters wouldn't leave her alone.

"Cinderella! Bring my face cream!" cried Drizella.

"Cinderella! My bath salts!" cried Anastasia.

Each time her stepsisters called, Cinderella had to stop whatever she was doing and take care of them.

When Drizella called for tea, Cinderella went down to the kitchen and put the kettle on. Then she let Bruno the dog in for a snack.

"Oh, Bruno," she said, tossing him a bone, "if my stepsisters don't get out of their bathtubs soon, I'll never get my chores done in time."

Bruno narrowed his eyes. Those stepsisters were the most selfish, lazy, nasty girls he'd ever known – and their cat was just like them. He wanted to help Cinderella. So, when the tea was ready, Bruno followed her up the stairs and down the long hallway.

Just as Cinderella walked up to Drizella's bathroom door, Bruno noticed Lucifer sleeping nearby.

"Woof, woof!" Bruno barked.

With a screeching yowl, Lucifer ran into Drizella's bathroom.

Splash! Bruno chased the cat right into Drizella's tub! Then Bruno jumped in himself!

Drizella screamed. Lucifer jumped out. And Bruno chased the cat down the hall and into Anastasia's bathroom.

Splash! Lucifer was now in Anastasia's tub. And Bruno jumped right in after him!

"Get out of your tubs this instant!" Cinderella's stepmother cried. "You don't want to smell like that dog, do you?"

Cinderella sighed in relief. Although she still had many jobs to finish before the ball, at least one job was now done. Thanks to Bruno, Lucifer had had his bath!

The Case of the Missing Vegetables

Of all the things Belle loved about the Beast's castle, the thing she loved the best was the garden at the back. She had read every one of the Beast's books about gardening, and every season she experimented with something new. This summer, she'd decided to try growing vegetables. And now they were ready to be picked.

"Don't tell the Beast," she whispered to Mrs Potts, "but today for lunch I'm going to make him a salad."

"Oh, really," said Mrs Potts.

"Mmm-hmm." Belle nodded proudly. "Yesterday, I saw so many things ready to be harvested. Lettuce, carrots, cucumbers, peas . . . even tomatoes! Can you believe it? The Beast is going to be so surprised!"

"Indeed," Mrs Potts smiled. "Lunch is definitely going to be a surprise."

Belle slipped on her gardening gloves and her sun hat, grabbed her biggest basket, and happily skipped out into the garden.

"First," she said out loud, to no one in particular, "let's get some lettuce!"

But, when she bent down where the lettuce should have been, she found a bed of empty soil.

"My lettuce!" she cried. "Where did it go?"

Rabbits? Deer? Bewildered, Belle moved on to where her tender, sweet, young carrots had been growing.

"Oh, dear!" she cried. "There's nothing here now either!"

There wasn't a single pea to be found. "I don't understand," she said.

But facts were facts. The garden was empty and there was nothing she could do . . . but go back to the castle and look for a book about building fences for next summer's garden!

As she walked inside, empty-handed and disappointed, Belle passed Mrs Potts and Chip.

"What's the matter?" asked Mrs Potts.

"Oh, everything!" Belle sighed. "My whole garden has been robbed." Then she shrugged. "So much for my salad idea."

"Don't feel sad, Belle," Chip said. "Come and have some lunch."

"I'm not hungry," Belle replied, smiling sadly.

"Oh, I don't know," said Mrs Potts, steering her into the dining room. "You might be . . ."

"SURPRISE!" called the Beast.

"What?" Belle gasped. There, laid out upon the table, was what looked like every possible vegetable from her garden, washed and sliced and arranged, just so, on fancy dishes.

"You've worked so hard in the garden," the Beast explained, "I thought it would be nice if I did something for you. I hope you like it."

Belle smiled. What a treat!

Trusting Trusty

"Tramp!" cried Lady one morning. "One of our puppies is missing!"

"Don't worry," said Tramp with a yawn. "Scamp is always getting into mischief."

"Its not Scamp," said Lady. "It's little Fluffy! She never gets into trouble. Tramp, what should we do?"

"You look inside. I'll look outside," said Tramp worriedly.

Tramp searched their back garden. Then he went to the next garden, and the next.

From a neighbour's porch, Trusty the bloodhound called, "Howdy! Whatcha looking for?"

"My daughter, Fluffy! She's missing," said Tramp.

Trusty's long floppy ears pricked up. "A missing puppy – now that's serious! And I should know. I used to help my grandpa track down missing persons through the swamps!"

"I know," said Tramp. He'd heard Trusty tell that story 100 times.

"Have you found a trail yet?" asked Trusty.

Tramp shook his head.

"Well, let me at it!" Trusty loped back to Tramp's garden. He put his big nose to the ground. _Sniff, sniff, sniff_ . . . .

"Tramp, have you found Fluffy?" Lady called from the dog door.

Tramp ran over. "No," he replied. "But Trusty offered his . . . uh . . . services."

"He can't smell any more," Lady whispered. "I know he tracked that dogcatcher's wagon and saved you – but he hasn't tracked anything since."

"He helped us once," said Tramp. "I think we should trust him again."

Just then, Trusty shouted, "Look at this!"

He had spotted a bluebird's feather below a window. "That's the window the puppies look out," said Lady.

"Look! A bit of puppy fur," said Trusty. "And footprints!" Trusty followed the trail of footprints to the back of a shed.

And that's where Trusty found the missing puppy! Fluffy was fast asleep under a big tree.

"Fluffy! What happened?" Lady cried.

"I woke up and saw a bluebird," said Fluffy with a yawn. "And I didn't want Scamp to bark and scare it away, like he always does. So I didn't wake anyone. I followed the bird all the way to this tree. Then I guess I got sleepy."

Lady walked over and gave Trusty a kiss.

"Thank you," she told the bloodhound.

"Aw, shucks," said Trusty, blushing. "It weren't nothin'."

As the bloodhound trotted home, Tramp turned to Lady. "See that," he said with a grin, "I told you we should trust Trusty!"

Baloo's Secret Weapon

Mowgli and his pal Baloo were taking a lazy afternoon stroll through the jungle. Suddenly, Mowgli stopped in his tracks. "Did you hear that?" he asked.

"Hear what, little buddy?" Baloo asked.

"It sounded like twigs snapping," Mowgli said. "I think somebody might be following us!"

"That was just your old Papa Bear's stomach growling," Baloo told him. "It's time for some lunch."

"And I know just where to get it," announced Mowgli. He shimmied up a tree, plucked a bunch of bananas, and tossed them down to the bear.

"That's my boy!" Baloo cried proudly.

But, as he was scrambling back down, Mowgli spotted a flash of orange and black.

"Shere Khan!" Mowgli whispered to Baloo. "We've got to get out of here!" The tiger had been after Mowgli ever since the boy had first set foot in the jungle.

The two friends didn't know which way to turn. Now that Shere Khan had their scent, it would be almost impossible to lose him. Then they both heard a lively beat drumming its way through the jungle.

"Oh, no," said Mowgli. "King Louie and his crazy band of monkeys. That's all we need!"

Baloo's eyes suddenly lit up. "That's *exactly* what we need, Little Britches!"

Still clutching the bananas, Baloo and Mowgli ran towards King Louie's compound. When they arrived, Baloo disguised himself as a monkey. The orang-utans were so busy dancing and singing they didn't notice his disguise. Then the bear quickly found a huge empty barrel, and filled it with the bananas.

"Look!" cried Baloo, peering into the barrel. "Lunch!" The monkeys ran over and jumped right into the barrel! They greedily ate the feast, tossing peels out as they made their way through the bunch.

Baloo signalled to Mowgli, who came out of hiding. "Come and get me, Shere Khan!" the Man-cub taunted.

Within seconds, the tiger appeared in the clearing, a fierce gleam in his eye. "Hello, Stripes," Baloo greeted him cheerfully. Then the bear picked up the barrel, heaved it, and sent King Louie's troop flying at Shere Khan. The orang-utans landed on the tiger's back, where they frantically jumped up and down, pulling on his tail and ears. Mowgli and Baloo watched as Shere Khan raced back into the jungle, trying to free himself from his shrieking passengers.

"Like I always say," Baloo declared as he grinned at Mowgli, "there's nothing more fun than a barrel of monkeys!"

How to Unpack for a Vacation

One morning, Donald Duck heard a knock at the door. When he opened it, he found his friend Mickey Mouse standing there.

"Today is the day!" exclaimed Mickey.

"Today is *what* day?" asked Donald with a yawn.

"Don't you remember?" said Mickey. "You're driving me, Minnie and Daisy to the beach for a week's vacation." Mickey held up his suitcase. "I packed last night. Aren't you packed too?"

"No," said Donald. "I thought we were leaving next week!"

"No," said Mickey. "We're leaving today. And Minnie and Daisy will be here in an hour."

"Oh, no!" cried Donald.

"Calm down," said Mickey. "You have time to get ready. Just pack your things now."

While Mickey relaxed on the porch in a rocking chair, Donald went back inside.

"What do I pack?" Donald muttered to himself as he raced through his house. "I'll need my toys, of course, in case I get bored." Donald ran to his playroom and placed all his toys in boxes.

"What else should I pack?" Donald asked himself. "Clothes!" He ran to his bedroom and took out every suitcase he owned. Then he emptied all his drawers and filled his suitcases.

Finally, Donald calmed down. "That should do it," he said with a sigh of relief.

Mickey couldn't believe his eyes when Donald began packing up his car. Just then, Minnie Mouse and Daisy Duck arrived. They each had one small suitcase.

Minnie and Daisy took one look at Donald's car and gasped. Boxes and baskets were crammed into the back and front seats. Daisy opened the boot and found it overflowing with Donald's suitcases.

"There's no room left for *our* suitcases!" cried Daisy.

"Forget our *suitcases*!" exclaimed Minnie. "There's no room for us!"

Mickey put his arm around Donald.

"It's okay, Donald," he said. "It's hard packing for a vacation. You have to leave some things behind – even some of your favourite things. But they will all be here when we get back. I guarantee it!"

"And besides," added Daisy, "don't you want to leave room in your car to bring back souvenirs, like seashells and T-shirts and saltwater taffy?"

Donald brightened. "Seashells and T-shirts and saltwater taffy!" he cried excitedly. "Oh, you bet!"

"Good," said Mickey. Then he pointed to Donald's overflowing car. "Now let's all help Donald *unpack* for this vacation!"

THE LITTLE MERMAID

A Working Holiday

Sebastian the crab loved his busy job as court composer to King Triton. He wrote songs, ran rehearsals, consulted with the King – and he even watched out for Ariel to make sure she stayed out of trouble.

One day, King Triton burst into the rehearsal hall and announced, "Sebastian! You need a vacation! I want you to relax and forget about work for a few days. And that's an order."

"Yes, sire," said Sebastian without enthusiasm. Sebastian wasn't very good at relaxing.

After Sebastian had gone, King Triton assembled his daughters and the court musicians. "Sebastian has been my court composer for many years," he announced, "and I've been wanting to honour him with a grand concert. Now that he's away, we can finally prepare a wonderful surprise for him." Triton smiled. "I can't wait to see the look on Sebastian's face when the big night arrives!"

Meanwhile, Sebastian was at the Coral Reef Resort. "Well, here I am at the most beautiful spot in the sea," he said to himself. "But I am bored out of my mind!"

When he couldn't sit still any longer, Sebastian decided that he would sneak back to the palace for a few minutes just to see how everything was going. He wandered into the concert hall, where he found the orchestra and Triton's daughters about to rehearse. "Sebastian!" cried Ariel. "What are you doing here?"

"Oh, nothing," he said. "I forgot my conducting baton. I never go on a vacation without it." He looked at Ariel. "And what are *you* doing here?"

Thinking quickly, Ariel told Sebastian that they were preparing a last-minute concert for her father. That was all Sebastian had to hear! He immediately set to work rehearsing the musicians. He worked harder than he had in weeks. And he loved every minute of it.

After the three days were up, Sebastian made a big show of returning to the palace. "I feel so refreshed!" he announced to the King. "Thank you, sire, that was just what I needed."

"That's grand, Sebastian!" replied the King. "Now follow me."

Triton led Sebastian to the concert hall, where the King gave a glowing speech about the crab's many contributions throughout the years. Then the elaborate programme of music began. The orchestra played beautifully, Ariel and her sisters sang exquisitely, and the King beamed proudly.

"What do you think?" Triton asked.

"It's perfect!" said Sebastian. "I couldn't have done a better job myself!"

The Good Old Summertime

The Seven Dwarfs were on their way back home after a long day at the diamond mine. Each swung a shovel in one hand and a bucket in the other.

As they marched through the forest, Happy enjoyed the sounds of the birds singing and the warmth of the summer sun on his face. "Summer is such a wonderful time of year!" he exclaimed.

"Oh, yeah?" snapped Grumpy. "What's so wonderful about it?"

"Well . . . the days are longer," said Happy.

"The days are hotter," complained Grumpy.

Doc spoke up. "I like the summertime too. It's a very healthy season."

"Healthy?" said Grumpy. "This heat?"

"Look at all the fresh vegetables and fruit you can eat all summer long," said Doc.

"Like what?" asked Grumpy.

"Like peaches," Sleepy said with a yawn. "I like them with cream before I go to bed."

"And just look at the melons on those vines," said Doc. "They're as big as Dopey's head!"

Dopey grinned and nodded.

Grumpy rolled his eyes and said, "Dopey's a melon head, all right!"

"Don't be such a grump!" scolded Doc.

"Yes, cheer up! Summer's a great season," Happy said with a grin.

"It's too hot, I say," Grumpy insisted. "And all those blooming plants make Sneezy sneeze even more!"

"Yes," said Sneezy. "Sorry, but . . . *Ah-choo!* I think Grumpy's right."

"No, he's not," said Happy. "Summer's the very best time of year."

"It's too hot, I say!" repeated Grumpy.

By this time, the Seven Dwarfs had reached a small bridge running over a brook.

"Well, if it's too hot for you, Grumpy, then I have a special warm-weather remedy," said Doc, stopping in the middle of the bridge.

"Yeah?" snapped Grumpy. "What is it?"

Doc motioned for the other Dwarfs to gather around him. They blocked Doc from Grumpy's view as he leaned over and filled his bucket with cool water from the stream.

"Well?" said Grumpy. "Are you going to give me your special remedy?"

"Of course," said Doc.

With a big "Heave-ho!" Doc dumped his bucket of water over Grumpy's head.

Splash!

"That should cool you off," said Happy.

Grumpy sputtered with surprise. But he had to admit, the soaking actually did cool him off!

THE PRINCESS AND THE FROG

The Frog Hunt

Deep in the bayou, the frogs Tiana and Naveen faced countless dangers. But of all the predators, the most frightening were the hunters – even the alligators were wary of them. Fortunately, Tiana and Naveen could count on the help of the friends they met along the way...

"My name's Raymond, but everybody calls me Ray!" announced the large firefly that had just joined them. Tiana and Naveen had got their tongues tangled after becoming hungry. The firefly helped Tiana and Naveen untangle themselves.

Tiana explained to Ray that Louis was guiding them to the home of Mama Odie, so that she could change them back into humans.

"Mama Odie?! Well you folks is goin' in the wrong direction! First rule of the bayou: don't take directions from a 'gator!"

And Ray whistled into the night, summoning his family of fireflies to the rescue. Shortly afterwards, Naveen, Tiana and Louis were following a long string of firefly lights across the bayou. In the romantic glow of the evening, Ray told Tiana about his true love, Evangeline. "She is the prettiest firefly that ever did glow."

"Just do not settle down too quickly," Naveen advised.

Tiana rolled her eyes and took to land. She blazed a trail through the bushes while Louis followed her, trying to escape the pricker bushes. Suddenly – *WHOOSH!* – a net swooped down and scooped up Naveen. Three frog hunters – Reggie, Darnell and Two Fingers – were out to capture the two frogs!

"Oh no!" panicked Ray. "Have courage, my fellow, a bug's got to do what a bug's got to do!" he cried as he shot straight up Reggie's nose.

Quickly, Naveen escaped while Ray was blown out of the hunter's nose. Meanwhile, Darnell and Two Fingers had captured Tiana! Naveen leapt in to save her.

While Naveen diverted the men's attention, Tiana jumped out of her cage. Naveen and Tiana jumped all over the place, and try as they might, the hunters only succeeded in knocking each other out.

"Those aren't like any frogs I've seen! They're smart!" Reggie marvelled.

"And we talk too!" called Tiana to him.

The hunters opened their eyes wide, speechless. Then they screamed in terror and ran off!

Now that's a frog hunt that they won't easily forget – probably the last hunt of their lives!

Bambi

Flower's Power

It was a warm summer afternoon in the forest, and a shy little skunk named Flower was playing a game of hide-and-seek, searching for his friend Thumper. He had been looking for quite a while.

"Come out, come out, wherever you are!" Flower called. "I give up."

"*Surprise!*" shouted Thumper, bursting out of a thicket. "Here I am! *Ugh!*" Thumper wrinkled his nose. "What's that *smell?*"

Flower blushed bright pink. "Sorry," he said miserably. "I sprayed. It happens when I get scared."

"*Whew!*" Thumper waved his paw in front of his face. "You should warn us before you let out that kind of stink!"

"Well *you* should warn *me* before you jump out like that," Flower said. "Anyway, it'll go away . . . in a day or two."

But a day or two was too long for his friends to wait. The smell was just too strong!

"Sorry," Bambi told Flower. "I, uh, think my mother's calling me," he said.

"Me, uh, too," Faline gasped. "See you later, Flower . . . in a day or two."

"Or three!" Thumper added, giggling.

And the next thing he knew, Flower was all alone.

Poor Flower. If only he weren't a skunk, he thought. If only he didn't *stink* so much whenever he got scared. What was the point? It only drove his friends away. But now it seemed he couldn't even play hide-and-seek! No matter what his mother and father said, as far as Flower was concerned, being a skunk stunk!

And that's why Flower wouldn't have been very surprised if, two days later, his friends had still stayed away. But, to his bashful pleasure, there, bright and early, were Bambi and Faline – with Thumper hopping close behind.

"Want to play?" Bambi asked Flower cheerfully.

"Anything but hide-and-seek!" said Flower.

"How about tag?" said Thumper. "Ready or not, you're It!"

But before the game could begin, a soft *crunch, crunch* of leaves made the friends turn.

"Wha-wha-what's that?" Bambi said, staring straight into a hungry-looking, red face.

"That's a fox!" said Thumper.

"A fox?" shrieked Flower. "Oh no!" He span around and lifted his tail and buried his head in fear . . . and the next thing the friends knew, the hungry fox was running away, whimpering and rubbing his nose.

"Sorry," Flower sighed, blushing.

"Don't be!" said Bambi and Thumper.

And do you know what? Flower wasn't!

Ask Nicely

"Steady, Samson," Prince Phillip said absentmindedly, tightening the horse's reins. "No need to hurry. We'll get there soon enough – and I need some time to think."

Phillip had a lot to think about. He was riding through the forest towards the castle of King Stefan and Queen Leah. Phillip's father, King Hubert, would be meeting him there. So would the girl Phillip was destined to marry.

Princess Aurora. Phillip had heard her name since her birth exactly 16 years earlier. Their parents had long planned their marriage. But Aurora had been cursed by the evil Maleficent at birth, and had been forced to go into hiding until her 16th birthday, when the curse would end.

That meant Phillip had never set eyes on his bride-to-be, nor spoken with her. He had always wondered what she might be like.

"I hope I like her," he murmured to his horse. Then another thought occurred to him. "I hope she likes me!" he added. "I'd better make sure I impress her." But how? he wondered

"I know!" he exclaimed. "I'll make a dramatic entrance. We'll gallop in and slide to a stop right in front of her. That will impress her for sure!" He whistled and gave Samson a little kick. "Come on, Samson! We've got to practise."

The startled horse snorted and gave Phillip a dirty look. He planted his hooves and stood stock-still.

Phillip frowned impatiently. "Come on!" he urged his horse. "Go, Samson!"

But Samson refused to budge.

"It's like you don't even *want* to help me," he muttered. Suddenly, Phillip blinked. "Wait a minute," he said. "Why should you want to help me when all I do is yell at you?" He patted the horse's shoulder. "Sorry, old boy."

He reached into his pocket for a carrot. He fed it to the horse, still patting him.

Samson finished the carrot and snorted. Suddenly, he galloped forward, then leaped up and kicked out his heels. Phillip hung on tightly, gasping with surprise as the horse skidded to a halt.

Phillip laughed. "Wow!" he exclaimed. "Thanks, Samson. That was perfect – I guess all I had to do was ask you nicely! Now if we can just repeat that for the princess–"

Suddenly, he stopped short. He heard the faint sound of beautiful singing. He listened carefully. Who would be out in the forest singing like that?

"Come on, Samson," he said. "Let's go see – if you don't mind, of course!"

Happy Campers

It was a warm, sunny day on Ant Island – the perfect day for Princess Dot and her fellow Blueberries to go on a camping expedition! Flik volunteered to be their leader.

"Single file! Forward march!" called Flik. "Follow me, Blueberries. Watch out for those twigs!"

"This is gonna be so much fun, Flik!" said Dot, marching behind him. "Pitching our tents! Making a campfire! Telling ghost stories all night long!"

"Well, we've got to get to our campsite first," Flik reminded her. "The perfect campsite for the perfect campout!"

"Where's that?" asked Dot.

"I'm not exactly sure," said Flik. "But don't worry! I'll know it when I see it."

So on they hiked, until they came to some soft moss beside a quiet stream.

"Is this it?" asked Daisy excitedly.

Flik shook his head. "Definitely not," he said. "Too out in the open."

"We're getting tired," Dot said.

"Chins up, Blueberries," said Flik. "We'll find the perfect campsite soon. I'll bet it's just across that stream."

Flik guided the Blueberries onto a broad leaf. Together they rowed across the water. But the other side of the stream was not quite perfect enough for Flik either.

"No worries," Flik said. "See that hill over there? I'll betcha the perfect campsite is just beyond it."

The Blueberries followed him up the grassy hill and down the other side.

"We made it!" the Blueberries cheered.

"Not so fast," said Flik, frowning. "The ground is too damp here. We'll have to keep looking."

"But Flik! We can't go any further," they complained.

"Nonsense!" said Flik, tightening his backpack. "You're Blueberries! C'mon!"

And so, with the Blueberries dragging their poor, tired feet, Flik hiked on. He looked behind a big rock, but it was too dusty. He looked near a hollow log, but a troop of boy beetles was already there. He even looked inside an old, discarded shoe, which might have actually worked . . . if it hadn't been so stinky.

Just when the Blueberries thought they couldn't walk another inch, Flik suddenly froze in his tracks. "The perfect campsite! We've found it! Let's pitch those tents, Blueberries, and get a fire started!"

But instead of cheers, Flik heard only silence. He turned around and saw that those poor Blueberries, still wearing their backpacks, were already fast asleep!

The Power of Dreams

Rapunzel had finally managed to leave the tower she'd been kept in her whole life, and now Flynn had taken her to a pub full of horrible ruffians!

Mother Gothel was right, she thought, the world was too dangerous. Rapunzel didn't realise that Mother Gothel had just been trying to scare Rapunzel into never leaving the tower.

Rapunzel had made a deal with a thief named Flynn – she had hidden his satchel and demanded he take her to see the floating lights she saw from her tower every year on her birthday.

She was just about to give up on her dream when a huge thug slammed the door shut, blocking their way out. He was holding a WANTED sign. Rapunzel was confused but Flynn knew their was a reward for anyone who could find him. He swallowed nervously – his plan had backfired.

"Run and tell the guard!" the thug told his sidekick. "This reward will come in handy: I could do with some money right now!"

"Me too," the landlord shouted, grabbing hold of Flynn.

"Calm down, my friends. I'm sure we can come to some sort of arrangement!" said Flynn.

Rapunzel, terrified, stammered, "Um, excuse me? Ruffians?" Rapunzel broke in. "Is it possible to get my guide back? I need him to show me the way…"

The thugs just ignored her and continued to pummel Flynn. Suddenly, Rapunzel forgot she was afraid.

CLANG! Rapunzel stood fiercely atop the bar and hit her pan against a giant pot.

"Put him down!" she shouted. The thugs stopped.

Rapunzel explained that she needed Flynn to take her to see the lights.

"Have some humanity. Haven't you ever had a dream?!" she asked

Everyone was stunned. Who would have believed that such a delicate young girl could get so angry? What's more, she was right!

"I've always wanted to play the piano," one good-for-nothing admitted, moved to tears. "I know I may not seem like it, but I'm really a sensitive soul!"

"Me too!" another thug continued. "I've always dreamed of falling in love…"

And little by little, everyone in the pub began to describe their hidden hopes and dreams. Flynn couldn't believe his ears, or eyes! The girl had managed to win over a room full of the meanest, toughest-looking men in the kingdom!

MULAN
Invincible Mushu

After helping Mulan defeat the Huns and restore the Fa family honour, Mushu had been given back his old job as family guardian. He was supposed to help guard the temple of the Fa ancestors.

One day Mushu was sunning himself on the temple roof, when a big lizard waddled up. He seemed to be staring right at Mushu.

Mushu frowned. "Who you lookin' at?" he said to the lizard.

The lizard flicked out his tongue.

Mushu was offended. "Oh, yeah?" he said. "Stick your tongue out at me, will you? Well, get a load of this!" Puffing out his tiny chest, Mushu spat out a miniature burst of fire, no bigger than the flame of a match.

The lizard just blinked.

"Not good enough for you, eh?" Mushu said. "All right, tough guy. Try this on for size!" Mushu cleared his throat dramatically. Taking a deep breath, he opened his mouth and spat a bigger flame at the lizard.

The lizard crouched, lowering his chest to the ground. Then he straightened his legs. Then he crouched again. The lizard was doing push-ups, as lizards will do.

"Oh-ho!" Mushu shouted. "Think you're tough, do you? Well, Scales for Brains, I didn't spend time in the Imperial Army for nothing!" And with that Mushu crouched down on all four legs and began to do push-ups, too.

". . . Ninety-eight . . . ninety-nine . . . one hundred!" Mushu counted, panting. He leaped to his feet and began to run circles around the lizard. "Just ask anyone," he told the lizard. "I'm the dragon that defeated hundreds of Huns. I could eat you for lunch, small fry."

The lizard just sat there.

Huffing and puffing, Mushu stopped in front of the motionless reptile. He began to box at the air, bouncing around on his hind feet. "Think you can take me on, do you? Well, watch out. I'm a three-time champion in the featherweight division. 'Float like a dragonfly, sting like a bee,' that's me all ri – "

Suddenly – *snap!* – the lizard snatched up a fly that landed on Mushu's nose.

"Ahhhh!" Mushu screamed. He was so startled, he leaped backwards . . . and fell off the roof. He landed on the ground in a puff of dust.

"Ha-ha-ha-ha-ha-ha-ha!" The air filled with the sound of roaring laughter. The ancestors had seen everything.

"Cheer up, Mushu," one ancestor said. "It looks like you have a new friend."

Sure enough, the lizard had followed Mushu down from the roof. "Well," Mushu said, "I always did want a pet."

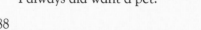

Market Day

"What's wrong, Abu?" asked Aladdin. The normally lively little monkey hadn't been himself lately. Abu sat at the window gazing longingly towards the village. "You're right," Aladdin said. "A trip to the marketplace is exactly what we need. Let's go right now!"

The pair had a wonderful afternoon visiting old friends. Abu played with Salim the goat, joked with Kahlil the ox and teased Gamal the camel. He and Aladdin stopped at each vendor's stall to say "hello." Aladdin saw how happy Abu was in the hustle and bustle of the marketplace.

"You know, Abu," said Aladdin that night, "you can invite your friends from the marketplace to the palace anytime you'd like." The monkey jumped up and down, hugging Aladdin and knocking off his hat. "Okay! Okay! You're welcome!" Aladdin laughed.

The next day, Abu disappeared first thing in the morning. When he returned, Salim and Kahlil were with him. "Welcome," said Jasmine. "Please make yourselves at home." But they already had. The goat was chewing on the curtains, and the ox was wandering in the garden, eating the tops off the flowers.

"We can always buy new curtains or plant new flowers. The important thing is that Abu is happy again," Aladdin said to Jasmine, who sighed and agreed reluctantly.

The following day, Gamal and several other camels arrived. Jasmine was not pleased when they spat on the new carpet. "Think of Abu," Aladdin told her.

The day after that, the fruit seller rolled through the palace with his cart. Another vendor came with a pile of smelly fish. Next came the lady who sold dates, and the man who sold pottery.

"Isn't it wonderful that Abu has so many friends?" said Aladdin.

"It is," Jasmine agreed. "But have you noticed that we only see his friends coming and not going?"

"Now that you mention it, I have," Aladdin replied. "Let's find out what's going on." The couple followed Abu as he led his guests out to the garden. What they saw made them gasp. There was the entire marketplace! Aladdin burst out laughing. "I guess the next time Abu is feeling homesick, he doesn't need to go any farther than his own backyard!"

Jasmine sighed. "Aladdin, these people can't stay here." But, when Jasmine saw the sad look on Aladdin's face, she added, ". . . Well, maybe they could come back next month."

And so began a new tradition – "Palace Market Day," which happened once a month. And *that* made little Abu *very* happy!

Disney Princess
Cinderella

The Prince's Dream

The Grand Duke was a little worried about Prince Charming. At tonight's ball, the Prince had finally met the girl of his dreams. But, at the stroke of midnight, she'd run away. And now it was impossible to reason with the Prince.

"You must bring her back!" the Prince told the Grand Duke.

"Of course, Your Highness!" said the Duke. "I've already sent the royal guards after her carriage . . . as I told you four times already!" he added under his breath.

But the guards returned without her. The captain bowed to the Prince. "I'm very sorry, Your Highness," he said. "I don't understand what happened. I could see her carriage ahead of us – and an extraordinary carriage it was. It actually seemed to shimmer."

The Prince remembered how the girl's gown and tiara had shimmered too. The Duke sighed as he watched Prince Charming's eyes glaze over. The Prince would clearly be distracted until they found this mystery girl.

"Then what happened?" asked the Duke.

"We turned a corner and the carriage simply . . . vanished," said the captain.

"I don't even know her name," said the Prince, in a daze.

"Well, for now, you must try to focus on your duties as the host of the ball," the Duke advised the Prince. "The ballroom is still filled with eligible maidens."

The Prince shook his head. "There is no other maiden. Not for me. If only she had left some clue!" he cried despairingly. "Some token to remember her by!"

The Duke rolled his eyes. "Your Highness might try investigating your right jacket pocket, then."

Startled, the Prince stuck his hand into his pocket and withdrew a glass slipper! He had been so distracted by his new-found love for the mystery girl that he had completely forgotten about the tiny glass slipper she had left behind on the stairs. He looked at the slipper, then at the Duke.

"I . . . I . . ." the Prince stammered.

"I suggest you allow me to see to the arrangements," the Duke said kindly, taking the slipper. "We'll find your mystery lass, Your Highness."

The Prince nodded gratefully, then turned towards the window and gazed out into the night. Somewhere out there, his princess was waiting for him. "Dreams can come true," he murmured. "After tonight, I'm sure of it."

Little did he know that on the other side of his kingdom, Cinderella was standing by her own window, holding the other glass slipper – and saying the very same thing!

How to Win at Hide-and-seek

"Belle," Mrs Potts called. "Oh, Belle!" Belle was sitting in the library, surrounded by a pile of books.

"There you are!" Mrs Potts cried.

"Hi, Belle," Mrs Potts's son, Chip, chimed in.

"Hello to both of you. Were you looking for me?" Belle asked Mrs Potts.

"As a matter of fact, I was," Mrs Potts told her. "I was just stopping by to enquire as to whether or not you would like some tea."

"Thank you," Belle said. "I would love some."

Mrs Potts poured Belle a piping hot cup of tea. Belle drank it, and thanked her.

"You're welcome, Belle," Mrs Potts said. "Come along, now," she called to Chip.

"But, Mama," Chip whined. "I want to stay here with Belle!"

"Belle is busy," Mrs Potts explained. "You'll just get in the way."

"That's all right," Belle said. "I was just about done for today. I'd love to spend some time with Chip."

"All right," Mrs Potts said. "But Chip, you come right back to the kitchen when Belle tells you to."

"Okay, I promise," Chip said.

"So," Belle began when Mrs Potts had left, "how about a game of hide-and-seek?"

"How do you play that?" Chip asked.

"It's simple," Belle said. "One person hides, and the other person tries to find him."

"I can do that!" Chip said.

"Of course you can," Belle told him. "So, do you want to be the hider or the seeker?"

"I want to be the hider," Chip told her.

"Okay," Belle said. "I'll close my eyes and count to ten. One, two, three . . . ."

Chip took off, darting behind the velvet curtains just as Belle called, "Ten! Ready or not, here I come! Hmm, now where could he be?" she wondered aloud.

Belle looked under the table. "He isn't there," she said. Then she looked in the corner. "He isn't there, either," Belle continued. She looked high. She looked low. But she just couldn't seem to find Chip anywhere. "I give up," Belle said. "Come out, come out, wherever you are!"

Chip silently giggled from behind the curtain, but he was careful not to make too much noise. He was having fun!

"It seems that Chip doesn't want to come out from his hiding place," Belle said. "I guess that means I'll have to eat a slice of Mrs Potts's chocolate cake all by myself."

And, upon hearing that, Chip jumped out from his hiding place and called after Belle, "Here I am! Wait for me!"

A Rainy Night Out

"Yip!" Scamp barked at the squirrel nibbling on an acorn in the grass. His brother and sisters were taking a nap under the big oak tree, and there was nobody else around to have fun with.

"Yip!" Scamp barked again, and the squirrel darted across the lawn. Scamp gave chase. The squirrel zipped up a lamppost and leaped onto a nearby tree branch. With a whimper, Scamp sat down and thumped his tail on the sidewalk. That was the problem with squirrels. They always got away too easily.

Disappointed, Scamp trotted along the pavement, stopping when he got to an open space. The grass here was tall, and butterflies flitted from wildflower to wildflower.

"Yip! Yip!" Scamp raced through the tall grass. He chased the butterflies to the end of the open space and back again.

It was getting dark. Scamp decided it was time to head home. He hadn't caught a single butterfly, but he'd had fun trying. He couldn't wait to get home and tell his brother and sisters about the new game he'd invented. They'd be so impressed!

Scamp trotted up to the front porch and tried to get through the doggie door. *Thunk!* His nose hit the wood, but it didn't move. The door was locked!

"Yip! Yip! I'm home!" he barked. "Let me in!"

Scamp sat there for several minutes, barking. Nobody came to the door. Suddenly – *boom!* – thunder echoed overhead. Lightning flashed and rain began to fall.

Scamp bolted over to the big oak tree, sat down and covered his eyes with his paws. Thunderstorms were scary!

"I'm not going to cry," he told himself as his eyes started to mist over. He shivered in the dark. He'd probably catch a cold by morning!

Scamp let out a little whimper and moved even closer to the tree trunk. He buried his wet nose in his wet paws and closed his eyes.

Scamp was just falling asleep when a sound made him start. Somebody was coming up the drive!

By the time Jim Dear and Darling were out of the taxi, Scamp was dashing across the lawn as fast as he could go. He bolted through the door just as it opened.

"Scamp, you're soaking wet!" Darling declared as the puppy found his brother and sisters napping in front of the fire. And, as he lay down among them, Jim Dear came over with a warm towel to dry him off.

Home, sweet home, Scamp thought happily, as he drifted off to sleep.

In Hot Water

Ariel could hardly believe that her plan was going so well. She had convinced Ursula, the sea witch, to change her from a mermaid into a human. Even though Ariel had paid for the transformation with her voice, she had already found her beloved Prince Eric. The only problem was that he didn't recognize her. And Ariel couldn't speak to explain who she was.

But Ariel wasn't worried. She knew he would fall in love with her, voice or no voice. And then they would be happy together forever.

"Come along, my dear," a female servant said, leading Ariel into a spacious room with sky-blue walls.

Ariel almost tripped on the edge of a rug, but caught herself just in time. She still wasn't used to her brand-new legs.

She put one hand into the pocket of her sailcloth dress to make sure that Sebastian was still inside. She was glad he was with her – having him nearby made her feel more at home.

"All right, let's get you cleaned up first," the woman said. "It'll be time for dinner soon."

As the woman bustled about, Ariel had a chance to look around the room. There were large windows along one wall and an ornate lantern hanging from the ceiling. There was also a large, shell-shaped bath filled with water.

Ariel watched curiously as the servant threw some white powder into the bath. Suddenly, the water fizzed with a huge pile of bubbles! Ariel gasped, delighted, as bubbles floated up out of the water towards the ceiling. She raced forward and leaped right into the bath, splashing water and bubbles everywhere.

Forgetting that she couldn't breathe under water any more, she dived beneath the bubbles. She came up coughing and wiped the water out of her eyes.

"Ahhhh!" Sebastian sputtered, swimming out of her pocket. He spat out a mouthful of bubbles. "What do these humans do to nice, clean water?"

The servant looked alarmed. "Oh, my! Did I see something move in there?"

Ariel shook her head, quickly shoving Sebastian back into her pocket.

"Well," the servant said. "You can't take a bath in that dress. Let's hang it up to dry."

Ariel was a little worried about Sebastian, but she did as the woman said. Soon the sailcloth dress was hanging on a towel rack.

Oh, well, Ariel thought. I'm sure Sebastian can take care of himself. Knowing him, he'll probably go and find the kitchen. I wonder what the cook is like? I hope he doesn't like seafood!

Snow White's Thank-you Present

"I don't know how I can ever thank them," Snow White said to her new husband, the Prince. The two of them were on their way to visit the Dwarfs and give them a special present – a meal fit for seven kings!

Snow White looked at the dishes and hampers filled with delicious food. "It just doesn't seem like enough," she said with a sigh. "They saved my life!"

"I'm sure seeing you happy is thanks enough," the Prince said, putting his arm around Snow White. "They don't want riches, and they seem quite happy living the way they do."

Snow White had to agree and, as the cosy Dwarf cottage came into view, she perked up. She could not wait to see her little friends! "Yoo-hoo!" she called as she dashed from the coach. "Sneezy? Happy? Bashful?"

Snow White knocked on the door, but there was no answer. "They must not be home yet," she said to the Prince. "We'll have just enough time to get everything ready."

Snow White went inside and set the table and tidied the house, humming while she worked. She was so excited to see her friends that she couldn't help checking the windows for a sign of them every few minutes. As the sun set, the princess began to worry.

"They're awfully late!" she said. The Prince agreed. It was getting dark.

"Perhaps we should go and find them." The Prince strode outside and unhitched one of the horses from the coach. Together the Prince and Princess set off to find the Dwarfs.

At last they reached the mine. Holding up lanterns, they saw at once what the trouble was. A tree had fallen over the mine entrance. The Dwarfs were trapped!

"Snow White, is that you?" Doc called through a small opening.

"Are you all right?" Snow White asked.

"We're fine, dear. Just fine," Doc told her.

"No, we're not," Grumpy said, rather grumpily. "We're stuck!"

"Don't worry," the Prince said. "We'll have you out in no time."

Hitching his horse to the big tree, the Prince pulled it away from the mine so the Dwarfs could get out.

Snow White embraced each dusty Dwarf as he emerged. She even hugged Dopey twice! "Now let's get you home," she said.

Back at home, the Dwarfs were thrilled to see the fine meal laid out on their table.

"How can we ever thank you?" Doc said, wringing his hat. "You saved our lives."

"Don't be silly." Snow White blushed. "Seeing you happy is thanks enough."

MICKEY MOUSE
Island Adventure

Mickey, Minnie, Donald and Daisy were on their way to their seaside holiday. As soon as they arrived, they put on their bathing costumes and ran down to the beach.

They came to a lovely cove. "I'm going to relax right here!" Minnie declared as she spread out her blanket.

"Me, too," said Daisy, opening her umbrella.

"Those waves are just perfect for surfing," said Donald.

"You boys run along," Minnie said.

"We're happy right here," said Daisy.

Mickey and Donald surfed and swam until the sun went down.

The next day was sunny too. On their way to the beach, Mickey and Donald spied a boat for rent. "Let's go fishing!" cried Donald.

But Daisy and Minnie shook their heads. "We want to relax," they said.

So Donald and Mickey went fishing alone.

On the third day, Mickey and Donald wanted to go for a long swim.

"No, thanks," said Minnie. "I want to take it easy."

"Me, too," said Daisy. "We're going to the cove to relax."

The boys went off to swim. Daisy and Minnie headed for the cove.

While she and Minnie were lounging under the palm trees, Daisy spied a bottle floating in the water. There was a map rolled up inside. She waded into the water to get it.

"It's a treasure map!" she exclaimed.

"The treasure is on an island!" cried Minnie, pointing to a big X on the map.

Minnie and Daisy decided to follow the map. They went up one hill and then down another. They crossed a stream and reached a dock with a boat tied to it.

"That's the island," said Daisy, pointing out to sea. They hopped into the boat and started to row.

They rowed and they rowed until they reached the island. Minnie and Daisy were very tired and very hungry.

"Look!" Minnie cried. "I see a fire!"

"Pirates!" exclaimed Daisy.

But there were no pirates. Just Donald and Mickey, waiting for Daisy and Minnie to arrive. A campfire was roaring, and fish sizzled on the grill.

"Looks like they found our map!" Donald exclaimed.

"*Your* map?" cried Minnie.

"It was the only way to get you two to have an adventure with us!" Mickey replied.

"Now, sit down by the fire," said Donald. "Lunch is served!"

A Big Buzz

Flit let out a big sigh. Pocahontas was spending so much time with John Smith that she never had time for him any more! He buzzed along behind the pair, following them everywhere. But Pocahontas was too distracted to play with him.

Buzzz, buzzz. Flit was grateful that his speedy wings made a noise when he flew. At least Pocahontas could hear him – even if she pretended she didn't.

"Look at this, John," Pocahontas said, crouching down in the path. "Fresh deer tracks."

John leaned over to inspect the prints left behind in the mud. Flit buzzed down too. There were two sizes of prints – large and small.

"A mother and her fawn," John said. He leaned forward for a closer look, accidentally pushing Flit out of the way.

"They're probably looking for food before the snows come, so they'll be fat enough to make it through the winter," Pocahontas explained.

John got to his feet. "I hope they find it."

Pocahontas smiled up at him, then stood too. Flit buzzed up a second later, just as John lifted his hand to push a lock of hair off Pocahontas's face. Once again, Flit was shoved away.

Buzzzzzzzz! Buzzzzzzzzz! That was it! Flit had had enough of being ignored!

Flit flapped his buzzing wings faster and faster. Then he began to fly in a circle around John and Pocahontas. *Zzzzzzzzzzz!*

"Do you think he's trying to tell us something?" John asked, leaning towards Pocahontas.

"I don't know," she replied. She leaned in closer to John too. Soon they were nose to nose, looking into each other's eyes.

Flit gave up. He stopped buzzing and flopped to the ground, landing in one of the deer tracks. He was exhausted.

"What was that about, Flit?" Pocahontas asked, scooping him up with a laugh.

Flit was still panting. He wasn't even sure he could fly any more. He gazed up at Pocahontas, his eyes wide and his shoulders slumped.

"That is one exhausted hummingbird," John said.

Pocahontas stroked Flit's blue feathers, then leaned forward and kissed him on the end of his long, pointed beak. Then she set him gently on her shoulder.

"You just ride here for a while," she told him. Flit grinned happily as John and Pocahontas continued on through the forest. Mission accomplished!

A Bear-y Tale

It was time for Mowgli, Bagheera and Baloo to go to bed.

"Good night, Man-cub," purred Bagheera.

"But I'm not sleepy yet," protested Mowgli. "I need a bedtime story."

"Bedtime story?" said Bagheera. "At this hour?"

Mowgli turned to the big bear. "Please, Baloo?"

"A bedtime story, huh ..." said Baloo. "Now, how do those things begin?"

"Once upon a time ..." purred Bagheera.

"Oh, right . . . Once upon a time . . . in a house not far from this very jungle, there lived a clan of men," Baloo began.

"Real men?" asked Mowgli.

"Yep," said Baloo. "A father and a mother, and a little cub, just like you. Well, now, this clan, they cooked their food, and one day, don't you know, they made a mighty tasty stew . . . only thing was, when they sat down to eat, it was just too hot. So the mother got an idea. They'd go for a walk in the jungle and, by the time they got back, their stew would be nice and cool. But do you know what happened next?"

"No," Mowgli said.

"Well, that family had barely been gone a minute, when an old bear came wandering up, and stuck his nose into the Man-house."

"He did?" gasped Mowgli.

"Well, now, can you blame him? That stew just smelled so awfully good. And the next thing you know, he was tastin' it – startin' with the biggest bowl, but that was still too hot. So next he tried the middle bowl, but that was too cold. So – he tried the littlest bowl, and, don't you know, it was just right! That old bear didn't mean to, but he ate the whole thing right up!"

"What happened next?" said Mowgli.

"Oh, well, after that, this bear, he started to get tired. Real tired. And, don't you know, Little Britches, that right there in that house, looking so soft and comfortable, were three cushy-lookin' pads . . . I think men call them 'beds.' Anyway, that bear, he had to try them, too. Naturally, he laid down on the biggest one first. But it was too hard. So he tried the middle one, but that was much, much too soft. So, he tried the littlest one, and, son, let me tell you, that thing was so comfortable, he fell asleep right then and there! And he would have slept clear through the next full moon . . . if only that family hadn't returned and . . ."

"And what?" Mowgli asked breathlessly.

"And startled that bear so much, he ran back into the jungle . . . full belly and all."

Mowgli smiled and tried to cover a big yawn. "Is that a true story, Baloo?"

The bear grinned. "Would I ever tell you a tall tale, Little Britches?"

Nani and David's Stitched-up Date

Lilo sat at the kitchen table, a frown on her face. "It's not fair that we have to spend the night at old lady Kingsley's house just because Nani and David want to go to a movie," she said.

Stitch nodded.

"How is she going to watch us, anyway, when she can barely see?" Lilo asked. "And," she continued, "do you know what movie Nani and David went to see? *Invasion of the Bug-Eyed Aliens, Part VI: The Sliming* – without us!"

Stitch made a noise of outraged agreement. Lilo stood and said, "Come on, Stitch. Let's go see the movie ourselves."

Lilo and Stitch sneaked past the snoring Mrs Kingsley. Lilo opened and shut the front door as loudly as she could. Then, doing her best impression of Nani, she shouted, "We're back, Mrs Kingsley! Thanks!"

Mrs Kingsley woke up, tottered to the door and peered blindly at Lilo. "Is that you, Nani? Well, I hope you had a lovely time." And with that, the two made a break for the cinema. But, once they got there, they had two problems – money and . . .

"Sorry, kid, no dogs allowed in the cinema," the ticket taker said.

Lilo had to think quickly. "He isn't a dog. He's my teddy bear."

"He sure doesn't *look* like a stuffed animal," the ticket taker said.

"They make them very lifelike these days," Lilo fibbed. "Now, can we go inside? My mother is looking for us and, if we don't find her soon, I think I may start to cry."

"Okay, okay," the ticket taker said.

By the time the two had got into the cinema, the bug-eyed aliens had begun the 'sliming,' and everyone in the cinema was screaming. Lilo and Stitch immediately joined in – perhaps a little too enthusiastically, since Nani and David noticed them right away.

"Excuse me, excuse me," Nani said as she made her way out of her row and down the aisle, cola spilling and popcorn flying.

Nani grabbed hold of Lilo's arm and dragged her out of the cinema. David and Stitch were right behind them.

"I'm so angry with you I'm going to . . . I'm going to–" Nani stuttered.

"–take you out for ice cream," David finished her sentence.

"Out for ice cream?" Nani said.

"It's a beautiful night, and I can't think of anything more wonderful than two sisters having ice cream together." David turned to Lilo and Stitch. "Don't you think?"

The Gift Horse

"I can hardly wait to see her!" Prince Phillip told his horse, Samson. He had just met the woman of his dreams singing in the forest. And she had invited him to her cottage that very evening.

Suddenly, the Prince pulled his horse's reins up short. Samson jerked to a stop and chuffed angrily.

"Sorry, boy," said the Prince. "But I just realized that I should bring her a gift tonight – something to show her how much I love her. Let's go to the village."

Samson shook his mane and refused to move a hoof. Shopping wasn't his idea of fun. He was tired and wanted to go back to the castle for some oats!

"C'mon, boy," pleaded the Prince. "I'll give you some nice crisp apples."

Apples! Samson's eyes widened. Suddenly, he wasn't so tired any more! With a bright whinny, he kicked up his hooves and took off.

When they reached the village square, the Prince scratched his head in thought. There were so many shops.

"What sort of gift do you think she will like?" he asked.

As a horse, Samson didn't care all that much. Yet he did his best to answer.

"Red roses?" asked the Prince, passing a flower shop.

Samson shook his head.

"Yes, you're right," said the Prince. "She lives in the forest. She must see flowers every day."

They passed a dress shop and the prince peered in at the window.

"How about a new dress?" he asked Samson.

Samson shook his mane in irritation.

"No, huh?" said the Prince. "Girls like to choose their own dresses, don't they?"

They passed more shops: a bakery, a hat shop and a blacksmith's.

Samson sighed. If he didn't help the Prince find a gift soon, they could be here all day! With a whinny, Samson took off down the street.

The Prince yelped in surprise. By the time he'd taken back control of the reins, Samson had stopped in front of a jewellery shop.

"Samson, you're a genius!" the Prince cried at the sight of the gems glittering in the window. "That sapphire ring sparkles as beautifully as her blue eyes."

The Prince bought the ring, slipped it in his pocket, then mounted Samson again.

"To the castle!" said the Prince. "I've got to tell my father I've found the girl of my dreams."

Samson whinnied and took off at a gallop. He didn't know what the King would say to the Prince, but one thing he was sure of – he had certainly earned those apples!

Pinocchio
Imagine That!

The carnival was in town. Pinocchio grabbed his friend Jiminy Cricket and off they went. Pinocchio was amazed at the marvellous sights. There were jugglers to see and games to play. He even saw an elephant doing tricks!

"That elephant is amazing!" Pinocchio cried.

"I suppose," said Jiminy politely.

Next they came to a lion's cage. The big cat opened his mouth and roared.

"Look at those teeth!" Pinocchio marvelled.

Jiminy Cricket nodded. "They're pretty big, it's true."

Then they saw a giraffe.

"What a long neck!" Pinocchio exclaimed.

"Giraffes are all right, I guess," said Jiminy with a shrug. Pinocchio was confused.

"If you don't like elephants, lions or giraffes, what kind of carnival animals do you like?" Pinocchio asked.

"Fleas," said Jiminy.

"Fleas?" Pinocchio said, even more confused.

"Come on! I'll show you," said Jiminy.

Jiminy led Pinocchio to a tent with a sign that read FLEA CIRCUS.

Inside Pinocchio saw a tiny merry-go-round and little swings. There were small animal cages and a little trapeze. There was even a tiny Big Top with three miniature rings. But no matter how hard he looked, Pinocchio could not see any fleas.

"That's because there *aren't* any fleas," Jiminy explained.

"What's the point, then?" Pinocchio asked.

"The point is imagination," said Jiminy. "Why, you can do anything with your imagination," he continued. "You can even see the fleas at the flea circus."

"But I don't see them," said Pinocchio, confused.

"You have to pretend to see the fleas, and pretty soon you can," said Jiminy. "Like that juggling flea over there. Oops, he dropped his juggling pins."

Pinocchio laughed and joined in the game.

"That flea is going to jump through a ring of fire," Pinocchio said. "I hope he makes it!"

"Now the fleas are doing acrobatics," Jiminy declared.

"They've made a flea pyramid," said Pinocchio. "And the flea on top is standing on his hands."

Finally, it was time to go home.

"What did you think of the Flea Circus?" asked Jiminy Cricket.

"It was the most amazing circus I ever saw, and I didn't really see it at all," Pinocchio replied.

"Yes, indeed. You imagined it," said Jiminy Cricket. "Imagine that!"

To The Rescue

Snow White and her prince spent nearly every day together. But one morning, the Prince told Snow White that he had an errand to take care of. The Prince saddled his trusty steed, Astor, and bid Snow White farewell.

That afternoon, Snow White spotted a cloud of dust on the road. A horse was rapidly approaching. She was excited that the Prince was home early. But imagine Snow White's surprise when she saw that Astor was alone! "Why, where's the Prince?" she wondered out loud. But the horse could not say.

Snow White's tender heart filled with dread. Surely the Prince is in trouble, she thought. She bravely decided she must go and find him. Astor stamped her hoof on the ground and nodded towards her empty saddle.

"Do you want me to get on?" Snow White asked. Again, Astor nodded. Goodness! thought Snow White. Maybe Astor can tell me where the Prince is, after all! The Princess barely had time to sit down before Astor was racing down the road towards the forest!

Astor ran deeper into the woods with Snow White tugging uselessly at the reins. If only she knew that the Prince was safe! Then, suddenly, Snow White spotted a piece of red cloth caught on a sharp thorn. Could it be? It was! A scrap torn from the Prince's very own riding cloak! And that wasn't all. As they continued through the forest, Snow White spotted petals from the rose she had given the Prince. Then she found his hat dangling from a tree!

Snow White gripped the reins with one hand. She clutched the Prince's hat and concentrated on thinking hopeful thoughts.

Finally, they emerged into a sunny clearing, and Astor slowed to a stop. Snow White spotted the Prince, lying on the ground. She slipped out of the saddle and raced across the clearing. Breathless, Snow White reached the Prince just as he sat up and stretched.

"What a nice nap!" he said. "I hope you're hungry!"

Snow White was bewildered. Next to the Prince lay a lavish picnic spread out on a soft blanket, and the Prince was as happy and healthy as ever!

"I knew Astor would get you here quickly," he said, beaming. "Tell me. Are you surprised?"

Snow White paused for a moment to catch her breath. "Oh, yes, very surprised," she said at last, smiling. She picked up an apple and offered it to Astor.

"And," she added, "I'm very glad you have such a dear and clever horse!"

Flik's Big Date

Flik loved Queen Atta very, very much. So, he decided to plan the most romantic evening for the two of them an ant could possibly imagine.

"I'll pick you up at eight tonight," Flik told Atta when he met her in the anthill early in the morning. Then off he hurried to get ready for their big date.

First, there was the dinner to prepare: sprouted wheat with sunflower seeds and wild truffles; free-range millet on a bed of dandelion greens; and Queen Atta's favourite dessert: gooseberry mousse.

The perfect menu! Flik thought. It was sure to impress Atta.

Then Flik went down to the stream to find the perfect leaf for a romantic moonlit cruise. "This elm leaf should do," Flik said as he tied the leaf to a root near the shore. "And I'll use this twig for my oar. Yes, Atta's going to love this."

But that wasn't all that Flik had planned.

"How's it coming?" he asked the circus bugs, who were back for a visit and busy practising their instruments just up the hill from the stream.

"Brilliant!" Slim replied. "Just brilliant. Don't worry about a thing. It's all under control. We'll have Atta's favourite song memorized by tomorrow night, no problem!"

"But our date is tonight," said Flik.

"Oh," said Slim sheepishly.

"Told you so," said Francis.

"Don't worry," said Slim. "Remember, we're professional entertainers. You want an orchestra to dance to, and you'll have an orchestra to dance to."

"Are you sure you wouldn't like some magic instead?" Manny the Magician asked. "I have found that nothing inspires romance in a lady quite like cutting her in half."

"Um, I think I'll stick with the dancing," said Flik. But, speaking of inspiring romance, he'd almost forgotten all about the fireflies!

"Come on, guys!" he called to the dozen or so he'd hired for that evening. "I want some of you in the trees, some of you along the water, and the rest of you over there by the picnic blanket . . . perfect!" he said as their thoraxes lit up the quickly falling night. "Dinner is ready. Boat is ready. Music is . . . almost ready. Everything is set to go!"

Suddenly, Flik looked down at his watch, and his heart skipped a beat. "Oh, no! It's eight o'clock!" he yelled. "I've really got to go!"

Can you believe it? Flik was so busy getting everything ready, he'd almost forgotten to pick Atta up for their date!

MULAN
A New Friend

Imagine Mulan's surprise when, while out in the meadow picking flowers for her grandmother, what should she spy in an old cypress tree, but a tiny grey kitten.

"Oh, you poor thing. Are you stuck?" Mulan said.

"Meow," replied the kitten.

So Mulan grabbed hold of the lowest branch, and pulled herself up into the tree. The climb was not easy, but at last she reached the kitten. Cradling it in one arm, she climbed back down to the ground.

"There," said Mulan, catching her breath. "Now you can go back home."

Gently, she lowered the kitten to the ground. With a quick tickle behind her ears, Mulan nudged her on her way.

But the grateful little kitten barely moved an inch – instead, it sat there, blinking up at her and purring.

"Go on," Mulan said, smiling. "I'm sure there's a bowlful of milk waiting for you."

But still the kitten would not budge.

"Very well, suit yourself," said Mulan, scooping up her flowers. "I'm late already and really should get home. Try to stay out of trees, little one!" She turned to go.

"Meow, meow, meow!"

Now, imagine Mulan's surprise when she looked down at her feet to find her new kitten trotting close beside her.

"Well, well!" Mulan laughed. "It appears the Fas are going to have a little house guest!"

But not everyone at Mulan's house was pleased to have company. Namely, Mulan's dog, Little Brother. Especially when the kitten walked in and lay down on his silk cushion!

"Ruff! Ruff! Ruff!" he barked.

"Now, now," Mulan said. "Our friend here has just been through quite an ordeal. Be a good host and let her rest, won't you?"

But then the kitten did something even harder to forgive. She walked right over and drank out of Little Brother's dish!

"Grrrr! Grrrrr! Grrufff!" protested Little Brother.

"Oh, dear," said Mulan. "She's probably thirsty too. Here, kitty," she said, setting down a bowl of milk. "Have some of this."

Now, imagine Little Brother's surprise when that tiny kitten pushed the dish of milk all the way over to Little Brother with her little black nose.

"Meow," said the kitten, giving it one more push.

"Look, Little Brother!" exclaimed Mulan. "She wants to be your friend."

And, from that moment on, that's what they were!

The End of the Tunnel

Flynn the thief was cunning. To frighten Rapunzel, he had taken her to a horrible pub full of thugs. It was the worst ruffians' hangout in the kingdom! He thought this would make her want to return to her tower straight away and give up on the idea of seeing the floating lanterns.

If Rapunzel hadn't confiscated his satchel with the golden crown inside, he would never have agreed to guide her through the forest in the first place!

Rapunzel is going to go home like a good girl and give me back my satchel, he thought to himself as they entered the pub. But in his plan, Flynn hadn't reckoned on the young girl bringing all these thugs to their knees in a matter of moments! They were even describing their life's dreams to her one by one... it really was an unbelievable sight!

While Rapunzel befriended the thugs, Mother Gothel arrived at the pub. She could not believe what she was seeing either. She mumbled, "At last I've found Rapunzel, but she seems to be managing perfectly well without me... I'm going to have to come up with a really clever trick to make her come back to the tower!" She was thinking this when a thug arrived at the pub with the royal guards.

"Where's Rider? Where is he?" demanded the Captain.

The Stabbington brothers entered the pub in shackles, followed by Maximus. The horse was still hot on Flynn's trail.

Luckily, Flynn and Rapunzel had time to slip behind the counter before anyone saw them!

Suddenly, the landlord leaned towards Flynn and grabbed him by the arm! The young thief was panic-stricken. The landlord was bound to hand him over to the guards to get the reward! But, instead, the he lifted up a heavy trap door concealed behind the bar, and whispered, "Go, live your dream."

"I will," Flynn replied.

"Your dream stinks. I was talking to her!" The thug nodded towards Rapunzel.

"Oh, thank you!" said Rapunzel.

Flynn slipped into the dark tunnel first. The young girl was reluctant to follow him. Perched on her shoulder, Pascal, her chameleon, gave her a little sign of encouragement. Rapunzel took a deep breath and plunged into the dark tunnel behind Flynn. The landlord closed the trap door.

Rapunzel shuddered.

"Don't worry," said Flynn as he managed to reassure her. "There's always light at the end of the tunnel."

The Great Garden Mystery

For the first time in many years, the Sultan of Agrabah had spare time. With Jasmine and Aladdin helping him run the kingdom, the Sultan could spend his afternoons in his vegetable garden. He grew aubergines, chickpeas, parsley, cucumbers, tomatoes and lettuce.

"Vegetables, yuck!" Iago the parrot squawked, perching on a beanpole as the Sultan watered his aubergines. "Give me a fig any day. You can keep your lettuce and parsley. Blech!"

One day, the Sultan came out to his garden and found that there was not one vegetable left in it! The chickpea plants were bare, the lettuce was gone and the tomatoes had vanished. There wasn't even one lonely sprig of parsley!

The Sultan, Jasmine, Aladdin and Rajah searched high and low for any clues. Finally, they found one: a set of muddy claw prints. The prints could belong to only one creature – Iago!

"I can't believe it," said the Sultan. "That parrot must hate vegetables so much that he decided to get rid of each and every one of them!"

They followed the claw prints over the garden wall and into the city. The royal family wound their way further and further into the city, until Aladdin recognized his old neighbourhood.

"I wonder why Iago would bring those vegetables here?" he said. "If he wants to sell them,

he's out of luck – no one here has any money."

Aladdin got his answer soon enough. Rajah led the family around a corner, and there, in a courtyard, was a poor family having a picnic. It was a jolly affair – they were talking and laughing and passing dishes around. And in the middle of it all was Iago.

"Iago!" cried Jasmine. "You gave my father's vegetables away?"

The father of the family stood up. "My apologies, Your Highness," he said. "We did not know that the vegetables belonged to the Sultan. This parrot saw how hungry we were and said he would give us something to eat. We would give them back, but we have already made *falafel* out of the chickpeas and parsley, and *baba ghanoush* out of the aubergines. However, there is plenty to go around, if you would like to join us."

Jasmine thought she had never received such a nice invitation. So they all sat down, and tucked in. The *baba ghanoush* was rich, and the *falafel* was tasty, and went very well with the Sultan's tomatoes and lettuce.

"I am delighted," said the Sultan, "that my garden is such a success. I think, however, that it would be even better if the garden was in the city, and belonged to everyone. Perhaps I will move the garden to this very courtyard."

Everyone thought that was a wonderful idea, except for Iago. "Vegetables, yuck!" he said.

No Work For Tinker Bell

Tinker Bell and her fairy friends from Pixie Hollow were on their way to bring summer to the mainland.

Summer was the busiest of all the four seasons – which meant the fairies would be away from home for months instead of days.

Tinker Bell was so excited! She had heard that the fairy camp where they'd be staying was an amazing place.

Once Tink and the others arrived, the nature fairies got right to work.

Vidia, a fast-flying fairy, made the summer grasses sway. Iridessa, a light fairy, bathed flowers in sunshine.

Rosetta, a garden fairy, helped bees find their way to the flowers' sweet nectar. Fawn, an animal fairy, greeted birds while Silvermist, a water fairy, frolicked with tadpoles.

Meanwhile, Tink landed in a peaceful clearing with her friend, Terence – a dust-keeper fairy.

"Where is everyone else?" she asked him.

Terence pulled back a tangle of leaves beneath a huge oak tree, revealing the bustling fairy camp. Tink couldn't wait to get right to work!

"Don't worry, you'll find something to fix," Terence told her. Then he flew off to make pixie dust deliveries.

The Fairy Camp was even more incredible than Tink had ever imagined! Hidden beneath the tree, an entire fairy community bustled with activity.

Tinker Bell wasn't going to waste her first summer on the mainland! She couldn't wait to start tinkering! She went over to a fairy who was painting stripes on bees.

"How's the bee striper working? Need any tweaks?" she asked.

The animal fairy shook her head. "It's working fine, Tink," she replied.

Tinker Bell was glad that her inventions were working well, but she really wanted something to fix. Her tinkering nature meant she only felt truly happy when she was busy fixing something.

Since there wasn't anything that needed to be repaired just yet, Tink decided to go and look for lost things.

The other fairies reminded Tink that she needed to stay hidden from humans. They couldn't believe that Tink wanted to get *closer* to the humans – they knew that it could be very dangerous if a human discovered a fairy.

But Tinker Bell – as curious as ever – was determined to do some exploring while she was on the mainland.

Dining Under the Stars

It didn't take the two frogs, Tiana and Naveen, long to arrive at the home of Mama Odie. The voodoo priestess would restore them to humans and finally it would all be over!

Tiana thought that the time had come to enjoy a rest.

"Let's take a break!" she shouted to Louis the alligator, Ray the firefly and Naveen. "Is anyone hungry?"

"I'm dying of hunger!" admitted Louis.

"How about swamp gumbo?" suggested Tiana. "It's my speciality!"

"That'll do!" said Naveen, leaning against a tree, his legs on a mushroom.

He placed a leaf on his knees as a napkin, and added, "Sounds delicious! I'll start with free dinner cocktail and something to nibble on while I wait, thanks."

"Oh no, no, no, Your Royal Highness!" protested Tiana immediately, with a hint of irony in her voice. "That's not how I go about things! Your job is to slice the mushrooms!"

"But I don't know how to slice," growled Naveen, slowly and carefully cutting a slice of mushroom.

Tiana chuckled, amused. "At that rate, we'll still be here tomorrow!"

So, standing behind Naveen, she guided his hand. Tiana was chopping very fast! Naveen winced.

"Yes, OK, OK, I'm not really used to doing this. Most of the time I had servants do everything for me: dress my clothes, brush my teeth, even help me get out of bed!"

"Aw, you poor baby." Tiana said mockingly.

However, Naveen sliced the mushrooms eventually and soon the swamp stew was ready.

Suddenly, Ray raised his eyes to the sky, seeing the Evening Star.

"There she is. The sweetest firefly in all creation... Evangeline!" he sighed. "So far above me, yet I know her heart belongs to me!"

Of course, no one wanted to spoil his happiness by telling him he was wrong and that he was actually talking to a star.

He began to sing softly, romantically, and Naveen invited Tiana to dance.

"Impossible!" she refused. "I don't know how to dance."

"If I can chop, you can dance," he retorted. Tiana gave in, and Naveen led her in a tender waltz.

He guided her steps, then he said, "You see? Dancing, chopping, what's the difference? The main thing is to give it a try!"

Cinderella

The Missing Slipper

"Oh, what a lovely morning!" cried Cinderella as she sat up in her bed in the royal palace. The sun was shining. The birds were singing. And the delicious smell of freshly baked cinnamon buns was drifting up from the royal kitchen.

"Mmm, breakfast," said Cinderella. She smiled down at the mice gathered on her satin bedspread. Then she stretched over and slipped on the dressing gown that lay at the foot of her bed. "Now, where are those slippers . . . ?"

"Here's one, Cinderelly!" said Jaq, jumping down to drag a silvery bedroom slipper closer to Cinderella's foot.

"Thank you, Jaq, dear," said Cinderella as she slid her toes inside. "But . . . where's the other one?"

Jaq turned and looked around. "I don't see it, Cinderelly!" Quickly, he bent down and peeked under the bed. Still nothing. Uh-oh!

"Mert! Bert!" Jaq shouted to his friends. "Has anybody seen Cinderelly's slipper?"

The other mice shrugged and shook their heads.

"Don't tell me I've lost my slipper," Cinderella said with a sigh. "Not again!"

"Don't worry, Cinderelly," a mouse named Suzy told her. "We'll find it."

Together, Cinderella and her friends searched her room from top to bottom. They peered under tables, behind bookcases, inside wardrobes and dressing tables – everywhere a missing slipper could possibly be.

"I'm beginning to think it walked away," Cinderella said sadly.

"Hmm," said Jaq. "That slipper was here last night . . ." Suddenly Jaq stopped in mid-sentence. "Gus-Gus!" he exclaimed, smacking his forehead. "That's right!"

"What's right?" said Cinderella.

"Follow me, Cinderelly," Jaq said.

With one slipper on, Cinderella followed Jaq as he tiptoed across the room and nodded towards a little mousehole. "Look here, Cinderelly," he said.

Curious, Cinderella knelt down and peered inside . . . and sure enough, there was her missing slipper – with a soundly sleeping Gus nestled cosily inside.

"Oh," said Cinderella, "what a little dear."

"Wake him up, Cinderelly!" said Jaq.

"Oh, no!" replied Cinderella. "Let's let him sleep."

"But Cinderelly needs her slipper!" he cried.

Cinderella thought for a moment. "Actually, no!" she told her mouse friends as she kicked off her other slipper. "I've just decided it's the perfect day for breakfast in bed!"

Enchanted Stew

Belle hummed to herself as she strolled through the castle. She had been living in the castle for a few months now and was finally beginning to feel at home. The enchanted inhabitants were truly good to her, and even the Beast seemed to be softening a bit.

Finishing her song, she stepped into the kitchen for a chat with Mrs Potts and the Stove. They were always pleased to see her, and Belle enjoyed talking to them while learning new recipes.

"Well, hello, dear!" Mrs Potts and the Stove called out together as Belle stepped into the large kitchen. The smell of roasting meat and vegetables greeted Belle as well, and her mouth watered. Dinner would be delicious, as usual.

"Hello," Belle replied.

"You're just in time for a spot of tea," Mrs Potts said.

Belle smiled as Chip hopped across the counter, stopping right in front of her. "I'll be your teacup," he said. "And no bubble tricks, I promise," he added seriously.

"All right then," Belle agreed. Mrs Potts filled Chip with steamy tea and dropped in a sugar cube.

"How was your morning in the library, dear?" Mrs Potts asked.

"It was wonderful!" Belle exclaimed. "I finished my book about knights in shining armour and started one about a prince who's disguised as a frog."

"A frog!" the Stove exclaimed. "Oh, my!"

Suddenly, black smoke began to billow out of the sides of the oven door.

"Oh, my!" the Stove said again, throwing open the door. Smoke poured into the room. When it finally cleared, Belle spied a scorched roast and crispy black vegetables inside.

"Oh, my!" the Stove exclaimed again.

"What are we going to feed the Beast for supper?" Mrs. Potts fretted.

The kitchen door opened, and Lumiere rushed into the room. "What is that awful smell?" he asked. A moment later, he spied the roast. "It's absolutely scorched!" he shouted. "We can't possibly feed that to the Beast! What will we do?"

Belle got to her feet. "Enchanted Stew," she said calmly. Taking down a large stew pot and a few vegetables, she began to chop and simmer. The last ingredient was the scorched roast.

"It adds the perfect smoky flavour," she explained. Just then the Beast came into the kitchen. "What smells so delicious?" he asked.

"Supper," Belle replied with a smile and a wink at the Stove and Mrs Potts. "It's called Enchanted Stew, and we cooked it together!"

Disney

Lady and the *TRAMP*

Like Father, Like Son

Tramp had a whole new life. He had gone from being a stray to becoming a member of the Dear household. And now, he and Lady were proud parents.

But Tramp was finding it difficult to change some of his old ways.

"Tramp," Lady said gently, "you need to set an example for the puppies – especially Scamp."

Scamp had an adventurous side just like his dad. So, it wasn't surprising that father and son often got carried away when they played together. They couldn't resist the urge to roll in a puddle of mud – and then chase each other across the clean kitchen floor.

Soon, Aunt Sarah and her two troublesome cats, Si and Am, were going to be visiting. Lady was worried.

"Don't worry. I promise to keep Scamp away from those troublemakers," Tramp said.

"And?" replied Lady.

"And I promise to stay away from them, too," Tramp added.

When the big day came, Lady and Tramp herded their pups into a bedroom and told them to stay put. But Scamp was curious. He slipped out of the room and hid behind the living room settee. Then he sneaked up behind the cats and swiped at their tails as they flicked back and forth. The cats turned and chased Scamp up and over the settee, under a table and into a cupboard.

Well, Tramp thought, I suppose I'm going to have to chase those nasty old cats whether I want to or not!

He enthusiastically dived into the cupboard. Seconds later, Tramp and Scamp emerged. Much to Aunt Sarah's horror, Si and Am were later found inside tied together with a scarf. When no one was looking, Tramp and Scamp shared a victory wink.

Tramp and Scamp were banished to the garden for their antics. When Lady came out that evening, she found that they had dug up the entire garden looking for bones. Father and son saw the look on Lady's face and knew that they were about to get a lecture.

Tramp looked at Lady innocently. "You want him to get exercise, don't you?" he asked.

"Try it, Mum!" Scamp cried. "It's fun."

"What am I going to do with you two?" Lady said, laughing.

Tramp and Scamp dragged a huge bone out from behind the kennel.

"Join us for dinner?" Tramp replied.

"Well, all right," Lady said. "But, as soon as we're done, we're cleaning up this yard."

"Yes, ma'am!" chorused Tramp and Scamp, looking very pleased with themselves.

"Stackblackbadminton"

After dinner at Prince Eric's castle, Ariel, Eric and Grimsby went into the drawing room to relax.

"My dear, do you play?" Grimsby asked Ariel. He pointed to a table. On it sat a red-and-black chequered board.

Of course, Ariel could not answer because she had exchanged her voice for legs. But she nodded eagerly.

"I'll make the first move," Eric said, and slid a black disk from one square to another.

That seems simple enough, thought Ariel. The game seemed similar to a merpeople game called 'Conch.' She reached over and pushed the same black disk to a third square.

Eric laughed. "No, no. I'm black. And you're red. *You* move the *red.* Understand?"

Ariel gazed at Eric and sighed.

"Perhaps I should show the young lady?" suggested Grimsby.

He took Ariel's seat, and the two men moved the disks all over the chequered board. But Ariel still didn't understand what they were doing – this game wasn't like Conch at all!

Suddenly, she heard a flapping sound on the windowsill. It was Scuttle!

Ariel pointed at the men and mouthed, *What are they doing?*

"They're playing Stackblackbadminton, a popular human game," said Scuttle.

Ariel's eyes widened. That sounded like something she had better learn if she wanted to fit into Eric's world.

"You see those disks?" asked Scuttle. "Those are *chips.* At the end of the game, players stack their chips. Then the dealer – the person *not* playing – "

Me? mouthed Ariel.

Scuttle nodded. "Yes. It's up to you to end the game by collecting all the chips off the board."

Ariel smiled. She would show Eric she *did* know how to play.

She walked right over to the two men. They seemed to have finished playing. They were staring hard at the board – and there weren't many chips left on it. So she bent down and swept all the pieces off the board.

Eric and Grimsby yelped. The little mermaid grinned. Eric didn't think she knew how to play his game but, from the stunned look on his face, she'd given him quite a surprise!

Ariel smiled and began to lay the 'chips' out as if they were shells in a game of Conch. This "Stackblackbadminton" game was all right, but she couldn't wait to teach Eric and Grimsby how to play a *really* good game. She picked up the first 'shell' and showed Eric how to move it. He smiled at her, and her heart fluttered. Things were starting to go well at last.

Rise and Shine!

"All right, Dwarfs!" Doc called one morning. "Is everyone ready to leave for work? Let's see. We've got Happy, Dopey, Sneezy, Bashful, Grumpy and Sleepy." Doc looked around. "Sleepy?" No answer. Sleepy was nowhere to be found.

"Oh, no, not again," Doc complained, leading the other Dwarfs up the stairs to their bedroom. There, just as Doc expected, they found Sleepy, dozing peacefully in his bed.

Doc walked to Sleepy's bedside. He pulled the covers off the sleeping dwarf. "Come on, Sleepy! Rise and shine!" Doc called. But Sleepy just rolled over and dozed on.

"Oh, this is ridiculous!" exclaimed Grumpy. "We go through this every single morning, dragging Sleepy out of bed, and I'm tired of it."

"Me, too!" said Dopey.

"Me, three!" said Sneezy. *"Ah-CHOO!"*

The Dwarfs stood around Sleepy's bed, looking down at him, wondering what to do.

"I have an idea!" said Doc. "We'll have to take the day off from the diamond mine and stay here today to work on my plan, but I think it will solve our problem – once and for all!"

The Dwarfs gathered into a huddle around Doc as he outlined the details. Then they got their tools and set to work. Soon the bedroom was filled with the sounds of

hammering, sawing and metal working. All of the activity centred on Sleepy's bed. Despite the racket, Sleepy slept on . . . .

He slept all morning. He slept all afternoon. He slept all evening. He slept through the night.

Then, bright and early the next morning, an alarm clock perched on top of Sleepy's bedside table sprang to life; its bell jangled noisily, shaking the clock.

With a rope tied to its handle, the clock bounced across the top of the table until it fell off the edge. The falling clock tugged on the rope, yanking a broomstick at the other end. When the broomstick moved, the large weight it was propping up dropped to the floor, activating a pulley that pulled up sharply on Sleepy's headboard. The head of Sleepy's bed lifted off the floor, and Sleepy slid down and off the foot of the bed, onto a smoothly carved wooden slide that carried him out of the window, down to ground level and – *splash!* – right into a wooden tub filled with cold water.

Wide awake, Sleepy sat in the tub, blinking and wondering what had just happened.

The other Dwarfs crowded around the bedroom window and peered down at him, grinning cheerfully (except Grumpy, of course).

"Good morning, Sleepy!" cried Doc. "Do you like your new alarm clock?"

Winnie the Pooh

Piglet's Night-Lights

Winnie the Pooh knocked on Piglet's door. "Ready for our camp-out, Piglet?" Pooh called.

Piglet opened the door and looked around anxiously. "It's getting awfully dark out there."

As Pooh and Piglet walked, Piglet got more frightened.

"What's that?" he asked suddenly, pointing to a scary-looking shape in the trees.

"Hello!" called a voice from above. Pooh and Piglet both jumped, startled.

"Who's there?" Pooh asked.

"Why, it's me – Owl," the voice answered. "I thought you two might need a little help finding the others. We owls can see quite well at night."

By the time the friends reached the campsite, it was completely dark.

"Have no fear, Tigger's here – with illuminagination!" Tigger said, holding up a lantern.

The friends set up the tent and Piglet climbed inside and began to unpack. A few minutes later, he poked his head back out. "Oh, no!" he wailed. "I forgot my night-light!"

"Don't worry, Buddy Boy," Tigger said.

"You can use my lantern!" But just then, the lantern flickered out.

Pooh pointed to Eeyore, who was standing next to Rabbit and Owl. "Can't have a camp-out without a campfire," Eeyore said. They went to gather some sticks, and minutes later a fire was burning.

"Campfires certainly are pleasant," Piglet said. "They make a very good sort of light."

The friends played shadow puppets until bedtime. Piglet wouldn't leave the light of the fire, though, so Pooh kept him company. Soon, the fire began to fade. "Maybe we should go to sleep now, Piglet," Pooh said, yawning.

"I can't sleep without a night-light, Pooh," Piglet replied.

Looking up at the night sky, Pooh thought of something. "The stars are night-lights, Piglet," he said, pointing up at the sparkling stars.

Piglet looked around. "You're right, Pooh!" he cried. Piglet pointed to the moon. "Look how bright the moon is tonight. I feel much better."

"Do you think you might be able to sleep now, Piglet?" Pooh asked with a huge yawn. "Piglet?"

But Piglet was already fast asleep.

Pinocchio
Fish Food

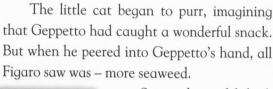

Figaro the cat was scared. He was also hungry. But he knew there wouldn't be any dinner. Figaro, Geppetto and Cleo the goldfish had just been swallowed by a whale!

"Don't worry, Figaro," Geppetto said, seeing the cat's worried look. "We'll get out of here somehow – and when we do, we'll keep searching for Pinocchio. We won't stop until we find him."

That Pinocchio! Figaro growled. After all that Geppetto and the Blue Fairy had done for Pinocchio, he had run away from home without a care in the world. That was how they ended up inside the whale! Now what would become of them?

Figaro decided then and there that if they ever found Pinocchio, he was going to use both of the wooden boy's legs as scratching posts. It would serve him right.

Meanwhile, Geppetto was peering into the puddle of water at the bottom of the whale's stomach. Figaro watched curiously.

"Let's see," Geppetto murmured, bending over and poking at the water. "There must be something in here . . . ."

"Aha!" Geppetto cried happily. He was clutching a small, soggy clump of seaweed.

Figaro blinked. Seaweed?

A moment later, Geppetto bent down again. "Aha!" he cried once more.

The little cat began to purr, imagining that Geppetto had caught a wonderful snack. But when he peered into Geppetto's hand, all Figaro saw was – more seaweed.

Seaweed was *fish* food, Figaro thought with a scowl. Surely Geppetto didn't expect *him* to eat that for dinner.

But, as he watched, Geppetto carefully divided the seaweed into three portions. He placed one portion in Cleo's bowl. He set one portion in front of Figaro. The third he kept for himself.

"Let's eat!" Geppetto said, smiling bravely.

Figaro sniffed his seaweed. He stirred it around with his paw. But he just couldn't eat the seaweed. With a twitch of his tail, Figaro turned away.

Geppetto watched the little cat with sad eyes. Figaro sighed. He couldn't help but feel ungrateful.

Reluctantly, Figaro turned back to his dinner. He nibbled at the seaweed. It was cold. It was slimy. But it tasted like – *fish*!

Figaro gobbled down the rest of his meal. With his belly full, the little cat felt better. He decided that if they found Pinocchio, he would only use *one* of the puppet-boy's legs to sharpen his claws on.

Probably.

101 DALMATIANS

Lucky's Last Laugh

It was getting quite late at Pongo's and Perdita's house, but their darling little puppies were still not asleep. Not that they didn't want to go to sleep. At least most of them. No, the problem was that one of them wouldn't let them go to sleep – Lucky!

"And then, don't you remember, you guys, the part at the very beginning, when Thunderbolt jumped across that canyon? Whoosh! Like a rocket! Clear to the other side!" Lucky said.

"Yes, Lucky, we remember," his sister Penny said with a groan. "How could we forget? You've reminded us 101 times!"

"Yeah! It was so great! And then there was that part when – "

"Lucky!" wailed Rolly. "We all watched the same episode of Thunderbolt tonight. You don't have to tell us about it."

"Yeah, I know, but I just wanted to tell you about the part when Thunderbolt found the little girl, then ran back to tell the sheriff – "

"Lucky! It's late! We want to go to sleep!" barked Patch.

Lucky laid his head on his paws. "Okay," he said. "I'll be quiet."

All the puppies closed their eyes.

"Oh! But what about the part when the sheriff told Thunderbolt to climb up that cliff, and he got to the top, and he grabbed that rope with his teeth, and he pulled up the little girl – "

"Lucky!" yelped Pepper. "We don't care about Thunderbolt. We want to go to bed!"

"Right." Lucky sighed, lying down once again. "Wait a sec!" He sat up. "Don't care about Thunderbolt? How could you not care that he carried that little girl across that broken bridge and through those raging rapids?"

"We mean," said Freckles, "we want you to be quiet so we can go to sleep!"

"You mean," said Lucky, "you don't want me to tell you about the last part where Thunderbolt ran back to the mountains and into that cave, and found that amazing thing?"

"Yes!" Lucky's brothers and sisters shouted together.

"Why didn't you say so?" said Lucky. "Good night."

And with that, Lucky closed his eyes. For a minute, everyone enjoyed the silence. Then Penny sat up.

"Hey, wait a minute," she said. "What thing did he find?"

"Yeah," said Patch. "I missed that part."

"Me, too," said Rolly. "What was it exactly that he found, Lucky? Tell us."

But there was no answer. Lucky was fast asleep. And now the *other* Dalmatian puppies were wide awake!

Beauty and the Beast

A Friend for Philippe

Belle loved life in the castle with her Prince, and she loved her faithful horse, Philippe. Lately, however, Philippe had been acting strangely. One morning, Belle decided to try and cheer him up. She asked her friends for some help.

First, Lumiere helped Belle to brighten up Philippe's stall. They covered the walls with wallpaper and trimmed them with gold. They piled pillows in the corners and hung a huge chandelier from the ceiling.

"Voilà!" Lumiere exclaimed. "What more could a horse ask for?"

But Philippe stared sadly out of the window.

"I wish I knew," said Belle.

Next, Belle saw to it that Philippe was treated to a bubble bath fit for a king. "If this doesn't make him smile," Belle told Chip, "I don't know what will!" But in the end, though he was shiny and sweet smelling, Philippe was just as glum – and Belle was just as puzzled. She asked the Prince if he had any suggestions.

"A good walk always used to cheer me up," the Prince said.

Belle thought that was a wonderful idea. She led Philippe to a wide, open meadow, but he wasn't interested in galloping.

"Oh, Philippe," Belle said in despair. "I just don't know what else to do!"

Then, all of a sudden, Philippe's ears pricked up. Belle barely had time to sit up before he charged off! Before long, they emerged into a clearing filled with wild, beautiful horses! Philippe whinnied, and several of the wild horses answered him. Finally, Belle realised what Philippe had wanted – to be with other horses!

All afternoon, Belle watched Philippe race and play. Soon, he had even made a friend. The two horses grazed, chased each other around the clearing, and dozed together in the warm sun.

All too quickly, the day was over, and the sun began to set. Belle put Philippe's saddle on and they started back towards the castle. Soon, Belle heard the sound of hooves behind them. Philippe's new friend was following them home!

"Welcome to our castle!" Belle told the new horse when they arrived. She hurried to fix up the stall next to Philippe's.

"There," she said when she was finished. "Now this looks like a stable where a horse (or two!) could really live happily ever after!"

And that is exactly what they did.

Small Fairies Come in Big Packages

Princess Aurora's wedding to Prince Phillip would take place in just a few days. The three good fairies, Flora, Fauna and Merryweather, wanted to give Aurora the perfect gift. They stood in front of an enormous box, trying to decide what to put in it.

"How about a pretty dress for Princess Aurora to wear on her honeymoon. Something pink!" Flora said decisively.

"What about a grand carriage?" Fauna put in with a smile.

Flora shook her head. "King Stefan is already having a carriage made for them. No, let's give her a dress."

"I've got it!" Fauna cried. "A flock of doves that we'll release just as Aurora and Phillip come out of the church. Perfect!"

"A tiara to wear with her wedding gown – that's what Aurora needs," Merryweather piped up. "With three jewels: one red for Flora, one green for Fauna and one blue for me. It will remind our sweet Briar Rose of how much we love her."

"A dress is much more practical than a flock of doves, dear," said Flora firmly.

"But a flock of doves is much more romantic than a dress," Fauna insisted.

Merryweather put her hands on her hips. "A tiara! What's wrong with a tiara?"

But neither Flora nor Fauna even glanced her way. That made Merryweather mad.

"It's settled. We're giving her a dress," Flora said.

"Doves," said Fauna.

"Why can't we give her a – " Merryweather began but, as she waved her arms, trying to get the other fairies' attention, she lost her balance and fell right into the big box. Flora and Fauna did not notice.

"We'll give her both!" said Flora.

They pointed their wands at the box, showering it with sparkles. A huge piece of satin ribbon appeared, wrapped itself around the box, and tied itself into a big bow.

Flora and Fauna put on their capes, ready to deliver the gift to Aurora. But where was Merryweather?

"Oh, well, perhaps she went on ahead," said Flora. "Let's be on our way."

At the palace, Flora and Fauna placed the gift before the Princess. When Aurora untied the ribbon, Merryweather burst out of the box. She presented the Princess with a beautiful tiara that sparkled with red, green and blue jewels.

"Oh, thank you, my dears! It's perfect!" Aurora said with a gasp.

Merryweather smiled. "That's exactly what I thought!" she said.

ALICE
in
WONDERLAND

The Queen's Way

"Goodness!" Alice took a few steps back. She had no idea a queen could bellow quite so loud! Alice had been excited to meet the Queen of Hearts, but the Queen was always shouting, "Off with his head!" It really wasn't very friendly.

"I guess since she's the Queen, she can do what she likes," Alice said to the flamingo croquet mallet she held firmly by the feet.

The flamingo nodded.

"Perhaps she'll be friendlier when we begin playing." Alice sighed.

"Only if she wins," the flamingo replied.

Alice didn't care if the Queen won. Besides, she wasn't really sure the game had rules. And the hedgehog she was supposed to use for a ball did not look as if he would stay put long enough for her to knock him under any of the playing-card wickets, anyway. Standing back, Alice watched the Queen take her turn.

Her Royalness bent over the hedgehog ball, swung her flamingo mallet high into the air, and brought his beak down with a whoosh. The prickly creature was off on a rolling run. He tumbled through wicket after wicket, getting dizzier as he went. He had nearly finished, when one of the wickets bent over the hedgehog's path too late. The hedgehog rolled off course, and the Queen's turn was over.

"Off with his head!" the Queen roared.

She pointed her terrified flamingo at the card.

"Oh, this is so unfair," Alice lamented to her own flamingo. "It wasn't his fault that the hedgehog got dizzy. And that is no way to treat anyone!"

"It *is* a way," her mallet whispered, looking terrified. "It's the Queen's way."

Unfortunately, the Queen had heard Alice. She turned to Alice. Her face was redder than a tomato. Alice knew what had to be coming. She cowered beside a rosebush and waited for the horrible order.

"Off with her – "

"M-m-my dear." The small King appeared from behind the Queen. "The wickets are out of line." He pointed at the cards that were nervously shuffling themselves off the croquet field.

"Get back here!" the Queen shouted. "I'll have your heads!" Forgetting all about Alice, the Queen marched towards the cards.

Alice breathed a sigh of relief and straightened her collar. "She wants everyone else to lose their heads," she whispered very softly. "But, clearly, she has already lost her own!"

At this, Alice's flamingo laughed so hard, she nearly lost her grip on it. Alice smiled. The Queen might be a living terror, but at least Alice had a friend in this crazy court – even if her friend was a croquet mallet!

A Silo Scare

Flik took a step back and gazed up at the giant silo he and a troop of ants had just finished building. Now that the colony was using his harvester, they had a surplus of wheat. The silo would store the wheat safely.

"Nice job, Flik," Queen Atta said.

Flik blushed. A compliment from Atta always made his face feel warm. Atta was the smartest and prettiest ant in the colony. She was also its new Queen.

"Thanks, Atta," Flik said, trying to sound casual. "It should keep our wheat dry all winter."

Suddenly, a voice called down from the top of the silo. "Hellooooo," it said.

Flik and Atta looked up. It was Dot, Atta's little sister. She and her Blueberry friends were sitting on top of the silo.

"The view up here is amazing!" Dot called.

"Dot! Be careful!" Atta said worriedly.

Dot grinned down at her sister. "We will!"

"Don't worry," said Flik. "I built in several safety – "

Atta interrupted him. "I have a meeting," she told Flik. "Stay out of trouble," she added in a louder voice. For a second Flik thought Atta was talking to him. Then he realized that she was talking to the Blueberries.

"I'll keep an eye on them," Flik said.

"Come on up, Flik," Dot called as Atta hurried away. "You just have to see the view!"

"Coming!" Flik replied. He did want to see the view, and he also wanted to keep a close eye on the Blueberries.

But, just as Flik got to the top, one of the Blueberries leaped into the silo.

"Wheeeeee!" she cried as she zoomed down towards the pile of wheat.

"The silo is not a playground," Flik told the other girls. "It's for storing wheat, and I built in all these extra safety devices – "

"Come on, Flik," Dot interrupted. "We don't need any safety devices!"

Grinning, she jumped into the silo and slid to the pile of wheat at the bottom. Two other Blueberries followed. But then – *whoops*! – another Blueberry accidentally pushed down a lever. A big pile of wheat tumbled into the silo, heading straight for the Blueberries below!

Panicked, Flik hit a switch. The falling wheat was caught halfway down by a handy-dandy wheat stopper – one of the safety devices he'd built into the silo.

The Blueberries stared at Flik. Just then, Atta walked by. "Dot, what are you doing?" she asked.

"Uh, Flik was just showing us his great safety devices," Dot said sheepishly.

"And they really work," said Flik, sighing with relief.

Disney
Princess
Cinderella

The Masquerade Ball

"Where could she be?" Cinderella asked. She looked around the grand ballroom. Hundreds of happy citizens were gathered there, each dressed in a splendid costume.

Cinderella and her new husband, the Prince, were holding a Masquerade Ball. Cinderella had sent a special invitation to her Fairy Godmother, who had promised to come.

But the ball had started almost an hour ago, and Cinderella still hadn't seen any sign of the plump, cheerful little woman.

"Don't worry, my love," the Prince said. "I'm sure she'll – what's this?"

A messenger handed Cinderella a note.
Never fear –
I'm here, my dear.
Just seek and you will find
Which mask I am behind!

Her Fairy Godmother was playing a trick on her! "I'll find you," Cinderella whispered.

Was her Fairy Godmother wearing that beautiful unicorn costume? Was she the princess with the pink mask? The dancing harlequin clown? The fuzzy brown bear? Cinderella felt a little dizzy as she turned around and around. How would she ever find her Fairy Godmother in the crowd?

Cinderella stared at a masked milkmaid with twinkling eyes standing near a fountain.

Could that be her? she wondered.

Cinderella looked around thoughtfully. When she turned back to the fountain, the milkmaid was gone! Instead, someone in a butterfly mask was standing there.

"Looking for someone, Princess?" the butterfly said in a deep voice.

"No – never mind," Cinderella said.

She wandered away, still searching. But she kept thinking about the twinkling eyes behind the butterfly mask. Then she remembered something – the milkmaid had the same twinkling eyes! Could it be . . . ?

She hurried back to the fountain. But there was no sign of the milkmaid or the butterfly. The only person standing nearby was wearing a beautiful white swan costume.

"Oh, dear," Cinderella whispered.

She stared at the swan. Mischievous eyes twinkled behind the feathered white mask.

Suddenly, Cinderella laughed out loud. "Aha!" she cried. "I caught you!"

She pulled off the swan mask. Her Fairy Godmother smiled back at her. "You win!" she exclaimed. "How did you find me?"

"I almost didn't, the way you kept magically changing costumes," Cinderella said. "Then I remembered how you magically changed *my* outfit not too long ago – and I figured it out!"

The Father of Invention

There was never a dull moment in the castle of Belle and the Prince. Friends came and went, Mrs Potts and the other members of the household bustled about, and Maurice, Belle's father, was always tinkering away on a new invention.

One morning, Maurice wheeled a complicated-looking contraption into the kitchen, and presented it to Mrs Potts. "Just a little something to make your life easier," he said proudly.

"Thank you, Maurice dear, but . . . what is it?" the housekeeper wondered.

"I call it a 'plate pitcher'," answered Maurice. He took a pile of clean plates and loaded them onto a mechanical arm. Then he positioned the machine in front of the open china cabinet. He pressed a button and stood back proudly. With a couple of loud clangs, the machine sprang to life.

The plate pitcher began to hurl plates this way and that. They smashed against walls and onto the floor.

"Look out, Mrs Potts!" shouted Maurice as a plate whizzed by her head. He crawled along the floor, reached up and hit the off switch. "I'll just go work out the kinks," he said, wheeling the machine out of the room.

The next day, Maurice had another surprise. "It's for cleaning the carpets," he explained as he pointed to a large metal box with a big hose coming out of it. "No more beating heavy rugs for you!"

"Well, it looks harmless," Mrs Potts decided. "How does it work?"

"Like so!" exclaimed Maurice. He picked up the hose and flipped a switch. Instantly, curtains, pillows and lamps were sucked towards the nozzle – and it looked as if Maurice himself was in danger of disappearing! Luckily, Mrs Potts came to his rescue and turned off the machine.

"Must have made it a tad too powerful," Maurice admitted.

The following day Maurice had yet another time-saving device for Mrs Potts. This one was a laundry machine that flooded the entire ground floor of the castle with water and soapsuds.

"Maurice," Mrs Potts said gently, "it is very sweet of you to want to make my job easier. But I enjoy it. By taking care of the castle, I'm taking care of the people I love." She looked thoughtful for a moment, then added, "But I have to admit, the one thing I would love is something that would make me a nice, hot cup of tea at the end of the day."

"I have just the thing!" Maurice replied with a twinkle in his eye.

Mrs Potts looked slightly worried. "You do?" she asked.

"Yes," Maurice answered. "Me!"

Mama Odie to the Rescue

The evil sorcerer, Dr Facilier was worried. With the help of his magic talisman, he had transformed Lawrence, the valet, into Prince Naveen, so that he could marry Charlotte. This way, the sorcerer hoped to get his hands on the girl's fortune!

But the talisman was losing its power. So he had to capture Naveen to refill its magic with a few drops of his blood...

"Come to me, Shadows!" he invoked. "Bring me the Frog Prince without delay!"

The clawed beasts flew out of the window and soon found Naveen's tracks in the bayou. He and Tiana were on their way to the home of Mama Odie, the good voodoo priestess. They were going to ask her how they could become human again.

But suddenly, the shadows grasped Naveen and carried him away. "Help!" he shouted.

Tiana, Louis the alligator and Ray the firefly tried to hold on to him, but in vain. No one could fight against the forces of darkness... no one but a powerful voodoo priestess! And *whoosh!* Mama Odie made the evil Shadows disappear!

"Not bad for a 197-year-old blind lady, hey?" she laughed.

Mama Odie and her snake Juju lived right here in a swamp boat that was wedged between the branches of a tree. The wise woman was a little eccentric. However, with all her knowledge, they couldn't help but respect her.

"Now, which one of you has been messing with the Shadow Man?" she said to Naveen and Tiana, unable to see them, as she stirred her pot of gumbo. "You want to be human, but you blind to what you need."

"What we want, what we need, it's all the same thing, yes?" Naveen insisted.

"No, you listen to your Mama now. The only thing important is what's under the skin...you got to dig a little deeper." Still Mama Odie knew that the frogs would have to learn that the hard way.

"Gumbo, gumbo, in the pot! We need a princess. What you got?!" Mama Odie conjured an image of Charlotte and her father in the tub of gumbo.

"Charlotte is not a princess!" said Naveen.

"But of course she is!" countered Tiana. "Her father was crowned king of Mardi Gras. So she is still a princess until midnight!"

"A Mardi Gras princess is better than no princess at all, isn't it?" Mama Odie pointed out in a mischievous tone.

Naveen blushed. Yes, a kiss from Charlotte would suit him very well!

Ariel's New Move

"Whoa." Prince Eric brought the carriage to a stop. Beside him, Ariel barely managed to keep from sliding off the seat. She had been human only for a short time, and she wasn't used to her legs yet.

"Are you hungry?" the prince asked. Eric gestured towards a restaurant and looked at Ariel expectantly.

Ariel smiled and nodded. She could not speak, and she was a little wary of eating. Humans ate fish, and she could not help but think of her best friend, Flounder, whenever she saw something scaly lying on a plate. But she wanted to please the prince.

The restaurant was nearly empty. Eric and Ariel sat at a table for two as the owner approached.

"What'll it be, dear?" a woman with warm brown eyes and white hair asked, looking kindly at Ariel.

"She'll have . . . the soup?" Eric looked at Ariel for confirmation. Ariel nodded. "And I will have the speciality of the house."

Ariel was glad that Eric didn't seem to mind talking for her, though she desperately wanted to speak for herself and tell him how much she enjoyed being with him.

When the owner walked away, the silence in the room seemed to grow. Ariel tried to communicate with gestures, but Eric didn't seem to understand and, after a few minutes, the poor girl started to feel foolish.

With a sigh of relief, Ariel noticed the owner coming back with their food. Eric seemed relieved too.

After she set down their plates, the white-haired woman walked over to a tall wooden piece of furniture near the wall. She sat down in front of it and placed her hands on the black and white keys.

Ariel had never seen a piano before. And she had never heard one either. She was enchanted by the music. She let her spoon drop into her bowl. The song was lovely – happy and sad at the same time. She wanted to sing along! But, of course, she could not. Still, she could not break away. The music reminded her of the rhythms of the ocean. She stood and began to sway, but her new legs were so awkward, she stumbled.

Suddenly, Eric's strong arm was around Ariel's waist. With his other arm, he took Ariel's hand in his. Ariel looked startled. "Haven't you ever danced before?" the prince asked.

Ariel shook her head shyly.

"I'll show you," the prince said, smiling at her. He whirled Ariel around the floor. The Little Mermaid was a natural. She spun and smiled, glad that they had found a way to communicate without words.

A Real Sleeper!

"Time for bed, Nemo," said Marlin. "It's a school day tomorrow," he added. "You need to get your rest."

"Okay, Dad," said Nemo. "But can you tell me a story? How about one when you were younger?"

"Well, just one then," said Marlin, swimming back over to his only child. He thought for a moment, then smiled broadly. "Did you know that when I was younger – much younger, actually – did you know that I wanted to be a comedian?"

Nemo's eyes widened with surprise. "*You*? A comedian? Aren't comedians supposed to be . . . funny?"

"Well, you see, son," said Marlin, "life is not easy for a clownfish. You may as well realize that right now. See, when you're a clownfish, everyone you meet assumes that you are funny. It's a common mistake. Anyway, years ago, I figured that as long as everyone expected me to be funny, I would try being funny for a living."

"But, Dad," said Nemo, "you aren't funny at all."

"Hey, now! Wait just a minute!" Marlin said, a bit huffily. "In my day, I was known as quite the crack-up! Let me see. I'm sure I can remember some of my old routine, if I just think about it for a minute." He thought for a moment. "All right, it's all coming back!" He cleared his throat. "Good evening, ladies and jellyfish! The ocean sure is looking *swell* tonight. Would you like me to give you a coral report about the latest happenings on the reef? Get it?" he said, looking down at Nemo. "You see, there's something called an oral report, and the words coral and oral sound quite a bit alike."

Nemo gave his father a pained look.

"So, the other day my appendix nearly burst," Marlin went on. "So I decided I'd better go to a sturgeon!"

Nemo blinked. "Dad, these really aren't that funny," he said with a yawn.

"A *sturgeon*. Get it? Rather than a surgeon?" Marlin sighed and continued his routine. "A funny thing happened on the way to the show tonight. I met a guy, nice fish and all, but he seemed to be a bit down on his luck. He told me he was living on squid row."

Nemo's eyes were starting to droop sleepily.

"Do you know why the whale crossed the ocean?" Marlin continued. "Now, don't try to guess. I'll tell you: the whale crossed the ocean to get to the other tide. The other *tide*."

Nemo's eyes were now completely closed, and a tiny snore escaped from him. Marlin smiled at his sleeping son.

"Works every time," he said with a chuckle.

Tangled

An Extraordinary Secret

Flynn and Rapunzel fled through the pub's secret passage – this was no time to hang around!

When she had made Flynn guide her to the floating lanterns, Rapunzel had never imagined for a moment she would find herself in a filthy tunnel hiding from the Royal Guards!

In the Snuggly Duckling, Maximus led the guards straight to the secret passageway. The horse and the guards all charged into the tunnel.

Meanwhile, Mother Gothel had watched the scene unfold, and approached a ruffian at the pub door.

"Where does the tunnel let out?" Mother Gothel demanded. She threatened the ruffian until he told her.

Flynn and Rapunzel ran along the tunnel, the guards hot on their heels. "Run!" Flynn cried.

They raced out of the tunnel and skidded to a stop at the edge of an enormous cavern.

Rapunzel lassoed her hair around a rock, swung through the air, and landed on a stone column. Flynn spun around and fought off Maximus and the guards with Rapunzel's frying pan!

Then Rapunzel threw Flynn her hair and held on tight as he leapt off the cliff. He swung right over the heads of the Stabbington brothers!

But Rapunzel and Flynn weren't safe yet! Maximus had a different plan. With one kick of his hoof he brought down the dam and water came flooding into the cavern.

The guards and the Stabbingtons were swept away by the raging flood!

Flynn and Rapunzel ducked into a cave, just as a stone column crashed to the ground, closing off the entrance. They were trapped!

Water quickly began to fill the cave. Flynn cut his hand trying to dislodge the large rocks surrounding them, but the boulders wouldn't budge. There was no way out.

"It's all my fault!" sobbed Rapunzel. "I'm so sorry, Flynn!"

"Eugene. My real name's Eugene Fitzherbert," Flynn admitted. "Someone might as well know."

"Eugene?" Rapunzel exclaimed. "Well, since we're telling secrets," Rapunzel declared, "I have magic hair that glows when I sing."

The thief stared hard at her, in shock. Then, Rapunzel suddenly realized that her hair may actually be able to save them!

Snow White
and the Seven Dwarfs

A Visit to the Castle

"Gosh," Bashful said bashfully. "Do you think the Princess will be glad to see us?"

"Of course!" Happy chuckled.

"All right, men," Doc said. "Here we are. Now, all we have to do is go up and dock on the floor. That is – knock on the door!"

The Seven Dwarfs had just reached the castle where Snow White lived. They had been so busy in the mines that this was the first time they'd had a chance to visit since Snow White had married the Prince.

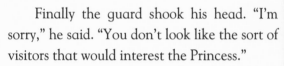

Sneezy looked up at the beautiful castle. "*Ah-choo!*" he sneezed. "Wow. This place sure is pretty."

"Time's a wastin'," Grumpy muttered.

He knocked firmly on the tall wooden door. A moment later a guard opened it.

"Er, good day," the castle guard said. "New servants around the back, please."

"Oh, we're not flu nervants," Doc spoke up. "Er, we're not new servants. We're here to see the Princess!"

"Yes! The Princess!" the other Dwarfs agreed. Dopey nodded eagerly.

The guard looked doubtful. "*You're* here to see the Princess?"

He looked them over. The Dwarfs stood up straight, glad that they'd remembered to wash that morning.

Finally the guard shook his head. "I'm sorry," he said. "You don't look like the sort of visitors that would interest the Princess."

"Oh, but we are!" Sleepy yawned. "She'll be interested in us."

"Sorry," the guard said. "You'll have to go."

But Grumpy held the door open. "Mark my words," he growled. "If you don't tell the Princess we're here, there'll be trouble."

"Who is it?" a sweet voice called from inside the castle. "Who's at the door?"

"Never mind, Princess!" the guard called. "It's just some strange little men who claim they know you."

"Little men?" Snow White cried, rushing forward. She peered around the door past the guard, and her lovely face lit up with joy. "Why, Doc – Grumpy – Sleepy – Dopey – Happy – Sneezy – even dear Bashful!"

Bashful blushed deeply. "Gosh," he said. "Hello, Princess."

The guard looked surprised. "You mean you know these fellows?" he asked the Princess. "I thought they were just riffraff."

"Riffraff?" Snow White cried. "Why, no – they may look a little different, but they're just like royalty to me! They're my very best friends!"

The guard apologized to the Dwarfs. Then Snow White invited her friends into the castle for a nice, long visit.

Sleeping Beauty

Pink or Blue?

On the wedding day of Prince Phillip and Princess Aurora's no one was happier for them than the three good fairies.

"Such a happy day!" exclaimed Flora from a balcony overlooking the crowded ballroom. "Fauna, don't you agree?"

When Fauna didn't answer, Flora looked over to find her weeping.

"Fauna, why are you crying?" asked Flora.

Dabbing her eyes, Fauna said, "I love weddings even more than happy endings! Both make me cry for joy!"

"It is a joyful day," said Merryweather. "Everyone in the kingdom is here. And look at all the wedding presents!"

"Oh, my!" said Flora. "It will take days for the bride and groom to open them all."

"Point them out again, dear," Fauna asked Merryweather. "I had tears in my eyes."

Without thinking, Merryweather used her magic wand to point, and when she did – zzzing! – she accidentally turned all of the white packages her favourite colour – blue.

"Merryweather!" snapped Flora. "Change those packages back this instant."

"I don't know," said Merryweather, tapping her chin. "I like them this way."

"Oh, do you?" said Flora. "Well, look again!"

Using her own magic wand, Flora sent a second blast of magic across the room. *Zzzing!* Now the wedding presents were *her* favourite colour – pink!

"Now, dears," said Fauna, trying to make peace. "Today is not a day for bickering."

"I'll stop, if she will," said Merryweather, after she'd already changed the pink packages back to blue again!

"You call that stopping?" said Flora. Then *zzzing!* went Flora's wand. And the presents turned pink again!

Fauna had had enough! Taking out her magic wand, she waved it around in a circle, and chanted:

"*Presents changing pink and blue,*
wed your colours, then stay true!"

With a final *zzzing!* Fauna sent her magic spell across the room, and the presents changed again.

"What did you do?" cried Flora and Merryweather.

Fauna shrugged. "I simply mixed your colours together and locked them in. Pink-and-blue-striped wrapping paper is all the rage this year," she said. "Now let's all go eat some wedding cake."

"Wedding cake?" said Merryweather. "Hmm … I wonder what colour the frosting is."

THE ARISTOCATS

Wherever You Go, There You Are!

"Oh, dear! Oh, dear!" said Amelia Gabble. The goose and her twin sister, Abigail, had been waddling along the road to Paris, when Amelia suddenly stopped.

"What's wrong?" asked Abigail, bumping into her.

"Just look and you'll see," said Amelia. Stretching out one big white wing, she pointed to the road ahead. Abigail looked, and then the two geese put their heads together and began to argue in low voices.

Behind the geese, Thomas O'Malley, Duchess and her three kittens gathered together.

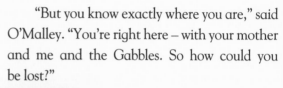

"I wonder what's wrong," said Duchess.

"Guess I'd better find out," said O'Malley.

He sauntered forward. "Ladies, ladies, what's going on?" he asked the twin geese.

"We know this is the road to Paris," Amelia explained. "But up ahead, the road divides."

Sure enough, the single road split in two.

"I think we should go right," said Amelia.

"And I think we should go left," said Abigail.

The three kittens began to worry.

"Mr O'Malley, are we lost?" asked Marie in a small, frightened voice.

O'Malley smiled down at the little white kitten. "Lost? What's lost? I don't know the meaning of the word."

"I do," said Berlioz. "If you're lost, then you don't know where you are."

"But you know exactly where you are," said O'Malley. "You're right here – with your mother and me and the Gabbles. So how could you be lost?"

Duchess shook her head and said, "Mr O'Malley, if we want to get to Paris and we don't know the way, then I do believe that we are lost."

"But Paris is just a place," said O'Malley. "And places are easy to find."

"Look, Mama, look!" Toulouse shouted. "I see something over that hill. It's the top of the Eiffel Tower!"

"Toulouse, you're right!" said Duchess.

"Nice going, little tiger," said O'Malley. Then he turned to the Gabble sisters. "Well, ladies, looks like Paris is thataway!"

Soon they arrived in Paris, where the Gabble sisters met up with their Uncle Waldo. The geese waved goodbye.

Marie sighed with relief. "I'm glad we're not lost any more."

"Aw, honey," said O'Malley, "someday you'll understand. Places may come and places may go but, when you're a free spirit, you can never be lost."

"Never?" asked Marie.

"Never," said O'Malley. " 'Cause wherever you go, there you are!"

Marie nodded. She liked the sound of that!

Eeyore Beats the Heat

One day, when it seemed the sun was shining even more sunnily than ever over the Hundred-Acre Wood, Eeyore sighed and wished that autumn – if it wouldn't be too much trouble – would hurry itself up and get there.

"Something the matter, Eeyore?" asked Roo.

"Oh, it's just that it's so terribly hot," replied Eeyore. "If I weren't stuffed with sawdust, I think I would melt."

"Well, come with me!" squeaked Roo. "I'm going to the swimming hole to cool off."

But Eeyore shook his head. "Can't do, Roo," he said. "Not with my sawdust and all . . . I'd probably just sink. And that's if I'm lucky."

And so Roo, who felt sorry for Eeyore, but who was also eager to swim, continued on his way.

Soon, another friend came along. And this friend was Winnie the Pooh.

"You're looking a little warmish, Eeyore," Pooh said.

"Same to you," said Eeyore with a sigh. "Same to you."

"Ah," said Pooh, "but I am off to catch a breeze – and pay a call on some bees – with my trusty balloon here. Care to join me?"

"No, thanks, Pooh," said Eeyore. "I never did like feeling like the ground was missing. And . . . I expect that with my luck, the balloon would probably pop."

"Well, Eeyore, I understand completely. Wish me luck, then, won't you?" Pooh replied.

"Good luck, Pooh," said Eeyore. "As if anything I ever wish comes true . . ."

The next friend to come upon Eeyore was little Piglet.

"Hello, there, Eeyore," said Piglet. "Whoo! Are you as uncomfortably hot as I am?"

"Oh, no," said Eeyore. "I'm sweltering. Parched. Smouldering. Torrid. Yes – 'uncomfortably hot' would be an understatement."

"Poor Eeyore," said Piglet. "Why don't you come play in the cool mud with me?"

But once again, Eeyore shook his head. "Afraid mud is not an option, Piglet," he explained. "Once I get dirty, I'll never get clean. No. Go enjoy yourself on this hot day like everyone else. All except me. As usual. I'll just suffer."

And suffer poor Eeyore did . . . until not too terribly much later when his friends all returned with something sure to cool even Eeyore off on this sultry day.

"Guess what we've brought you, Eeyore!" Roo squealed with delight.

"It's ice cream," whispered Pooh.

"Ice cream, huh?" Eeyore sighed. "I suppose I'll have to eat it all before it melts."

And do you know what? He did!

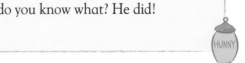

DUMBO
'Ears a Job for You, Dumbo!

It had been a hard day for little Dumbo. It was bad enough that everyone made fun of his ears except his mother, but then they had put his mother in a cage, so Dumbo couldn't even be with the one person who loved him and treated him decently.

What made things even worse was that Dumbo didn't have anything to do. It seemed that he was the only creature in the circus who didn't have a job. Everyone had a purpose except Dumbo. All he could do was feel sad and be laughed at.

Dumbo heaved a sigh and went for a walk through the circus tents. Soon, he found himself among the refreshment stands. Everyone here had a job too. Some were squeezing lemons to make lemonade. Others were popping popcorn or roasting peanuts. Wonderful smells filled the air.

Finally, Dumbo came to a little candyfloss wagon. The puffy cloud of sugar looked tempting, and Dumbo wanted a taste, but there were so many customers he couldn't get close enough.

Suddenly Dumbo heard a loud buzzing. Then all the customers waved their hands over their heads and ran away.

The smell of sugar had attracted a swarm of nasty flies!

"Scat!" cried the candyfloss man. "Go away before you scare off my customers."

Dumbo reached out his trunk to smell the delicious candyfloss.

"Not you, Dumbo!" the candyfloss man cried. "It's bad enough chasing flies. Do I have to chase elephants too?"

Poor Dumbo was startled. With a snort, he sucked candyfloss right up his nose.

Ahhh-choo!

When he sneezed, Dumbo's ears flapped – and something amazing happened.

"Remarkable!" the candyfloss man cried. "All the flies are gone. They think your ears are giant fly swatters!"

The candyfloss man patted Dumbo's head. "How would you like a job?"

Dumbo nodded enthusiastically and set to waving his ears. Soon, the candyfloss stand was the most popular refreshment stand in the circus – and had the least flies. But, best of all, Dumbo now had something to do to take his mind off his troubles. He was still sad, but things didn't seem quite so bad. And, who knows, perhaps soon he'd have his mother back.

"I wonder what other amazing things those big ears can do?" said the candyfloss man, giving Dumbo a friendly smile. "I'll bet they carry you far . . . ."

Hide, Dude!

"Come on, Squirt!" Nemo cried happily. "Race you to the coral shelf!"

Nemo took off, pumping his mismatched fins as hard as he could. His young sea turtle friend laughed and swam after him.

Squirt was visiting Nemo at his home on the reef. "This way, dude!" Squirt yelled, flinging himself through the water. "I'm catching some rad current over here!"

Nemo hesitated for just a second, watching as his friend tumbled along head over heels past some stinging coral. Squirt was so brave! Even after all that Nemo had been through – being captured by a scuba diver, then escaping from a tank to find his way home again – he still got scared sometimes.

With a deep breath, he threw himself into the current. He tumbled after Squirt, fins flying as the water carried him along. Finally, he came out the other end of the current, landing in the still ocean beside Squirt.

He giggled. "Hey, that was fun!" he cried. "Let's do it again! Squirt? Squirt, what's wrong?"

The sea turtle was staring into the distance, his eyes wide. "Hide, dude!" Squirt cried.

Before Nemo could respond, Squirt's head and legs popped into his shell and he landed on the sea floor with a flop.

Nemo started trembling. What had scared Squirt so much? He stared around, expecting to see a shark or something equally frightening. But all he could see nearby were a few pieces of coral with a lone Spanish dancer floating along above them.

He swam down and tapped on Squirt's shell. "Hey," he said. "What is it? There's nothing scary here."

"Whew!" Squirt's head popped out. He looked around, then gasped and hid again. When he spoke, his voice was muffled. "It's totally still there!"

Nemo blinked and looked around again. Again, all he saw were the coral and the Spanish dancer.

"Hey, wait a minute," he said, suddenly realizing something. "Haven't you ever seen a Spanish dancer before?"

"A – a Spanish wha-huh?" Squirt asked, still muffled.

Nemo knocked on his friend's shell again. "It's a kind of sea slug," he explained. "Don't worry, Spanish dancers are nice – you don't have to be scared. I promise."

Finally Squirt's head popped out again. He smiled sheepishly at Nemo.

"Sorry, dude," he said. "I never saw one of those before. It totally freaked me out."

"It's okay." Nemo smiled back. He already knew that new things could be scary – and now he knew he wasn't the only one who thought so. "Come on, let's go play."

The GREAT MOUSE DETECTIVE

A Lesson in Confidence

"Oh dear!" Olivia, a very worried little mouse, sat with Dr Dawson next to the fireplace in Basil of Baker Street's home.

"What's the matter?" Dr Dawson asked.

"What's the matter?" Olivia repeated indignantly. "My father's been stolen by a peg-leg bat! Have you forgotten already?"

"No, no, dear," Dawson reassured her. "Of course not. I know you must be quite upset."

"Quite upset!" Olivia cried angrily. "I couldn't possibly be more upset!"

"But we're at Basil's now, and he's the best. You even said so yourself," Dawson said.

"But what if he doesn't want to help me?" Olivia asked.

"Why wouldn't he want to help you?" Dawson asked.

"You heard him," Olivia answered. "'I simply have no time for lost fathers,'" she said, quoting the detective.

"He didn't mean it," Dawson said reassuringly. "He's just in the middle of something. Perhaps we caught him at a bad time. But, whatever the circumstances, my dear, you must try not to fret."

"I know you're trying to help me, Dr Dawson," Olivia said, as politely as she could manage. "But I don't know if I can really avoid fretting. My father is out there somewhere, and I just *have* to find him!"

"You're right!" Dawson said. "You do have to find him. You have to help Basil track down your father and, in order to do that, you are going to need a clear mind. Now, can you have a clear mind while you're fretting?"

"Well, it probably doesn't help," said Olivia reluctantly.

"Can you think logically while you're upset?" Dawson asked.

". . . Probably not," Olivia said.

"Can you work side-by-side with Basil of Baker Street, the great mouse detective, to save your beloved father while you are *worried*?" Dawson asked.

"No!" Olivia paused as the truth sank in. "No, I can't. I owe it to my father to be level-headed. I can be sad and scared later – right now I have to be a detective, like Basil!" she finished triumphantly.

"That, my young lady, is the smartest thing you could have said. And, if you can hold on to that attitude, your father will be found in no time." Dawson smiled at Olivia.

Just then, Basil came swooping back into the room. "Of course he will. I never miss my mark. Your father is as good as found, because I am just that good!"

Olivia smiled secretly. She knew *she* was just that good too.

My Side of the Story

Perhaps you know the story of how Pocahontas and John Smith made peace between their people. Well, I've got a much more interesting story for you – mine.

My name is Percival, but my friends call me Percy. Once upon a time, I was the pet pug of a very important man named Governor Ratcliffe. I lived a life of luxury. My meals were served in sterling silver bowls. I had ten different kinds of bones to choose from. I wore perfume, for goodness' sake! But life felt, well, pretty boring.

That all changed the day we arrived on the shores of America. Ratcliffe was after one thing and one thing only – gold. And Ratcliffe didn't care about the people who lived in this new land. John Smith did, but I didn't care much for John Smith. He was always trying to pat me on the head. "Grrrrr!" I would growl at him. You have to be firm with these humans. Make sure they know their place.

Not long after we had arrived in the New Land, I was having a bubble bath when suddenly – *splash!* – a raccoon landed in my tub! Well, if there's one thing my mother taught me, it was to avoid all animals without a pedigree. This wild creature could be rabid! The raccoon ate my cherries and then ran off. After that I had one thing on my mind – revenge!

The next time I saw the raccoon, he was eating bones out of my personal bone collection. So I had to chase him – it was a matter of pride! But wouldn't you know it, the brazen little devil trapped me in a hollow log. There I was, stumbling around the woods with a log stuck on my head. It was hours before I got that thing off.

That's when I ran into John Smith and Pocahontas. And guess who was with them – that bone-thieving raccoon! He grabbed a little hummingbird and started waving him at me like a sword. It would have been funny if it wasn't so annoying!

And then the weirdest thing of all happened – a tree talked to me! Grandmother Willow said I shouldn't chase Meeko. By chasing him, I had started trouble between us; now, it was time to stop the fighting. Of course, I understood immediately. I'm pretty clever, you know.

It took the humans a little longer to get the picture, and John Smith got hurt. But it all worked out okay in the end. I decided I didn't need my fancy, high-falutin' life, so I became a settler with my new friends!

John, however, had to go back to England. I knew he would miss me. So when he reached out to pat my head, I actually let him.

After all that he had been through, I felt he finally deserved it.

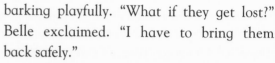

Beauty and the Beast

Belle and the Castle Puppy

Belle was strolling through the castle garden one day when she saw a puppy huddled outside the castle gates. He looked cold and dirty.

"Oh, you poor thing!" Belle cried. "Let's get you warmed up and fed!"

Once inside, Belle gave the puppy a bath. When he was clean and dry, the puppy ate a bowl of warm stew.

"I hope we can keep him!" Chip exclaimed.

All the enchanted objects were happy to have a guest. But the ottoman remembered when he had been a real dog. What if Belle liked this dog more?

"Do you want to play?" Belle asked, letting the puppy outside. As Belle and the others followed, the ottoman slinked out behind them.

A while later, the Beast walked up to Belle. "Someone has dug up my roses!" he exclaimed. Then the Beast saw the puppy. "Get rid of him – NOW!" the Beast roared as he stomped away.

Just then, the ottoman ran past Belle and chased after the Beast – his legs were muddy. Belle suddenly understood.

"The ottoman dug up the roses! He just wanted some attention, too!" Belle realized.

The puppy raced after the ottoman, barking playfully. "What if they get lost?" Belle exclaimed. "I have to bring them back safely."

"I'll come and light your way." Lumiere called to Belle.

Belle, carrying Lumiere, walked along a dark path. "Puppy! Ottoman!" she called.

Suddenly, Belle heard barking and followed the sound to a clearing where she saw the ottoman and puppy – who was barking loudly. Belle gasped. A large wolf was sitting nearby.

"The puppy is protecting the ottoman!" Lumiere exclaimed.

Quickly, Belle put Lumiere on the ground and lit a large stick she'd found.

"Get away! Get away!" she shouted swinging it towards the wolf.

Just then, the Beast showed up, roaring loudly. The wolf yelped with fear and ran away.

Later that night, everyone settled by the fireplace. Belle watched the Beast stroke the ottoman and feed biscuits to the puppy.

"May the puppy stay until I can find him a home?" she asked.

The Beast cleared his throat. "His home is here – with us," he answered gruffly.

Belle smiled. She loved the Beast's gentle, caring side that he was starting to show.

A Mouse in the House

Alice was a daydreamer. When her older sister tried to read Alice her lessons in the meadow by their house, Alice did everything but pay attention. Once, she fell asleep and dreamed of a silly place called Wonderland.

When Alice woke up from her dream, her sister gave up on lessons for the day and suggested they have tea instead.

Sitting at the dining room table, Alice began to tell her sister all about Wonderland. "I know I was only dreaming," said Alice, "but it all seemed so real!"

"What happened?" her sister asked.

"Well," said Alice. "I attended the strangest tea party at which the Mad Hatter and the March Hare – they were the hosts of the party – kept offering me tea, but refused to serve me any." Alice picked up the teapot to refill her own cup. "And you won't believe it, but inside the teapot lived a little–"

The lid of the pot Alice was holding flew open and a little whiskered face popped out. "Eek!" yelled Alice, slamming down the lid. Her mind raced. How could the Dormouse from her dream have crossed over into her real life?

Alice finished her tea and biscuits as quickly as possible. When her sister went to pour more tea, Alice grabbed the pot and insisted, "I'm sorry, but there isn't any more!"

"My goodness!" Alice's sister declared. "Now *you're* acting like the Mad Hatter and the March Hare!"

Alice slipped outside with the teapot as soon as she could. With her kitten Dinah following close behind, she went straight to the tree where she had fallen asleep that very afternoon. "Maybe if I doze off again," she told Dinah, "I can dream this little fellow back where he belongs."

But Alice couldn't fall asleep. She tried counting sheep, and reading the boring book her sister had left by the tree. Nothing seemed to work. Finally, she lifted the lid of the pot. "I'm sorry," she told the Dormouse. "I'm not sure what else to do." But the Dormouse knew. He jumped out of the teapot – and was chased by Alice's kitten! The Dormouse ran into the stump that led to the rabbit hole of Alice's dream, but Dinah stayed behind. The inside of the stump looked too dark and scary to the little cat. Alice waited, but the Dormouse did not come out again.

That night, as she slept, Alice dreamed of Wonderland again. She was back at the un-birthday party, waiting to be served a cup of tea. The Dormouse threw open the teapot and gave Alice a sleepy grin. "Thank you, miss!" he said. "And, whatever you do, please don't dream about your cat!"

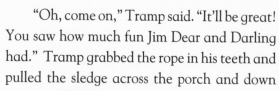

Sledging

Lady stood on the porch as Jim Dear and Darling walked up the front path. Jim pulled a sledge and Darling held their son. They were all covered in snow, rosy cheeked and smiling from ear to ear.

"That was fun! Wasn't it, Darling?" Jim asked.

"I don't know the last time I had so much fun," Darling agreed, patting Lady on the head.

"But we should get out of these wet clothes before one of us catches a cold," Jim said, leaning the sledge against the side of the house.

"I agree," Darling said. And the three of them hurried inside.

Just then, Tramp came walking up the front path. "Hey, Pidge," he said to Lady. "What do you say we take this old thing for a spin?"

"What is it, anyway?" Lady wanted to know.

"A sledge!" Tramp told her.

"What do you do with it?" she asked.

"You ride down hills," Tramp explained.

"That sounds dangerous," Lady said hesitantly.

"Nah, it's fun!" Tramp cried. "So, what do you say?"

"It's awfully cold out here," Lady said. She wasn't convinced at all.

"Oh, come on," Tramp said. "It'll be great! You saw how much fun Jim Dear and Darling had." Tramp grabbed the rope in his teeth and pulled the sledge across the porch and down the steps.

Lady took off after him. "Wait for me!" she cried anxiously.

"Come on, Pidge!" Tramp encouraged her. "Jump on!"

Lady jumped onto the sledge, and Tramp pulled her down the snow-covered street and up to the top of a nearby hill. "What a view, huh?" he said.

"What a view indeed," Lady agreed. "What now?"

"Now, we ride," Tramp said. He pushed the sledge forward and took a running leap onto it, sending them racing down the hill.

"Oh, dear!" Lady yelped as they plummeted down the hill, the wind blowing her ears back.

"Just hold on!" Tramp instructed.

Lady squeezed her eyes shut, and Tramp barked with excitement. But suddenly they hit a patch of ice, the sledge spun, and they went flying – right into a snowbank!

Tramp jumped to his feet. "Pidge, are you okay?" he asked anxiously.

"Okay?" Lady asked. She was already pulling the sledge back up the hill. "Hurry up, Tramp! Let's do it again!"

Red Alert!

"Nice work with the wheat husker," Flik said. He smiled with satisfaction as he watched a troop of ants lower the contraption that lightly smashed the wheat kernels. How had the colony got along without his clever inventions? Flik wondered.

"How's it going with the berry masher?" called a voice. It was Atta, the colony's Queen.

"I was just heading over to take a look," Flik said, smiling at Queen Atta. "Care to join me?"

"Sure," Atta said as she led the way to the berry-mashing area. Mashing berries was messy, so the ants did it in a special part of the anthill.

"Cowabunga!" called a large ant. Ten dozen ants leaped off a rock onto a giant lever. The lever lowered, pressing a flat rock onto a pile of berries. Sweet red juice squirted out from the sides and dripped into carved wooden bowls.

When all the juice was squeezed out of the berries, Atta dipped her finger into a bowl for a taste.

"Delicious," she said. Red juice stained her mouth and chin.

"The berries were especially sweet this year," Flik said modestly.

"And with your new invention we should have plenty of juice for this year's feast," Atta said. "As long as Dot and the Blueberries don't drink it all first," she added.

Flik laughed. Dot and her Blueberry friends loved berry juice and were always trying to dip into it before the feast. They had been shooed away from the berry masher more than once in the last week. Three times, in fact!

"Good work, masher ants!" Flik called to the horde that was climbing back up to their jumping rock. Another group was making a pile of fresh berries.

They had nearly finished piling a huge mound of berries, when suddenly the alarm sounded.

"Alert, alert!" a guard ant called through a megaphone made from a rolled-up leaf. "Red fire ants are storming the colony!"

Flik, Atta and the masher ants fled the food area as fast as their legs could carry them. Sure enough, they soon ran into half-a-dozen red ants. Flik was about to charge when he heard a familiar voice.

"Flik, it's me!" it said. The voice sounded like . . . Dot's.

"Hold on!" Flik shouted. The ants stopped. Flik quickly wiped the first red ant's sticky face. "These aren't fire ants," Flik explained. "They're Blueberries – covered in berry juice!" He smiled at Atta. "Maybe we should call them Redberries, instead!"

Jasmine's Jewel Thief

"This is so much fun!" cried Jasmine. She and Aladdin were flying all over the desert on their favourite flying carpet.

Jasmine leaned back against Aladdin and reached up to smooth back her windblown hair. But, as her fingers brushed past her ears, she noticed something missing. Sitting up, she felt again. One of her gold earrings was gone!

"What is it?" Aladdin asked when he saw Jasmine searching the Carpet.

"It's nothing. Just an earring," Jasmine said. She tried to be casual about it, but her eyes gave her away.

"Just an earring?" Aladdin said. "Didn't your father give them to you?"

"Yes," Jasmine confessed. "They are my favourites. At least, they were."

"Are," Aladdin said firmly. "We'll find the other one. Home, Carpet," he instructed.

Back at the palace, Aladdin and Jasmine looked everywhere. They searched their chambers, the gardens, even the fountains. They were about to search the kitchen when Abu scampered by.

Aladdin looked at the monkey suspiciously. "You haven't seen a shiny gold earring, have you?"

Abu shrugged, but did not look Aladdin in the eye. Aladdin knew he was on to something.

The monkey was crazy for anything that glittered. He'd spent too many years as a poor thief.

"Are you sure?" Aladdin asked sternly.

Slowly, Abu motioned Aladdin to follow him.

When he saw the monkey's bed, Aladdin almost started to laugh. Why hadn't he noticed before how lumpy it was?

When Abu pulled back the covers, Aladdin could not help himself. He laughed out loud. Abu's bed was covered with shiny objects! There were spoons, goblets and coins. And, from beneath his small pillow, Abu pulled out Jasmine's earring.

Aladdin shook his head and smiled at Abu. "You don't have to scavenge any more. We live in the palace!"

So they took the earring to Jasmine. "You found it!" she cried. She leaned down and gave Abu a kiss. The little monkey blushed.

"Here, Abu, take this ring as a reward for finding my earring," Jasmine said. She removed a gold ring from her finger and gave it to the monkey, who gave a happy jump and tucked it into his hat.

"Actually, Abu didn't really–" Aladdin began. But just then he caught Abu's deadly glare. "Well," he continued, amused. "Yes. Um, good job, Abu."

Bambi

Night-time is for... Exploring!

As the moon rose above the forest, Bambi snuggled close to his sleeping mother. What a day it had been! Exploring new places, learning new words and meeting new friends. Bambi yawned and closed his eyes . . . .

"Bambi! Oh, Bambi!"

Bambi slowly opened his eyes. "Thumper?" he whispered. "Why aren't you asleep?"

"Asleep? Come on!" cried Thumper. "Sleep is for the birds! How can you sleep when there's so much to see and do at night?"

"But everybody knows that night-time is for sleeping," Bambi said.

"Oh, brother," Thumper said. "Do you have a lot to learn! Follow me, Bambi, and I'll show you how the night is a whole new day!"

And suddenly, at the prospect of an all-new adventure, Bambi's sleepiness disappeared. Quietly, he stood up and let Thumper lead the way.

Thumper was right – the forest was as busy at night as it was during the day, but with a whole new group of animals. Owls, opossums, raccoons and badgers – all those animals that Bambi thought spent most of their lives asleep – were now as lively as could be.

"Wh-wh-what's that?" Bambi exclaimed, as a dot of light landed on his nose.

"Don't worry, Bambi, it's just a firefly,"

Thumper said with a giggle.

"'Firefly'," Bambi said. Then suddenly, the little light disappeared. "Hey, where'd it go?"

"There it is!" cried Thumper, pointing to Bambi's tail. "No, wait. It's over there."

Happily, Thumper and Bambi chased the firefly as it flitted from one friend to the other. "I think he likes us!" Thumper cried.

But their game was soon interrupted by a flurry of sound. Thousands of leathery wings were suddenly beating overhead.

"Duck, Bambi!" hollered Thumper, just as the whole group swooped around their heads.

"Boy, that was close!" said Thumper.

"Were those fireflies too?" Bambi asked.

"Naw," Thumper laughed. "They didn't light up! Those were bats."

"'Bats'," repeated Bambi. "They're really busy at night."

"You can say that again," agreed Thumper, trying to stifle a yawn. And, since yawns are contagious, Bambi's own yawn was not far behind.

"This was fun," Bambi told his friend. "But what do you say we go home and go to bed?"

But there was no answer . . . for Thumper was already fast asleep!

MULAN
Such a Shame

Mulan nudged Khan into a gallop and kept her eyes straight ahead. She was on her way to town to go to the market for her family. It was a regular trip for her, but the people working on the sides of the road did not seem to think so. Without even looking at them, Mulan knew that she was causing whispers. But they weren't just talking about her. They were talking about the man riding with her – Captain Li Shang.

The captain didn't seem to notice the whispering, even as they entered the town and a group of girls giggled behind their fans. Mulan did her best to ignore it. Everyone had been making a fuss over her since she returned from the Emperor's palace. They all said she was a hero, but inside she just felt like . . . Mulan.

Shang swung down from his horse and offered to go inside to buy the rice. Mulan was about to object. She didn't need Shang's help at the market. The only reason she'd brought him along was because he wanted to see more of her town. But Shang was already inside the tiny shop.

Mulan sighed. She held the Captain in high esteem. She liked him – she really did. But she was always disagreeing with him. Even when she didn't need to.

"Shame!" Across the street, an older woman pointed at Mulan, startling her out of her thoughts.

"Shame!" the woman said again. "Don't think I have forgotten you."

Mulan blushed, recognizing the woman. It was the Matchmaker! Mulan looked at the ground as her cheeks grew even hotter, but they were not as hot as they had been on the day that she first met the Matchmaker – the day she accidentally set the woman on fire!

The Matchmaker continued, pointing and screeching at Mulan as she waddled across the street. "You!" she scolded. "Just because all of China thinks you are a hero does not mean you can escape your fate. I predict you will bring shame to your family. I feel it."

Mulan did not know what to say to the old woman.

"There is not a matchmaker in the world who could ever find a match for you!" the woman screeched.

"Then it is a good thing she will never need one," Shang said. As he walked past the Matchmaker, he accidently stepped in a puddle, splashing the Matchmaker from head to toe!

The Matchmaker was speechless, her face twisted into a scowl. Mulan could not think of a thing to say either. But, instead of wearing a scowl, her face was set in a wide smile.

August 26

Bedtime for Duchess

"Come, my precious ones!" Duchess called to Berlioz, Toulouse and Marie. "It's time to go to sleep."

"Oh, Mother!" Toulouse complained.

"But I'm not tired!" Marie joined in.

"I'm not going to sleep," Berlioz added. "Night-time is just when things start happening for us alley cats." Berlioz crouched down low, hindquarters in the air, and pounced on an imaginary opponent.

"Who does he think he's kidding?" Toulouse whispered to Marie, who rolled her eyes in agreement.

"Now, now, it's been a long day," Duchess told them. "I don't want to hear any more protests."

"Mother!" Berlioz whined.

"We need a bedtime story!" Marie insisted.

"A story? My darlings, it's way past your bedtime, and I'm just too tired tonight," replied Duchess.

"Then why don't we tell *you* a story?" Toulouse offered.

"Yeah!" Berlioz chimed in.

"What a lovely idea," said Duchess.

"Once upon a time . . ." Marie began.

"There was a big, mean, ferocious alley cat," Berlioz continued.

"Berlioz!" Marie protested. "It's not supposed to be scary. She'll have nightmares!"

"Sorry, Mama," Berlioz said.

"That's quite all right," Duchess told him.

"Now where were we?" Toulouse asked.

"Once upon a time . . ." Marie began again.

"Yeah, once upon a time there was this amazing kitten," Toulouse said. "And he could paint like no other kitten you've ever seen."

"And that's because the model for his paintings was the most beautiful kitten you've ever laid eyes on," Marie added.

"Give me a break!" Berlioz said, grumbling under his breath. He and Toulouse snickered.

"Very funny." Marie was not amused. "Can we get back to the story?"

"This kitten was a painter by day and a smooth-talking, alley-hanging, danger-seeking hepcat by night," Berlioz continued.

Toulouse tapped Berlioz with his paw. He looked up and saw what both Toulouse and Marie were seeing. Duchess herself had fallen asleep!

Berlioz, Toulouse and Marie each gave their mother a kiss good night.

"Good night, Mama," said Marie.

"Good night, Mama," said Toulouse.

"Good night, Mama," said Berlioz.

Then all three curled up beside Duchess and promptly fell asleep too.

Beauty and the Beast

A Wintry Walk

"It's so beautiful," Belle murmured as she gazed out of the castle window. Snow had been falling for hours and hours, covering everything in a deep blanket of white. "You know what would be nice? A wa –"

Suddenly, a heavy red cape was draped over her shoulders. "How about a walk?" the Prince asked.

Belle smiled into his blue eyes. "I was just thinking that!" she said.

"Aha," he replied mischievously. "But were you thinking of a walk on these?" He pulled a pair of large showshoes out from behind a chair.

"Snowshoes!" Belle cried, clapping her hands together. She and her father used to go showshoeing together in the woods when she was a little girl, and she loved it. No matter how deep the snow was, the special shoes allowed her to walk over the huge drifts.

Minutes later the pair were in the castle courtyard, strapping the snowshoes onto their boots. Belle walked forward gracefully, heading through the gate towards the forest, pausing to scatter birdseed for the neighbourhood birds.

But the Prince was having trouble, tripping over the giant shoes with every step.

"When I was a beast, I just walked through the snow," he said, panting. "I didn't have to bother with silly contraptions like these!" He stepped forward and tumbled headfirst into a deep snowbank.

Belle laughed. At first, the Prince scowled but soon he was laughing too.

"You're thinking too much," Belle said. "It's actually a lot like walking in regular shoes. You just have to keep your feet a little further apart so they don't get caught up on each other."

"Hmm," the Prince said. He stepped forward. But, when he lifted his other foot, it caught on the icy top layer of snow, and he fell again.

Belle stifled a giggle as she helped him to his feet. "Step lightly," she suggested.

"I'll say," the Prince grumbled. He stepped more lightly this time, and moved easily across the snow. Soon he was keeping up with Belle, who led him all the way through the forest. It was a wonderful, wintry walk. And, when they got back to the castle, they found hot chocolate and biscuits waiting for them in front of the fire!

"Oh, good," said the Prince. "Eating! This is one thing I'll always be good at." He picked up a biscuit, which broke and fell with a *plop!* into his cup.

"Aw," he said, crestfallen.

"You know," Belle said with a teasing smile, "you aren't so different from the clumsy beast I fell in love with!"

True Love

Time was running out for Tiana and Naveen to return to the town. They had to find Charlotte and get her to kiss Naveen while she was still the Mardi Gras princess – and that was only until midnight. After that, her kiss wouldn't lift the evil spell, and Tiana and Naveen would be frogs forever!

"But surely we aren't going to swim across the bayou?" worried Tiana.

"I've got an idea!" declared their friend Louis, the alligator.

He led them to the steamer, a paddleboat that was coming downriver, taking costume-clad revellers to the New Orleans carnival. Tiana, Naveen, Louis and Ray the firefly climbed on board. Fortunately, a jazz band took Louis for a trumpet player in disguise and invited him to play with them! The alligator's own dream had at last come true!

Naveen sighed. He would like to have his dream come true too! And Mama Odie had helped Naveen realize something important. He had finally discovered what mattered more than anything else to him – Tiana.

"She is the love of my life, Ray!" he confided to his friend. "She's the one I want to marry, not Charlotte! I will ask her to marry me tonight!"

Of course, Naveen was renouncing Charlotte's fortune, but with Tiana he would be rich in love!

"And then I will help Tiana to buy her restaurant anyway," he resolved as he prepared a candlelit dinner on the roof of the boat. "I will work hard, and I will earn all the money she needs."

Full of good intentions, he ran in search of Tiana.

"Oh, Naveen!" she enthused when she saw the pretty table. "What are we celebrating?"

"Errm... our last hours as frogs!" he replied in embarrassment.

He was seeking the courage to make his declaration... when she cried, "We're arriving at the port, Naveen, and there's the building that I'm going to buy for my restaurant! Thanks to your marriage to Charlotte, I will be able to pay the estate agent! It's my last chance – if I don't settle the amount tomorrow, the sugar mill will go to the other buyer!"

On hearing these words, Naveen quickly changed his mind. He would rather sacrifice himself and marry Charlotte; otherwise Tiana would be so unhappy at losing her restaurant – her only dream.

I really love Tiana, he thought. *All I want is her happiness.* Yes, he was sure now. She was definitely his true love!

Tinker Bell
AND THE GREAT FAIRY RESCUE

The Automobile

Tinker Bell arrived in Pixie Hollow last spring, where she had discovered her talent as a tinker fairy. Now, she was on a mission on the mainland, the world of humans, where the fairies were setting up summer. But Tinker Bell couldn't find anything that needed to be repaired, so she wanted to look for lost things.

The other fairies reminded Tinker Bell that they needed to stay hidden from humans – because humans could be dangerous to fairies.

Just then, a loud *CRACK* went through the fairy camp! Fawn was startled and knocked over some paint she was using to decorate butterfly wings, and the splattered butterfly took off.

The loud noise made Tinker Bell very curious. The other fairies hid, but Tinker Bell went to see where the noise came from. She was intrigued by the sight of an automobile making its way down the winding road – and took off after it! Tinker Bell had never seen a car before.

Tink followed and watched as the car stopped at an old house in the country.

Then she saw a little girl, her father and their cat get out.

"Could we have a tea party in the meadow? Please?" Lizzy, the little girl, pleaded.

"Not today," Dr Griffiths said wearily. "I have quite a bit of work to do."

After the three had gone inside, Tink flew under the car to examine it. Suddenly, Vidia appeared. "You shouldn't be this close to the house!" she scolded.

But Tinker Bell was already poking around the engine. She found an interesting-looking lever and turned it. Outside of the car, Vidia got showered with water! She was furious! Tink knew fairies couldn't fly with wet wings!

Moments later, Lizzy and her father returned to the car – and the fairies froze in fright. Luckily, the humans were busy examining a strange-looking butterfly.

"I guess that's just the way the fairies decided to paint it," Lizzy said.

"Fairies do not paint butterfly wings, because fairies are not real," Dr Griffiths insisted as he captured the creature with a net. Lizzy sighed. Her father was a scientist and he didn't believe in magic or fairies. He was also often too busy to spend much time with her.

Tinker Bell had heard the humans' conversation and she almost wanted to prove fairies existed right there and then! But she knew that could be dangerous, so she stayed hidden – for now.

Disney
THE
LION KING
The Very Best Fisherman of All

Simba and his friends Timon and Pumbaa were hungry. They wandered through the forest until they came to an old, rotten tree. Timon knocked on the trunk.

"What's it sound like, Timon?" Pumbaa asked.

"Like our breakfast!" Timon replied.

He yanked at the bark and hundreds of grubs slithered out.

Timon handed Simba a grub.

"No, thanks." Simba sighed. "I'm tired of grubs."

"Well, the ants are tasty," said Timon. "They come in two flavours. Red and black."

Simba shook his head. "Don't you eat anything but bugs?"

"Fish!" Pumbaa declared.

"I love fish!" Simba exclaimed.

"Why didn't you say so?" said Timon. "There's a pond at the end of this trail." The three friends started off down the trail.

"What now?" asked Simba when they arrived at the pond.

"That's the problem!" said Timon. "We're not the best fishermen in the world."

"I'll teach you!" Simba said.

The lion climbed up a tree and crawled onto a branch that hung over the water. Then he snatched a fish out of the water.

"See!" Simba said, jumping to the ground nimbly. "Not a problem. Fishing's easy."

"Not for me!" Timon cried. He dangled from the branch, but his arms weren't long enough to reach the fish.

Simba laughed. "Better let Pumbaa try."

"What a joke!" cried Timon. "Pumbaa can't even climb this tree."

"Want to bet?" asked Pumbaa.

"Stay there," Timon warned. "I don't think this branch is strong enough for both of us."

With a hop, Pumbaa landed on the branch next to Timon. The limb started to bend.

"Yikes!" Timon cried as he leaped to another tree.

Crack! The branch broke under Pumbaa. With a squeal, he landed in the pond. The splash was enormous!

Simba, sitting on the bank, was soaked. Timon was nearly blasted from his perch. Pond water fell like rain all around them.

Simba opened his eyes and started to laugh. So did Timon.

Pumbaa was sitting in a pool of mud where the pond had been. He'd splashed so much of the water out that dozens of fish squirmed on the ground, just waiting to be gobbled up.

"Wow!" Timon cried. "I think Pumbaa is the very best fisherman of all!"

A Prize-winning Pair

Max and his dad, Goofy, were sitting at the breakfast table. Max looked at the funny pages, while Goofy leafed through the rest of the paper. "Listen to this!" said Goofy. "Channel 10 sponsors the Father & Son of the Year Contest. The father and son who can prove that they have achieved something truly incredible together will appear on national TV on Father's Day to accept their award."

"Too bad Bigfoot ruined that video we took of him last summer," said Max. "Finding him and living to tell about it – now that was incredible!"

Max paused for a moment. "Hey, I know! Why can't we go back and find him again? And this time we'll make sure we have proof."

"Okay, Maxie. Count me in!" said Goofy. "And we can even get a little fishing in too."

Goofy and Max reached the campsite that night, pitched their tent, and went to sleep. Soon they were awakened by a loud crash.

"It's him!" cried Max. "Get the camera!" But, when they poked their heads out, they saw it wasn't Bigfoot at all, but Pete and P.J.

"I'm sorry," said P.J. "I told my dad about your trip, and now he wants *us* to win that prize. We're out here looking for Bigfoot too."

The next day, Pete set up a barbecue with several juicy steaks. "This will lure him out for sure," he told P.J. The trick worked. In a matter of minutes, Bigfoot crashed through the trees and made a beeline for the meat. "Tackle him, P.J.!" yelled Pete.

Though he was scared, P.J. did as he was told. Bigfoot threw him around like a rag doll while Pete turned on the camera. "The judges are going to love this!" cried Pete.

"Help!" P.J. begged.

Goofy and Max heard P.J.'s cries and came running from the lake. Without saying a word, Goofy jabbed the monster in the backside with a fishing lure while Max threw a fishing net over the monster's head. Howling, the monster dropped P.J. to the ground.

"You were awesome," Max told Goofy.

"Right back at you, son," Goofy replied.

"Got it!" Pete said triumphantly. "Here, P.J., take some footage of me." He struck a hero's pose in front of the captive monster.

Back at home, Pete sent the video to Channel 10. But, after viewing the tape, the judges decided it was Goofy and Max who deserved the award instead.

But on Father's Day – the day they were to appear on TV – Goofy and Max decided to go to the beach together instead. They realized they didn't need anybody to tell them what an incredible father-and-son team they were. They knew it already!

Disney
Sleeping Beauty
The Wedding Gift

Aurora was busily preparing for her wedding day, and the whole castle was abuzz with excitement. The gardeners were gathering the most fragrant flowers. The chefs were cooking up the grandest of banquets. And the royal dressmaker had the most honoured job of all – sewing the wedding dress.

"If you please, Your Royal Highness, what did you have in mind?" the dressmaker asked Aurora.

"Well," Aurora began.

"You'll want white, of course," the dressmaker broke in, "I see something more vanilla, to complement your lovely skin."

"Actually," Aurora said, "I –"

But the dressmaker wasn't done yet. "And you'll want a train!"

That wasn't what Aurora had had in mind at all. But before Aurora could say anything, the fairy Merryweather spoke up.

"But what if she doesn't want a dress that colour?" she said, pointing to one of the samples. "What the dear girl needs is something blue," Merryweather said.

"Oh, no!" Flora scolded. "A wedding dress shouldn't be blue. It should be pink!"

"Just a minute now!" King Stefan declared. "I hereby decree that the colour of the gown be left to the bride."

Aurora smiled at her father. Then the king went on. "The most important thing is that the dress be covered with lots of jewels!"

"Why, of course, Your Supreme Highness," the dressmaker said. "Lots of jewels."

Aurora sighed. While her father and the dressmaker talked about various designs, she felt a soft hand take hold of hers.

"Come, darling," her mother whispered, smiling. "I have something to show you."

Together, they walked into the Queen's dressing room. And there, Aurora watched her mother pull out a long, beautiful gown, edged with delicate lace and tiny pearls.

"This was my wedding dress when I was a princess," the Queen explained. "And my mother's before me. I had hoped one day you'd wear it – if you'd like to."

"Oh, Mother!" Aurora exclaimed. "It's just what I had in mind!"

Moments later, Aurora went downstairs, wearing her mother's wedding gown.

"Oohh!" The fairies gasped.

"Perfect!" declared her father.

All agreed that the dress looked as if it had been made especially for Aurora – and, in a very special way, it had been.

Tangled

Incredible Tales

Flynn and Rapunzel were trapped in a cave. The water was rising and it had already reached as high as their chins!

Flynn tried diving under the water to find a way out, but it was so dark that he couldn't see a thing. He cut his hand trying to dislodge the large rocks surrounding them, but the boulders wouldn't budge. It wasn't easy feeling his way along the walls.

"My hair glows in the dark!" Rapunzel suddenly remembered.

Flynn gave her a strange look, convinced that she'd gone crazy.

"I promise you. If I sing, my hair will glow!" Rapunzel insisted.

Flynn was still in shock when Rapunzel broke into a beautiful song and then dived underwater. He quickly joined her and was stunned to see her hair glowing so brightly it lit up the entire cave!

Flynn spotted an opening in the rocks and swam towards it, pulling Rapunzel along with him. They soon emerged into the open air and found themselves on the river bank.

"We made it! We're alive!" exclaimed Rapunzel, as she helped revive Pascal.

She looked over at Flynn who was in a state of shock – but not because they had just nearly drowned.

"Her hair glows," he murmured. Then he turned to Pascal. "I didn't see that coming. Why does her hair glow?"

Rapunzel pulled her hair from the river and began wringing the water out of it. "It doesn't just glow," she said calmly.

They started walking to find somewhere to dry off. Flynn gathered some wood to light a campfire.

"Just don't freak out," Rapunzel told Flynn once the fire was lit, and she wrapped her hair around his hand, which he had wounded getting out of the cave. As Rapunzel began to sing, her hair once again glowed brightly. Within moments Flynn's hand was healed.

"Your hair really is magic," he muttered in bewilderment. "It's incredible! How long has your hair been like that?"

"Always. That's why my mother kept me in the tower, because people might steal it. How long ago did you change your name?"

Flynn blushed with embarrassment.

"Flynn was my favourite storybook hero when I was young, at the orphanage. I always wanted to be a swashbuckling hero like him!"

Rapunzel burst out laughing.

"One thing's certain, Eugene, each of us, in our own way, has an incredible tale to tell!"

Tinker Bell Never Gives Up

While they were setting up summer on the mainland, the fairies based their camp under a large oak tree, away from the prying eyes of humans.

But shortly after Tinker Bell arrived, a car had backfired with a bang as it was driving past on a nearby road.

The noise had made everyone jump and Fawn accidentally spilled paint on a butterfly's wing!

The other fairies had hid, but Tinker Bell just had to see what had made the noise. Vidia went after her, trying to get Tink to come back. But Tink wouldn't listen.

The car had stopped outside of a county house. A little girl, Lizzy, and her father had got out of the car and gone into the house with their bags.

Tink had flown into the car's engine to investigate and had accidentally showered Vidia with water! Vidia was upset, because she couldn't fly with wet wings.

Just then, Lizzy and her father returned to finish unloading the car. Tink and Vidia froze, but the humans' attention was focused on a butterfly – the very one that had been splashed with paint when the car backfired.

Lizzy thought that fairies had decided to paint the wing differently, but her father,

Dr Griffiths, disagreed. He didn't believe in fairies. He caught the butterfly in a jar to show to the museum.

If Vidia hadn't stopped her, Tink would have flown out and proven that fairies existed right then and there!

Meanwhile, Lizzy was pulling a little fairy house out of the back of the car. She hoped a real fairy would come to live in her miniature house one day.

Lizzy invited her father to help her set it up in the meadow, but – as usual – he was too busy. He had to get ready for a meeting he was having at the museum the next day.

When the humans had left, Tinker Bell apologized to Vidia for getting her wet.

"Maybe if you spent less time causing disasters," Vidia snapped, "you wouldn't have to help everybody so much."

But Tinker Bell wouldn't listen. She was too excited! The pair set off together into the meadow, where they soon spotted Lizzy's fairy house! Tink flew over to investigate.

"Tinker Bell, we're not supposed to go near human houses!" warned Vidia.

"Human houses are a lot bigger," Tink replied.

Vidia sighed, knowing Tink wouldn't give up on her plan to explore.

Peter Pan
A 'Snappy' New Ship

"**M**y ship, my beautiful ship!" Captain Hook moaned. It had not been a good day for the pirate. Peter Pan and the Darling children had stolen his ship. And now, Hook was stranded on an island with Smee and the other pirates, their rowing boat having been chomped to bits by the crocodile.

"It's a nice island, Captain," offered Smee, trying to cheer up his boss. "And you could use a vacation. Why, look at those dark circles under your eyes."

Captain Hook turned to Smee with a furious look on his face. "Pirates don't take vacations!" Hook boomed. "Pirates seek revenge! Which is precisely what we are going to do, as soon as we have a new ship to sail in."

Smee looked around. "Where are we going to find a ship around here, Sir?" he asked.

"*We* aren't going to find one," Captain Hook answered. "You and the rest of this mangy crew are going to *build* one! And I don't mean a little one either. I mean a big, menacing, fit-for-a-magnificent-pirate-like-me one!"

For weeks, the pirates chopped trees and cut them into planks for the ship. They whittled thousands of pegs to use for nails, and crushed countless berries to use for paint. "You're not moving fast enough!" Hook complained as he sat in the shade, sipping juice out of a pineapple.

Finally, an exhausted Smee fetched Hook as he awoke from his afternoon nap.

"It's ready, Captain!" he announced.

Even Hook had to admit the ship was magnificent. Shaped like a gigantic crocodile, it was painted a reptilian shade of green. "No one will dare come near this ship. Not even that pesky crocodile. He won't want to tussle with anything this terrifying," Smee assured him.

Captain Hook was delighted. "We set sail tomorrow!" he crowed.

That night, Smee couldn't resist putting one more finishing touch on the ship. He painted a row of eyelashes on the crocodile's eyelids.

The next morning, Captain Hook and the crew climbed aboard and pushed off. The ticking crocodile soon appeared.

"Smee!" yelled a terrified Captain Hook. "I thought you said he wouldn't come near us!"

"But look how calm he is," said Smee, puzzled. "He's even smiling!"

Smee leaned over the side of the railing. "You know, it might be those eyelashes I painted. Maybe the croc thinks the ship is its mother."

Hook lunged at the roly-poly pirate. "You made my ship look like a *mother* crocodile? This vessel is supposed to be terrifying!"

"Mothers *can* be terrifying, sir," said Smee. "You should have seen mine when I told her I was going to become a pirate!"

The Twilight Bark

Rolly, Patch, Lucky and the rest of the puppies were watching the end of "The Thunderbolt Adventure Hour". As the credits began to roll, Pongo turned off the TV.

"Aw, come on, Dad!" Patch complained.

"We let you stay up late to watch the whole show," Pongo said.

Lucky sat staring at the blank television screen, hoping it would magically turn itself back on.

Perdy licked his face encouragingly. "Sit down, children," she said. "Your father and I need to speak with you."

"Uh-oh," Penny said worriedly.

"Oh, it's nothing like that," Pongo assured her. "We just think it's time to tell you about the legend of the Twilight Bark."

"Sounds cool!" Pepper cheered.

"What's the Twilight Bark?" Freckles asked.

"Legend has it," Perdy began, "that there's a special way that dogs can send each other messages. It stretches from the farthest side of the city all the way to the farthest part of the countryside."

"Wow!" Penny gasped. "Why would you need to do that?"

"Sometimes," Pongo began, "you need to communicate information from one place to another quickly, and you don't have time to go

to the other place yourself."

"I don't need any Twilight Bark!" Patch said. "I can take care of myself."

"Fat chance!" Lucky said under his breath.

"What do you know?" Patch barked.

"If you ever get into any trouble," Perdy told the pups, "just go to the top of the highest hill you can find, and bark out your message, and the members of the Twilight Bark will pass it along until someone can come and help you."

"That sounds like a bunch of baloney," Patch told his parents.

"Patch!" Pongo scolded his son. "That isn't very nice."

Just then, Lucky started howling at the top of his lungs.

"What's got into you?" Perdy asked.

"I'm trying out the Twilight Bark," Lucky said. "To get us rescued from Patch."

"Lucky," Perdy scolded him, "apologize to your brother."

"That's okay," Patch said. "I don't need his apology. I was right anyway. All that howling and no word from the Twilight Bark."

Just then, the doorbell rang. All the puppies gasped and turned to look at Patch.

Perdy and Pongo smiled at each other, knowing it was actually Roger returning from the shop with milk for tomorrow's breakfast.

An Out-of-this-world Party

Every year, one of Lilo's classmates had a party to celebrate the last day of school. This year, Lilo begged Nani to let her have the party at their house. She wanted to show off her new friends Jumba and Pleakley to her classmates – and to prove to them that even though Stitch wasn't a very good dog, he was a great alien!

Lilo gave invitations to all her classmates – even Myrtle, but only because Nani said Lilo had to invite her. Myrtle didn't want to go to the party any more than Lilo wanted to have her there, but she didn't want to be left out either.

On the big afternoon, everyone went straight to Lilo's house after school.

Lilo ushered all the children to a stage in the garden. Then she pulled back the curtains to reveal Stitch in a fancy rock-and-roll costume. Stitch crooned into a microphone while swivelling his hips and strumming his guitar. All the children thought he was cool – except Myrtle. When Stitch tried to give her a kiss on the cheek during a love song, she shrieked, "Ooooh! Yuck! Dog germs!"

"Time for crafts!" Pleakley called. "Today, you are each going to make your own intergalactic communicator. You'll need to decide which planet you would like to contact so we can program your device accordingly."

A little while later, one boy shouted, "Hey, I called Jupiter!"

Another child yelled, "I'm talking to Mars!"

Myrtle stamped her foot. "This dumb thing doesn't work," she said. "All I've got is static!"

Jumba turned to Lilo and gave her a wink. "Who wants to play Pin the Smile on the Man in the Moon?" he asked.

"I do! I do!" shouted Myrtle.

Jumba hustled Myrtle into a small spaceship with no windows. Then he handed her a large, paper smile. "When you pass by the moon in a few hours," said Jumba, "try to pin the smile in the correct position. Remember that you will be travelling at several thousand miles per hour, so act quickly!" Then he shut the cockpit door.

"But the spaceship is fake," Lilo said to Jumba. "It's not moving or anything."

"Ah, but Myrtle doesn't know that," Jumba replied. "Inside the ship, it looks like she's heading to the moon. This should keep her busy for a few hours while we enjoy ourselves." He smiled. "Now, who's up for cake?"

The kids cheered, and everyone moved over to a picnic table, leaving the spaceship behind. As she followed them, Lilo heard Myrtle grumble from inside the little ship, "This is the most boring party game ever."

252

A Magical Surprise

It was a lovely day in Agrabah. In the palace garden, Princess Jasmine was pouring a bowl of tea for her pet tiger, Rajah. It was, in fact, just like every other lovely day in Agrabah – and that was the problem.

"Sorry to be so glum," Jasmine said to Rajah. "I was hoping to spend some time with Aladdin, but I can't find him anywhere."

Rajah nodded his furry head sympathetically.

Just then, to Jasmine's surprise, the Magic Carpet zoomed into the garden and stopped in front of her – all alone.

"Where's Aladdin, Magic Carpet?" But when the Magic Carpet did a quick flip, Jasmine realized it wanted her to jump on for a ride. Soon Jasmine was riding high above land.

"Oh, Magic Carpet, it's beautiful up here," Jasmine said with a sigh. "But I'm worried about Aladdin. Can you take me to Aladdin?" Jasmine asked. But the Magic Carpet didn't respond.

Taking matters into her own hands, Jasmine urged the Magic Carpet on a search for Aladdin, riding everywhere she could think of. Yet, nearly an hour later, they still had not found Aladdin. At last, the princess told the Magic Carpet to return to the palace.

Before long, the Magic Carpet landed right in the middle of the castle garden.

"SURPRISE!"

As Jasmine stood, surprised, all of her friends and family leapt out from behind the bushes, carrying presents. Delighted, Jasmine smiled from ear to ear. But what was this all about? It wasn't her birthday.

Suddenly, Aladdin popped out from behind a large cake. "Happy anniversary, Jasmine!" he said, beaming. "Are you surprised?"

"Surprised?" Jasmine replied. "Of course I am!" Then she added to Aladdin with a whisper, "It's not our anniversary!"

Aladdin smiled and whispered back, "It's the anniversary of the day we first met in the marketplace. I thought it was cause for a celebration."

Jasmine smiled and kissed Aladdin on the cheek. But when she looked at the Magic Carpet, she stopped abruptly.

"Why, you sneaky thing!" she said. Then she smiled. "You were in on this surprise all along, weren't you?"

Then she turned to Aladdin, "This party – it's wonderful."

This would certainly be a day she would never forget.

The Mysterious Necklace

It was a fine summer morning, just right for a walk along the seashore.

With joy in her heart, Ariel strolled along the beach and soon found herself a long way from the castle.

Suddenly, she stumbled against a hard object buried in the sand.

"Ouch!" she cried, discovering a shiny object. She dug it up.

"It looks like one of those delicious things that humans are so fond of," said her friend Scuttle, licking it.

"Do you mean a 'sweet'?" laughed Ariel. "No, it's a jewel! Scuttle, go and find Sebastian. Tell him to call my father!"

A moment later, Ariel's father, King Triton, emerged out of the sea.

"Father," said Ariel. "I've just found this wonderful jewel and –"

"Where did you find it?" asked King Triton, amazed.

"On the beach," explained Ariel. "Do you know where it comes from?"

"I'm going to show you something," said her father solemnly, before transforming her into a mermaid.

Holding the jewel in her hand, Ariel dived into the water after her father. Soon, they arrived at the throne room.

"A tidal wave carried off the treasure of Atlantica," explained the king. "I fear this jewel is the only one that's left."

"I'll help you find the others!" said Ariel.

First of all, the Princess searched the wreck of a ship and collected almost a dozen jewels!

Then, with the help of Flounder and his friends, she found even more gems in the coral reef.

Hidden among the seaweed, which was every imaginable colour, the jewels had gone unnoticed!

Soon, the Atlantica treasure chest was full to the brim once more, thanks to Ariel.

"Ariel, on behalf of the kingdom, thank you," said King Triton, opening the chest to take out the wonderful precious stone that she had found on the beach that morning.

And, giving her a kiss on her forehead, King Triton fastened the necklace around her neck.

Soon it was time for Ariel to turn back into a human and return to her castle, where Eric was waiting for her.

That night, Ariel looked out at the ocean while touching the jewel hanging from her neck. Her family was never very far away, but she found it reassuring to have a little piece of Atlantica with her forever.

Lizzy's Fairy House

Tinker Bell was a very inquisitive tinker fairy. She always wanted to investigate everything – and nothing interested her as much as the mainland. Humans had such unusual inventions!

The fairies were bringing summer to the mainland. Almost as soon as Tink arrived, she saw a car speeding past on the road. She couldn't help but follow it to take a closer look.

Soon the car stopped in front of a house. The driver was a scientist called Dr Griffiths and he had a little girl called Lizzy.

Vidia had followed Tinker Bell, trying to get her to come back to the fairy camp. The two set off into the meadow near the house, and Tink spotted a row of buttons lined up like stepping-stones. She started picking them up to take back to camp.

"I'm not carrying this human junk...." began Vidia, but then she spotted something that made her stop in her tracks. It was a fairy house that Lizzy had made!

Tinker Bell was excited.

"Tinker Bell, we're not supposed to go near human houses!" warned Vidia.

"Human houses are a lot bigger," Tink replied. She went inside and looked around, delighted by the tiny furnishings.

"It's perfectly safe," Tink called.

"Oh, really?" asked Vidia. To teach Tinker Bell a lesson, she whipped up a gust of wind that slammed the door shut!

Tink didn't mind. She was having fun exploring.

But suddenly, Vidia saw Lizzy approaching in the distance. She pulled on the door to let Tink out – but it was jammed shut!

"Tink, someone's coming!" cried Vidia. "Get out of there!"

Tink ignored her. She was sure Vidia was just trying to scare her.

Vidia hid, watching as Lizzy got closer. "Oh, no! What have I done?" she cried as the little girl peeked into the house.

"A ... a ... a fairy ...," Lizzy whispered.

Tinker Bell saw Lizzy's huge eye staring at her through the window. It was terrifying! Lizzy snatched up the fairy house and raced back home. Vidia followed at a safe distance.

Dr Griffiths was busy studying a butterfly he had captured earlier. "Now, dear," he said. "What did you want me to see?"

"Um, never mind ...," Lizzy answered. She worried that her father might try to study the fairy the way he was studying the butterfly.

Lizzy ran upstairs to her room with the little fairy house and Tinker Bell inside. What would happen to the curious fairy now?

Winnie the Pooh

Playing School

Now, it just so happened that when the wind changed ever so slightly, and the leaves began to turn scarlet or golden, depending on their preference, and the days grew ever so much more eager to be over and done, this was also the time that Christopher Robin returned to school, as well as the time, not so surprisingly, when his friends in the Wood felt as if they should really do the same.

But *playing* school, as you might suspect, is not as similar to real school as perhaps it should be. First of all, there's no teacher to tell you what to do. And, after sitting at their desks for what seemed like a good three and a quarter hours (but was really just five or so minutes), Winnie the Pooh and his friends came to the conclusion that something rather important in their game of school was missing.

"Perhaps it's time we had a snack," suggested Pooh.

"I don't think that's it, Pooh," said Piglet.

"Our problem," announced Owl, "is that we do not have a teacher. No classroom is complete – and this is a well-known fact – without a teacher. Which is why I'm quite happy to offer my considerable expertise."

"Just a minute, Owl," Rabbit broke in. "And why is it, exactly, that we should let you be the teacher? Some might say – myself included – that I'm better suited to the job."

"You?" Owl scowled.

"Perhaps we should have a vote," said Piglet. "I'd like to nominate Pooh."

"Me?" Pooh said. "Why, thank you, Piglet. I gladly accept. Now . . . what's a 'teacher' again?"

"Really!" said Owl, with no small amount of scorn. "A 'teacher,' my dear Pooh, is the someone who stands before the class."

"To give out snacks?" asked Pooh hopefully.

"No," said Owl. "To give out knowledge."

"Oh," said Pooh. "I don't think I'd enjoy that nearly so much."

"Well, if it's all the same to you, and if anyone cares, I'll be the teacher," Eeyore said glumly. "I probably wouldn't have made a good student anyway."

"That will never do!" exclaimed Rabbit.

"Hi-ho!" said Christopher Robin, returning from a thoroughly enjoyable, and very well-taught, day at school. "Whatever are you up to?"

"Playing school . . . I think," said Pooh.

"Only we don't have a teacher," Piglet explained.

"I could teach you. I learned ever so many things today," said Christopher Robin.

"Hooray!" cheered Roo. "Let's start right away!"

Pinocchio
A Bright Idea

One day, Geppetto told Pinocchio, "I am off to deliver these puppets. I will be gone for a few hours. Stay out of trouble!" But Geppetto had not been gone for 15 minutes before Pinocchio became bored. "I have nothing to do," he said.

"You could clean the shop," said Jiminy Cricket.

"That's no fun," said Pinocchio. "I'll paint a picture instead."

"Where will you get paint?" Jiminy asked.

"From the workbench," said Pinocchio.

"You know you're not supposed to go near Geppetto's workbench," warned Jiminy. But the cricket's warning came too late.

"Oops!" Pinocchio cried.

He'd spilled red paint all over the workbench. Hurriedly, he grabbed a rag and tried to clean up the mess, but the paint just smeared. He'd made the mess even bigger!

Pinocchio looked around desperately. When he noticed Geppetto's kitten, Figaro, sleeping by the hearth, he had an idea.

"I'll say Figaro did it," Pinocchio said.

Jiminy shook his head. "That would be wrong," he said.

"What else can I do?" Pinocchio asked. "The workbench is ruined, and my father will be furious!"

"Why don't you paint it?" suggested Jiminy.

"That's a very good idea!" said Pinocchio.

So he set to work. First, he painted the bench top bright red. Then he painted the drawers green and yellow.

Figaro woke up and investigated, getting paint all over his whiskers.

Soon, the job was done.

"It looks wonderful," said Jiminy.

"Yes, it does," Pinocchio agreed. But he did not feel proud at all.

"It's a work of art!" Geppetto cried when he got home. "It's so colourful it makes the whole shop cheerful."

Then Geppetto saw the paint on Figaro's whiskers. "Did Figaro knock over the paint again?" he asked. "Is that why you painted the workbench?"

"No," Pinocchio said. "I spilled the paint. I couldn't clean it up, so I painted the whole workbench. I'm sorry."

Geppetto was quiet for a moment, and then he said, "I'm proud of you, Pinocchio."

"Because I painted the workbench?" Pinocchio asked.

"No," said Geppetto. "I'm proud of you because you told the truth and apologized instead of telling a lie. That takes courage. Now, every day, when I see my beautiful workbench, I'll remember you did the right thing, and that will make the colours seem even brighter!"

MICKEY MOUSE
Spring Cleaning

Mickey Mouse hummed as he straightened up his messy house. He swept up some leaves that had blown in through the front door. Then he shook the mud off his doormat.

He was picking up some old magazines when one of them caught his eye.

"'Make a Fresh Start with Spring Cleaning,'" Mickey read aloud. "Hmm. Spring cleaning, eh?"

He looked out of the window. It wasn't spring – it was autumn! What was he doing cleaning his house?

"Whew!" he exclaimed as he dropped his broom and flopped onto the sofa. "Looks like I have a whole day free now. I think I'll see if Minnie wants to come over!"

A short while later, Minnie Mouse rang the doorbell. "Hi, Mickey!" she said cheerfully. "What do you want to do to – "

She gasped. Mickey's house was a mess! There was mud on the floor, dust on the shelves, dirty dishes on the table, laundry piled here and there, books and magazines everywhere . . . .

"What's wrong?" Mickey asked.

"Mickey," Minnie said, "er, when was the last time you cleaned your house?"

Mickey laughed. "Don't be silly, Minnie!" he said. "I don't need to clean this place for months."

"M-m-months?" Minnie gasped. She couldn't believe it. In a few months, Mickey's entire house would be buried in mess!

"Sure!" Mickey shrugged. "Haven't you ever heard of spring-cleaning?"

Minnie wasn't sure what to do. She didn't want to be rude, but she had to convince Mickey to clean his house – and it couldn't wait until spring!

"You know, Mickey," she said casually, "I just read something about a fun new trend."

"Really?" Mickey smiled. "What's that, Minnie? Maybe it's something we could do today, since we have the whole day free!"

"Oh!" Minnie pretended to be surprised at the idea. "Why, I suppose we could! I hadn't thought of that."

"So, what's the trend?" Mickey asked eagerly. "Waterskiing? Rock climbing? Fondue parties?"

"No," Minnie said cheerfully. "Autumn cleaning! It's the newest rage."

"Autumn cleaning?" Mickey said doubtfully. He blinked, then smiled. "You know, that's so crazy, it sounds like fun! Come on, let's try it!"

Minnie smiled and picked up the magazine with the spring-cleaning article in it. "Good," she said. She stuffed the magazine into the dustbin. "I'll start right here!"

101
DALMATIANS

One Lucky Pup

"Where are we going?" Penny asked.

"Why do we have to get in the car? We're going to miss 'Thunderbolt'!" Pepper pouted. The puppies all hated to miss their favourite dog hero TV show. They groaned in disappointment.

"This will be even more fun," Perdy said soothingly as she coaxed the puppies into the car. "I promise."

Roger and Anita got into the front seat. It didn't take long to get out of the city. Soon the car was winding down a country lane. The puppies smelled all kinds of good things. They smelled flowers and hay. Then they smelled something sweet – peaches!

"Here we are!" Anita opened the car door.

"Where's here?" Freckles asked Lucky.

"It looks like an orchard!" Lucky yipped. He loved to eat fruit.

Roger stretched. "You dogs run and play," he said. "We'll call you when it's time for our picnic."

"Don't eat too many peaches," Pongo barked, but the puppies were already running off.

All morning, the puppies romped and played in the green grass until Pongo and Perdy came to call them. "Time for lunch!" Pongo barked.

"I'm not hungry," Rolly said, rolling over in the grass.

"I hope you didn't eat too much," Perdy said.

The big dogs herded their puppies up the hill towards the spot where Roger and Anita were laying out a picnic. Perdy scanned the group. "Wait a minute," she said to Pongo. "Where's Lucky?"

The black-and-white pack stopped in its tracks. Pongo counted them. Lucky was definitely missing!

Perdy sighed and began to whimper.

"Don't worry, Mother," Pepper said sweetly. "I have an idea." He turned to his brothers and sisters. "Hey, everyone. Let's play 'Thunderbolt'!" he barked. "We have to find Lucky!"

All of the puppies yipped excitedly and tumbled over one another to find Lucky's trail. Soon every nose was sniffing the ground.

Penny sniffed around a tree and behind a patch of tall grass. She'd caught the scent! "Here he is!" Penny barked.

The rest of the dogs gathered around to see the puppy asleep in the grass. Lucky's ears covered his eyes, but there was no mistaking the horseshoe of spots on his back, or the pile of peach stones by his nose!

"Lucky is lucky we found him," Perdita said with a relieved sigh.

"And," Pepper joked, "he'll be *really* lucky if he doesn't wake up with a tummy ache!"

Disney Winnie the Pooh

The Ups and Downs of Babysitting

"Roo, I have to go out tomorrow evening," said Kanga. "So you'll need a babysitter. Who would you like?"

"Tigger!" shouted Roo.

Kanga was not surprised. Tigger was the only animal she knew who liked to bounce more than a baby kangaroo!

The next day, Tigger came over to Kanga's house.

"Now, Tigger, I know you and Roo like to bounce," said Kanga. "But a good babysitter must know when to put the bouncer to bed."

"Don't worry, Kanga!" said Tigger.

For hours, Tigger and Roo had a fine old time bouncing around. Then Tigger looked at the clock and said, "Time for bed!"

Roo hopped right into his room.

"That was easy," Tigger said to himself. "Now I'll just tuck you in and – hey! I said bounce *into* bed. Not *on* it!" cried Tigger. But Roo wouldn't stop. So Tigger gave up and started bouncing too.

Then Tigger remembered Kanga. "Wait a minute! I'm the babysitter!" said Tigger. "I'm supposed to be tucking you in!"

"I don't want to be tucked in!" said Roo.

"What if I read you a story?" asked Tigger.

"No," said Roo. "I'm not even sleepy. I could bounce all the way to Pooh's house!"

"But it's time for *bed*, not bouncing," said Tigger. "I'll get you some milk. That will make you sleepy."

But when Tigger came back to Roo's bedroom, Roo was gone!

"Uh-oh!" said Tigger. He rushed to Pooh's house.

"I'm sorry, Tigger," said Pooh, "but Roo isn't here."

Then Tigger rushed to Piglet's house. But Roo wasn't there either. And he wasn't at Owl's or Rabbit's.

Finally, Tigger returned to Kanga's house. Where could Roo be? Just then, Tigger passed Roo's room – and saw Roo in his bed!

"Where were you, Tigger?" asked Roo.

"Where was I?" said Tigger. "Where were *you?*"

Roo explained that when Tigger had gone to get the milk, Roo had decided he did want to hear a story. But his favourite book was under the bed.

"You were *under* the bed?" cried Tigger.

"I'm home!" called Kanga at the front door.

Tigger sighed with relief.

"How did it go?" she asked Tigger.

"Kanga," said Tigger, "the wonderful thing about Tiggers is bouncing – and from now on I'm sticking with that. Babysitting just has too many ups and downs!"

Cinderella

Cinderella and the Sapphire Ring

It was one year since the Prince and Cinderella had married. To celebrate, the Prince was to hold a ball, and he gave Cinderella a gold ring set with a blue sapphire – Cinderella's favourite stone.

However, the ring was too large and somehow, it had slipped off her finger.

"Oh, no!" cried Cinderella, "My ring! Where is it?" She checked inside her gloves, but it was nowhere to be found.

"Don't worry, Cinderelly," her mouse friends Jaq and Gus piped up. "We'll help you find it!"

"Where have you been today?" Jaq asked.

Cinderella thought. "The first thing I did was go to my bedroom to write in my diary." So, they hurried to Cinderella's room.

"No ring," Jaq said with a sigh.

"Let's try the kitchen," said Cinderella. "I went there next to make a pot of tea." But the only ring in there was a day-old doughnut.

"Perhaps we should try the library. I read there this afternoon," said Cinderella. They searched high and low, but they could not find Cinderella's sapphire ring.

"I also went to the stables to feed Frou. Perhaps I lost my ring in his stall." The three friends sifted through piles of straw. But there was still no ring.

Cinderella scratched her head. "There's one more place to look," she said. "The garden!"

The friends searched every blossom. Until Gus exclaimed, "Cinderelly! I see it!" He picked up a shiny, blue object.

"Sapphire, Cinderelly?" Gus asked. Cinderella shook her head. It was just a marble.

"Wait a minute," she said as they stopped by the well. "After I drew some water from the well, I noticed my ring was gone. Could it have fallen in there?"

"I hope not," said Gus, trembling.

Jaq rolled his eyes. "Don't be such a scaredy-cat. Get into this bucket!"

Cinderella lowered Jaq and Gus into the well. "Do you see anything?" she called down.

"Eek!"

Cinderella pulled up the bucket as fast as she could. "What did you see?" she cried.

"Oh, nothing," said Gus slyly. "Nothing but Cinderelly's ring!"

"My heroes!" cried Cinderella. "Wait until I tell the Prince how you saved our special day!"

At the ball, Cinderella and the Prince raised their glasses to Gus and Jaq, their guests of honour, and thought how lucky they were to have such wonderful friends.

Sleeping Beauty

Aurora's Slumber Party

One day, Prince Phillip had to visit another kingdom for a few days. "Why don't you have friends over while I'm away?" he suggested.

"That's a wonderful idea!" Aurora replied. "I'll invite them to a slumber party." The princess worked all evening making invitations. Flora, Fauna and Merryweather were excited when they received them. The fairies arrived at the castle with their wands, ready to use their magic.

"We don't need magic to have fun," said Aurora. "There are all kinds of things to do." A little while later, the fairies began to get hungry. "I'll use a spell to make some food," said Merryweather.

"We have bread, butter, strawberries and cream right here," Aurora pointed out. "You can make a snack without using magic."

"This is fun!" Merryweather exclaimed as she made herself a triple-decker berry sandwich. It looked so good, the other fairies raced over to make their own. When Flora bit into hers, a dollop of cream flew across the room, right onto Aurora's face!

"Oops," Flora said. "I'm sorry, Princess." But Aurora wasn't upset. In fact, it made her giggle. Soon everyone was laughing.

A little later, Fauna had an idea. "Let's make a surprise for the morning," she suggested.

"Why don't we make some cinnamon rolls?" Aurora offered. They began to make the dough. While they waited for the dough to rise, the friends went upstairs. Flora grabbed a pillow and swung it at Aurora. The princess ducked and grabbed a pillow of her own. A few minutes later, feathers covered the room and Aurora and the fairies were out of breath from laughing.

"It's probably time to finish the rolls," Aurora said. She and the fairies went down to the kitchen and saw that the ball of dough had become the size of a table!

"I may have used a teensy bit of magic," Merryweather admitted.

"That's all right," Aurora said with a yawn. "We'll have enough for the whole kingdom."

Fauna pulled her wand out. "I think a little more magic would make this a lot faster." A few minutes later, all the rolls were done.

Aurora and the fairies went back upstairs. "Let's read a story," the princess suggested. Flora began to read and after a few minutes, everyone was sleepy.

"This has been a wonderful slumber party," Aurora said. "Good night, fairies."

"Good night, Princess," the fairies replied. And very soon, they all drifted off to sleep.

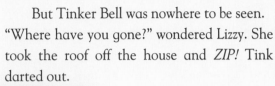

Fairies to the Rescue

Tinker Bell has been captured by a little human girl called Lizzy!

The fairies were bringing summer to the mainland, and Tink had flown off to investigate a car that had passed by the fairy camp.

The car stopped at a county house, and Tink watched as the humans spotted a butterfly with a splattered wing. Lizzy's father, Dr Griffiths, was amazed, but wouldn't believe Lizzy when she said the fairies must have painted it that way. Dr Griffiths was a scientist and didn't believe in fairies.

Vidia, who had followed Tink, was upset. She knew humans could be dangerous and she wanted to go back to the fairy camp. But then Tink had found a little fairy house that Lizzy had made. She went inside to explore and Vidia, wanting to teach Tink a lesson, slammed the door shut with a gust of wind.

Just then, Vidia had seen Lizzy approaching, but the door of the little house was stuck! Vidia could do nothing but hide as Lizzy picked up the fairy house and spotted Tinker Bell.

The little girl was so excited, she took the house – and Tink – straight up to her bedroom.

Lizzy placed the fairy house on the bed and peeked in one of its windows.

But Tinker Bell was nowhere to be seen. "Where have you gone?" wondered Lizzy. She took the roof off the house and *ZIP!* Tink darted out.

Mr Twitches, the family cat, immediately lunged for the fairy. As Vidia watched at the window, Lizzy put Tinker Bell in a birdcage for safekeeping.

"Don't worry," Lizzy told her. "Mr Twitches won't bother you as long as you're in there."

Vidia knew that she had to free Tink, but she couldn't do it alone. She flew as fast as she could towards fairy camp, but a rainstorm slowed her down.

When Vidia finally arrived at fairy camp, she explained to her friends what had happened. She said that Tinker Bell had been captured in a cage, and that they had to go and save her.

"We can't fly in the rain," Fawn said. "And the meadow's already flooded!"

Clank and Bobble weren't worried, they had a plan. They were going to build a boat!

Under Clank and Bobble's direction, the entire camp set to work creating a hull out of bark, a mast out of reeds and twigs, and a sail out of a lily pad.

It was going to be a challenge, but the fairies were determined to rescue their friend.

DUMBO
A Tail Tale

Dumbo and Timothy Mouse has made a new friend, called Eeny. He lived at the circus with his brothers Meeny, Miny and Mo. Like Dumbo, with his great big ears, Eeny also had something special about him: a very, very long tail!

"I wish my tail was just like every other monkey's," Eeny sighed.

"Don't be silly," said Timothy. "Your tail is terrific. Isn't it, Dumbo?"

Dumbo nodded, flapping his great big ears.

"But my brothers are always making fun of me," said Eeny.

Timothy Mouse told Eeny how Dumbo was also teased. Until they realized he could do special things – like fly!

"I bet your tail can do some spectacular things!" said Timothy Mouse.

"I doubt it," replied Eeny, gloomily.

"Well, first you've got to cheer up!" exclaimed Timothy. Dumbo nodded and tootled a happy little tune with his trunk.

Eeny brightened up. Holding his tail like a string bass, he plucked it to get a tune. Together, he and Dumbo continued their song.

Right away, Meeny, Miny and Mo ran up to investigate. "Eeny's making music with his tail!" they cried.

Miny and Mo loved Eeny's musical tail.

But Eeny's brother, Meeny, wasn't as impressed.

"What's so great about thumping a tail?" he muttered to himself.

"Hey, Dumbo," said Timothy Mouse, "grab the end of Eeny's tail."

Holding Eeny's tail in his trunk, Dumbo twirled it around like a skipping rope. Miny and Mo jumped in.

Suddenly, a yell came from inside the big top.

Eeny, Miny and Mo ran into the tent, followed by Timothy Mouse and Dumbo. Meeny was hanging by the tip of his tail from the highest trapeze. He was jealous of Eeny, and he had wanted to show what his tail could do. But it hadn't gone as planned.

"Dumbo," Timothy Mouse cried, "we've got to fly up there!" But before Dumbo's ears could even start flapping, Eeny had climbed the pole and was lowering his tail to his brother. "Just grab my tail and I'll pull you up," Eeny shouted. Meeny held on, and a few minutes later, the two monkeys were safe.

"Boy, am I lucky to have such a brave brother," Meeny said with a sigh.

That afternoon, in honour of their brother the hero, Meeny, Miny and Mo put on a tail-band concert of their own. And from that day on, they never, ever made fun of Eeny's long, long tail again.

264

Quincy's Dream

The Little Einsteins met in the clubhouse after school one day to talk about their upcoming mission. Everyone was excited, except Quincy. "Are you daydreaming, Quincy?" teased Annie.

"I'm really tired." Quincy said. Quincy told his friends what was bothering him.

"I had this scary dream last night, and now I'm afraid to go back to sleep," Quincy said. "I used to think I was really brave, but now I just feel silly."

"I'm sure even the bravest knight in the world has a scary dream sometimes," said Leo. "We all have them!"

"But what should I do if I have another bad dream?" he asked.

"Do what I do," offered June. "Use your imagination to change what happens in your dream. If I have a dream about a big, scary tiger, I just use my imagination to turn him into a cuddly orange kitten."

Annie spotted something she thought could help Quincy.

"A dream catcher!" she shouted. "We can use it to catch your bad dream, Quincy!"

Quincy was puzzled. "It looks like a spiderweb with feathers hanging from it."

"Some Native American tribes believe that if you hang a dream catcher over your bed, you can 'trap' your bad dreams in its web," explained June.

"I've got a plan!" exclaimed Leo. "Catch your bad dream in this dream catcher tonight, and then bring it to the clubhouse tomorrow."

The next morning, Quincy brought the dream catcher to the clubhouse. Leo, Rocket and the team were all going to jump into Quincy's bad dream and show him how to change the ending. With his friends by his side, there was nothing to be afraid of!

When the team landed in Quincy's dream, he was dreaming that a famous painting had come to life.

"Yikes!" Annie gasped. "It's a monster!"

"Hey, you can't say I didn't warn you!" Quincy said.

"Okay," June said to the team, "Everyone concentrate on the monster. Imagine, that instead of stomping his feet in anger, he's actually dancing!"

Suddenly, the angry monster changed into a graceful ballerina.

"We did it!" shouted Leo.

Quincy was proud of himself, too. "You were right, guys. When you use your imagination, anything is possible!"

Snow White
and the Seven Dwarfs

A Big Surprise

One spring day, Snow White went to the Dwarfs' cottage. Snow White knew the Dwarfs worked hard. That day, she wanted to make sure that when they got home, they didn't have to do any more work. Once the Dwarfs had left, she and her animal friends hurried into the cottage, and set to work. The birds chirped while they picked up crumbs. The squirrels used their fluffy tails to dust. And the chipmunks washed and dried the dishes. With so many helpers, Snow White had the downstairs gleaming in no time. Next, they went upstairs, and the Princess made the beds.

Before long, every inch of the Dwarfs' cottage was neat and tidy. Snow White and the animals went to gather fresh berries to use in the Dwarfs' supper.

"They'll be very hungry after their long day, so we'll make Blueberry Pie for dessert!" Snow White told the rabbits.

Back inside the cottage, Snow White and her friends fixed supper. There was soup to be simmered, bread to be made and pie to be baked. Before she knew it, the late-afternoon sun was casting long shadows across the windowpanes. *Tweet! Chirp!* A bluebird was singing outside the window. That was the signal to say the Dwarfs were almost home. Snow White and the animals hurried outside and hid. She peeked in through a window.

When they got inside, the Dwarfs could not believe their eyes. The floors were swept, the room was tidy and there was even a freshly baked pie cooling on a windowsill!

"What is that delicious smell?" Doc wondered.

"Look!" cried Grumpy. He went to the pot of soup.

The Dwarfs were confused. They tried to guess which Dwarf had done this. Doc noticed that Happy's smile was especially big. Was he keeping a secret? Dopey pointed out that Sneezy seemed supersneezy. Maybe because he had dusted and swept the cottage?

Snow White giggled as she listened outside the window. "They'll never guess that we did it," she whispered to her animal friends. When the Dwarfs started to eat their pie, Snow White quietly headed home.

After a long workday, their tummies pleasantly full, all Seven Dwarfs were ready for bed. When they climbed the stairs, the Dwarfs found one last treat: seven neatly made beds. As they drifted off to sleep, the Dwarfs decided to tell their good friend Snow White about this wonderful surprise the very next time they saw her.

Tinker Bell
AND THE
GREAT FAIRY RESCUE

Make-believe

The fairies were bringing summer to the mainland. Curious Tinker Bell had left the safety of fairy camp to follow a car along a road – she wanted to see how it worked.

Vidia had followed Tink, trying to get her to come back. She knew fairies weren't supposed to go near humans. But Tink hadn't listened. The car soon stopped at a house, where a girl, Lizzy, and her father had got out. Lizzy believed in fairies, but her father, who was a scientist, did not.

Tink found a fairy house that Lizzy had made. Tink was exploring it when Vidia accidentally trapped her inside! Lizzy found Tinker Bell and was very excited – she had finally found a fairy. She took the fairy house, with Tink inside, up to her room. To keep Tinker Bell safe from the family cat, Lizzy put the fairy inside a birdcage.

Vidia watched from the window and thought Lizzy was keeping Tink prisoner! She rushed back to fairy camp to get help and the fairies built a boat in order to rescue Tinker Bell – it was raining, so they couldn't fly.

Back at the house, Lizzy let Tinker Bell out of the cage and showed off her collection of fairy artwork. But as Lizzy described what was going on in each picture, Tink realized that the little girl had her fairy facts all wrong!

Tink tried to tell Lizzy, but all Lizzy heard was a jingling sound. "So that's how fairies speak!" she exclaimed. Tink went over to the fairy house to fix the door.

"Why, you're quite the little tinker, aren't you?" asked Lizzy.

Tink pointed to herself, then rang the little house's fairy bell. "Tinker Bell?" Lizzy cried. "What a lovely name!"

Just then, Lizzy's father came upstairs to fix some leaks in the roof. "Lizzy," he said, "it sounds like you're talking to ... a fairy?"

Tinker Bell hid. Lizzy quickly held up a fairy drawing to show her father. "Oh, yes, but she's make-believe," she replied.

"Quite right," her father said. "For that reason, I would like to see you spending less time in the fantasy world and more time in the real world. This summer you have an excellent opportunity to learn all sorts of wonderful things. Here is a blank field journal. I'm sure you'll be able to fill it with your own scientific research." Satisfied, her father went back to repairing the house.

Lizzy sighed. She hadn't wanted to put Tinker Bell in danger by telling her father about her. But she hoped one day she could convince her father that fairies really did exist!

Sleep Tight, Nemo!

It was late at night at the bottom of the sea – but little Nemo was wide awake.

"Nemo," said Marlin, poking his head into the anemone, "you should be asleep!"

"But I can't sleep," said Nemo. "I need another story."

"No more stories," said Marlin. "I told you five already."

"Then maybe another snack?" said Nemo.

But Marlin rolled his eyes. "No, Nemo. You just had a plankton snack five minutes ago. What you

should do now, young clownfish, is go to sleep!"

"Okay, Dad," said Nemo. Then he did as his dad told him and closed his eyes. But, seconds later, they popped open again.

"Dad!" Nemo called out. "Daaaad!"

"Nemo!" Marlin groaned. "I'm beginning to lose my patience!"

"But, Dad," said Nemo, "I . . . I . . . I heard a noise."

"What kind of noise?" Marlin asked.

"Um . . . a . . . a spooky noise," answered Nemo.

"*Hmph.*" Nemo could tell Marlin did not like this reason for being awake either. But still, Marlin stopped and listened . . . and listened . . . and listened.

"I don't hear anything, Nemo," he said after a moment.

So Nemo tried his best to shut his eyes really tight and get comfortable. He wiggled this way . . . then that way . . . then this way again. But nothing worked.

"Daaaaaaaaaaaad!" he called out.

"Nemo," Marlin said. "For the last time, it's time to go to sleep. If you call for me again, it had better be a good one or . . . or . . . or *else*. Good night!"

Now, Nemo knew his father well, and he knew when Marlin was just a teeny, tiny, itsy, bitsy bit angry with him. But Nemo also knew that when you can't go to sleep, you can't go to sleep. And no matter how many moonfish or angelfish or sea stars you count; no matter how tightly you close your eyes; no matter how mad your dad gets – you'll never go to sleep until you're absolutely, positively, no-doubt-about-it ready. And Nemo wasn't. But why not?

Suddenly, Nemo bolted up. "Dad!" he shouted. "Dad! Oh, *Daaaaad*!"

"All right. That's it, Nemo!" Marlin said.

"But, Dad," Nemo said. "There's one more thing I really, really, truly need. Then I promise, I'll go to sleep."

And with that, he snuggled into Marlin's fins for a great big good-night hug.

"I love you, Dad," he said. "See you in the morning."

Tangled

A Professional Thief

Mother Gothel was angry. Rapunzel – the girl she had kidnapped and kept hidden her whole life – had dared to leave the tower! Even though Mother Gothel had warned the girl about the dangers of the world outside, Rapunzel had still followed that thief Flynn into the forest!

"She can manage perfectly well without me!" Mother Gothel realized with irritation.

Mother Gothel followed Rapunzel's trail to the pub where the Rapunzel had befriended a group of ruffians. They had helped Rapunzel to escape with Flynn when the guards came to arrest him for stealing the royal crown.

"How can I persuade Rapunzel to return to the tower now?" wondered Mother Gothel. "She will never believe my stories about monsters any more!"

Mother Gothel went on thinking and soon she had hatched a plan. Spying on the ruffians at the pub, she had discovered that the Stabbington brothers had been Flynn's partners in crime. But Flynn had tricked them by keeping the crown for himself, so now the Stabbingtons wanted revenge… And, as Mother Gothel had found the crown hidden in the tower, she had an offer for the two brothers.

"I promise to give you the crown back. In return, you must capture Flynn and hand him over to the guards. Then I won't have much of a problem bringing Rapunzel back home…"

The Stabbingtons immediately agreed. Mother Gothel then headed off to find Flynn and Rapunzel.

Flynn had just gone to gather firewood, and Mother Gothel surprised Rapunzel, jumping out angrily from behind a tree.

"Oh, Mother! How did you find me?"

"I followed the trail of lies and treachery," Mother Gothel replied scornfully. "Come with me, we're going back to the tower."

"But I'm not in any danger here!" the girl protested. "Flynn really likes me and…"

"He's making fun of you, you silly little girl: he's a professional thief! As soon as you give him back the crown he will forget you completely! Here's the crown. Give it back to him and you'll see how quickly he abandons you!"

Then Mother Gothel ran off before Flynn returned.

Rapunzel sighed. Her mother really was so mistaken! Flynn was indeed a professional thief, but he had not needed to steal her heart – she had given it to him freely. She knew she would prove Mother Gothel wrong.

Tinker Bell
AND THE
GREAT FAIRY RESCUE

Something to Fix

All the fairies knew that Tinker Bell was too curious for her own good! That explained why she went into the little house made by Lizzy, a little girl from the mainland. Then Vidia played a joke and accidentally trapped Tink inside!

Lizzy found Tinker Bell and was very excited. She took the fairy up to her bedroom and put her in a cage – so that the family cat couldn't catch her. Vidia had watched from the window and then quickly flown back to fairy camp to get help.

But then a storm had begun! The fairies couldn't fly in the rain and the meadow was flooded, so they decided to build a boat. As they set off to rescue Tinker Bell, Silvermist, Rosetta, Fawn and Iridessa remembered that with 'faith, trust and pixie dust', anything was possible. As Bobble steered them into the fast-moving current, Rosetta looked out at the distance they had to travel, hoping that Tinker Bell was all right.

But Tinker Bell was fine – and being questioned non-stop by an excited Lizzy about what it was like to be a fairy. Lizzy couldn't understand Tink's tiny voice, so Tink answered with hand movements.

Next, Tink opened a blank field journal that Lizzy's father had given her – he didn't believe in fairies and had wanted Lizzy to record her research about 'real' things in it. But it was perfect for her fairy facts!

Lizzy wrote the words "Scientific Fairy Research" on the first page. Then Lizzy asked questions and Tinker Bell acted out the answers.

Soon the journal was filled with drawings of Tink's fairy friends and Pixie Hollow, and descriptions of the fairies' special talents.

Now that Lizzy's fairy field journal was complete and the rain had eased off, it was time for Tink to go and find her friends. Tinker Bell was sad about leaving Lizzy, but excited about going back to fairy camp.

Tink flew out of the window, but stayed and watched while Lizzy tried to show her father the journal they had made.

"I made it especially for you, father. It's just like your field journal, it's filled with lots of facts...."

But Dr Griffths was too worried about the leaks in the roof to look at her book. He had to fix them to stop water damaging their house.

Tink saw how sad Dr Griffiths was that he couldn't spend more time with his daughter. She decided she had to stay and help them. After all, fixing was her talent!

Laugh, Cobra Bubbles!

Lilo thought she was a very lucky girl. She had a lot of good friends, who she loved to laugh with. Stitch had a funny, scratchy laugh, to go with his scratchy voice. Pleakley giggled, and Jumba shouted out big guffaws. But as for Cobra Bubbles, well, the truth was, Cobra Bubbles just didn't laugh. Ever. And Lilo was just dying to find out what his laugh sounded like.

So Lilo tried to get Cobra Bubbles to laugh. She showed him the latest episode of "The World's Funniest Lobster Videos," but he didn't crack a smile, even when a lobster ate an entire jar of pickles. She made funny faces at him until her face hurt, but he just looked at her, expressionless. She even tried (at Stitch's suggestion) a whoopee cushion. But she was too busy running away to see if he laughed or not when he sat down on it.

Clearly, something had to be done. It just wasn't healthy for a person never to laugh. She explained the problem to Nani.

"Nani, Cobra Bubbles is one of my best friends. He's practically family! But he never laughs. I think I need to help him," Lilo said.

"Well," Nani said thoughtfully. "What have you tried?"

"I tried lobsters, funny faces and a whoopee cushion," said Lilo, ticking the items off on her fingers. "But none of them worked! He didn't even blink!"

"Hmm," said Nani, "I think I see the problem. Do *you* think those things are funny?"

"Well, no," Lilo admitted. "I'm scared of lobsters, my face still hurts from making funny faces, and I think whoopee cushions are silly."

"Maybe Cobra Bubbles thinks so too," said Nani. "You know, he might laugh if he is having a good time. Why don't you start out by doing something fun?"

So, the next day, Lilo enrolled Cobra Bubbles in her hula class. The music started, and the dancers came out on stage, swinging their hips and swirling their grass skirts. And there, in the middle of them, was Cobra Bubbles. He did his best to follow the complicated steps of the dance, and Lilo did her best to keep a straight face. But it was impossible. Cobra Bubbles in a grass skirt was the funniest thing she'd ever seen. The other kids in the class thought so too. Soon they were all laughing – even the hula teacher!

Then, to Lilo's surprise, Cobra Bubbles began to smile. And then he chuckled. And, soon enough, Cobra Bubbles was actually laughing! Lilo thought that Cobra Bubbles's laugh was somehow both quiet and big, and very nice. Just like him.

Carl's Promise

Carl and Ellie had been best friends since they first met as children. They grew up, got married and dreamed of becoming explorers.

But Carl and Ellie didn't become explorers. They both worked at the zoo. However, they still dreamed of travelling to Paradise Falls in South America. They saved all their spare change in a jar to pay for the trip. But they could never quite collect enough.

The years went by, and Carl and Ellie grew older. After Ellie passed away, Carl kept all her things just as they had been. But it wasn't the same. He missed Ellie. To make matters worse, the neighbourhood around their beloved home was being torn down to make room for tall, modern buildings.

One day, Carl heard a knock at his door. A boy in a uniform was standing on his porch.

"Good afternoon," said the boy. "My name is Russell, and I am a Junior Wilderness Explorer. Are you in need of assistance today, sir?"

"No," replied Carl. He didn't want help. He just wanted to be left alone.

But Russell wouldn't leave. He wanted to help Carl so that he could earn his Assisting the Elderly badge.

"If I get it, I will become a Senior Wilderness Explorer," Russell explained.

To get rid of Russell, Carl gave him a task. He asked him to find a bird called a Snipe. "I think its burrow is two blocks down," Carl said.

Russell eagerly set off to find the bird, not knowing that it didn't really exist. Carl had made the whole thing up!

Not long after that, Carl received some bad news. He was being forced out of his house and sent to live in a retirement home. Carl didn't want to leave his house. All his memories of Ellie were there.

That night, Carl sat in his living room, looking through Ellie's adventure book. He remembered Ellie's dream of going to South America. He had promised her he'd take her there in an airship.

The next morning, two nurses arrived to drive Carl to the retirement home. "I'll meet you at the van," he told them. "I want to say one last goodbye to the old place."

As the nurses walked back to their van, a huge shadow fell over them. They turned to see thousands of balloons tied to Carl's house! A moment later, the whole house rose into the air! "So long, boys!" Carl yelled out of the window. He was going to South America!

Aurora and the Helpful Dragon

Princess Aurora went riding on her horse, Buttercup, with Prince Phillip close behind. As they rounded a bend, a small dragon popped out from behind a tree.

"Oh, he's so cute!" Aurora exclaimed.

Phillip was worried. "Dragons can be dangerous!" The little dragon shook his head.

Aurora laughed. "Let's take him home. I'm going to call him Crackle!"

"He does seem like a harmless little fellow," Phillip agreed.

When Phillip and Aurora rode into the courtyard, the three good fairies were hanging banners for a ball. King Stefan and the queen were coming to the castle.

Flora gasped when she saw Crackle. "Dragons can be dangerous."

"Remember the last one!" Fauna added.

"Oooh, I think he's sweet," Merryweather spoke up.

Just then, Crackle noticed a kitten in a basket of yarn. Crackle listened to it purring. Then he tried to purr. "Purrgrr, purrgrr!" Clouds of smoke streamed from his nose and mouth.

Crackle looked sad. "Oh, Crackle," Aurora said gently. "You're not a kitten. You're a dragon."

Aurora noticed that Crackle looked unhappy, so she took him to the castle.

But King Hubert heard Crackle and rushed into the room. "Oh, my, my, my! How did a dragon get in here?" he shouted. Frightened, Crackle ran to the garden. Aurora, found the little dragon sitting beside a fountain, watching a fish. *Splash!* Before Aurora could stop him, Crackle jumped into the water.

"Crackle, you're not a fish!" Aurora exclaimed. "You're not a kitten either. Do you think no one will like you because you're a dragon?" she asked. Crackle nodded.

"You can't change what you are," Aurora said kindly. "But you you can be a helpful dragon."

Suddenly thunder boomed. Rain began to pour down. Everyone was gathered in the grand hallway, watching the storm.

"I'm afraid King Stefan and the queen might lose their way," Prince Phillip said.

Aurora looked at Crackle. "Fly to the top of the tower and blow the largest, brightest flames to guide my parents to the castle."

Suddenly, gold and red flames lit up the sky above the watchtower. Crackle had done it! And thanks to Crackle's flame, the king and queen got safely home.

Too High A Price To Pay

The evil sorcerer had managed to capture the frog Naveen! He had poured several drops of Naveen's blood into his talisman. This allowed his accomplice Lawrence to continue looking like Prince Naveen. He was going to be able to marry Charlotte, the richest young lady in New Orleans!

"I am going to become master of the world!" the sorcerer roared with laughter. From his balcony he was watching the Mardi Gras parade go past.

The main float looked like a wedding cake, which was occupied by Charlotte and the fake Prince Naveen, as they prepared to get married for real. The priest had already begun to bless their union.

"I haven't got a second to lose!" whispered the frog Naveen, double-locked in a sorcerer's casket. He had to stop Charlotte marrying the fake Prince! He bravely managed to launch the casket onto the float, and at the same moment, Tiana – who was also a frog – saw the fake Prince Naveen in the process of marrying Charlotte...

"Oh! I thought that Naveen loved me!" she sobbed.

"But of course he does!" cried Ray, her firefly friend. "There's something wrong. I'm going to sort this out!"

Landing on the float, Ray heard the frog Naveen calling from inside the casket. Ray quickly rescued him and, in a flash, Naveen jumped onto the false prince and tore the talisman from his neck! The villain immediately changed back into Lawrence.

"Ray!" shouted Naveen as he threw the talisman to the firefly for him to look after. But the sorcerer's evil Shadows immediately sprang forward in pursuit. As they rapidly caught up, Ray found Tiana and in threw the talisman to her. Tiana tried to run away... but the evil sorcerer barred her way.

"Give the talisman back to me, Tiana, and I will give you the means to open your own restaurant!" he whispered. "You'll be able to honour the memory of your poor father who was never able to achieve his dream."

"My father taught me to recognize the things that are really important in life!" Tiana replied sharply. "And opening my restaurant at the cost of your success would really be too high a price to pay!"

As she spoke, she broke the talisman and the evil sorcerer disappeared into thin air.

"I will probably just stay a waitress forever now," sighed Tiana. "But at least I'm an honest waitress!"

Tinker Bell
GREAT FAIRY RESCUE

A Muddy Rescue

Tinker Bell's curiosity had led her to a human house and to a little girl named Lizzy.

Lizzy lived with her father, a scientist called Dr Griffiths who didn't believe in magic or fairies and was often too busy to spend time with his daughter – even though he wanted to.

Another fairy, Vidia, had tried to stop Tink from exploring the house – she knew humans could be dangerous – but Tink had ignored her. Vidia had raced off back to fairy camp to get help.

But a storm had started and fairies couldn't fly in the rain! So, they built a boat and set off to rescue Tinker Bell.

What the other fairies didn't realize was that Tink was fine! She was a having a lovely time with Lizzy, who loved fairies.

Tink had decided to stay and help Lizzy spend more time with her father. She had an idea – if she could help Dr Griffiths with the house repairs, he would have more time to spend with Lizzy!

Meanwhile, back on the fairy boat, the rescuers were in a panic. They were heading straight for a waterfall!

"Hang on, we're going straight down!" yelled Bobble.

Then Silvermist, a water fairy, reached into the waterfall and made the water rise up so that the drop wasn't as steep. After a wild ride, the boat crashed onshore.

The fairies were all right, but the boat was ruined. They had no choice but to continue their mission on foot.

Vidia finally spotted the muddy road that led to Lizzy's house. Vidia helped her friends across, but then got stuck in the mud herself! Silvermist, Fawn, Rosetta and Iridessa grabbed onto her and pulled.

Then, suddenly, they saw the lights of a car coming towards them! "Pull! Pull!" cried Rosetta – but Vidia was trapped.

Iridessa knew what she had to do. She walked towards the car, then held up her hand and bounced the headlight beams back at the driver. He thought another car was coming straight for him and slammed on his brakes.

Moments later, the driver got out of his car. "Hello? Is somebody out there?" he asked.

Fawn grabbed his shoelace and instructed the others to hold on tight. When the driver turned to leave, he pulled them all out of the mud!

The fairy friends were so relieved. They made sure everyone was okay, then continued on their way to rescue Tinker Bell.

Bambi
Winter Nap

Bambi nosed under the crunchy leaves, looking for fresh grass. There was none. He looked up at the trees, but there were no green leaves there either. Food was getting scarce in the forest.

"Don't worry, Bambi," Thumper said when he saw the confused look in Bambi's eyes. "We'll get through the fall and winter. Dad says we always do. We find what we can when we can, and we always make it until spring."

Bambi sighed and nodded. Thumper's dad was smart. He knew lots of things about the forest.

"Besides, it's better to be awake than napping all winter. Yech!" Thumper hated to go to bed, even at bedtime.

"Napping?" Bambi didn't know that some animals slept through the winter months.

"Sure. You know, like Flower, and the squirrels, and the bears. They hole up for months. Haven't you noticed the chipmunks putting their acorns away the past couple of months?" Thumper pointed towards an oak tree.

Bambi nodded.

"That's their food for the winter. As soon as it gets cold enough, they'll just stay inside and sleep," Thumper explained.

"But how will they know when it's time to wake up?" Bambi couldn't imagine life in the forest without all the other animals.

Thumper tapped his foot to think. It was a good question. And, since he had never slept through the winter, he wasn't sure of the answer. "Let's go ask Flower." They headed for the young skunk's den.

"Hello," Flower said.

"Flower, you sleep all winter, right?" Thumper asked.

"It's called hibernation." Flower yawned a big yawn. "Excuse me," he said, blushing.

"So, Bambi wants to know who wakes you up in the spring," Thumper said.

"You'll be back, won't you, Flower?" Bambi asked worriedly.

The little skunk giggled. "Oh, we always come back. Just like the grass and the flowers and the leaves," Flower explained. "I never thought about what wakes us up before. It must be the sun, I guess."

Bambi smiled. He didn't know the grass and leaves would come back in the spring too! He was feeling much better about the forest's winter nap.

Suddenly, Thumper started laughing. He rolled on his back and pumped his large hind feet in the air.

"What is it?" Bambi and Flower asked together.

"You really are a flower, Flower!" Thumper giggled. "You even bloom in the spring!"

Peter Pan

A Feather in His Cap

Peter Pan and Tinker Bell were off on an adventure and the Lost Boys were bored.

"Never Land is a dull place without Peter Pan," Slightly complained.

Then Rabbit spoke up. "We can play Pirates! That's always fun."

"Can't," said Slightly. "I lost the feather off my pirate hat."

"We could find another feather," Tootles suggested.

"An extraordinary feather," Cubby said. "Like Captain Hook's."

"That it!" Slightly cried. "I'll steal Captain Hook's feather!"

A short time later, the Lost Boys were sneaking aboard Hook's pirate ship. Luckily for them, the pirates were taking a nap!

There, hanging from a peg on the mast, was Captain Hook's hat.

"There it is," whispered Tootles. "Get it!"

"M-m-m-me?" stammered Slightly.

Smee, Hook's first mate, awoke with a start. He thought someone had said his name. "Smee you say! That be me. But who be calling Smee?"

He opened his eyes and spied the Lost Boys. "Ahoy!" he cried, waking up the others. Quick as a flash, the Lost Boys were caught.

Captain Hook burst from his cabin. "Lash them to the mast!" he commanded. "We'll catch Peter Pan when he comes to save his friends."

Floating high on a cloud, Peter Pan and Tinker Bell saw their friends being captured.

They flew down to Pirates' Cove and landed on the ship's mast. Peter cupped his hands around his mouth and made a most peculiar sound.

"Tick tock," Peter went. "Tick tock!"

Down on deck, Captain Hook became very frightened. "It's that crocodile!" he cried. "The one that ate my clock and my hand! Now he's come back to eat me!"

"Tick tock…tick tock," went Peter.

"Man the cannons!" Hook cried. "Shoot that crocodile!"

The Lost Boys, tied to the mast, were forgotten. As the pirates ran in circles, Tinker Bell began to flap her wings. Fairy dust sprinkled down onto the Lost Boys. Soon they floated right out of the ropes and up into the clouds. On the way, Slightly snatched the feather from Hook's hat and stuck it in his own.

Peter Pan, Tinker Bell and the Lost Boys met on a drifting cloud.

"Thanks for saving us!" exclaimed Tootles.

"You helped me scare old Hook!" Peter Pan cried. "That's a feather in all your caps."

"But the best feather of them all is in mine," Slightly said, as he showed off Captain Hook's prized feather!

Monkey Trouble

"Hey, let me go!" Mowgli cried. "Baloo!" But the big bear couldn't help him. Mowgli was being carried off through the treetops by a band of wild monkeys!

The monkeys laughed and chattered as they swung Mowgli from one tree to another. One monkey dropped him, and Mowgli yelled. But another monkey caught him by the ankles just in time. Then a third monkey pulled him away by one arm, swinging over to another tree on a large vine, where more monkeys grabbed at him.

Soon Mowgli was out of breath and confused. "Hey!" he yelled. "Quit it! I want to go back to Baloo! Let me go!"

The monkeys laughed. "Sorry, Man-cub!" one shouted. "We can't let you go. You might as well forget about that bear!"

"Yeah!" another monkey said, catching Mowgli by the arm. "You're with us monkeys now. We're better than any old bear! You'll flip for us monkeys."

He tossed Mowgli straight up. Mowgli felt himself flipping head over heels.

A second later a pair of monkeys caught him by the legs. "See, Man-cub?" one of them said. "Monkeys know how to have fun!"

Mowgli laughed, feeling dizzy. "That was kind of fun!" he cried. "Do it again!"

The monkeys howled with laughter. They tossed Mowgli up, over and over. Mowgli somersaulted through the treetops until he couldn't tell up from down any more. After that, the monkeys taught him how to swing from branch to branch and vine to vine. They even showed him how to shake the trees to make bananas fall into his hands.

"Being a monkey is fun!" Mowgli exclaimed through a mouthful of banana.

Maybe it was good that the monkeys had found him, Mowgli thought. Being a monkey might even be more fun than being a wolf or a bear. And it was definitely more fun than going to the Man-village.

Mowgli swallowed the banana and looked around at his new friends. "What are we going to do next?"

A monkey giggled. "We're going to see King Louie."

"Yeah!" another monkey said gleefully, clapping his hands. "He's the most fun of all!"

"King Louie?" Mowgli said suspiciously. He didn't like the way the monkeys were grinning at him. "Who's that?"

"You'll see, Man-cub!" the monkeys cried, swinging through the treetops.

Mowgli shrugged. How bad could this King Louie be?

Lilo's Riches

Stitch stretched his blue arms and folded them behind his head, soaking up the rays on the wide Hawaiian beach.

Flash! Lilo snapped his photo. *Flash!* Lilo turned and snapped a picture of Nani and David riding their surfboards.

Suddenly Stitch stood up. He grabbed Lilo's camera. Lilo struck a hula pose and – *Flash!* – Stitch caught it on film.

"Let's take some more!" Lilo giggled, running toward the shoreline. Stitch was right behind her, snapping picture after picture. *Flash!* He got two kids splashing. He turned quickly and – *Flash!* – he momentarily blinded a bald man holding an ice-cream cone.

The man looked at Stitch, dazed. Lilo had seen that look before. Most people didn't know what to make of Stitch. Then, as the man stared, his mint-chocolate-chip ice cream rolled off his cone and splatted in the sand.

"Sorry," Lilo muttered. She grabbed Stitch's arm and tried to lead him away, but Stitch strained against her, pulling her closer to the melting green blob.

With one swipe of his tongue, Stitch lapped the mess up. "Ptooey!" He spat it out, all over the man's feet. It was too sandy. "Ptooey! Ptooey!" Stitch continued spitting out sand as Lilo dragged him away.

As soon as he stopped spitting, Stitch pointed at the snack shack.

"Sorry, Stitch. I don't have any money for ice cream," Lilo explained. "How about if we play a few songs instead? Here, you play," Lilo tossed Stitch the ukulele. "I'll dance."

At first, Stitch just plucked a few sour notes. But soon the rhythm got him and he was playing like a real-life rock star.

Lilo was enjoying dancing so much, she didn't even notice that the tourists had begun to toss coins to them.

Stitch hammed it up, tossing his head and wiggling his hips. Lilo waved her arms and smiled her most winning smile. When the song ended, the two took a bow. Quickly, Lilo gathered the coins.

"We've got enough! Come on!" Lilo went running towards the snack shack.

"Three mint-chocolate-chip cones, please," Lilo said.

Lilo handed one cone to Stitch. She took a quick lick of the second one as she scanned the beach. Spotting the bald man, she hurried over and thrust the third cone towards him. "Here," she said. "Sorry about before."

The man smiled and he took the cone. Then Lilo handed him her camera. He snapped a picture – *Flash!* – of Lilo and Stitch eating ice cream.

Disney Pinocchio
In a Tangle

One night, while Pinocchio was sleeping, a loud crash woke him. He jumped up and raced downstairs to Geppetto's workshop.

"Is anybody here?" Pinocchio called nervously.

"Meow!" came the reply. It was Geppetto's little kitten, Figaro.

"I hear you, but I can't see you!" called Pinocchio.

Suddenly, the puppets above Geppetto's workbench began to move.

"Yikes!" cried Pinocchio, startled.

Pinocchio looked up to see Figaro tangled in the puppets' strings. Pinocchio began to laugh.

"That's funny!" he said.

"Meow!" cried Figaro. He didn't think it was funny! The kitten struggled to get free, but he only became more tangled in the strings.

Pinocchio just laughed harder.

Jiminy Cricket hopped down from the hearth. He rubbed his tired eyes. "What's going on?" he asked.

Pinocchio pointed to the little kitten.

"Pinocchio, maybe you should help poor Figaro instead of laughing at him," Jiminy said.

"Maybe I should leave him there," replied Pinocchio. "Then Geppetto can see how naughty he's been."

"Meow!" poor Figaro wailed.

"That's not very nice," said Jiminy. "How would you feel if you were all tangled up?"

Pinocchio sighed. "I guess I wouldn't like it very much."

He was about to free the kitten, when he suddenly exclaimed, "Hey, Jiminy, look at that!"

Figaro's paws were now wrapped around the strings in such a way that when his paws moved, the puppets began to dance!

"That's a neat trick," said Pinocchio. "Figaro can work the puppets!"

The kitten moved his paws some more, and all the puppets danced on their strings.

"I have an idea," said Jiminy Cricket. "Do you want to hear it?"

Pinocchio and Figaro both nodded.

The next morning when Geppetto awoke, he got a surprise.

"Look, Father!" Pinocchio said. "Figaro can make the puppets dance!"

Pinocchio winked at Figaro, and the cat leaped onto the puppet strings again.

"Amazing!" Geppetto cried, watching the show. "We can put on a puppet show for all the children of the town!"

Pinocchio was thrilled to see Geppetto so happy.

"But when did you discover Figaro's talent?" asked Geppetto.

"Just last night," said Pinocchio, "when I found him in your workshop . . . uh, hanging around."

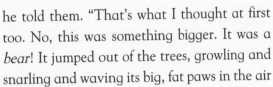

Tiger Lily

It was a hot summer night in Never Land – so hot, in fact, that the poor Lost Boys couldn't sleep. And so it was decided that instead of trying to stay in their hideout in Hangman's Tree, Peter Pan and the Lost Boys would camp out for the night in the wild, wild wilderness.

Certainly, they thought, the woods would be cool and shady, and the tall trees would catch any breeze kind enough to blow through. But little did they know how mysterious – and downright spooky – a forest could become once the sun went down.

"It's dark out here," said Cubby.

"And awful quiet," said Tootles.

"Won't you tell us a story, please, Peter?" asked Slightly, who was shivering in his fox suit despite the sticky heat.

"Very well," agreed Peter. "If it will make you all be quiet! I will tell you the story of the very first time I ever camped out in the wilderness – which, by the way, was the first time I met Tiger Lily . . .

"I had made myself a fire, a great big one, 'cause it was fall and the nights were getting cool. I'd just laid my head down on a patch of nice, soft moss, when all of a sudden I heard a rustling in the shadows."

"*Indians?*" the Lost Boys gasped.

But Peter shook his head. "Not Indians," he told them. "That's what I thought at first too. No, this was something bigger. It was a *bear*! It jumped out of the trees, growling and snarling and waving its big, fat paws in the air like Captain Hook swattin' blue flies. I've never seen such a mean, angry beast, before or since!"

"So wha-wha-what did you do?" asked the Lost Boys.

"Told him to get lost, of course. To *scram*! Apparently, he didn't understand English, however, 'cause he just kept charging. Well, I'm not going to lie to you; I started to get nervous. And then, there she was – Tiger Lily – as quiet as a mouse. Without a 'hi' or 'how do you do', she grabbed a stick from my fire and waved it at the bear. And the next thing I knew, the bear had turned around and was running off crying! I suppose Tiger Lily saved my life that night," said Peter. "And it wasn't the last time either. The end. Good night."

"Um . . . Peter," said Cubby, peering out into the darkness, "do you know what ever happened to that bear?"

Peter thought for a moment. "Nope," he said and shrugged. "Probably still out there, wandering around, I guess." He yawned a big, mischievous yawn. "Now stop yer yammerin' and close your eyes and go to sleep!"

Buttercup the Brave

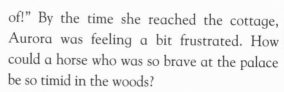

"Which horse would you like to ride today?" a stable groom asked Princess Aurora. Aurora looked around. There were so many horses! It was always hard to choose. But then a fine palomino caught Aurora's eye. Aurora rode him around the palace courtyard. The horse marched as confidently as if he were the king himself.

"What's this horse's name?" Aurora asked.

"We call him Brutus, Your Highness," the groom replied.

"Oh, no!" Aurora exclaimed. "That won't do at all. I think I'll call him Buttercup."

Aurora smiled. "Do you like your new name, Buttercup?" The horse snorted happily.

Aurora rode Buttercup around the castle grounds. When a carriage rumbled past, he stood to attention. When Aurora asked him to jump over a stone wall, he cleared it effortlessly.

The next day, Aurora decided to ride Buttercup to the fairies' cottage. But the moment they entered the woods, Buttercup became a different horse. He began to walk slowly and look around nervously. When some of Aurora's woodland friends appeared, Buttercup tried to run away!

"What's the matter, Buttercup?" Aurora asked. "Why, there's nothing to be frightened of!" By the time she reached the cottage, Aurora was feeling a bit frustrated. How could a horse who was so brave at the palace be so timid in the woods?

Flora, Fauna and Merryweather hurried out of their cottage. "Oh, what a beautiful pony!" Merryweather exclaimed.

Aurora sighed. "He is beautiful," she said. "But he seems to be afraid of the woods!"

"I'm sure it will be all right," Flora said. "You'll just need to be patient with him."

Soon it was time to say goodbye to the fairies and they made their way through the forest. Suddenly, Buttercup stopped abruptly. "What is it this time?" Aurora asked with a sigh. Then she looked ahead and gasped in horror. An enormous mountain lion was blocking their path! To Aurora's surprise, Buttercup didn't panic or try to run. Instead, he stood proudly and puffed himself up to look even bigger than he was. He planted his hooves and snorted angrily at the mountain lion. Then he marched forwards and struck out at the lion with his front hooves! The lion let out a yowl. Then it raced away. Buttercup had been brave when it really counted.

"Good boy!" she praised him. "You know, Buttercup, I think we make a perfect team!"

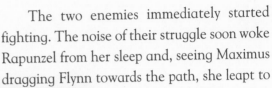

The Horse Charmer

Flynn and Rapunzel were camping in the woods. The royal guards were hot on the thief's heels, but he was escorting the young girl to the town all the same. To begin with, he had just wanted to get back the crown that she had taken from him. Now he genuinely wanted to help her make her dream come true: to see the floating lanterns being launched.

"Good night blondie!" he said, lying down by the fire.

"Good night Eugene!" Rapunzel said, using his real name.

They soon fell peacefully asleep. But at dawn Flynn woke up with a start, feeling what he thought was rain. *Plip!* A drop of water splashed on his forehead. *Plop!* Another fell on his cheek.

The thief opened his eyes... and found himself face to face with Maximus, the captain of the guard's horse! Maximus was soaking wet because he had just come out of the flooded tunnel where he had been chasing Flynn the evening before...

"Well I never! The proud steed of the head guard!" exclaimed Flynn mockingly. "I hope you've come to apologize for your shocking behaviour yesterday!"

But of course, Maximus had really come to arrest him and Flynn was well aware of it!

The two enemies immediately started fighting. The noise of their struggle soon woke Rapunzel from her sleep and, seeing Maximus dragging Flynn towards the path, she leapt to her friend's aid. The horse was holding Flynn by the foot. Rapunzel took hold of Flynn's arm and, stuck in the middle, Flynn had the feeling that he would end up being torn in half!

Then, *pop!* Maximus accidentally pulled off Flynn's boot. The thief was free and quickly ran off. Maximus rushed after him, but Rapunzel stood on the path and blocked his way. "There now. Calm down, my beauty. Nice horse! Sit!" she said.

Maximus was enchanted by the pretty young girl and, as Flynn looked on, the horse began to obey her like a well-behaved dog!

"There, there!" Rapunzel continued. "You've had enough of running after this naughty Eugene, haven't you? You're a good horse. You know, it's my birthday today. It would make me really happy if you'd leave Eugene in peace until tomorrow. What do you say?"

Maximus stretched out his hoof as a gesture of peace. The thief agreed to shake his hoof, wide-eyed in disbelief – he had heard stories about snake charmers, but never about a horse charmer!

Tink Causes Trouble

The fairies were on the mainland to bring the season of summer. Tinker Bell had found herself with no work to do, because all of her inventions were working perfectly. She had nothing to fix, so she had entertained herself by flying after an automobile! She had followed the car all the way to a house where a little girl called Lizzy lived with her father.

Vidia had tried to teach Tink a lesson, trapping her inside a tiny fairy house that Lizzy had made. But then, the little girl discovered Tinker Bell. Vidia panicked. She hadn't meant to put Tink in danger. She flew back to the fairy camp to get help.

But Vidia didn't realize that Tinker Bell had become friends with Lizzy. She had chosen to stay and help Lizzy and her father, Dr Griffiths. The scientist didn't believe in fairies and he was often too busy to spend time with his daughter. When Lizzy tried to show him her special fairy journal, he said he had no time – he had to fix some leaks in the roof.

So, Tinker Bell decided she would fix the leaks herself. She flew up into the attic and, in no time at all, she rigged up a system to take the water back outside. Then she flew back inside and couldn't help but notice a butterfly fluttering in a jar on Dr Griffith's desk. The scientist had caught it earlier to study. Tink felt terrible seeing the poor creature trapped, so she set it free.

The next morning, Dr Griffiths came by to check on his daughter.

"All the leaks have stopped," he said. "It's as if they mended themselves."

After he had gone, Tinker Bell tried to tell Lizzy to go and show her father the fairy field journal. "I would like to show him this," Lizzy said. "He has so much to learn about fairies."

But when Lizzy got downstairs, her father was very upset. "The butterfly is gone," he announced. "I was going to present it at the museum tonight. I didn't let it go, and since there is no one else in this house, it must have been you."

"I didn't," replied Lizzy. "It must have been...." Tinker Bell headed towards the office, but Lizzy waved her away.

"It must have been who?" he asked.

"I could tell you, father," Lizzy declared, "but you wouldn't believe me."

"Very well," Dr Griffiths said, "off to your room. I'm very disappointed in you."

Tinker Bell felt very bad for getting Lizzy into trouble. She wanted to show herself to Dr Griffiths, but Lizzy wouldn't let her new friend put herself in danger.

The Midnight Gift

Midnight was about to strike in New Orleans! Quickly, Tiana – who had turned into a frog – hopped to St Louis Cathedral where her friend Charlotte was about to marry an imposter masquerading as Prince Naveen.

Fortunately, when she arrived in front of the cathedral, the imposter was already being taken away by the police and the real Prince Naveen, who was still a frog too, was talking to Charlotte.

"But is it like the fairy tales then?" Charlotte was saying. "If I kiss you, will the sorcerer's evil spell be lifted, and will you become a handsome prince again?"

Naveen nodded. "Yes, because until midnight you're princess of the carnival," he explained. "And in that way Tiana will also become human again...."

Charlotte clapped.

"Oh wow! It's too marvellous for words! I have to kiss a frog, who will be transformed into a prince, and we will get married and live happily ever after, and on top of that, I will save my friend Tiana, and..."

"Wait Charlotte," interrupted Naveen, suddenly looking sad. "You must promise me that by tomorrow you will give Tiana all the money she needs to buy her restaurant. Because Tiana's happiness is very important to me...."

Tiana had dreamed of opening her own restaurant her whole life. Prince Naveen had fallen in love with Tiana, and wanted to help her.

Charlotte was about to kiss Prince Naveen... when Tiana leapt in front of them. "No don't do it, Naveen, I beg you!"

"What? But it's your last chance to achieve your dream, Tiana!"

She shook her head and replied, "There would be no point realizing my dream without sharing it with you by my side, Naveen... because I love you as much as you love me!"

They threw themselves into each other's arms, and Charlotte burst into tears! "It's so moving," she sniffed. "Tiana... all my life, I have hoped for a big fairy-tale love story. And you have found it! Of course I will kiss you, Naveen, and then you can marry Tiana!"

But it was too late: the bells chimed midnight! Charlotte desperately placed one, two, ten kisses on the lips of the frog Prince. But she was no longer a princess!

Naveen and Tiana looked at each other, madly in love. They could remain frogs forever now. What did it matter? They were contented with simply having each other.

The Desert Race

"Drat!" the Sultan cried. "Drat that dratted Desert Race!" Jasmine was surprised. Usually her father loved the Desert Race! The Sultan shook his head. "Prince Fayiz will be riding for Zagrabah again. His horse is so fast, he's won the last three years!"

"I have an idea!" Jasmine said eagerly. "I could ride Midnight in the Desert Race. He's the fastest horse in Agrabah!"

"Oh no!" The Sultan looked shocked at the suggestion. "The Desert Race can be dangerous."

"How about if I ride Midnight in the race?" Aladdin spoke up. The Sultan's face brightened. "What a splendid idea!" he cried.

The next day, Aladdin and Jasmine went to the stables. As soon as Aladdin was on Midnight, the horse threw him. Nobody but Jasmine had ever ridden him.

"Sorry," Jasmine told Aladdin. "Let me ride in the race, Father," Jasmine urged. The Sultan didn't seem to hear her.

The day of the race arrived. Fayiz rode in on his impressive white stallion, Desert Warrior. The riders took their places at the start line. "What an odd-looking horse Aladdin is riding," the Sultan said. But the princess was nowhere to be found. "We can't wait any longer." The Sultan started the race.

A black horse with a veiled rider took the lead. As soon as they were out of view, the rider threw off the veil. It was Jasmine! "I just had to prove that you were the fastest," she whispered to Midnight.

Aladdin's horse spotted an oasis of water and jumped in. "Now that's more like it!" exclaimed the horse. Except the horse was actually the Genie!

On land, Jasmine and Midnight galloped off without a backwards glance. Fayiz and Warrior stayed on Midnight's heels, until the horses had to jump a ditch. Midnight sailed over easily, but Warrior skidded to a stop!

Now there was nothing to keep Jasmine and Midnight from winning. But then Jasmine heard the sound of hoofbeats close behind her. It was Aladdin! He and Jasmine were neck and neck. But neither could keep the lead. And so, the two horses crossed the finish line at the same time.

"Congratulations!" Aladdin said.

"Same to you," Jasmine replied. "But where did you find such a fast horse?"

"Er..." Aladdin looked at his feet.

"Surprise!" the Genie cried, transforming back into his usual form.

"Sorry, Princess," the Genie said, winking. "We were just horsing around!"

Faith, Trust and Pixie Dust

The fairies were bringing summer to the mainland and Tinker Bell was very excited to be there. She was curious about the human world. Her curiosity had led her to a little fairy house, made by a girl named Lizzy.

Vidia, feeling frustrated that Tink was putting them in danger and wanting to teach her a lesson, had slammed the door of the fairy house shut. Then the door got stuck and Tink was found by the little girl! Vidia panicked and quickly flew to get help.

A storm had broken out, so Vidia and the other fairies had built a boat to reach Tinker Bell. They had sailed through the flooded meadow, survived a crash and saved Vidia from being stuck in the mud. Now, they were trudging silently through the rain.

"I was just thinking if Tink were here," said Silvermist, "how not quiet it would be right now. I really miss her."

"Tinker Bell getting trapped is all my fault," Vidia admitted. "I'm so sorry."

To Vidia's surprise, the other fairies weren't upset with her.

"Tinker Bell can get into plenty of trouble by herself," Rosetta declared.

They gathered around and chanted the fairy motto: "Faith, trust and pixie dust!"

They vowed to work together to save Tinker Bell.

Vidia loved feeling part of the group. She usually liked to be by herself and was sometimes even mean to the other fairies. But she was finally beginning to understand the importance of friendship.

Back in Lizzy's room, Tinker Bell was apologizing to Lizzy. She had got the little girl in trouble with her father, who didn't believe that fairies existed.

Lizzy understood.

"I wish I were a fairy just like you," Lizzy told Tink. "Then I could fly around with the other fairies all the time."

Tink knew how to make Lizzy's wish come true: pixie dust!

She told Lizzy to close her eyes and spread out her arms. Then the fairy hovered above Lizzy's head and showered it with pixie dust. It was time for some flying lessons!

Lizzy was so happy to have a friend like Tinker Bell. She knew her father loved her and wanted to spend more time with her, but, being a grown-up, he found it hard to believe in magic and especially in fairies.

Lizzy hoped that, one day, her father would believe in magic and that they could spend lots of time together.

Winnie the Pooh

The Sleepover

"Comfortable, Piglet?" Pooh asked. The two friends were having a best-friend sleepover.

"Oh, yes," Piglet replied. "Goodnight Pooh Bear."

Piglet lay in the darkness of Pooh's room. Although, the darkness at Pooh's house was much, much darker than it was at Piglet's house. Then he noticed it was much quieter than Piglet's own room at night.

"Pooh Bear?" Piglet whispered. There was no answer. He heard a soft, low rumbling. It was curiously similar to the sound of a sleeping bear snoring. The sound grew louder and then softer, over and over again! *Was it the sound of an approaching heffalump?* Piglet wondered.

"Oh dear!" Piglet shouted, running to Pooh's bed. "Wake up! P-p-please, P-P-Pooh!"

"Hmm?" Pooh said drowsily, sitting up. Piglet was hiding under the covers in Pooh's bed.

"Why, Piglet," said Pooh. "What's the matter?"

"It's that horrible n-n-noise, Pooh," he stammered. Piglet listened for the noise, then realized he couldn't hear it.

"That's funny," said Piglet. "The noise stopped as soon as you woke up, Pooh."

"Hmm," said Pooh. He shrugged. Then he yawned. "I guess that means we can go back to sleep."

"Pooh Bear," said Piglet timidly, "I don't mean to be a bad best friend. But could we, well, have the rest of our sleepover another night? I'm just used to sleeping in my own house."

Pooh put his arm around Piglet. "I understand, Piglet," he said.

Pooh helped Piglet gather his things, then hand in hand, they walked to Piglet's house.

Piglet was happy to be at his own house. "Thank you so much for understanding," he said. "I suppose you'll need to get home to bed now?"

"That does sound like the thing to do," Pooh replied. "But first I might sit down for a little rest."

While Piglet put away his things, Pooh sat down in the chair.

By the time Piglet came back, Pooh was making a soft, low rumbling sound. But in the comfort of his own house, it did not strike Piglet as anything other than the sound of one sleeping bear snoring.

"Sweet dreams, Pooh Bear," he whispered. Piglet climbed into his own bed and drifted off to sleep. It seemed that he and Pooh were having their best-friend sleepover, after all.

Disney
MICKEY MOUSE
An Uncle Mickey Day

Morty and Ferdie Mouse were oh-so-very excited. Today was their number one favourite kind of day. An Uncle Mickey day! That meant their Uncle Mickey was going to take them out to do all kinds of special, surprising things.

"Uncle Mickey!" the twins shouted when he came to pick them up. "What are we doing today?"

"What *aren't* we doing today, you mean," said Mickey. "I thought we'd start with bowling."

"Hooray!" cheered Morty and Ferdie.

At the bowling alley, Morty and Ferdie discovered that if they rolled the bowling ball together, they could knock at least four or five pins down every time.

Then it was off to the park for some hide-and-seek and a game of catch. Uncle Mickey didn't mind being the finder in hide-and-seek every time. And he didn't mind chasing the balls that Ferdie sometimes threw way, way over his head.

"I'm hungry," said Morty when at last they stopped to rest.

"Me, too," said Ferdie.

"How about some pizza?" suggested Mickey.

"Okay!" the twins shouted together.

At the pizza parlour, Mickey let Morty and Ferdie choose their favourite toppings. Morty picked pepperoni. Ferdie picked black olives. Mickey, meanwhile, had his usual: extra cheese!

"All finished?" asked Mickey. "We'll have to hurry if we're going to go to the carnival."

"All right!" the boys shouted.

After the carnival, where they each won a prize, the boys told Mickey what a great day it had been.

"Well, it's not over yet," Mickey told them.

"Really?" said Morty.

"What's next?" asked Ferdie.

That's when Mickey held up three tickets – and a mitt. A baseball game! Oh, wow!

There was nothing in the whole, wide world that Mickey's nephews liked better than baseball games . . . and popcorn . . . and peanuts . . . and ice cream. And to make things even better, Uncle Mickey caught a foul ball, and their favourite team won. They even watched fireworks at the end of the game.

"Wow, Uncle Mickey! Thank you so much!" said the twins when they finally returned home, tired and full and very, very happy. "This has been one of the best Uncle Mickey days ever!"

"Oh, this was nothing," said Uncle Mickey. "Just wait until next time!"

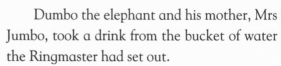

DUMBO
Lend Me Your Ears

"I think I can, I think I can, I think I can," chugged Casey Jr, the circus train. The train moved slowly around a bend. "I think I can. I think I . . . *Ah-choo!*" he sneezed. Suddenly, he came to a halt. "I know I can't," he admitted finally. The animals and the performers poked their heads out, wondering what was wrong.

"Well?" asked the Ringmaster.

"Casey Jr here has a cold," the engineer replied. "He's going to need some rest before he can take us any further."

The Ringmaster frowned. "But we're due at the fairground in a few hours. What will we do? After all, the show must go on!"

The engineer just shrugged and turned his attention back to the sneezing, coughing and spluttering little engine.

The Ringmaster went down the train, swinging open the doors to all the cages and cars. "Come on, everyone," he said. "Might as well stretch your legs."

The animals lumbered, scampered and pranced onto the wide open field. Next, the clowns and acrobats and animal trainers sauntered out. Some set up crates in the grass and played cards, others rehearsed and a few pulled out packed lunches and sprawled on the ground.

Dumbo the elephant and his mother, Mrs Jumbo, took a drink from the bucket of water the Ringmaster had set out.

Mrs Jumbo gazed around. "Looks like we're in the middle of nowhere," she said. "I do hope poor Casey Jr is feeling better soon."

"Me too," Dumbo's friend Timothy Q. Mouse said hopefully.

Just then a clap of thunder sounded. Raindrops began to fall from the sky. The animals and performers ran for the shelter of the circus wagons. Dumbo held on to his mother's tail, but just as they were about to board, the wind picked up. The gust caught Dumbo's huge ears and sent him flying backwards.

"That's it!" yelled the Ringmaster over the howling wind. "Dumbo, come with me!" He led Dumbo over to the train, climbed onto the front wagon, and motioned for the little elephant to join him.

"Now spread out those great ears of yours!" the Ringmaster said. Dumbo's ears billowed out, catching the wind like giant sails and pushing Casey Jr along the tracks. "The show will go on!" the Ringmaster shouted happily.

"I know I can. I know I can. I know I can," chanted Casey Jr. And then he added, "Thanks to Dumbo!"

Nemo's Best Shot

"Come on, Dad! We're going to be late!" cried Nemo.

Nemo and Marlin were hurrying through the busy swimming lanes of the colourful Great Barrier Reef.

"Are you sure you want to play pearl volleyball?" Marlin asked nervously. "There are lots of other things you can do. Sponge jumping, for example. Or maybe reef dancing."

"Reef dancing!" cried Nemo, horrified. "No way! That's for babies! I want to play pearl volleyball!"

After they arrived at Sea Urchin Stadium, Mr Ray gave the opening announcements. "Hello and welcome, everyone! Before we get started, let's give a big thank you to Ms Esther Clam for donating today's ball."

Everyone applauded as Esther opened her shell and spat out the pearl.

"Let's play pearl volleyball!" cried Mr Ray.

"Good luck, son," said Marlin. "Just remember what I told you – "

"I know! I know!" said Nemo, rolling his eyes. "When you give it your best shot, even if you lose, you win."

The players lined up on either side of the sea fan net. Ray's Raiders were on one side, and Nemo's team, the Fighting Planktons, were on the other.

Marlin watched anxiously. He was sure that Nemo wouldn't be able to play as well as the other fish because of his small fin.

Marlin wasn't the only one who had doubts. Turbot Trout sidled up to Nemo on the court.

"Coach may be letting you play today," Turbot snapped, "but you better not mess up the Planktons' winning streak."

Nemo narrowed his eyes. Turbot didn't know that Nemo had spent many hours smacking around pebbles in a dentist's office aquarium.

"Just watch and learn," murmured Nemo.

Suddenly, the pearl came right to Nemo. *Smack!*

Using his good left fin, Nemo sent the pearl flying right over the net. The pearl flew so fast, the other team couldn't return it. Nemo scored his first point for the Planktons!

Nemo played like a pro. He scored again with his good fin, then with his tail. And, just to show his father and Turbot Trout, he scored the winning point with his little fin.

"Go, short fin!" cried Turbot Trout. "With a player like you, we're going to go all the way to the Lobster Bowl Clam-pionship!"

"Wow, Nemo," said Marlin after the game. "That was amazing."

"Thanks, Dad," said Nemo. "I gave it my best shot, like you said. And we actually won too!"

THE
LION KING
The Hic-hic-hiccups

"What a day!" Pumbaa said as he led Simba and Timon through the forest.

"What a day, indeed," Timon agreed.

"*Hic!*" said Simba.

"What was that?" Timon cried.

"Don't be scared. It's just that I have the – *hic!* I have the hiccups," Simba explained.

"I'll tell you what to do," Timon said. "Forget about it! They'll go away – eventually."

"Forget about it? *Hic!* But I can't roar," Simba explained. And to demonstrate, he opened his mouth really wide. But, just as he was about to roar, he hiccupped! "See?" he said sadly.

"Have you tried licking tree bark?" Pumbaa asked.

"Licking tree bark?" said Simba.

"It always works for me," Pumbaa explained. "That or closing your eyes, holding your nose and jumping on one foot while saying your name five times fast – backwards."

Timon watched Simba hop around on one foot, holding his nose with his eyes closed. "Abmis, Abmis, Abmis – *hic!* It's not working!" Simba cried.

"Maybe there's something caught in his throat," Timon offered.

"There's nothing caught in his throat," Pumbaa said.

"How do you know?" Timon asked.

"I just know about these things," Pumbaa answered.

Suddenly, right on cue, Simba interrupted their argument with the biggest hiccup of all.

"HIC!"

And, wouldn't you know, just then the biggest fly you've ever seen came soaring out of Simba's mouth. It flew right into a tree and crashed to the ground. The fly stood up groggily and shook itself off.

"It's about time, buddy!" the fly said to Simba.

Simba was about to reply, but he was interrupted by two voices, shouting in unison –

"DINNER!"

The fly gave a frightened squeak and flew off, as Timon and Pumbaa both pounced on the spot where it had been just a moment earlier.

Peter Pan

Where's Tink?

Peter Pan was in a hurry to meet Tinker Bell. (Because you know how Tinker Bell gets if you keep her waiting.) Today they had a date for a game of tag.

"Tink!" he called as he arrived at his hideout. He took off his hat and placed it on the table. "I'm home!"

But there was no reply.

How strange, thought Peter. Tinker Bell was never late. He called her name again as loudly as he could. But still no answer. He started to worry.

"Wake up! Wake up!" he shouted to the Lost Boys, who were napping in hammocks. "Tinker Bell is missing!"

"Tinker Bell?" Cubby yawned. "I know I saw her flying around here this morning."

"Yeah," said Rabbit. "She helped me fix my slingshot."

"Well, she's not here now," said Peter.

"Where would she go?" asked Tootles.

Peter thought for a moment. He knew that Tinker Bell liked to fly around Never Land. And she especially liked paying visits to other fairies. But not when she had a game of tag to play with Peter. No, that was not like Tinker Bell at all.

"The question," Peter Pan finally declared, "is not where would she go, but who could have taken her!"

"Oooh . . ." the Lost Boys shuddered.

"Do you mean . . ." the Raccoon Twins began.

"Indians?" finished Peter. "I certainly do. I can see it right now. While you were sleeping, a whole band crept in and stole our Tinker Bell away."

Then Slightly spoke up. "Or what if it was . . ."

"Pirates!" cried Peter. "Of course! Those dirty, rotten scoundrels! It would be just like them to lure Tinker Bell outside, ambush her and kidnap her and hold her for ransom! They probably have her chained up in the deep, dark hold of their ship at this very moment!

"Men!" Peter cried. "We can't just stand here while Tinker Bell suffers in the grimy hands of bloodthirsty pirates – in mortal danger! I hereby declare that a rescue mission be formed at once. Are you with me?"

"Hoorah! Hoorah!" the boys cheered.

"Then let's go!" said Peter. And with that, he grabbed his hat and—

Ring-a-ling! Ring! Ring! Rrrring!

"Tink!" Peter exclaimed as his missing (and furious!) friend shot up into the air. "Where have you been? You had me worried sick!"

Tinker Bell just jingled angrily at Peter. She hadn't been kidnapped. She'd been trapped under Peter's hat the whole time!

Cinderella

The Lost Mice

One winter night, the Prince led Cinderella out to the balcony. "I have a surprise for you," he said, handing her a box. Inside was a beautiful new coat.

"Oh, it's lovely!" Cinderella exclaimed.

The next morning, the princess showed her coat to Suzy, one of her mouse friends.

A few minutes later, Jaq went into Cinderella's room. It had been a chilly night in the attic.

"Cinderelly!" Jaq called. If he told the princess how cold the attic was, she would help them. But she was on her way out and didn't hear. Jaq sighed. He was sure she wouldn't mind if they sat in front of the blazing fire in Cinderella's room.

Soon, the new housekeeper came in. When she saw the mice, she shrieked. She didn't know that the mice were Cinderella's friends. She chased them with a broom and the mice ran into the castle gardener. Before they knew what was happening, he had trapped them. "Take them outside!" the housekeeper said.

Meanwhile, Cinderella and the Prince were out riding. As their horses trotted through the countryside, they saw the castle gardener in one of the fields.

"Hello!" the Prince called out. But the gardener did not answer. The Prince turned to Cinderella. "That was odd," he said. "Why wouldn't he answer?"

"Perhaps he was lost in thought?" Cinderella replied.

Cinderella was right. The gardener was making a decision. He should let the mice go but he was worried about them. Finally, he took the mice to the stables. "Don't tell the housekeeper," he told the stable workers. "These poor mice need warmth and a bite to eat." The mice were very grateful.

Later that night, Cinderella was starting to worry. She hadn't seen the mice all day. She was searching for them when she ran into the Prince.

"I am looking for our new housekeeper. Apparently she threw the mice out of the castle today!" said the Prince.

"Oh, no!" Cinderella cried. "Poor dears. They'll freeze outside!"

"Don't worry," the Prince said. He told Cinderella about what the gardener had done.

Together, Cinderella and the Prince went to the stables. They thanked the gardener and the stable workers. She was relieved to see her little friends safe and sound. From then on, the mice always had a warm place of their own – in one of the main rooms of the castle.

A Scientific Discovery

Tinker Bell was a very curious fairy. She loved discovering new things and exploring new places. This is why, while the fairies were bringing summer to the mainland, Tink flew off after a car. Vidia had followed and tried to get Tink to come back to fairy camp, but Tink had ignored her.

Tink ended up being discovered by the little girl who lived in the house. The girl's name was Lizzy and her father was a scientist called Dr Griffiths. He didn't believe in fairies and found it hard to find time to spend with his daughter, because he was so busy working and repairing the house.

Tink decided to help Lizzy and her father. She fixed the leaks in the roof of their house, so that Dr Griffiths would be able to spend time with Lizzy instead. But then Tinker Bell got Lizzy in trouble by freeing a butterfly Dr Griffiths had captured. To make it up to Lizzy, Tink sprinkled her with pixie dust so that she could fly around her room!

Meanwhile, Vidia and the other fairies had been travelling from fairy camp to rescue Tinker Bell. They had just arrived at the house. "Okay," began Vidia. "Tinker Bell is upstairs."

But before they could move, Mr Twitches, the family cat, appeared!

Mr Twitches headed for the staircase and blocked the way.

Vidia had an idea. She shot a stream of pixie dust at a plate, which began to hover in the air. The others joined in, sprinkling the magic dust on dishes and silverware.

Now the fairies hurried across their flying bridge to reach the stairs – but Mr Twitches was right behind them.

"You know where Tink is," Rosetta told Vidia. "You go. We'll take care of the cat."

Meanwhile, Dr Griffiths could hear strange noises coming from Lizzy's room. "What's going on in here?" he demanded. "Look at this room! How did you get footprints on the ceiling? The truth this time."

"Well, I....," began Lizzy. "I was flying. My fairy showed me how."

"You've got to stop this nonsense!" insisted Dr Griffiths. Just then, Vidia sneaked into the room, but he didn't see her. "You will never convince me that fairies exist!" he added.

Tinker Bell couldn't stand it any longer. She flew out of hiding and hovered directly in front of his face! "It can't be!" Lizzy's father cried. He stared at Tink in wonder. "This is going to be the discovery of the century!"

Vidia saw him raise a glass jar. "Watch out!" she warned. Now that her wings were dry, she was able to fly over and knock Tink out of the way. *SLAM!* The jar came down on Vidia instead.

Now it was Vidia that needed rescuing!

Patch's Plan

"Whoa!" Patch said, "Look at all these other puppies!"

His brothers and sisters were still whimpering with fear. They had just been dognapped and, after a long, bumpy ride in a car, they had arrived at a big, draughty house. But Patch was already trying to work out a way to get back home. He looked around the large shabby room. "Hey," he asked the closest stranger. "Where are we?"

The spotted puppy smiled at him. "Oh, you must be new!" he said. "Which pet shop did you come from?"

Patch scowled at the strange new puppy. "We're not from a pet shop – we were stolen from our house."

Several other puppies heard him and moved closer. "Stolen? Really?" they exclaimed.

The first puppy shrugged. "Well, bought or stolen, we're all stuck here now."

"Maybe *you're* stuck here," Patch said boldly. "Our parents and their human pets will be here soon to rescue us, just see if they don't!"

"I hope so," Patch's sister Pepper said. "I wonder why someone would want to steal us, anyway?"

Patch didn't know. But he was sure that their parents would find them soon. In the meantime, he wanted to make sure he and his siblings stayed well away from all the pet-shop puppies, so there wasn't any confusion.

"We don't know why there are so many of us," the strange puppy told Pepper. "I guess Cruella just really likes puppies."

Patch gasped aloud. "Cruella?" he cried. "Do you mean Cruella De Vil?"

His brothers and sisters shuddered. Their parents had told them scary stories about that nasty woman. Could it be true?

"Yes, she's the one who bought us," several of the other puppies spoke up, while others nodded their heads.

This changed everything! "We have to get away," Patch declared.

Rolly sighed. "We know," he said. "Mum and Dad will be here soon. I just hope we get home in time for breakfast . . . ."

"No, you don't understand!" Patch shook his head. "Cruella is bad news – that's what Dad always says. We have to get away from her now – all of us!" He gestured to the entire group of puppies, bought and stolen. It didn't matter where they'd come from. What mattered was they were in this mess together. "We have to work as a team."

The first puppy smiled at him. "I'm with you!" he exclaimed. "When we're done with her, Cruella will be seeing spots!"

First Day of School

It was the first day of a brand-new school year for Nemo and his friends.

"Hey, Tad! Hey, Pearl!" called Nemo as he swam into the playground. "Isn't it great to be back at school?"

"Well," said Tad, "I wouldn't go *that* far."

"What do you mean?" asked Nemo. "It's gonna be awesome! I heard this year we get to learn how to sub-tract and speak Prawn."

"Sure," said Tad, "but did you also hear who's gonna be teaching us all that?"

"No," said Nemo. "Who?"

Just then, up swam Sheldon, Jimmy and Jib.

"Hey, Sheldon," Tad called out. "Why don't you tell Nemo here about our new teacher, Mrs Lobster?"

"Mrs Lobster?" said Nemo.

"Yeah," said Sheldon. "Ooooh, they say she's the worst!"

"Who says she's the worst?" asked Nemo.

"Well, Sandy Plankton, for one. He says his cousin, Krill, had her last year – and that she was so mean, he'll never go to school again!"

"And you know what I heard from Sandy," said Tad. "I heard she has these great big claws, and that she uses them to grab students real hard when they give the wrong answer!"

"Oh!" said Pearl. "Don't say that. You're going to make me ink!"

"Yeah," said Nemo. "That sounds awful!"

"I know," said Jimmy. "Sandy says Mrs Lobster never goes on field trips like Mr Ray did. And she sends you home with tons of homework, and makes you stay after school if you forget to bring it in the next day!"

Oh, no! Nemo shud-dered. All summer long he'd been looking forward to this day. And now school hadn't even started yet and already he wished it would end!

"Don't look now," Sheldon whispered, "but I think she's coming!"

"I'm gonna ink!" whimpered Pearl.

Nemo shut his eyes and wished with all his might for his dad to come and take him back home . . . .

"Hello there," said a warm voice. "You must be my new pupils! I'm Mrs Lobster."

Huh? thought Nemo. Surely, this wasn't the Mrs Lobster the kids had been talking about. And yet, when he opened his eyes, there she was, taking the register.

"Jib, Jimmy, Nemo, Pearl, Sheldon, Tad . . . my, what a smart-looking class. I do hope you kids are ready to have fun."

Nemo sighed. That silly Sandy Plankton – they should know by now not to believe every-thing he said. Because now Nemo was pretty sure: this was going to be a great year, after all!

THE JUNGLE Book

Mowgli's Nap

Mowgli leaned forward for a better look. When Baloo yawned, you could almost see his tonsils. The big bear closed his gaping mouth and blinked sleepily.

"Am I ever sleepy." Baloo stretched, leaned against a tree trunk and scratched his back as he slid to the ground. "I think it must be time for an afternoon snooze."

"Good thinking, my friend." High above them, stretched out on a branch, Bagheera the panther dangled a limp paw. His golden eyes were half closed in the heat of the day.

"A nap? Not for me!" Mowgli shook his mop of dark hair. "I'm not tired."

"Now, hold on a second there," Baloo said. "Don't you want to go hunting with us after it cools off? You're going to need energy."

"I have plenty of energy," Mowgli insisted. "I have energy right now!" He started to walk away from the bear, but Baloo stretched out a paw and grabbed the boy's ankle.

"Not so fast," Baloo said.

"You may have energy but, if you use it now, you will not have it to use later," Bagheera said wisely.

"Listen to the cat." Baloo yawned. "He knows what he's talking about." And with that, Baloo pulled Mowgli onto a pile of leaves and held him down with one great paw.

"I have energy for now *and* later," Mowgli grumbled. He struggled to get out from under Baloo's big arm. But he couldn't move the bear.

"Good nap, Man-cub," Bagheera purred at the scowling Mowgli.

A moment later, the panther and the bear were sleeping soundly. As soon as Mowgli heard their snores he hoisted up the arm that was pinning him down.

"Good nap, yourself," Mowgli whispered. And he tiptoed off to swing in the trees and drop sticks on the animals below.

Baloo's snores shook the jungle for an hour, perhaps two, before Mowgli returned to the shady napping spot again. He'd had a grand time in the treetops, but the sun and the swinging had tired him. The great grey bear looked so soft and peaceful lying against the tree that Mowgli could not help himself. He curled up against his friend and closed his eyes.

Not two minutes later, Bagheera awoke and stretched his inky paws. The panther flicked his tail under Baloo's nose.

"I'm up. I'm up and ready to go!" Baloo sat upright. Then, spying Mowgli, the bear gave the boy a good shake. "How about you, Man-cub? You awake?"

But the only sound that came from Mowgli's mouth was a loud snore.

Disney
Lilo & Stitch

Homework Helper

Stitch didn't care for weekdays much now that Lilo was back in school. To Stitch they were the longest and most boring days of the week, spent waiting . . . and waiting for Lilo to come home.

And so you can imagine Stitch's excitement when three o'clock finally rolled around and Lilo's school bus dropped her off.

"Lilo!" Stitch would shriek, racing down to meet her. "Play time! Play time! Lilo and Stitch play time!" And, usually, Lilo would toss her backpack onto the porch and they would hop on her trike.

But then, one day, Lilo didn't drop her backpack. And she didn't run after Stitch. "Sorry, Stitch," was all she said. "My teacher says if I don't start doing my homework, she's going to have a talk with Nani!" And Lilo certainly didn't want that to happen! Her sister had enough to worry about – and so did Lilo.

And so, with that, Lilo went inside her house, took out her schoolbooks, and sat down at the dining-room table to study.

Stitch didn't understand. "Homework?" he said, peeking into Lilo's backpack. "What's that?"

"Homework," said Lilo, "is maths problems and a book report and a week's worth of spelling words that I have one day to learn! Now please, Stitch, be a good alien and shoo."

But Stitch wasn't about to give up so soon.

He was back in less than a minute with a basket full of Lilo's favourite action figures.

"You've got to be kidding," said Lilo. "I am not playing superheroes. Can't you see I'm busy?!"

"Noogy Bay!" muttered Stitch. This was very frustrating! But Stitch loved a challenge. Off he ran again. And this time he came back wearing a catcher's mask and vest, carrying a baseball, a bat and Lilo's glove.

"Play ball!" Stitch shouted.

And, for a second there, Lilo almost got up. Then she shook her head. "No, Stitch," she sighed. "If I don't start these spelling words now, I'll never finish them tonight."

Stitch thought for a second, then dashed off once again. Lilo could hear all sorts of banging and slamming coming from her room. It sounded as though Stitch was turning it upside down! Oh, great, she thought to herself. But at least he's leaving me alone . . . .

Then, to Lilo's surprise, Stitch once more appeared before her, carrying a book of crossword puzzles under his arm.

"Lilo play *and* spell words!" Stitch cheerfully told her.

"Why didn't I think of that!" said Lilo. "Stitch, you can help me with my homework any time!"

Just Believe

The fairies from Pixie Hollow were bringing summer to the mainland when they hear a loud *CRACK*. Tinker Bell just had to see what had made the noise – it was a car! She followed the car to a house where two humans lived – a girl called Lizzy and her father, a scientist called Dr Griffiths.

Tinker Bell had been discovered by the girl and the two had become friends. Tink had decided she would help Dr Griffiths to spend more time with his daughter. But so far, her plan hadn't worked.

Meanwhile Vidia had flown to get help to rescue Tink. All the fairies had travelled in the rain to the humans' house. But just as Vidia arrived upstairs, Tink had revealed herself to Dr Griffiths! Tink wanted to prove to him that fairies did exist. He too often scolded Lizzy for believing in them.

Dr Griffiths was about to capture Tink in a glass jar, when Vidia pushed her out of the way. Now Vidia had been caught instead!

"I must get this to the museum right away!" declared Dr Griffiths.

"Father, you can't do this!" cried Lizzy – but it was no use. Dr Griffiths ran out of the house, jumped into his car and drove off.

When the other fairies arrived upstairs, Tink told them that Vidia was in danger.

It was still raining, though. The fairies wouldn't be able to fly. "We can't fly," said Tink, "but I think I know somebody who can."

The fairies swirled around Lizzy and showered her with pixie dust. "All aboard!" cried Tink.

The fairies tucked themselves into Lizzy's coat and off she flew down the road that led to the city. Shortly after nightfall, the magnificent streets of London came into view.

"There he is!" cried Lizzy as she spotted her father's car.

Tinker Bell flew down and bravely darted into the engine. After some quick tinkering, the car stopped. Dr Griffiths jumped out and raced off towards the museum on foot. Tinker Bell – and Lizzy – were right behind him. "Father!" Lizzy called.

Dr Griffiths turned to see his daughter flying towards him. "Lizzy ... you're ... flying!"

"But I don't understand," he continued.

"You don't have to understand," Lizzy told her father. Dr Griffiths looked at all the tiny magical fairies hovering around him. His eyes filled with wonder.

"I just need to believe," he said. He handed the jar to Lizzy. Seconds later, Vidia was reunited with her relieved and grateful friends. And Dr Griffiths hugged his daughter, realizing she had been right all along....

Disney
Pinocchio
Boy's Best Friend

Like all little boys, Pinocchio wanted a puppy. And, like all little boys, he promised to feed it and walk it and do everything and anything required to care for it.

"Puppies are a lot of work," Geppetto told his son. "And puppies like to chew things, like slippers – and wood." The toy maker glanced over at the rows and rows of wooden toys on his workbench. "No, I don't think a dog is a good idea," he said finally.

That afternoon, when Pinocchio returned from school, Geppetto had a present waiting. The boy wasted no time in opening the box. "It's a dog," Pinocchio said, trying to hide his disappointment. "A wooden dog." Not wanting to hurt Geppetto's feelings, Pinocchio thanked his father and placed the toy on his bed.

A few days later, as Pinocchio was walking home from school, he heard a puppy whimpering in an alleyway. With a little coaxing, the puppy emerged. "Why, you look just like the wooden dog my father carved for me," Pinocchio said.

Pinocchio wondered what to do. "Well, I can't leave you here all by yourself," he decided. The boy went home and tied the dog to a tree a few doors up the street. Then he sneaked the puppy a bowl of food and went back inside.

After Geppetto had fallen asleep,

Pinocchio slipped outside and scooped up the dog. "Now, you're going to have to be very quiet," he warned.

Once inside, the puppy sprang from Pinocchio's arms and made a dash for Figaro. As the dog bounded after the fleeing cat, they upset chairs and knocked over crockery. "Look out!" cried Pinocchio. Geppetto soon appeared in his night clothes. "What's going on here?" he asked.

"Well," Pinocchio began. Suddenly, the puppy sprang onto Pinocchio's bed, knocking the wooden dog beneath it. Geppetto blinked. The puppy looked just like the toy he had made for his son!

"Could it be?" the toy maker asked. "Pinocchio! You wanted a puppy so much that the Blue Fairy must have turned your toy dog into a real one!"

Pinocchio just picked up the pup and brought it over to meet Geppetto. A day later, when Pinocchio finally found the courage to tell Geppetto the truth, the little puppy was in no danger of becoming an orphan again. "Well," Geppetto said affectionately when he found the pup carrying the wooden dog around the house, "I suppose we have room for two dogs here – especially if one of them walks the other!"

Cruella Sees Spots

Cruella looked around the living room of the old De Vil mansion and rubbed her hands together. The room was full of Dalmatian puppies. Everywhere Cruella looked she saw spots, spots, spots! At last, her dream was coming true! Cackling with glee, Cruella thought back to the day this had all started . . . .

It had begun as a perfectly miserable day. Cruella had been shopping for fur coats all morning and she hadn't found a single thing she liked.

"Too long! Too short! Too black! Too white!" she screeched, knocking an armload of coats out of the shop assistant's hands. "I want something unusual! I want a coat that has never been seen before!"

Cruella stormed out of the shop, slamming the door so hard that the glass cracked. She needed something to cheer her up. Just then she remembered that her old school friend, Anita, lived nearby.

Soon Cruella stood at the door, ringing the buzzer impatiently. She could hear cheerful piano music coming from an open window.

Just then, a pretty brown-haired woman answered the door. Her eyes opened wide when she saw the skinny woman covered in fur standing on her doorstep. "Oh, Cruella!" she cried. "What a surprise!"

"Hello, Anita, darling," Cruella said, walking into the sitting room. At that moment, a tall, thin man strolled down the stairs, smoking a pipe. But, when he caught sight of Cruella, he leaped back in fright!

"Ah, prince charming," Cruella said, smirking at Anita's new husband. Roger scowled. Suddenly something else caught Cruella's eye. Two black-and-white spotted dogs were sitting in the corner of the room.

"And what have we here?" Cruella asked.

"Oh, that's Pongo and Perdita," Anita explained. "They're wonderful pets." But Cruella wasn't looking at the dogs. She was looking at their coats. Their glossy fur wasn't too long or too short. It wasn't too black or too white. Cruella had never seen anything like it before. It was perfect.

"And soon we'll be even happier," Anita went on. "Perdita is going to have puppies!"

"Puppies!" Cruella shrieked. Suddenly she had an idea that made her smile an evil smile.

"Oh, Anita, you have positively made my day. Now, you must call me just as soon as the puppies arrive. I think they are *just* what I have been looking for."

Pongo snarled, but Cruella didn't notice.

"What a perfectly *marvellous* day," Cruella said to herself as she strode out of the door.

. . . And *that* was how it all started.

Winnie the Pooh

Tigger's Moving Day

After breakfast, Tigger likes to bounce. Sproing! Sproing! Sproing! He likes to bounce all day long, but he is always bumping into things. Thump!

"Tigger, you don't have enough bouncing room in this little house," said Rabbit. "We've got to find you a bigger house. That's all there is to it!"

By evening, everyone was excited about the big new house they had found.

"It IS a bouncy house," said Tigger. "The kind of house tiggers like best!" He bounced, and he didn't bump into anything. "But," he said, sighing, "I won't live next door to little Roo anymore."

"I know you'll miss being neighbours with Kanga and Roo," said Christopher Robin, "but now you'll live much closer to me. We can have fun being neighbours."

Kanga told Tigger she would bring Roo to visit. Tigger felt better and invited everyone to stay awhile. Rabbit put his paws on his hips. "We aren't finished yet. We need to move all your things from your old house to this house," he explained. Rabbit told everyone to bring all the boxes they could find to Tigger's house. Then he told Eeyore to get his donkey cart.

"Wow! Boxes are fun!" cried Roo as he and Tigger bounced in and out of the boxes everyone brought.

"There'll be time for fun later," grumbled Rabbit.

Tigger packed all his games and his stuffed animals in a box. He took his favourite lion out and hugged him. Rabbit packed Tigger's dishes. Kanga packed Tigger's hats and scarves. Pooh and Piglet packed Tigger's food. Soon Eeyore arrived with his donkey cart. Christopher Robin and Owl hoisted Tigger's bed and table and chairs onto the cart.

"Now my new home will be perfect," Tigger said, as they unloaded the cart and carried everything inside. "Thanks for your help, everyone!"

After his friends had gone, Tigger put all his things just where he wanted them. When he was finished, he sat down to rest. Hmmm. Seems like an awfully quiet house, he thought. He tried out a few bounces, but decided he wasn't in such a bouncy mood, after all. But just then, Tigger heard a little voice.

"Hallooo!"

"Roo!" cried Tigger. "Kanga! Come on in!"

"Hallooo! Hallooo!" Tigger soon heard all his friends calling outside his new door. Everyone had brought housewarming presents!

"Our work's all done," said Rabbit. "Now it's time for fun!"

Disney
The Fox and the Hound

Wild Life

Tod the fox had just arrived at the nature reserve, a vast, beautiful forest where wild animals were protected from hunters. Widow Tweed had brought him there to keep him safe, since her next-door neighbor, Amos Slade, had vowed to hunt him. Amos was angry with the fox because his beloved dog, Chief, had been injured while chasing after him.

At first, Tod didn't understand why his kind owner, Widow Tweed, had left him in the middle of this strange forest, alone and afraid. But she had seemed to be as sad about leaving him as he was about being abandoned.

The first night was dreadful. It had poured with rain and, although he tried to find shelter in different hollows and caves, they were always inhabited by other animals. There was no room for the poor, wet little fox. But the next morning, things began to look up. Tod met a pretty young fox named Vixey. She showed him around the forest, which had many beautiful waterfalls and streams full of fish.

"I think I'm going to like it here, Vixey," said Tod. Having lived his whole life with the Widow Tweed, he had never met another fox before, least of all one as lovely as Vixey.

But Vixey had lived the life of a wild fox, and she knew more about the world than Tod. "You must be very careful, Tod," she warned him. "Remember, we're foxes, and we have many enemies. You must always be on the alert for danger!"

"Come on, Vixey," scoffed Tod. "We're in a game preserve! I heard the Widow Tweed say that there's no hunting allowed in this forest. What could possibly happen to us here? We don't have a care in the world!"

Suddenly, a huge shadow fell over the two foxes. A look of great fear crossed Vixey's face. Turning around slowly and cautiously, Tod saw why. A huge bear was standing up on its hind legs. And it was staring straight at them!

"Grrrr!" the bear growled.

"Run!" yelled Vixey.

Tod didn't need to be told twice. The two foxes dashed away from the bear, scampering over hills, racing through a hollow tree and jumping over a narrow stream. When they were well away from the bear, they stopped and leaned against a rock, panting hard.

"Okay," Tod said, when he had caught his breath a bit. "I see what you mean about the dangers, Vixey. From now on, I'll be a lot more careful."

"Mmm-hmm," she replied. Then she smiled. "Come on," she said to Tod. "Let's go fishing!"

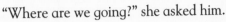

From Dream To Reality

Rapunzel had been locked away in a tower her entire life, and now she had acheived her dream of discovering the outside world, with the help of a thief called Flynn Rider. When they finally reached the town, she was amazed. There was a castle standing high above the kingdom, as if keeping watch over the people below – and what a lot of people there were!

One group of girls were entranced by Rapunzel's hair as she passed by. But people were treading on it. "We can help you braid it!" the girls shouted.

Laughing, Rapunzel accepted their offer and was soon able to admire her new hairstyle: a magnificent braid studded with fresh flowers. And no one could tread on it!

Being careful to stay hidden from the guards, Flynn accompanied Rapunzel to a stage, where an entertainer was inviting people to come and dance in honour of their lost princess. Rapunzel was enjoying herself and Flynn offered to show her around the town. He took her to the dressmaker where she tried on a wonderful dress. They treated themselves to some delicious cakes. At the bookshop, Rapunzel admired the hundreds of books. The day went happily by and, when evening fell, Flynn led Rapunzel onto a boat.

"Where are we going?" she asked him.

"Out by the castle. We'll see the lanterns better from there. It's time for your dream to come true: soon we'll see the lanterns float up into the sky!"

Suddenly, the young girl seemed terrified. If her greatest dream came true, what would she dream about then?

But already, the King and the Queen were launching the first lantern from their balcony. As soon as Rapunzel saw it, she forgot her fears. It was so beautiful! Even more beautiful than she had imagined! Soon the sky was filled with hundreds of lanterns. Rapunzel stared into Flynn's eyes and smiled.

"I wish this moment would never end!" she thought. "I could stay here forever!"

Flynn handed her a lantern so they could launch it together into the sky. "You know what?" said Rapunzel. "I'm going to give you back your crown. I should have done it sooner but I was afraid that you might leave. Now I know I can trust you. Do you understand?"

"I understand perfectly," Flynn replied, and he placed the crown in the bottom of the boat. He no longer cared about getting rich. Now his only dream was to be with Rapunzel, and this amazing dream seemed to be about to come true.

A Fairy-Tale Marriage

Deep in the Louisiana bayou, there was a lot of excitement. Naveen and Tiana – two frogs who were madly in love – were about to be married, and all of their animal friends were there to help.

Mama Odie, a good and powerful 197-year-old wise woman, conducted the ceremony. Naveen and Tiana had gone to Mama Odie when they'd been desparate to be human again. Now they were in love, they didn't mind being frogs so much.

"And by the powers vested in me, frogs, I now pronounce you... frog and wife! Naveen, you may kiss your pretty little bride!" Mama Odie announced.

Naveen took Tiana in his arms and placed a tender kiss on her lips, which she returned without hesitation...

Then, a cloud of multicoloured sparks crackling with magic began to swirl around them – and they became human again!

The couple looked splendid – Prince Naveen in a suit, and Tiana in a long, green dress... they looked at each other with surprise and astonishment.

Mama Odie laughed, "I told you that the only way to overturn this evil spell was to kiss a princess!"

"But of course, Tiana!" Prince Naveen exclaimed. "By marrying me, you have become a princess!"

"And then we kissed! You just kissed yourself a princess!" exclaimed Tiana.

"And I'm about to do it again," laughed Naveen as their friends cheered.

Shortly afterwards, Naveen and Tiana married again, but this time at a Cathedral in New Orleans, in the presence of their families. It was a beautiful ceremony. When Tiana came out of the church and climbed into her carriage, she threw her wedding bouquet into the crowd, and it was her best friend Charlotte who caught it!

Charlotte laughed, knowing this was a good sign for her: it meant that the next wedding would be hers!

It goes without saying that Tiana and Naveen lived together happily ever after... and soon there was a new restaurant in town – Tiana's Palace. The happy couple had bought the old sugar mill and turned it into the best place to go for good food, lively music and fun with friends and family.

Tiana had dreamed of owning a restaurant her whole life – a dream she had shared with her father. Now Tiana had everything she had ever wished for.

Disney
**Sleeping
Beauty**

The Crown of Diamonds

It was Aurora's seventeenth birthday, and she had some surprises awaiting her.

Her mother, the Queen, came in to wish her happy birthday. She led Aurora to a huge portrait hall.

"Why, Mother! Is that you?" exclaimed Aurora, pointing to a portrait. The Queen was wearing a crown with a pink, heart-shaped diamond.

"Indeed, I was 17," said the Queen. "It's a tradition that on a princess' 17th birthday, this crown is to be passed down by her mother, and worn until the princess becomes queen. However, she must answer three riddles," her mother said with a smile.

The three fairies, Flora, Fauna and Merryweather, flew in. "Happy birthday, Princess!" said Merryweather. "We're here to give you your clues!"

Flora recited the first riddle: "To the eyes, it's a treat; to the nose, a delight. To the hand it can be quite a fright. Though few think to taste it, its sweetness still shows. To this first riddle, the answer's a..."

"Let's see," said Aurora. "'To the eye, it's a treat. To the nose, a delight.' So it's pretty and smells good. 'To the hand quite a fright.' Like a thorn – on a rose. That's it!" She hurried off to the garden, and picked the biggest rose.

"Very good!" exclaimed Fauna. "And now for the second one: Some plant it, some blow it away. Some do it several times a day. Some may blush getting this on their cheek. Can you guess?"

"It's a kiss, isn't it?" Aurora cried. She kissed each fairy, causing them to blush.

"Now it's my turn!" exclaimed Merryweather. "What only gets stronger the longer it lives? Some say it's blind, some say it's true, some simply say, 'I feel this for you.'" Aurora thought hard. Just then Prince Phillip walked by.

"Happy birthday, my love!" he called. Instantly, Aurora knew the answer. She hurried up to her mother's sewing room.

"I've solved the riddles!" Aurora announced. She handed her the pink rose and gave her a kiss on the cheek.

"Very good!" declared the Queen. "And the answer to the third riddle?"

"It's love," said Aurora.

The Queen proudly placed the crown on Aurora's head.

That afternoon, Aurora had her portrait painted, so it could be hung in the portrait hall alongside her mother's.

"Happy birthday, Aurora," her mother warmly told her. "May you have many more!"

Bambi
The Secret Adventure

Early one morning, Thumper hopped over to a thicket and woke Bambi up.

"Let's go. Where we're going is a secret," he said.

On the way, Bambi and Thumper spotted their skunk friend, Flower.

"We're going on a secret adventure," Bambi said. "Do you want to come?"

"Oh, gosh! I do," Flower said shyly.

Thumper then said proudly, "I want to show you what the beavers build on water!"

Bambi and Flower smiled. It sounded exciting. Above them, a red bird sat unnoticed. *They are heading out all by themselves,* the bird thought. *I'd better tell their mothers.*

Meanwhile, Bambi, Thumper and Flower reached a meadow.

"Shhh!" Thumper whispered. "We are close to where all the bunnies graze – including my mama."

But Thumper's sisters had seen everything. They wanted to know what their big brother was up to, so they followed him. So did Red, the bird.

Soon the three friends came to a stream. A beaver walked up to them. "My name is Slap," the beaver said. "Where are you going?"

"I wanted to show my friends what you build on the river," Thumper explained.

"We call it a dam," said Slap. Carefully the three friends stepped out onto the logs.

"Why do they call you Slap?" Flower asked their new friend. Slap slapped the logs with his flat tail. The dam shook so much that a log broke loose and started drifting downriver.

"Help, Thumper!" four little voices cried. It was Thumper's younger sisters! The log they were sitting on was floating away!

"Oh, no! My sisters!" Thumper cried. "We have to rescue them!"

All the beavers jumped into the water and quickly swam towards the log. High above, Red saw the whole thing and went to get help.

Thumper's sisters held on but they were getting close to a waterfall! The beavers eventually reached the log. They slapped their tails with all their might and got the log to the riverbank. Thumper pulled his sisters to safety and thanked the beavers.

After a while, it began to get dark. Just then, Bambi and Thumper's mothers arrived!

"Oh, I'm so glad you are safe!" cried Bambi's mother. "Luckily, Red was keeping an eye on you."

"I'm very happy to see you too mother," Bambi said, glad that the adventure was over.

Street Cats

"Oh, Mama!" said Marie dreamily. "Paris is so pretty in the morning! May we please go explore just a bit?" The kittens and their mother had spent the previous night in Mr O'Malley's swinging bachelor flat, and were now making their way through the streets of Paris back to Madame's house.

"All right, darlings," their mother replied. "But just for a few minutes. Madame must be missing us terribly. Be sure to stick together!"

They passed a doorway to a jazz hall, where the previous night's party appeared to be still in full swing. "Oh, yeah!" said Toulouse as he danced in the doorway to the swinging beat.

"Come on, Toulouse," said Berlioz crossly. "I'm hungry!"

A few steps down the block, a fishmonger was just setting out his wares in the window of his shop. The three kittens put their paws on the windowsill, licking their lips as they watched him lay out the gleaming fish. The fishmonger smiled at them through the window, then came out of his shop and tossed them each a sardine. "Here you are, my pretty cats!" he said to them.

Yum! Sardines! The three meowed back a thank you and gobbled up the tasty treat.

"The streets of Paris are the coolest place on Earth!" said Berlioz as they continued walking. "I don't want to go back to Madame's house!"

"Berlioz! You mustn't speak like that!" said Marie. "You know how much Madame needs us...." Suddenly, she broke off. Her brothers followed her gaze, which was directed at the window of a fancy pet shop. "Oh, my!" she cried out delightedly. "Look at those!" In the window of the shop were several jewelled cat collars, all in different shades of the finest leather. Marie thought they were simply beautiful – especially the pink one. "I must say, the streets of Paris are a wonderful place!" Marie said dreamily.

Just then, they heard a deep barking. A moment later, a huge dog came bounding around the corner. The kittens froze in fear for a moment. Then all three of them turned and scampered back down the street in the direction of their mother and Mr O'Malley, with the dog hot on their heels.

"Paris is a fine city," said Berlioz, panting, as he raced down an alleyway. Darting behind some dustbins, the kittens were able to lose the snarling dog.

"Yes," replied Marie. "But I'm not sure how I feel about the Parisians – particularly the canine kind!"

DUMBO
Dumbo's Parade Pals

When Dumbo's circus came to town, the animals and circus folk marched in a big parade. The crowd loved seeing all the circus animals marching down the street.

Well, it may have been fun for the crowd, but it was no fun for Dumbo. His feet hurt, and he was *hungry*.

Then Dumbo noticed a peanut on the ground. He picked up the peanut with his trunk and ate it. Then Dumbo saw another peanut, and another. Leaving the parade, Dumbo followed the trail of peanuts all the way to a playground.

"See, the peanuts worked!" exclaimed a little girl with pigtails. "Now we have our own elephant to play with."

The girl and her friends surrounded Dumbo, patting his head. They marvelled at his long trunk and big ears. "What a wonderful little elephant!" they cried.

"Let's have our own circus," said a boy.

"I'll be the ringmaster!" cried the little girl. She led Dumbo to the middle of the playground. "Ladies and gentlemen! Presenting our star attraction – The Little Elephant!"

Dumbo knew just what to do. He stood up on his two back legs. Then he juggled some balls with his trunk. The children cheered.

Suddenly, Timothy Q. Mouse appeared. "Here you are!" he said to Dumbo. "We have to get back to the circus camp and get ready for the show!"

Dumbo nodded, and waved goodbye to his new friends. The children watched him go, looking terribly disappointed.

"I wish I could go see him in the circus tonight," one of them said. "But I don't have enough money for a ticket."

"Me neither," said the other children.

Dumbo was sorry that the nice children he had met would not be able to go to the circus. That night, he felt very blue as he put on his stage makeup and warmed up his ears. Finally, he tucked Timothy into the brim of his hat, then climbed onto a tall platform.

"Ladies and gentlemen!" the ringmaster cried. "I give you *Dumbo, the Flying Elephant!*"

Dumbo leaped off the platform, and his giant ears unfurled. The crowd cheered as Dumbo flew around the tent.

Suddenly, Dumbo spotted his playground friends. They were sitting in the first row! He swept by them, patting each child on the head with his trunk. The girl with pigtails waved at Dumbo. "Your mouse friend gave us free tickets!" she cried.

Dumbo smiled and reached his trunk up to the brim of his hat, where Timothy was riding. He gave Timothy a pat on the head too. He was the luckiest elephant in the world to have such wonderful friends!

The Ghost-Light Fish

Nemo loved school. So did his friends, Tad, Pearl and Sheldon. Mr Ray made everything so much fun. He took his students all over the reef.

That day, Mr Ray was taking them exploring.

"Okay, explorers," Mr Ray said. "Let's see if each of you can find a shell."

Tad was the first to find something. "Hey, guys!" he cried. "Look at this!"

Everyone stared at the gleaming white shell Tad held in his fin.

"Cool!" said Sheldon.

"It's heart-shaped!" Nemo exclaimed.

Minutes passed when suddenly Nemo heard an odd noise. He looked up and saw his friends Tad, Pearl and Sheldon bolting out of the cave, screaming loudly.

"What's the matter?" Nemo asked.

"It's a g-g-ghost fish!" Sheldon replied fearfully.

"Yeah, right," Nemo replied. He noticed Tad's fin was empty. "Where's your shell?" he asked.

Tad looked down. "I must have dropped it in there. But I'm not going back for it!"

"Don't worry," said Nemo. "I'll find it." So Nemo swam bravely into the cave.

"See?" he said to himself. "Nothing to be afraid of."

Nemo froze. On the cave wall was a huge, fish-shaped shadow! He took a deep breath. "Uh, excuse me, Ghost Fish?" he asked.

"A ghost fish?!" a tiny voice said nervously.

Nemo followed the voice and to his surprise, the ghost fish was actually a tiny glow-in-the-dark fish!

"Don't be afraid," Nemo said. "My name's Nemo. What's yours?"

"I'm Eddy," replied the little fish. "You mean there's no ghost fish?"

Nemo explained the whole funny story.

"By the way," said Nemo. "How do you glow like that?"

Eddy shrugged. "I just do," he replied.

Nemo thought of someone who would know more about Eddy's glow – Mr Ray! So, Nemo invited Eddy to meet everyone.

Outside, Nemo rejoined his friends. "I didn't find your shell," Nemo said to Tad. "But I did find your ghost fish!"

Everyone wanted to know what made Eddy glow!

"Good question, Nemo," Mr Ray replied. "There are tiny glow-in-the-dark organisms inside these patches on either side of Eddy's jaw."

Everyone ooohed and aaahed.

Mr Ray smiled at Nemo. "I think you deserve an A in Exploring today, Nemo!"

MICKEY MOUSE
A Wonderful/Terrible Day

"What a wonderful day!" Mickey Mouse said to himself. He hummed as he strolled through the outdoor market. The air was crisp. The leaves were pretty shades of red, yellow and orange. And the perfect hunk of cheese was right in front of him.

"I'll take that cheese and a loaf of bread," he told the market seller.

"You're just in time," the seller replied. "I'm about to close up shop."

Meanwhile, Donald Duck was just leaving his house. "What a terrible day!" he said in a huff. He had overslept and woken up with a crick in his neck. He hurried to cross the street, but had to stop for a red light.

When the light turned green, he stepped into the street.

H-o-n-n-k-k! A big truck roared past, just missing Donald.

"Watch where you're going!" Donald shouted. He raced ahead to the market.

"I'll take a loaf of bread," he told the seller.

"Sorry," the seller replied. "I'm sold out."

"Sold out?" Donald's eyes bulged in his head. "Sold out?"

Down the block, Mickey Mouse was having a friendly chat with Goofy. "How have you been, Goofy?" he asked.

"Fine," Goofy said as he peeled a banana. He ate the whole thing in one bite and dropped the peel on the ground.

In the market, Donald sulked. He was hungry!

"This is so unfair!" he said. Slumping his shoulders, he started off towards the park at the end of the street. But a second later he slipped on a banana peel.

"*Ooof*!" Donald fell to the ground with a thud. Scowling, he got to his feet.

Not far away, Mickey was spreading out his picnic blanket in the park. All around him, children were laughing and playing.

"Hey, kids!" he called with a friendly wave. He took a big bite of his cheese sandwich and chewed happily. "What a wonderful day," he said again.

Donald kicked a pebble on the sidewalk while his tummy growled. And then, all of a sudden – *thunk*! – a ball hit him on the head.

"Watch it, kids!" Donald shouted. He rubbed his sore head. "What a terrible day."

Just then, Donald heard a familiar voice call out, "Hey, Donald! Come have a cheese sandwich with me!"

Donald saw Mickey waving to him from under a tree. Donald wanted to stay mad. But the truth is that no duck can resist a cheese sandwich. He smiled and ambled over. Maybe it wasn't such a bad day after all!

THE
LION KING

Timon and Pumbaa Tell It All

It was a very hot day on the savannah, Simba, Timon and Pumbaa were lying in the shade, barely moving. It was too hot for the three friends to do anything except talk. Pumbaa had just finished telling a story about the biggest insect he had ever eaten (to hear him tell it, it was the size of an ostrich) and a silence fell over the little group.

"I know," said Simba. "Hey, Timon, why don't you tell me the story of how you and Pumbaa met each other?"

Timon looked at Pumbaa. "Do you think he's ready for it?" he asked.

"Knock him dead," said Pumbaa.

"It all started in a little meerkat village far, far away," began Timon.

"No," interrupted Pumbaa. "You've got it all wrong. It all started near a little warthog watering hole far, far away."

"If I recall correctly, Simba asked *me* to tell the story," said Timon. "And this is the story as told from *my* point of view."

"All right," said Pumbaa sulkily.

"And in that little meerkat village there was one meerkat who didn't fit in with the rest. All the others were content to dig, dig, dig all day long," said Timon. "*I* was that isolated meerkat. How I hated to dig! I knew I needed to go elsewhere, to find a home of my own, a place where I fitted in. So I left. Along the way I ran into a wise old baboon who told me what I was seeking – *hakuna matata* – and pointed me in the direction of Pride Rock. So I boldly set off towards this rock of which he spoke. And on my way there, I . . ."

"Met me!" Pumbaa interrupted.

Timon gave him a dirty look and continued. "I heard a strange rustling in the bushes. I was scared. What could it be? A hyena? A lion? And then I found myself face to face with a big, ugly warthog!"

"Hey!" said Pumbaa, looking insulted.

"We soon realized we had a lot in common – our love for bugs, our search for a home to call our own. So we set out for Pride Rock together. A lot of bad things happened along the way – hyenas, stampedes, you name it. But before long we managed to find the perfect place to live. And then we met you, Simba!"

"That's a nice story," Simba said with a yawn. "Now I think I'm going to take a nap . . . ."

Pumbaa cleared his throat. "It all started near a little warthog watering hole far, far away," he began.

"You always have to get the last word, don't you?" said Timon.

"Not always," said Pumbaa. And then he continued with *his* side of the story.

Tangled

Tricked

Flynn Rider had realized that he was in love with Rapunzel. Now, nothing mattered to him any more except being with her. So he decided to put his life as a thief behind him. Farewell crown, farewell wealth, farewell gold coins! At last he had found his true treasure. From now on he would take care of his precious Rapunzel with all of his heart.

As they floated along in their boat, admiring the lanterns, Flynn was getting up the courage to finally kiss Rapunzel, when he suddenly spied his old partners in crime, the Stabbington brothers, on the shore. The villains wanted to get hold of the crown he had refused to share with them, and Flynn knew they would do anything to get their revenge. He needed to give them back the crown straight away. Flynn turned away from Rapunzel.

"What's the matter?" she said in surprise, disappointed to have not had her first kiss.

"Oh, nothing important. Just a small matter I have to attend to. I'll be back!" And Flynn headed to the shore before running off, carrying with him the satchel with the crown. Pascal, Rapunzel's pet chameleon, was worried. What if Flynn didn't come back, as Mother Gothel had predicted?

"He will come back," Rapunzel said.

But Rapunzel didn't know that the Stabbington brothers were in fact following Mother Gothel's orders! When Flynn showed them the gold crown and explained that he was giving them his share, they refused to take it!

"We know that you have found treasure a thousand times more valuable than this. This Rapunzel has magic hair that cures illnesses. It's her we want!" The Stabbingtons knocked Flynn out, tied him in a boat and set him sailing. Then they rushed to capture Rapunzel!

Rapunzel dodged the brothers and ran into the forest. She didn't get far before her hair got tangled on a tree branch! As she tried to free herself, she heard a scuffle and then Mother Gothel's voice. "Rapunzel!"

"Mother?" Rapunzel ran back and found Mother Gothel standing over the brothers. They lay unconscious at her feet. Rapunzel believed Mother Gothel was her real mother, but in fact the wicked woman only wanted Rapunzel' magical hair to keep her young.

"You were right, Mother," said Rapunzel.

"I know, darling, I know," said Mother Gothel as she led Rapunzel back towards the tower where she'd been hidden her whole life.

TinkerBell
AND THE GREAT FAIRY RESCUE

A Happy Ending

Lizzy, a little girl, loved fairies. And one day she came across a curious little fairy called Tinker Bell!

Tink had been on the mainland with the other fairies from Pixie Hollow, helping to bring summer. But Tink was never completely happy unless she was tinkering – and she couldn't find anything to fix!

Suddenly the fairies had heard a loud noise. It was a car! Tink, as curious as ever, had followed it. Lizzy and her father were inside. Vidia had tried to get Tinker Bell to go back to fairy camp, but Tink hadn't listened. Vidia had tried to teach Tink a lesson, but had accidentally trapped her inside Lizzy's little fairy house!

Luckily, Tinker Bell and Lizzy became friends and Tink realized that the little girl was sad because her father was always so busy. He was a scientist called Dr Griffiths and he didn't believe in fairies. He wanted Lizzy to concentrate on things that were real. He even gave Lizzy a field journal to record her scientific research – but Tinker Bell had helped Lizzy make a fairy field journal instead!

In the end, Tink finally revealed herself to Dr Griffiths – to prove that Lizzy had been right all along. Dr Griffiths tried to catch Tink, but she had had some unlikely help from Vidia.

Vidia was usually a bit of a loner, but she had realized the importance of friendship.

But Dr Griffiths had caught Vidia instead! He raced off to the museum, but Lizzy and the fairies managed to catch up with him.

Finally, Dr Griffiths realized that Lizzy was right – he just had to believe.

Vidia was reunited with her fairy friends and then everyone – including Dr Griffiths – received a generous sprinkling of pixie dust to fly back home.

The next day, everyone enjoyed a picnic.

"Isn't this pleasant, father?" asked Lizzy.

"I can't imagine anything better," he answered. "Although flying over London Bridge is a close second."

Tink and Vidia sat together, sipping their tea. Not only did they know each other better now – but they had actually become good friends!

A little while later, everyone settled in to hear Dr Griffiths read from Lizzy's fairy field journal.

Just then, Terence returned from his pixie dust deliveries. "Well," he said to Tinker Bell, "you found something to fix after all."

Tink looked at Lizzy snuggled close to her father. "I guess I did," she replied with a smile.

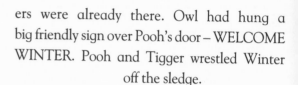

Pooh Welcomes Winter

Pooh had heard that Winter was coming soon, and he was very excited about having a visitor. Pooh and Piglet decided to throw a party to welcome Winter to Hundred-Acre Wood. The two friends set off to tell everyone.

Outside, it was snowing. They met Tigger along the way, and they walked to Kanga and Roo's house together. They all decided to go by sledge to the party. Owl landed on a branch overhead.

"Winter has arrived!" he declared. "I heard Christopher Robin say so."

Pooh told Owl about the party, then they all jumped on the sledge and slid down the hill towards Christopher Robin's house.

"There's Winter!" Tigger cried. "Tiggers always know Winter when they see him. That big white face – that carroty nose. Who else could he be?" said Tigger.

"Well," said Pooh, "he looks shy. We should be extra friendly." He walked right up to Winter. "How do you do? We are giving a party in your honour." Winter did not say anything.

"Oh d-d-dear," said Piglet. "He's frozen!"

"Quick!" cried Tigger. "We'd better get him to the party and warm him up." They hoisted Winter onto the sledge. When they slid up to Pooh's house, the oth-ers were already there. Owl had hung a big friendly sign over Pooh's door – WELCOME WINTER. Pooh and Tigger wrestled Winter off the sledge.

"Give him the comfy chair by the fire!" said Rabbit. Still, Winter did not say a word. His carrot nose drooped.

Just then, Christopher Robin tramped up to the door in his big boots. "Has anyone seen my snowman?" he asked.

"No," said Pooh glumly, "but we brought Winter here for a special party. He doesn't seem to like it."

"Silly old bear!" Christopher Robin laughed. And he explained to Pooh that Winter was not a person, it was a season. A time of year for cold snow, mistletoe, warm fires and good friends.

Pooh scratched his nose thoughtfully. "Yes, I see now," he said. "Of course, I am a bear of very little brain."

"You're the best bear in all the world," said Christopher Robin. "Come on, we'd better get the snowman back outside before he melts completely."

They undrooped the snowman's nose and stuck his hands back in. They decided to have the party anyway, to celebrate Winter. So everyone sang songs and danced around the snowman until they couldn't dance any more.

Disney
Lilo & Stitch

Travelling at the Speed of Stitch

Stitch was bored. Everyone seemed to have somewhere to go and something to do during the day but him. Lilo went to school. Nani went to work. And Jumba and Pleakley headed off to serve beach-goers at their new snack stand, the Galactic Burger.

So Stitch decided he needed a job. He and Lilo looked through the news-paper, searching for a job just right for a small, blue alien with a huge love of adventure. "Listen," said Lilo, pointing to an advert. "'Wanted: tour guide. Must have an outgoing personality and lots of energy.' That's you!"

So, the next morning, Stitch arrived at the tour agency, wearing his best Hawaiian shirt and a big smile. The woman doing the inter-view thought he was pretty scary-looking, but a group of tourists was arriving from the airport any minute and no one else had turned up to apply for the job. "You're hired!" she said.

"Aloha!" Stitch exclaimed when the holidaymakers arrived. He stacked leis on them up to their eyeballs and shook their hands enthusiastically. "Welcome onto the Hawaiian galaxy!" He showed them to a tour bus and pressed down on the accelerator as far as it would go. "Palm trees!" he yelled as the scenery passed by in a blur. "Pineapples!" he shouted as they drove through a fruit stand. Finally, the bus screeched to a stop at the beach.

"Surfing!" Stitch announced, hurling his group onto surfboards and pushing them out to sea. After being battered by the waves, the tourists were eventually tossed onto the beach.

Stitch herded them over to a barbecue. "Luau!" he explained.

"Now, that's more like it!" an elderly woman said, collapsing onto a bench.

"I'm starving," admit-ted a man with a lobster still hanging on to his Bermuda shorts.

But, instead of food, Stitch returned with several flaming torches. Nani's friend, David, had taught Stitch how to juggle fire. The little alien was sure the tourists would want to learn too. Thank goodness Stitch just happened to bring along a fire extinguisher!

The last stop on Stitch's tour was the 24-hour Hula Marathon. He gave his guests grass skirts and insisted they dance until they dropped as he played the ukulele.

When the holidaymakers returned to the tour agency that night, they emerged from the bus exhausted, battered, bruised and confused. The first thing they saw was the sign on the front of the tour agency: HAWAII: THE MOST RELAXING PLACE ON EARTH. Unless, of course, your tour guide happens to be from the planet Turo!

We're Going on a Picnic

"Cap'n?" Mr Smee knocked softly on Captain Hook's door. There was no answer. The chubby first mate pushed his way inside, carrying a breakfast tray. "I've got breakfast, Cap'n."

"I'm not hungry!" Captain Hook replied. "Go away!"

"But, Cap'n. You have to eat." Smee was getting worried. The Captain hadn't eaten in days. In fact, he hadn't even got out of bed! "I know you feel bad about Pe–" Smee stopped himself from saying the dreaded name just in time, "–that flying boy. And the croc – I mean – that ticking reptile, too." Captain Hook was really angry about being beaten by Peter again. Even worse, Peter had set the crocodile right back on Captain Hook's trail. "But we haven't seen hide nor scale of either of them for a week. I think the coast is clear."

There was no reply from Captain Hook.

Smee thought for a minute. "I know how to cheer you up!" he cried. "We'll have a nice old-fashioned picnic! Won't that be lovely!"

Again, silence from Captain Hook.

"Ah-ah-ah! No arguments!" Smee left the breakfast tray and hurried down to the galley. A picnic on Mermaid Island was just what the doctor ordered!

Smee whistled merrily as he made herring-and-pickle sandwiches (Captain Hook's favourite) and packed them in a wicker basket. This was Hook's day! Smee carefully folded a gingham tablecloth and placed it in the basket, along with his tin whistle. He was going to make sure that Hook had a good time, whether he wanted to or not!

Once the picnic basket was packed, Smee called down to Hook, "It's time to go, Cap'n!"

After a while, Captain Hook finally appeared on deck, blinking in the sunlight. "Fine," he said grumpily. "But I know I'm not going to have fun!"

Smee let the rowing boat down into the water and Hook began to climb down the rope ladder. Once he was safely in the boat, Smee picked up the picnic basket.

TICK TOCK TICK TOCK TICK TOCK.

"Smee!" cried Hook. "Help me!"

Smee peeked over the side of the ship. The crocodile was about to take a bite out of the boat!

In a panic, he threw the only thing he had on hand – the picnic basket. It landed right in the crocodile's open mouth. The crocodile stared at Smee in surprise. Then, without a sound, it slipped back under the water.

"My picnic!" cried Smee. "My tin whistle!"

"Next time you have any smart ideas about cheering me up," said the Captain, glaring at his first mate, "keep them to yourself!"

THE
LION KING

Hot on the Trail

"Over here!" Simba said, sniffing the trail. "It's going this way!"

"Yup, this way," Nala said with a nod, sniffing a stick. "And not long ago."

"I saw that stick first," Simba said. Nala was a good tracker, but Simba had learned from an expert – his mum. She was one of the best hunters in the pride.

"Hmm," Nala said with a sniff. "So what are we following then, master tracker? Can you tell me that?"

Simba was silent. They had seen some footprints, but they weren't clear enough to read. They'd also seen some dark wiry hair on a log, but that could belong to lots of animals.

"Something that isn't very graceful," Simba said. They had seen lots of crushed grass and broken sticks.

"Mmm-hmm." Nala nodded impatiently.

"A rhino!" Simba said confidently.

"A rhino?" Nala rolled onto her back, laughing. "Simba, you crack me up!"

"What?" Simba couldn't hide the hurt in his voice. It *might* be a rhino!

"The footprints aren't big enough," Nala said. "It's Rafiki, the baboon."

Now, it was Simba's turn to laugh. "Rafiki likes the trees, he doesn't use trails like a hyena!" The giggle died in Simba's throat and he felt the fur on the back of his neck stand up.

Hyenas were clumsy and had dark wiry hair . . . .

Nala didn't say anything, but her fur was standing up a little too.

The two lions walked in silence. Ahead of them they heard noises – thrashing and grunting.

"Simba," Nala whispered, "maybe we should turn back."

"Just a little further," Simba whispered. They were almost there!

The young lions crept through the grass on their bellies as quietly as they could. The grunting and thrashing grew louder. They could see a dust cloud rising. Simba stifled a growl. Something about the smell and the sound was familiar, but Simba could not put his paw on it.

As they crept closer, two bodies came into view by the side of a termite mound. Simba pounced!

"Pumbaa! Timon!" he shouted, landing between his friends.

"Simba!" the warthog said, grinning. Termites dripped out of his muddy mouth. "Want some?"

Timon held a handful of wriggling insects towards Nala. "There are plenty to go around."

"Uh, no thanks," Nala said as she came out of the grass, giggling. She shot a look at Simba. "I think I'll wait for the master tracker to hunt me up some lunch!"

MULAN
Jin's Treasure

After Mulan had saved China from the Huns, she returned to her village. She helped out her family the way she always had, and in time, people forgot how brave Fa Zhou's daughter really was. Then one day, a group of frightened children came running towards her.

"Help! Help!" they shouted. "Our friend Jin is trapped in a cave!"

"Hurry – take me to him!" exclaimed Mulan. She called to her little dragon friend, "Mushu, you've got to come, too!"

The children led Mulan to the other side of the mountain. "A boulder has fallen, blocking the entrance to the cave," Wang, the blacksmith, explained. "But what are you doing here?" he asked Mulan. "This is no place for a girl! It will take muscles of steel to move this boulder."

"Yes!" agreed Chung, the carpenter. "If you want to do something useful, go back to the village and fetch us some water."

Mulan returned to the village, but not to fetch water. Instead, she found a shovel and ran back to the cave. "That boulder is too heavy to be moved," Mulan told the men. "Let's try another way."

At last, the large men shook their heads and reluctantly stepped aside. Mulan began to dig at the base of the boulder.

"If you can't move an obstacle," she said, "you can always try to go around it."

And slowly but surely, Mulan formed a tunnel beneath the rock. Once the tunnel was finished, Mulan and Mushu climbed under the boulder, into the cave.

"Boy, am I happy to see you!" the boy exclaimed.

"We're happy to see you, too!" said Mulan. "But what made you come in?"

"I saw something shiny and I wanted to know what it was," Jin explained.

Mulan looked around. "You mean that?"

There, in the back of the cave, lit up by Mushu's fire, were many shiny objects. The cave was full of hidden treasures!

"Think of what this fortune could mean for our village!" exclaimed Mulan.

"Come on!" Jin said. "Let's go and show the others."

They each grabbed an armful of treasure and headed for the tunnel.

As the pair emerged, followed by Mushu, the crowd let out a cheer. Then they noticed the gold and jewels.

"What have you found?" asked Wang.

"It's treasure," she told him. "Now I'll go back to the village and fetch some water," she continued, grinning. "I'm pretty thirsty after all that digging."

The Secret Gourmet

When the sun shines in New Orleans, the whole town sings and dances! And it's reason enough for Charlotte's father to want to share a meal with friends.

"Charlotte, darling," he said to his daughter one sunny evening, "what would you say to going to eat at Tiana's restaurant?"

"Fantastic!" says Charlotte happily. "I'll go and put on my pink silk dress!"

The young woman never missed a chance to go and visit Tiana. They were very fond of each other! And now that Tiana had married Prince Naveen and they had opened a restaurant together, it was even more fun to visit her!

"I hope Naveen's parents will be there!" Charlotte exclaimed shortly after getting into the car with her father. "I always enjoy chatting to a king and queen!"

As they drove down the road, no one noticed Stella, Charlotte's dog, fast asleep on the back seat.

Stella woke with a start when the car pulled up in front of the restaurant. Usually, Stella didn't like to leave the house. She was about to bark, but then she recognized the delicious smell of Tiana's beignets!

Stella suddenly didn't want to go back to the mansion after all. She snuck quietly into the restaurant kitchen at the back of the building.

Meanwhile, Charlotte and her father were joining Eudora, Tiana's mother, who was dining with Naveen's parents. "I will serve you the new House Gumbo!" Tiana suggested.

At the back of the room, Louis the alligator and his band were playing jazz music. The atmosphere was fantastic.

Charlotte clapped with joy. "We're going to have an amazing evening! All that's missing is Stella. What a shame she doesn't like going out."

Poor Charlotte! She had no idea what was happening in the kitchen...

Stella was so happy to be there and was simpering and begging so much that the chef gave her lots of beignets!

"We have a secret gourmet in the kitchen," he laughed. "Her appetite does me proud! Serve her as many beignets as she wants, she's my guest!"

Stella barked with happiness. A secret passenger in the car, and a secret gourmet in the kitchen – it was good to get out of the house after all ... but only if you're a secret guest!

Disney
THE LITTLE
MERMAID

Ariel to the Rescue

"Oh, Eric! This is wonderful!" Ariel said excitedly as she twirled around the ballroom with her prince. "I can dance with you and see the ocean!"

"Do you miss your sea friends?" he asked.

"Sometimes," Ariel replied. "But I love being with you."

A few weeks later, Eric took Ariel to the lagoon. Ariel noticed that it now had a big wall around it. The wall would keep out dangerous sea creatures, but it also had a gate for Ariel's friends to enter the lagoon. In fact, Flounder, Scuttle and Sebastian were there to greet her.

Ariel was so excited that she waded into the water to greet her friends. Then she saw something in the lagoon.

"Look!" she exclaimed. As they watched, a small dolphin leapt out of the water!

"He's just a baby. I wonder where his mother is," Flounder said. He swam across the lagoon, but the baby dolphin raced away.

"Poor little guy," Flounder said. "He seems scared of me."

But the princess wouldn't give up. Soon she had coaxed the baby to swim over to her.

"I wish there was something we could do," Ariel said.

"I bet his mother is on the other side of that wall." Flounder said. "We'll find her!"

But a few days later, Sebastian and Flounder still hadn't found her. Tomorrow, Ariel would ask more of her friends from under the sea to help with the search.

Later that night, Ariel awoke to the sound of thunder. When she and Eric arrived at the lagoon, Flounder was trying to calm the scared baby dolphin.

Ariel climbed onto the lagoon wall and called to the sea creatures. "Help me, please! I am Ariel, princess of the seas. I need my father, King Triton."

Below the surface, sea creatures raced to find King Triton. Suddenly there was a flash of light! King Triton had arrived.

The storm quieted down. The baby dolphin's mother was at the lagoon gate, frantically trying to get in.

"Oh, dear!" Ariel exclaimed. "The gate won't open! She can't get in!"

Eric looked at King Triton. He raised his trident and blasted down the wall. The dolphins swam to each other, then the baby went to Triton to thank him. That night, the moon rose. But there was no royal ball at the palace. Instead, Eric and Ariel returned to the lagoon. They were so happy to have somewhere Ariel could see her friends.

Paradise Falls

Carl had wanted to be an explorer ever since he was a child. So had his friend and wife, Ellie. He had promised Ellie that he'd take her to see Paradise Falls in South America one day.

But they were never able to save enough money to go. When they grew older, Ellie sadly passed away, and Carl was told he had to move out of his house.

But Carl decided he had to keep his promise to Ellie. He tied thousands of balloons to their little house and slowly it lifted into the sky.

Carl steered the flying house using ropes attached to the weather vane. He checked his compass and map, and set a course to Paradise Falls in South America.

"We're on our way, Ellie," he said happily.

Suddenly, there was a knock at the door. Carl was shocked. He was thousands of feet up in the air! Who could be at his door?

It was Russell! A Junior Wilderness Explorer who had knocked on his door a few days before. Carl had told him to find a Snipe – a bird that didn't really exist – just to get rid of him. Russell had been under Carl's porch, looking for the snipe, when the house lifted off.

"Please let me in!" Russell begged.

What choice did Carl have? He let Russell come inside.

Carl hated to stop, but he knew he had to land and send Russell home. He started to cut some of the balloons free.

Meanwhile, Russell was watching the clouds out of the window. "There's a big storm coming," he said. But Carl didn't hear him.

A flash of lightning lit up the room. Carl desperately tried to steer the house away from the storm, but it was too late. The little house tossed in the wind. Carl ran this way and that, trying to save Ellie's belongings. Finally, exhausted, he fell asleep.

When Carl woke up, the storm was over. "I steered us down," Russell told him proudly. "We're in South America."

As Carl and Russell stepped out onto the porch, the house crash-landed and sent them both flying. "My house!" Carl cried as it started to drift away from them. Grabbing hold of the garden hose, he and Russell managed to pull the house back down. Just then, the fog cleared. There, a short distance ahead, was Paradise Falls! It looked just like Ellie's picture!

"We made it!" Carl shouted. "We could float right over there!"

Carl was amazed. He had finally made the trip he and Ellie had always dreamt about.

Disney
LiLo & STiTcH
Knock, Knock! Who's There?

Standing in her brand-new bedroom, Lilo grinned. The walls were almost complete. In her mind, Lilo could see it all finished. Her bed would be against one wall, and Stitch's little bed would sit right beside hers. Lilo hugged herself with excitement. She wasn't quite sure that the wardrobe was in exactly the right place, but she loved everything else, so she didn't mind.

"Lilo, I want you to stay out of the workers' way," Nani said. "And keep an eye on Stitch! He keeps licking our nice new windows!"

Nani was worried. Cobra Bubbles was coming today to see how they were doing.

"We'll stay out of trouble," Lilo smiled angelically. "Right, Stitch? Stitch?" Lilo looked around.

Stitch wasn't exactly staying out of trouble. He had a tool belt around his waist, and his mouth was full of nails. With amazing force, Stitch spat the nails into the floor, accidentally fastening the end of his own belt to the ground.

"That'll keep you out of trouble." Lilo shrugged. Just then there was a knock at the door. "I'll get it!" Lilo called. She opened the new door. Cobra Bubbles filled the door frame.

"Hello," he said, without removing his sunglasses.

"Hey, come on in and see our new digs!"

Lilo cried, happy to see her friend.

Cobra Bubbles stepped over a power cord and walked around a pile of flooring. "You don't actually live here yet, do you?" he asked slowly.

"Not yet," Lilo chirped. "It's supposed to be finished next month."

"And where is . . . Stitch?" Cobra Bubbles peered around Lilo's room.

"Lilo?" Nani asked with a fake smile.

Lilo frowned. Stitch was no longer nailed to the floor.

Suddenly, they heard a knock. Lilo and Nani looked at each other. It wasn't coming from the front door – in fact, it sounded as if it was coming from Lilo's room!

"Who is it?" Lilo asked quietly.

With a monumental crash, Stitch burst through one of the new walls in Lilo's bedroom. "Here he is!" Lilo shouted.

"I see." Cobra Bubbles tried to keep frowning, but couldn't.

"Yes," said Nani nervously. "Stitch sure is, uh, helping out with the construction. Why, here he's decided on a new spot for Lilo's closet. We didn't really want it there, anyway." Nani gave Cobra Bubbles a weak smile, then turned to look at Stitch's handiwork.

"Actually," Nani said with a real smile, "this is a much better spot for the closet. Thanks, Stitch!"

Bambi

First Frost

Slowly, Bambi opened his eyes. Curled next to his mother, he was toasty warm in the thicket. Bambi blinked sleepily, peering past the brambles. Something was different. The forest did not look the same. The air was crisp and cold, and everything was frosted and sparkling.

"Jack Frost has been here," Bambi's mother explained. "He's painted the whole forest with ice crystals."

Bambi was about to ask his mother who Jack Frost was and how he painted with ice, when he heard another voice, an impatient one.

"Get up! Get up! Come look at the frost!" It was Thumper. He tapped his foot impatiently. "We haven't got all day!"

Bambi stood and looked at his mother. When she nodded approvingly, he scampered out of the thicket. Bambi looked closely at the colourful leaves on the ground. Each one was covered in an icy white pattern. He touched his nose to a big orange oak leaf. "Ooh, it's cold!" he cried.

"Of course it is!" Thumper laughed.

"I think it's beautiful," said Faline, as she stepped into the clearing.

"Me, too," Bambi agreed.

"Well, come look at this!" Thumper hopped away and the two young deer followed, admiring the way the sun sparkled on the frost-covered trees and grass.

Thumper disappeared under a bush; then Bambi heard a new noise. *Creak, crack.*

Faline pushed through the bushes with Bambi right behind her. There was Thumper, cracking the thin ice on a puddle with his feet.

Bambi had never seen ice before. He pushed on the icy thin puddle covering with his hoof. It seemed to bend. Then it shattered!

Soon the three friends were stomping on the ice-covered puddles. When all the ice was broken, Faline had an idea. "Let's go to the meadow!"

Bambi thought that was a great idea. The grass would be sparkling! They set out at a run, bounding and racing each other through the forest. But when they got to the meadow's edge, they all stopped.

They looked, sniffed and listened quietly. They did not sense danger – no, the trouble was that in the meadow, nothing was different. There was no frost.

"What happened?" Bambi asked.

"Frost never lasts long," Thumper explained. "It melts as soon as the sun hits it. But don't worry. Winter is coming, and soon we'll have something even better than frost. We'll have snow!"

Disney
MICKEY MOUSE
Scrooge's Nature

"Would you look at that!" Huey pointed to a picture of a Junior Woodchuck relaxing in a hammock, while another camper fished in a nearby lake.

"And that!" Dewey's eyes widened. He pointed at a picture of a star-filled sky in the same brochure.

"Camping at Faraway Lake sure looks fun," Louie agreed. "Do you think Unca Scrooge would . . . ?"

"You never know. He might pay for us to go," Huey said. The three boys looked at one another.

"Nah!" they said in unison. Uncle Scrooge may have been the richest duck in the world, but he did not part with his money easily.

"Let's show him, anyway," Huey said. "It's worth a shot."

The other boys followed Huey into their uncle's study.

Dewey nudged Huey forward. "Look at this, Unca Scrooge." Huey thrust the brochure into his uncle's lap.

"Humph." Uncle Scrooge scowled at the glossy photos. "What have we got here, lads?"

"It's a camp, Unca Scrooge. It's educational," Huey stammered.

"Looks like a waste of my hard-earned money," the old duck said.

"But . . . but we could camp out under the stars," Dewey said.

"And cook over a fire," Louie put in.

"And see nature," Huey added.

Uncle Scrooge's eyes narrowed. He looked from the brochure to his nephews' hopeful faces and back to the brochure. So, they wanted to learn about nature, did they?

"Here you are, boys," said Uncle Scrooge a short time later. He smiled from the safety of the screened-in back porch. "You have tents . . ." He indicated the three small leaky tents set up in the garden. "You can see the stars . . ." In fact, only one or two stars were visible through the branches of the tree the tents were under. "And you're cooking over a fire," Scrooge finished, pointing at the tiny, smoky little flame.

Huey slapped at a mosquito on his arm. Dewey shook his head to chase away a cloud of gnats. Louie yelped as he was dive-bombed by a bat. Who knew the garden had so much nature in it!

"This is much better than that Junior Woodchuck nonsense, isn't it, boys?" Uncle Scrooge asked, with the smile of a duck who has saved himself a penny.

"Yes, Unca Scrooge," Huey, Dewey, and Louie said. Then they turned back to the fire.

"I think . . ." said Huey.

". . . next time," continued Dewey.

". . . we ask Unca Donald!" finished Louie.

A Helping Paw

The dairy barn was warm and cosy, and 99 exhausted, hungry pups were taking turns to drink warm milk from the motherly cows.

"We'd nearly given up hope that you would get here," the kindly collie said to Pongo and Perdita, who had just arrived with the puppies.

"We're so very grateful to you for your hospitality," Perdita murmured wearily.

"Just look at the little dears," said one of the cows. "I've never seen so many puppies in one place before!"

Pongo, Perdita and the puppies had just come in from a long and weary march in the cold. It was very late, and the pups waiting for a drink of milk could barely keep their eyes open. The puppies had recently managed to escape from the dreadful old house owned by Cruella De Vil. They had been held prisoner there, guarded by two villains named Horace and Jasper. Cruella was planning to make a fur coat out of their lovely spotted fur. Luckily Pongo and Perdita had rescued them all just in the nick of time.

The pups had their dinners and gathered around the collie, thanking him for his hospitality.

"Not at all, not at all," the collie replied. "Do you have warm milk for supper every night out here in the country?" asked Rolly.

The collie chuckled. "No, but we do eat very simple country fare. I'm sure it's plainer than the food you eat in the city, but we eat big meals because of all the chores we do."

"And is it always this cold in the country?" asked Patch.

"Well, now," replied the collie. "I suppose most of you come from the city. No, it isn't always this cold, but there are plenty of differences between living in the country and living in the city. Take leashes, for instance. We don't keep our pets on leashes here, the way you do in the city, since our pets have a lot of wide-open space to roam around in. There aren't as many dogs nearby, but there are certainly other sorts of animals that one doesn't see in the city. Take cows, for instance. And then there are sheep and horses and geese, and . . . ."

Suddenly, the collie stopped talking. A tiny snore escaped one of the pups he had just been talking to. He looked around and realized that every one of the pups, as well as Pongo and Perdita, had fallen into a deep sleep.

"Poor little things," he said quietly, as he trotted outside to stand guard. "They've been through so much. I do hope they get home safely soon."

The Firebird

Once there lived the most magical bird – the Firebird! The Firebird sprinkled music from her feathers, filling the land with song and dance. But there was one person who didn't like music – the mean ogre, Katschai. He trapped the Firebird and locked her in a birdcage in his secret palace. But there was a single magical feather that a gust of wind carried far away...

Rocket saw the Firebird's feather, and caught it in his Mini Grab Nabber. He knew that his friend was in trouble and needed help.

"To save the Firebird, we'll need to get past Katschai," June said. "And he'll use plenty of magic spells to try and stop us."

"Stupendous!" exclaimed June. "We've got the magical feather which means we have the musical power to get past Katschai!"

Thanks to the Look-and-Listen Scope, the team made their way to the Instrument Forest. When they arrived, not a single instrument was playing its music! Rocket waved the Firebird's magical feather over the forest. When Katschai heard the music, he became angry. He created spooky animals to scare away the Little Einsteins.

"I've got a plan," Quincy said. "Leo, play the flute to make the bats disappear. I'll play the violin to get rid of the mosquitoes. June, play the xylophone to make the spiders leave. Annie, make the bear go away with a trumpet." It worked! The spooky animals disappeared.

Rocket continued his search for Katschai's secret palace. They saw a sad-looking seal who couldn't sing. Rocket had an idea. He sprinkled the little seal with the magical feather's musical power and helped him sing again.

But Katschai created a snow storm to stop Rocket from going any further.

"Rocket is stuck under that huge pile of snow – he can't fly!" cried Quincy.

"Don't worry, Rocket," Annie said. "I know a special song that can make the sun come out and melt the snow." And it did.

The team finally reached the secret palace. Rocket found the special rainbow key and unlocked the birdcage. The Firebird was free! She soared through the sky, sprinkling her musical power everywhere.

"The Firebird's even sprinkling her musical power on Katschai." Leo giggled.

Quincy laughed. "It's time for Katschai to finally face the music – he can't escape it now!"

"It's true," June said. "Never underestimate the power of music."

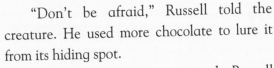

Strange Animals

Carl Fredricksen and a Junior Wilderness Explorer named Russell had just arrived in South America! Carl had dreamed of seeing Paradise Falls his whole life. He had promised his wife, Ellie, that he'd take her there one day. Sadly, Ellie had died before they could take the trip.

When Carl was told he had to move out of their home, he decided it was time to keep his promise to Ellie. He tied thousands of balloons to their house, and it lifted into the air!

But Carl hadn't planned on taking a companion along – Russell had been on Carl's porch when the house took off. They hit a storm and crash landed near Paradise Falls.

There was just one problem: the crash had sent them flying, and they couldn't get back into the house! It was hovering too high off the ground.

Russell had an idea: they could walk the house to the falls. They made harnesses out of the garden hose so they could pull the house.

"This is fun already, isn't it?" Russell said as they trudged along. "Don't you worry. I'm gonna assist you every step of the way."

After a while, they stopped to take a break. As Russell nibbled a chocolate bar, a beak poked out of the bushes and began to nibble it too!

"Don't be afraid," Russell told the creature. He used more chocolate to lure it from its hiding spot.

When the creature emerged, Russell gasped. It was the biggest bird he had ever seen! The bird liked chocolate. It liked Russell, too. Russell named the bird Kevin. He couldn't wait to show his new friend to Carl! But Carl yelled with fright when he saw the bird.

"Can we keep him?" Russell asked.

"No," said Carl.

Carl and Russell set off again. But Russell didn't want to leave Kevin behind, so he dropped a trail of chocolate for the bird to follow.

They hadn't gone far when they met a dog. "Hi there," said the dog. "My name is Dug." A talking dog? Carl and Russell were stunned! "My master made me this collar so that I may talk," Dug explained. "My pack sent me on a special mission. Have you seen a bird? I want to find one. I have been on the scent."

Suddenly, Kevin flew out of the bushes and tackled Dug. "Hey, that is the bird! May I take your bird back to camp as my prisoner?" Dug asked Carl.

"Yes! Yes! Take it!" Carl told him. He didn't want to deal with all these strange animals – he just wanted to reach Paradise Falls. But would he ever get there?

Disney
Winnie the Pooh

Eeyore's New Old House

One blustery, cold November day in the Hundred-Acre Wood, the blustery, cold November wind blew so strongly that it knocked Eeyore's house right over!

So Eeyore went to Pooh's house. "Well, Pooh," Eeyore said, "it seems that November just doesn't like me. Or my house. So I'm afraid I will have to stay here with you. If you don't mind, that is."

Pooh assured Eeyore that he didn't mind and offered him some honey.

"I'd prefer thistles, if you have any, which you probably don't," Eeyore said. "Oh, well. Perhaps Rabbit has some."

Well, Rabbit did have some thistles, so Eeyore settled down to stay with Rabbit. But Rabbit's house was so full of vegetables and gardening tools – rakes and shovels and baskets and twine – that there was scarcely room in the burrow for Eeyore. "I suppose Piglet might have more room, though I doubt it," said Eeyore.

Piglet told Eeyore he was welcome to stay with him, and even made Eeyore a little bed next to the pantry, which was full of haycorns. But Eeyore was allergic to haycorns, and soon his sneezing almost knocked Piglet's own house down.

"One house knocked down today is more than – *ah-choo*! – plenty," said Eeyore. "I'll just have to try Kanga and Roo."

Kanga and Roo were happy to put Eeyore up in their house. Roo was so excited to have a guest that he couldn't stop bouncing. Soon Eeyore was feeling dizzy just from watching him. But, just as Eeyore was about to try Owl's house, Piglet, Rabbit and Pooh arrived.

"Eeyore, we've found you the perfect house to live in!" Piglet cried.

"I doubt that," Eeyore said as they led him through the Wood. "The perfect house would have thistles, and enough room, and no haycorns, and, above all, no bouncing. But where am I going to find a house like that?"

Soon, they arrived at a snug little house made of sticks, with a pile of thistles in it. "Here it is, Eeyore," said Piglet.

"That's *my* house," said Eeyore, hardly able to believe his eyes. "But my house got knocked down."

"Piglet and I put it back together again," Pooh said, "and Rabbit donated his thistles, so now you have a house with thistles, and enough room, and no haycorns, and, above all, no bouncing."

Eeyore looked at his house, and then at his friends. "It looks like November doesn't dislike me so much after all," he said. "Maybe, that is."

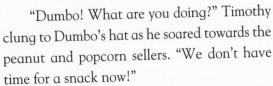

DUMBO

Dumbo's Daring Rescue

Dumbo stood on his platform high above the floor of the circus Big Top. Below him, the clowns looked the same size as peanuts. He could hear them calling for him to jump.

"All right, kid. You're on," Timothy said from the brim of Dumbo's hat.

Dumbo was ready. He knew what he had to do because he did the same thing every night. When the firefighter clowns called, Dumbo would leap from the platform and plummet towards the ground. Then, at the last possible moment, Dumbo would spread his tremendous ears and fly. The audience would cheer. And the show would be over.

"Hey, kid, that's your cue!" Timothy squeaked in Dumbo's ear.

Taking a step forward, Dumbo began to fall. He sped faster and faster towards the floor of the tent. The audience swam into view. They were screaming and laughing. Then, all of a sudden, Dumbo saw something else.

There, in the first row, was a little girl sitting all by herself. She was crying and holding on to a stick of candyfloss.

In an instant, the little elephant forgot all about the act. Spreading his ears, he swooped away from the shouting clowns. He scanned the seats intently. Why was the girl all alone? Where were her parents?

"Dumbo! What are you doing?" Timothy clung to Dumbo's hat as he soared towards the peanut and popcorn sellers. "We don't have time for a snack now!"

Dumbo ignored his friend. The little girl needed help!

At last, Dumbo saw what he was looking for. There, next to the candyfloss stand, were two very worried-looking parents.

"Clara, where are you?" the father called. His voice was lost in the hollering crowd. His daughter would never hear him calling to her!

Dumbo circled the tent again, turning back towards the bench where the little girl sat sobbing. How could he tell her that her parents were looking for her? He had to bring them together. Swooping low, Dumbo stretched out his trunk and scooped up the little girl.

"Dumbo, what are you doing!" Timothy cried again.

Dumbo sailed back and placed the girl gently beside her parents.

Immediately, the little girl's tears were dried. She was safe in her parents' arms!

The crowd went wild as Dumbo soared high over the arena. Even the clowns were smiling.

"Nice work, kid," Timothy said. "Good show."

Disney · PIXAR
FINDING
NEMO

Who's in Charge?

"Now, Dory," said Marlin, "you have to promise you'll keep a close eye on Nemo while I'm gone. Can you do that?"

"I can do that!" Dory said confidently.

But Marlin was a little worried. Everyone knew that Dory forgot things.

"Now remember," Marlin instructed. "Nemo needs to do his –"

"Science homework, practise playing the conch shell and clean the anemone," interrupted Nemo. "I got it, Dad."

Finally, Marlin waved goodbye and swam off to do his errands. As soon as he was gone, Dory began swimming in circles around the anemone. "Nemo, betcha can't catch me!"

Nemo chased Dory around the anemone a few times. It was fun, and Nemo wished they could play all afternoon. But he knew they couldn't.

"Dory, come on," Nemo called to her. "That was fun, but now I have to do my science homework."

Nemo explained his assignment to Dory: he had to find a sand dollar to bring into class the next day. So Nemo and Dory swam around the reef. Before long, Nemo spotted one.

"That's great!" replied Dory. "Now we can play!"

"No, Dory," he said. "Now I need to practise playing my conch shell."

They swam back to the anemone, where Nemo put his sand dollar away and got out his conch shell. Dory kept time while he played the songs that he needed to memorize for band practice.

"Thanks, Dory!" he said at last. "We're done."

"Yippee!" Dory cried, swimming around Nemo. "Now it's playtime!"

But Nemo remembered their work wasn't done yet. "Not quite, Dory," he said. "I have to clean the anemone before I can play."

"Clean?" Dory said with a frustrated sigh.

Nemo shrugged. "Dad said I should do it before he got home," he replied.

Together, Dory and Nemo cleaned up the zooplankton crumbs. When they were finished, the place was spotless.

"Thanks for helping me, Dory," said Nemo. "That went fast with the two of us working together."

"You're welcome," Dory replied. "So, what do you want to do now?"

Nemo laughed. "What do I want to do now?" he echoed. "I want to play!"

"Play, huh?" Dory said, weighing the idea. "Now, that's a crazy idea. I like it!"

One Part Hakuna, One Part Matata

"Why are you so sad?" Pumbaa asked Nala.

"I'm not sad," Nala said. "I'm just a little more on the serious side than the two of you."

"I think you could use a little *hakuna matata*," Pumbaa said.

"A whona mawhatta?" Nala asked.

"You really think she can handle it?" Timon whispered to Pumbaa out of the side of his mouth.

"Of course I can handle it!" Nala said, raising her voice. "I just need to know what it is first."

"Ahhhh, *hakuna matata*," Pumbaa said dreamily. "It's the problem-free way of dealing with all of life's inconveniences."

"It means, 'No worries'," Timon explained.

"Oh, I get it," Nala said. "Instead of dealing with your problems, you pretend they don't exist."

"*Hakuna matata* helps you relax," Pumbaa offered.

"It sounds like your *hakuna matata* is just another way of saying 'uninspired and lazy'," Nala continued.

"I think she might have just insulted us," Timon whispered to Pumbaa.

"There you are." Simba came walking towards them. "What are the three of you up to?"

"I was just learning about a strange little notion called *hakuna matata*," Nala explained.

"Isn't it great!" Simba said with a grin.

"Well, sure," Nala said. "If you don't ever want to get anything done."

Simba frowned. "It's not like that. *Hakuna matata* helps you get through things."

"Sure," Nala continued. "*Hakuna matata* – I don't have to worry. I don't have to try."

"I guess you could look at it that way," Simba said. "But, for me, it means, 'Don't worry about it right now. It's okay.' It gives me the strength to get through the bad times."

"Wow, I hadn't thought about it like that," Nala said.

"So, are you ready to join us now?" Timon asked.

"Absolutely!" Nala smiled.

"Bring on the crunchy beetles!" shouted Pumbaa.

"Let's go tease some elephants!" cried Timon.

"Everyone to the mudhole for a mud fight!" Simba yelled, and the three of them started off.

"Oh, dear," murmured Nala, "this isn't exactly what I had in mind." But she smiled, and ran after her carefree friends. "Last one to the mudhole is a rotten egg!" she cried.

Peter Pan

Tink Learns a Lesson – Or Does She?

Tinker Bell was cross. She and Peter Pan had made plans to explore Skull Cave, but he was still playing "Pirate Treasure" with the Lost Boys. When she jingled impatiently by his ear to let him know it was time to go, he said, "Just a minute, Tink." So, she decided to teach him a lesson. She flew inside a hollow tree.

"Help, help me!" she jingled as loudly as she could. "I'm stuck!"

A moment later Peter appeared. He was out of breath from flying at top speed.

"What is it, Tink?" he gasped. "Are you in trouble?"

Tinker Bell couldn't help laughing at the worried expression on his face. She laughed so hard that she fell right out of the tree.

Peter Pan frowned. "That's not funny, Tink," he said. "I really thought you were in danger! And you interrupted my game!"

He flew away. Tinker Bell stopped laughing. Obviously Peter hadn't learned his lesson yet. He was still leaving her behind to play with his other friends!

She flew to the lagoon and hid among the reeds at the edge.

"Help!" she jingled. "I've got wet!"

Peter rushed over to the lagoon as quickly as he could. He knew how dangerous it was for Tink to get her wings wet.

"Where are you, Tink?" he cried.

Tink couldn't help herself. He sounded so worried. She laughed and laughed, until she rolled right out of the reeds.

Peter looked very, very stern. "Tink, this isn't funny!" he cried. "You're scaring me! I know you want me to finish my game, but the more you interrupt me, the longer it's going to take!"

He flew off. Tinker Bell stopped laughing. (Peter was really testing her patience!)

Tink sat down under a mushroom and thought about how to get even with Peter. One last scare would make him sit up and take notice.

But, as she thought, she became sleepier and sleepier. She leaned back against the mushroom stem and closed her eyes . . .

The next thing Tink knew, she was suddenly snatched up by a hungry hawk! Tink jingled and jingled – but Peter didn't come!

"I'm not fibbing this time, Peter!" she jingled. "I'm about to become lunch! I'm sorry I ever tried to fool you. This time it's real!"

Then she woke up. Tink was very relieved to discover that she was safe and sound under the shady brim of the mushroom.

Tink took a deep breath. That was very scary, she thought. I think perhaps I learned my lesson. . . .

Then she thought about it again. Nah!

Jasmine And The Star Of Persia

Princess Jasmine loved stories about the stars. Every night, her and Aladdin would gaze up at the sky.

"What's that star?" Jasmine asked one evening.

"The Star of Persia," said Aladdin. "It belonged to a kind and beautiful queen. When she died, they hid the jewel away in a tower, sure that no-one would be worthy of its beauty again."

Jasmine's eyes twinkled. "Is that story true?" Aladdin shrugged. "I don't know. But there is one way to find out."

The next morning, Jasmine and Aladdin set off on the Magic Carpet. Before long, a tall tower rose from a plaza in a tiny Kingdom.

"Let's fly down and see if there's a way in," Aladdin said.

But they discovered that the tower was locked. Without a key there was little chance of getting in.

All of a sudden, a guard spoke up. "What do you want?" he demanded.

"We've heard about the Star of Persia," Jasmine explained, "and we've come to see the jewel."

"That's impossible," the guard said. "No one can see the jewel except a queen as lovely and worthy as our own."

"Well," said Aladdin, "this is Princess Jasmine. She's not a queen, but she will be."

"I'm very fair," Jasmine assured him.

The guard's eyes searched the plaza. "Fair enough to solve the argument happening over there?" he asked.

Jasmine made her way across the plaza and solved the argument.

"You did well," said the guard. "But the answer is still no. For our queen was also kind."

Jasmine turned to Aladdin. "Let's not bother him," she said. "I'll go and get him a drink from the fountain. Then we'll leave."

Jasmine found the fountain dry. However, as she held a jar under it, a stream of water came out. Everyone in the plaza stared.

"The fountain!" blurted the guard. "It hasn't had water since our queen was alive!"

The people bowed, and the guard unlocked the chains on the tower door. He led Jasmine to the highest room where the gleaming Star of Persia sat. The guard offered the jewel to Jasmine. "You have proved you are worthy enough to keep it. But promise to come and visit us whenever you can."

"Oh, I will!" exclaimed Jasmine. And because she was not only fair and kind, but also honest, she most certainly did.

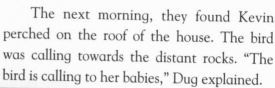

Meeting a Hero

Carl and a young boy called Russell were in South America. They had flown there in Carl's house with thousands of balloons tied to it! Carl had been married to a woman called Ellie for many years. They had always dreamed of becoming explorers and visiting Paradise Falls in South America. Sadly, they were never able to save enough money to take their trip, and Ellie had passed away. But Carl still wanted to make their dream come true.

Since arriving in South America, Carl and Russell had met a strange, huge bird – Russell named him Kevin – and a talking dog called Dug! Dug was on a mission to find Kevin and wanted to take the bird prisoner.

They were walking to Paradise Falls, holding on to the house with the garden hose. That night, they stopped to rest. "Dug says he wants to take Kevin prisoner. We have to protect him!" Russell told Carl while the others slept. Carl agreed that Kevin could come with them to the falls.

"Promise you won't leave Kevin? Cross your heart?" Russell asked Carl.

Carl thought for a moment. The last time he'd crossed his heart was when he'd promised Ellie he would take her to Paradise Falls.

"Cross my heart," he finally told Russell.

The next morning, they found Kevin perched on the roof of the house. The bird was calling towards the distant rocks. "The bird is calling to her babies," Dug explained.

"Kevin's a girl?" Russell asked in surprise.

Soon Kevin set off for her home. Russell wanted to go with her. But Carl was in a hurry to get to the falls. "She can take care of herself," he told Russell.

Suddenly, three fierce dogs burst from the bushes. They surrounded Carl, Russell and Dug, and demanded the bird. The dogs were part of Dug's pack. When they realized that Dug had lost the bird, they wanted to take the travellers to their master.

The dogs led Carl and Russell to a huge cave. An old man stood in the entrance, surrounded by more dogs. When the man saw Carl's house, he laughed. He had thought that Carl and Russell were explorers – but real explorers wouldn't come in a floating house! "My dogs made a mistake," he told Carl.

Carl thought the man looked familiar. "Wait," he said. "Are you... Charles Muntz?"

Carl couldn't believe it – Muntz was his and Ellie's childhood hero! "My wife and I, we're your biggest fans!" he said, shaking Muntz's hand. Carl wished that Ellie was there – he knew she would have been thrilled.

Pinocchio

A Nose for Trouble

School was out for the day, and Pinocchio was ready to have some fun.

"Wait for me!" Jiminy Cricket called. Jiminy caught up with Pinocchio in front of the small shop where he lived with Geppetto, his father.

"Father, I'm home!" Pinocchio called. "What are you making?"

"A cuckoo clock," Geppetto replied. "I even brought home a live bird for a model." He pointed to a birdcage.

"May I take the bird out and play with him?" Pinocchio asked.

"I'm afraid not," said Geppetto. "You aren't the only one who's been watching him."

Geppetto nodded towards Figaro the cat who was following the cuckoo's every move. At the end of the day, Geppetto went out to the market. As soon as he left, Pinocchio hurried over to the birdcage.

"Pinocchio?" Jiminy said. "What are you doing?"

"Taking the bird out," the puppet replied. As Pinocchio opened the cage door, Figaro jumped onto the table.

"Watch out!" Jiminy cried as the cat leapt towards the birdcage. The bird zipped out of the cage, spotted an open window and flew out. Just then, Geppetto walked in. He glanced at the empty birdcage. "Pinocchio!" he yelled. "I told you not to open the cage!"

Panicked, Pinocchio lied. "I didn't do it! It was Figaro! He opened the birdcage!"

"Figaro!" cried Geppetto. He picked up the cat to scold him.

At that moment, the puppet's nose began to grow. Pinocchio didn't want his father to know that he had lied. "Father," Pinocchio said, "I'm going to bed. I'm not well."

The next morning, Pinocchio got up early and spent the day looking for the cuckoo. Pinocchio told lie after lie. At the end of the day, Pinocchio's nose was longer than ever before – and he still hadn't found the cuckoo. Pinocchio headed home, determined to tell the truth.

"Figaro didn't open the cage," Pinocchio told his father. "I opened it and the cuckoo flew away. I'm sorry I disobeyed you, but most of all, I'm sorry I lied."

As Pinocchio spoke, his nose became shorter and shorter.

"I'm glad you finally told the truth," said Geppetto. "And the cuckoo came back. I was working on the clock today and he flew in through the window. I think he likes it here!"

"He should," Pinocchio said. "It's the best home anyone could ever want."

101 DALMATIANS

Puppy Trouble

Pongo and Perdita were joining Roger and Anita for a picnic with friends.

"I'm not sure we should leave the puppies," Perdita said. "Will Nanny be able to handle all fifteen of them by herself?"

Pongo reassured Perdita as she followed him out of the door.

Soon after, Lucky wanted something to do. "Let's get Nanny to take us for a walk!" he urged the other puppies. Nanny turned and saw fifteen puppies holding their leashes in their mouths.

When they reached the playground, Nanny unhooked their leashes and breathed a sigh of relief as the puppies scampered off to play.

They were so busy playing, that they didn't see Lucky chasing a butterfly and jump from the top of the wall and disappear. Lucky landed in the back of a fire engine, as it started speeding down the road!

"Woof! Woof!" Lucky barked. "I'm a fire dog!" Lucky enjoyed his ride, but he was glad when the fire engine stopped. He knew thathe had to get back to the playground, so he jumped off the fire engine.

"A puppy!" someone squealed.

Lucky looked up and saw a little girl pushing a doll pram. She stroked him.

"You can be my new dolly," the little girl said as she put him in the pram.

Suddenly, the little girl spotted something on the ground. "A button!" she cried. As she bent down to pick it up, Lucky jumped out and ran away as fast as he could.

Lucky raced across the street. He heard a honk as a car swerved to avoid him. Then dirty water splashed all over him, but he kept running until he reached the playground.

Nanny looked up. "Why, hello, little pup," she said to Lucky. "Too bad you can't come with us – you're not a dalmatian."

Lucky was confused, but then he spotted his reflection in a puddle. He was covered with dirt. He looked like a labrador puppy – Nanny didn't recognize him!

Lucky ran over to some children who were playing in a fountain. The children giggled as the little dalmatian splashed about in the fountain.

Lucky ran towards home. He grinned as he spotted Nanny in front of the house, unhooking his brothers' and sisters' leashes.

Later, when Pongo and Perdita came home, they found Lucky sleeping in his basket.

"You see?" Pongo whispered to Perdita. "I told you nothing would go wrong."

DUMBO
Happy to Help

"Whee!" cried Timothy Mouse as he flew through the air, seated inside Dumbo's hat. The young elephant used his big ears to fly around the circus tent. "Way to go!" Timothy said.

Dumbo smiled as he landed softly on the ground. "We had a great rehearsal," Timothy told Dumbo.

Just then some of Timothy's fans spotted him. "You can have the rest of the morning off, Dumbo. Take a nap, we'll practise later."

Dumbo was looking forward to a long nap, when suddenly he heard someone shout: "Oh, no! My beautiful balloons!"

Dumbo looked up. A bunch of colourful balloons were drifting away from a balloon seller. The elephant quickly sprang into action. He flew after the balloons, grabbed the strings with his trunk and flew back to the ground.

"You're the best!" the balloon seller said.

Happy to have helped, Dumbo made his way towards his train car to take his overdue nap. As he walked, he saw a crowd gathering. Using his trunk, he politely nudged his way in to see what was going on. A little girl stood in the middle of the crowd crying.

"I think the poor kid is lost," said a magician. "We must help her. But how?"

Dumbo walked over and tapped the girl on the shoulder with his trunk.

"Great idea, Dumbo!" said the juggler. "You could spot the little girl's mum from above!" He picked up the girl and put her on the elephant's back.

Dumbo and the little girl flew up above the circus tents. They looked down at the crowds of people.

"Mummy! There's my mummy!" the girl shouted.

Dumbo landed gently. The girl climbed off his back and ran into her mother's arms.

"Thank you, Dumbo! Thank you!" said the girl's mother. Dumbo was glad to have been able to help.

Suddenly a pie went whizzing by! Dumbo turned to see some circus clowns throwing pink cream pies at each other. They were covered from head to toe!

"What a mess!" said one of the clowns. "I think it's time for a shower," said another.

Dumbo had an idea! He flew over to the water tank and filled his trunk. Then he sprayed water all over the clowns! The clowns laughed as Dumbo rinsed away the gooey pink pie. Then Dumbo nodded and went off to finally take his long-awaited nap!

Disney
**MICKEY MOUSE
CLUBHOUSE**

Up, Up and Away!

Donald and his friends were standing outside the Clubhouse on a bright day.

"Oh, Donald," Daisy said, "look at the sky! It's lovely!"

"Shhh!" Donald whispered. "Don't make a move! Something is following me!"

Daisy giggled. "Oh, my!" said Daisy. "There is something following you! It's wearing a sailor's cap – just like yours. And when you move, it moves, too."

"Aw, phooey," Donald quacked as he turned around and saw his shadow. "That is a fine-looking shape, but I still don't trust it!"

"Cheer up, buddy," Mickey said. "Why don't we all leave our shadows on the ground and fly our hot-air balloon?"

Soon, the friends were floating high above the Clubhouse.

"Look, everyone!" yelled Minnie. "There are so many shapes below us. I see a triangle and a rectangle. What do you see?"

"What's a triangle?" asked Goofy.

"A triangle is a shape with three sides that all have points at the ends," Minnie explained.

"Like that?" Goofy questioned, pointing to a huge triangle. It was the top of a mountain and they were headed straight for it!

"We need help," cried Mickey. "Oh, Toodles!"

Toodles appeared with a ladder. Mickey dropped it over the side of the balloon and the friends headed down one by one. Everyone was happy to be standing on firm ground again. But they had to hike back home! The friends trudged along, growing more and more tired.

"I think we've been walking in circles," Mickey finally said. "I'm sure I've seen this tree before. Oh, Toodles!" And Toodles appeared, showing three pictures of Mickey. Mickey shared them with his friends.

"I'm standing in front of the Clubhouse and my shadow is different in each picture. In the morning, my shadow falls in front of me. At noon, I have no shadow. In the evening, my shadow falls behind me. Do any of you know what this could mean?"

"I've got it!" Donald shouted. "Right now, it's late and the sun is setting behind us. Toodles shows that in the evening, our shadows point towards the Clubhouse. If we follow them, they'll lead us back home."

Donald was correct. The shadows helped the friends head in the right direction. Soon, they arrived back at the Clubhouse.

"Well, Donald," Daisy said, "do you trust your shadow now?"

Tangled

Operation Rescue

The Stabbington brothers had once been Flynn Rider's partners in crime. They helped him steal the royal crown, but Flynn refused to share it with them. Flynn then changed when he met Rapunzel, and tried to return the crown to the brothers.

But the Stabbingtons knocked Flynn out and tied him in a small boat. They placed the stolen crown on his knees and sent the boat off towards the castle. Their plan worked perfectly: when the guards saw Flynn arriving with the crown, they immediately arrested him and threw him in the dungeon!

"Rapunzel!" moaned Flynn as he woke up. "I must rescue her!"

Fortunately, their horse friend Maximus had seen everything. He knew that Flynn had changed and that he didn't deserve to be in prison. He also knew that Rapunzel had been held in the tower by wicked Mother Gothel...

So, Maximus galloped to the pub full of ruffians they had visited earlier. He needed them to help Flynn to escape!

Meanwhile, Flynn had discovered that the Stabbington brothers were locked up in jail too. Mother Gothel had betrayed them. To get them to agree to trap Flynn and give up the crown, she had promised them Rapunzel's magic hair in exchange. Of course, she was lying! As soon as the Stabbingtons arrived to claim their reward, she knocked them out and handed them over to the guards.

Now Flynn understood everything. He begged the guards, "Please let me go! Rapunzel needs help!"

But at that moment, the gang of pub thugs came rushing into the prison. They fought with the guards and dragged Flynn out into the main courtyard. There, one of them pushed him onto a cart tipped at an angle.

"Put your head down," the ruffian told him. "Hold your arms against your sides. Open your legs wide."

Wham! The ruffian jumped on the other end of the cart and Flynn flew into the air! He went shrieking over the prison wall and landed right on Maximus' back – the horse had been waiting for him at the dungeon entrance.

Flynn was amazed – the horse that had once been desparate to catch him had ended up rescuing him!

They both cared deeply about Rapunzel and wanted to save her from Mother Gothel's evil clutches.

Flynn patted the Maximus and the horse galloped off towards the tower. But would they be too late to save Rapunzel?

The Monster of Paradise Falls

Carl Fredickson had dreamed of becoming an explorer since he was a boy. He had met a girl called Ellie who shared his dream, and they grew up and got married.

Carl had promised Ellie he'd take her to Paradise Falls one day. But they never managed to save enough money to go. When Ellie passed away, Carl missed her very much. One day, when he was being forced to move out of their home, he tied thousands of balloons to the house and flew to South America – to Paradise Falls. And he accidentally took a young boy called Russell along with him.

Carl and Russell had met a big, strange bird – Russell had named it Kevin, but then discovered it was a girl! They also met a talking dog called Dug. He had been sent by his pack to capture Kevin. More dogs had appeared and taken Carl and Russell to their leader. Much to Carl's surprise, their leader was Charles Muntz – a famous explorer who had been his and Ellie's childhood hero!

Muntz invited Carl and Russell into his giant airship – the Spirit of Adventure! When Dug tried to follow, the other dogs blocked his way. "He has lost the bird," declared Alpha, the leader of the pack. Dug was left outside.

On board the airship, the dogs served dinner while Muntz told Carl and Russell about the Monster of Paradise Falls.

"I've spent a lifetime tracking this creature," Muntz said.

"Hey, that looks like Kevin!" said Russell, noticing a bird skeleton.

"Kevin?" Muntz asked.

"That's my new giant bird pet," Russell explained. "I trained it to follow us."

Muntz became very angry. He thought Carl and Russell were trying to steal the bird from him.

At that moment, they heard a wail outside. Kevin had followed Carl and Russell into the cave! All the dogs began to bark. In the confusion, Carl and Russell slipped away.

"Get them!" Muntz roared at his dogs.

Carl and Russell untied the house and started to run. The snarling dog pack came racing after them. Kevin scooped Russell and Carl onto her back and raced for the cave opening, with the house still floating behind.

But Kevin wasn't fast enough to stay ahead of the pack. The dogs were closing in. Suddenly, an avalanche of rocks tumbled down and blocked the dog pack. "Go on, Master. I will stop the dogs!" someone cried.

It was Dug! He had come to rescue Carl and Russell. But would Carl, Russell and Kevin be able to escape…?

Bambi
The Winter Trail

One winter morning, Bambi was dozing in the wood when he heard a thumping sound nearby. "C'mon, Bambi!" his bunny friend Thumper cried. "It's a perfect day for playing."

Bambi followed Thumper through the forest. The sky was blue and the ground covered in a blanket of new snow.

"Look at these tracks!" Thumper said excitedly. He pointed to a line of footprints in the snow. "Who do you suppose they belong to?" Bambi didn't know, so they decided to follow the trail. They soon came to a tree.

"Wake up, Friend Owl!" called Thumper.

"Have you been out walking?" Bambi asked.

"Now why would I do that?" Friend Owl replied. "My wings take me everywhere."

Bambi and Thumper continued on. Next, they spotted a raccoon sitting next to a tree, his mouth full of red berries. "Hello, Mr Raccoon," Bambi said shyly. "Did you happen to see who made these tracks in the snow?"

The raccoon shook his head and began tapping the tree. "I know!" Thumper cried. "He thinks we should ask the woodpeckers."

Soon, Bambi and Thumper had found the woodpecker family. "Did you make the tracks in the snow?" Thumper called up to the birds.

"No, we've been here all day," the mother bird answered.

"If the tracks don't belong to the woodpeckers or the raccoon and they don't belong to Friend Owl, whose can they be?" Bambi asked.

"I don't know," Thumper replied, frustrated.

They soon reached the end of the trail, and the tracks led all the way to a snowy bush, where a family of quail were resting.

"Did you make these tracks?" Thumper asked.

"Why, yes," Mrs Quail answered. "Friend Owl told me about this wonderful bush. So this morning, my babies and I walked all the way over here."

Thumper and Bambi happily joined the quail family for a snack. Soon, it was time for the friends to go home. They'd spent all day following the trail. When they turned to leave, a big surprise was waiting for them – their mothers! Bambi bounded over to his mother and stretched his nose up for a kiss.

"How'd ya find us?" Thumper asked.

Thumper's mother looked down at the tracks in the snow.

"You followed our trail!" Bambi cried. His mother nodded.

"Now, let's follow it back home," Bambi's mother said. So that's just what they did.

Disney
THE
LION KING
Why Worry?

Zazu didn't know what to do with Timon and Pumbaa! Ever since they had come to the Pride Lands, he'd been trying to find the perfect jobs for them.

"Zazu," said Simba, "I think you should forget it. Timon and Pumbaa are used to taking life as it comes. *Hakuna matata* – no worries – that's their philosophy."

"Well, it's certainly not mine!" said Zazu.

That afternoon, the hornbill told Timon and Pumbaa that they would be in charge of watching the cubs while the lionesses went off to hunt. "No problem!" said Timon.

"Can we go to the water hole by ourselves?" asked Kiara, Simba's daughter.

"Sure," said Timon. "Have fun!"

"Do we have to take a nap?" wondered another cub.

"Not if you don't want to," said Pumbaa.

The cubs thought Timon and Pumba were the best babysitters on Earth. But Zazu didn't. He was furious.

"Aw, Zazu," said Timon. "Loosen up!"

"Things are loose enough around here as it is." Zazu sniffed. "Too loose, if you ask me."

The next day, Zazu put Timon and Pumbaa in charge of clearing the brushes around the water hole. As they uprooted each plant, they found an insect feast in the soil underneath. Pretty soon they were stuffed. It was time for a nap.

"What's this?" shouted Zazu. "Sleeping on the job?"

"Don't get your feathers in a ruffle," replied Timon. "What is it with you, anyway? You seem kind of tense all the time."

"Tense? Of course I'm tense!" Zazu shouted. "I'm Simba's right-hand man. It's up to me to see that the kingdom is in perfect order!"

Pumbaa spoke up. "And you do a very good job of it too."

"Thank you," said Zazu.

"But," added Timon, "what good is an ordered kingdom if you never stop to enjoy it?"

Zazu admitted that Timon had a point. The other members of the kingdom always seemed to head in the other direction every time they saw Zazu coming. Maybe he was too hard on everyone, including himself.

"Gentlemen," Zazu said. "I finally have the perfect job for you. I'm making you the ministers of *hakuna matata*. You are in charge of keeping things from getting too serious around here."

Simba was delighted when he found out. "Zazu, you're a genius!" he said.

"Thank you, sire," said Zazu. "I always said there was something special about those two!"

The Mysterious Voyage

Aladdin and Jasmine had just married and were taking a romantic trip.

"Madame, the Magic Carpet awaits you," said Aladdin, bowing before his bride.

"Won't you tell me where we're going?" Jasmine asked.

"You are going to see things you've never seen before – a whole new, exciting world," Aladdin replied.

Jasmine, Aladdin and Abu settled onto the Magic Carpet. Then they took off, soaring high above the palace.

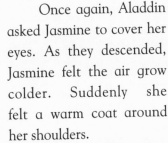

After a little while, the Magic Carpet began its descent.

"Are we there?" asked Jasmine.

"Almost," said Aladdin. "Close your eyes. I want this to be a surprise."

Suddenly, the Magic Carpet landed on top of a high cliff. Jasmine heard a loud noise that sounded like crashing water.

"Okay. Open, sesame!" said Aladdin. "This, Jasmine, is the ocean!"

Jasmine couldn't believe her eyes. The water was a brilliant shade of turquoise. Dolphins leaped in and out of the water. Huge ocean waves crashed onto a white sandy beach.

"It's magical!" said Jasmine. They had a wonderful time swimming.

When Aladdin and Jasmine were ready to go, he snapped his fingers for the Magic Carpet. "Time for our next destination!" he said.

Once again, Aladdin asked Jasmine to cover her eyes. As they descended, Jasmine felt the air grow colder. Suddenly she felt a warm coat around her shoulders.

"You can open your eyes now!" said Aladdin.

This time, everywhere that Jasmine looked, she saw white!

"Oh... what is it?" she asked, bending down to touch the cold, white powder.

"It's snow!" answered Aladdin. "Isn't it wonderful? It falls from the sky when it's cold."

"It's amazing!" cried Jasmine. "It looks like soft, white clouds!"

They spent the rest of the day playing in the snow. They built snowmen and made snow angels. Soon the sun began to set. "I think it's time to go," said Aladdin.

"You've shown me there are plenty of brand-new worlds for us to share," said Jasmine happily. As they made their way back to the palace, Jasmine smiled. She knew that this was just the beginning of their wonderful life together.

Hanukkah Fun

"Happy Hanukkah, Pooh Bear!" Roo exclaimed as he opened the door for his first guest. It was the first night of Hanukkah, and Roo and Kanga were having all their friends over to participate in some Hanukkah customs.

"Happy Hanukkah, Roo!" Pooh replied. Just then a delicious smell wafted by his nose. "Something smells yummy!" Pooh cried.

Kanga was making little potato pancakes called *latkes*, a special Hanukkah treat. "Try to be patient, Pooh," Kanga said with a smile. "We'll have these latkes a little bit later."

Before long, Piglet, Eeyore, Rabbit, Tigger and Owl had also arrived and it was time to light the Menorah, a candleholder that could hold nine candles.

"First," Kanga explained, "we light this centre candle, called the *shammosh*. Then, we use the shammosh to light one other candle for the first night of Hanukkah."

Tigger noticed that there weren't any candles in the other seven candle holders of the Menorah. "When do we light the other candles?" he asked Kanga.

"Well, Tigger," Kanga said, "Hanukkah lasts for eight nights. So tomorrow, on the second night, we will light two candles with the shammosh. On the third night, we will light three candles, and so on . . . until, on the eighth night, we will light all the candles!"

Everyone watched the candles burning. Then Pooh said, "Um, Kanga? Is it a little bit later . . . now?"

Kanga understood: Pooh was hungry for a latke! Kanga brought the potato pancakes to the table and everyone enjoyed the delicious treats.

When they were all eaten, Roo said, "Now let's play *dreidel*!" He got out a four-sided, clay spinning top. Kanga made a pile of sweets, nuts and pennies in the centre of the floor. She also gave a little pile of goodies to each guest.

Roo explained the rules, then each player took turns spinning the dreidel. Depending on what side the dreidel landed on, the player might win more treats from the centre pile, or lose treats from their own pile and have to add them to the centre pile.

"This is fun!" Piglet exclaimed. "And to think: there are seven *more* nights of Hanukkah!"

"Hey, Mama," said Roo, "there are eight of us and eight nights of Hanukkah. Can our friends come over every night of Hanukkah, and take turns lighting the Menorah?"

Everyone, including Kanga, thought that was a wonderful idea.

So that was exactly what they did.

A Difficult Decision

Carl Fredricksen and Russell had flown to South America in Carl's house. Carl was an old man who had dreamed of being an explorer since he was just a boy. His best childhood friend, Ellie, had had the same dream. They grew up and got married, and Carl promised Ellie he would take her to see Paradise Falls. But they never managed to save enough money to go, and sadly Ellie passed away.

Carl was being forced to move out of their home, so he decided to take the trip that he and Ellie had dreamed about. He accidentally took Russell along for the ride. Whilst walking towards Paradise Falls with the house in tow, they had met a strange bird called Kevin and a talking dog called Dug. Dug was part of a pack of dogs who wanted to capture Kevin for their leader – the great explorer, Charles Muntz!

But Charles thought Carl and Russell were trying to steal the bird from him, and he sent his pack of dogs after them. Luckily Dug was on their side and he blocked the other dogs' path with some rocks. But he couldn't stop the pack for long. One dog – Alpha – shoved him aside and jumped over the rocks. Up ahead, Carl, Russell and Kevin had come to the edge of a cliff. They were trapped!

Luckily, Carl and Russell were holding onto the house by the garden hose. Just then, the wind lifted the house into the air – taking Carl and his friends with it! Alpha grabbed Kevin's leg, but he lost his grip. The house floated to safety.

Carl and his friends had escaped, but Kevin's leg was badly injured. Russell realized that the bird needed help to get back to her babies. Out of nowhere, a spotlight appeared and shone down on the bird. Muntz had followed them in the Spirit of Adventure! Before Kevin could escape, a net shot from the airship and trapped her. Carl sawed at the net with Russell's pocketknife, trying to set her free.

"Get away from my bird!" Muntz snarled. Then he set Carl's house on fire!

Carl couldn't let his house go up in smoke – it held all his memories of Ellie. So he quickly made the decision to give up Kevin instead. The dogs dragged the wounded bird onto the airship. As Muntz lifted off with his prize bird, Carl ran to his house and beat back the flames.

"You gave away Kevin," Russell said.

Carl felt terrible, but what could he do? "I didn't ask for any of this!" he snapped. "Now, whether you assist me or not, I am going to Paradise Falls if it kills me."

Russell watched sadly as Carl walked away, pulling the house behind him.

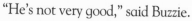

THE JUNGLE Book

"Hey, Hey, We're the Vultures!"

"Nothing exciting ever happens around here," Buzzie complained to his vulture singing buddies.

"That's not true," said Flaps. "What about that fight we had with the tiger Shere Khan last week?"

"Blimey, you're right," said Ziggy. "That was pretty exciting."

"But what are we gonna do now?" asked Buzzie.

"Let's sing," suggested Ziggy.

"Hey, good idea!" said the other three vultures.

"Only one problem," said Dizzy. "We need a tenor."

"Awww, you're right," said Ziggy. "That little Man-cub fellow, Mowgli, would have been a great tenor. Too bad he left the jungle."

"So, what are we gonna do?" asked Buzzie.

"How 'bout we hold an audition?" suggested Ziggy.

"Good thinking," said Flaps.

So the vultures put the word out in the jungle and, a week later, there was a line of animals ready to try out for the group.

"Name?" Buzzie asked the first applicant.

"Coconut," the monkey replied.

"All right, Coconut, let's hear ya sing," said Flaps.

Coconut shrieked for a few minutes, and the four vultures huddled together.

"He's not very good," said Buzzie.

"And he's a monkey," added Flaps.

"Next!" said Dizzy.

The vultures auditioned a lemur, two sloths, a wolf, a hippo, a toad and an elephant. None seemed like the right fit. Finally, the last animal stepped up.

"Name?" asked Buzzie.

"Name's Lucky," said the vulture. "Hey, aren't you the four fellows that helped that little Man-cub scare away that tiger Shere Khan?"

"Yeah," said Buzzie. "We are."

"Then I guess you four might be called 'lucky' yourselves!" cried Lucky. He began to laugh at his own joke.

"Go ahead and sing," said Ziggy, rolling his eyes.

Lucky sang for a few minutes and the four vultures huddled together.

"He's not bad," said Dizzy.

"Plus, he's a vulture," said Ziggy.

"And he's the last one left," pointed out Flaps. That settled it.

"You're hired!" the vultures sang.

"See, told you I was Lucky!" cried the vulture.

"But only with auditions," said Dizzy.

"Yeah," said Buzzie. "When we meet Shere Khan again, we'll see how lucky you really are!"

Peter Pan

Tinker Bell's Bedtime Story

"Shove over!"

"No. You shove over."

The Raccoon Twins were at it again. Peter Pan knew the bickering wouldn't stop until one of the boys had pushed the other out of the hammock.

"Hey!" Cubby yelled. The twins had tumbled out and landed right on top of the bear-suited boy.

Peter sighed. Every evening had ended like this ever since Wendy left.

As the tussle grew, Peter had an idea. He went to look for Tinker Bell.

"Say, Tink," Peter said when he found her, "how'd you like to be the new mother to all of us boys?"

Tink looked at Peter as if he was crazy.

"Aw, c'mon," Peter said. "You've seen the guys since Wendy left. They're fighting something awful. They need someone to tuck them in at night and tell them a bedtime story."

Tink was silent for a moment.

"I guess I could ask Wendy to come back," Peter said, looking at Tinker Bell slyly.

That did it. The last thing Tink wanted was for Wendy to return! The little fairy flew into the hideout and shook a finger at the Lost Boys.

"Gosh, Tink. What is it?" Slightly sat up, straightening his fox ears.

"Tink is going to tell us a bedtime story," said Peter.

The boys settled down. "Go ahead, Tink," Peter smiled. His plan was working perfectly!

Tink sat down and crossed her arms over her chest. She began to jingle.

"Once upon a time," Peter translated, "there was a beautiful fairy who, against her better judgement, lived with a pack of dirty, unruly, silly boys. And the dirtiest, unruliest and silliest of them all was Peter Pa– hey!" Peter interrupted his translation. "That's not nice, Tink!"

Tinker Bell jingled spitefully at him. "Okay," Peter said with a sigh, "I know it's your story. Go ahead." Tink continued and Peter translated, "One day, as the lovely Tinker Bell was minding her own business, the very smelly and unpleasant Peter Pan – *Tink*! – asked her to tell a bedtime story. Well, Tinker Bell didn't know any bedtime stories, so she went to fetch Captain Hook, so *he* could tell one."

With that, Tinker Bell flew out of the window.

"Tink! Tink, come back!" Peter cried. Tinker Bell returned and hovered in the window, jingling with laughter. "That was a dirty trick!" Peter scolded. "And besides, that's no way to tell a bedtime story." He sat down next to the boys' beds. "You have to do it like Wendy did. Like this."

Now it was Tink's turn to smile. While Peter told a bedtime story, and the Lost Boys drifted off to sleep, Tink curled up in her own little bed and closed her eyes. Her plan had worked perfectly!

Pinocchio
The Greatest Gift

Pinocchio was the luckiest boy in the world – and he knew it. No longer a wooden puppet, at last he was a real, live boy! And Pinocchio knew he owed it all to Geppetto for believing in him.

"I wish I could give Papa something in return," Pinocchio said to himself one day.

Pinocchio didn't have any money, so he decided to make a gift for Geppetto.

"Perhaps I should use Papa's tools and carve a present for him out of wood!" said Pinocchio.

So, one afternoon, while Geppetto was out, Pinocchio sat down at the woodworking bench. The only problem was, Pinocchio did not know the first thing about woodworking.

"That looks dangerous," said Pinocchio, eyeing a chisel. "I don't think Papa would want me to use that on my own." He decided he needed another gift idea. "I know!" he said. "Maybe I can cook something for Papa!"

Pinocchio went over to the hearth, where Geppetto did all of the cooking.

But he soon realized that he didn't know how to cook either. "And Papa is always telling me to stay a safe distance away from the fire," he reminded himself.

Pinocchio looked around the little house and spotted Geppetto's accordion sitting on the table.

"Of course!" cried Pinocchio. "Papa loves music. I could write him a song as a gift and then perform it for him!"

So Pinocchio picked up the accordion and began to play. But the sounds that came out were . . . well . . . just awful!

"Hmph," Pinocchio said in frustration. "I don't know how to play the accordion *or* write a song." He put the accordion down and stood in the middle of the room. Tears were welling up in poor little Pinocchio's eyes when Geppetto came in through the front door.

"My dear boy," Geppetto said, hurrying to Pinocchio's side, "what is the matter?"

Through his tears, Pinocchio explained how he had wanted to make a gift to show Geppetto how much he appreciated everything his father had done for him.

As Geppetto listened, his look of worry softened into a smile, and then *his* eyes welled up with tears. "My son," he said, "don't you know that you, and you alone, are the greatest gift a father could ever want?"

"I am?" Pinocchio asked.

"You are," replied Geppetto.

"Well, in that case," said Pinocchio with a sly grin as he hugged his papa, "you're welcome!"

Then Geppetto picked up the accordion and they sang and danced all the rest of the day.

The Real Adventure

Russell was a Junior Wilderness Explorer, and he had knocked on Carl Fredricksen's door to see if he needed help. Carl had been in a bad mood – he was being forced to move out of his home. He told Russell to find a bird called a Snipe.

Carl had been married to his childhood friend, Ellie. They both dreamed of being explorers and Carl had promised her they'd visit Paradise Falls in South America. But they had never managed to save enough money to go. When Ellie passed away, Carl missed her very much.

Then Carl decided he had to keep his promise and go to Paradise Falls. He tied thousands of balloons to his house and it lifted into the air. He didn't realize that Russell was still on the porch, looking for the Snipe!

Soon the pair landed in South America. They pulled the house along as they walked towards Paradise Falls. Before long, they met a strange bird called Kevin – who was actually a girl – and a talking dog called Dug. There was a whole pack of dogs who were controlled by the great explorer Charles Muntz – he wanted to capture Kevin. Russell and Carl managed to escape with Kevin, but then Charles set Carl's house on fire! Carl couldn't let all his memories of Ellie go up in flames, so he gave up Kevin.

Russell was very upset, because Carl had promised to protect Kevin. They wanted to help her to get back to her babies.

Carl told Russell he no longer needed his help, then he towed the house the rest of the way to Paradise Falls by himself. He placed the house exactly where it appeared in Ellie's drawing of Paradise Falls.

Russell was still angry with Carl. "Here," he said bitterly, throwing his Wilderness Explorer sash on the ground. "I don't want this anymore."

With a sigh, Carl picked up Russell's sash and went into his house. Carl found Ellie's adventure book. He had kept his promise. But he still felt sad. He wished Ellie were there with him.

Carl started to close the book, but something caught his eye. It was a photograph of their wedding day. Carl turned the page. He had never looked through the whole book before. To his astonishment, it was filled with photographs of the two of them over the years. On the last page, there was a message from Ellie:

Thanks for the adventure. Now go and have one of your own.

Carl smiled, realizing that Ellie had got her wish after all. Their life together had been the real adventure.

Cinderella

A Royal Friend

A crowd of girls looked on excitedly as Cinderella's coach came to a stop outside of their school. The headmistress hurried to open the door. "Welcome, Your Highness!" she exclaimed.

"It's so nice to see you all again," said the Princess. Everyone was happy to see Cinderella. But no one was more excited than a little girl called Emma.

When it was time for Cinderella to go, she made an announcement. "In one week, there will be a party at the castle – held in your honour." Cinderella smiled as she told them their dresses would be made for them.

The next day, the headmistress took them to the meadow near the royal estate. While her classmates ran and played, Emma noticed several seamstresses walking towards the castle gates.

Without thinking, Emma ran up and slipped inside! She wandered the hallways until she heard a seamstress call out, "Come in! Stand here, dear." She began draping fabric around Emma. When Cinderella stopped by, Emma was wearing one of the dresses.

"You look beautiful," exclaimed Cinderella. The Princess invited Emma to have tea with her.

"It must be wonderful to be a princess," Emma said between bites. "You get to wear fancy clothes and go to parties all day."

Cinderella laughed. "There's more to being a princess than clothes and parties. Help me this afternoon and see what a princess really does."

That afternoon, Emma and Cinderella put together baskets of donated goods. Then, they delivered the baskets to the orphanages.

When they arrived at her school, the headmistress gave Emma a big hug.

"Where have you been?" she cried. "We've been so worried."

"But I thought the seamstresses brought you to work?" Cinderella said, puzzled.

Emma apolgized, saying, "I just wanted to be a princess for a day."

"Being a princess means being responsible." Cinderella told her.

Cinderella decided Emma should help plan the party. So Emma helped to bake the cake. Cinderella was so impressed that she asked her mouse friends to make a special dress for Emma.

"Because you've worked so hard, I'm going to make you an honourary princess for the evening," Cinderella said. Emma was thrilled that she'd get to be Princess Emma for one magical night.

Tiana and the Jewel of the Bayou

One morning, Tiana, Naveen, Eudora and Charlotte were discussing Tiana's Birthday party. Prince Naveen was worried – he still hadn't found the perfect gift for his princess!

Nothing had seemed special enough for Princess Tiana. But luckily, Naveen had overheard Tiana and Charlotte in the kitchen.

"When my daddy and I used to go fishing in the bayou, we'd sometimes find a piece of swamp amber," said Tiana. "It was the most precious thing!"

"That's it!" whispered Naveen. Naveen met with the jazz-loving alligator, Louis. They were going to find Tiana some swamp amber!

As the birthday party was about to begin, Tiana couldn't find Naveen anywhere. A guest said he saw the prince down by the old, mossy tree in the bayou. Tiana was afraid Naveen was in trouble.

She ran to the river and climbed into a rowboat. She saw Naveen in the distance. He dove into the water by the old tree.

"Naveen!" Tiana called out. When the prince didn't reappear, she dove into the water!

She found Naveen in a tangle of roots. Tiana grabbed his hand and pulled him to the surface.

Naveen reassured her that everything was fine and gave her a hug. He opened his hand to reveal a plain, muddy rock. "I was expecting a sparkling jewel, but this is just..."

"Swamp amber!" Tiana exclaimed. "What a wonderful birthday surprise!"

Later, when Charlotte saw the birthday gift she screamed in fright. But Tiana explained that the rock brought back loving memories of her father. "That is the most precious gift of all," said Tiana.

Mama Odie picked up the swamp amber. "A little sparkle couldn't hurt," she said, tossing the rock into a pot of gumbo. "Gumbo, gumbo in the pot, we need some sparkle. What you got?"

In a puff of magic, the swamp amber became a dazzling golden jewel set in a fine necklace.

"Mama Odie!" Naveen exclaimed. "How did you do that?"

Mama Odie winked at Tiana. "Oh, it's just a talent we have down here in the bayou. We like to take things that are a little slimy and rough around the edges and turn 'em into something wonderful!"

"Like turning a frog into a prince!" Naveen agreed, as he and Tiana danced the night away.

Tangled

The Real Prisoner

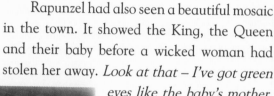

With a heavy heart, Rapunzel found herself back at the tower with Mother Gothel – the wicked woman that Rapunzel thought was her real mother.

Alone in her room, the young girl thought sadly about Flynn, who had helped her to finally leave the tower. Even Pascal, her pet chameleon, was finding it hard to keep her spirits up. But suddenly, he changed colour to match the kingdom flag that Rapunzel had brought from the kingdom, with the golden sun emblem. Rapunzel watched as he climbed along the wall, and as he passed over the pictures she had painted, the young girl was taken aback. My goodness! Without realizing it, she had painted the emblem of the kingdom all over the walls – and yet she had never seen it before she left the tower!

"How do you explain that, Pascal?"

Rapunzel thought about it. Somewhere, deep down inside her, she must have already known about this emblem, as golden as her own hair. Perhaps that was why she was so keen to find out about the lanterns that appeared in the sky every year on her birthday. Flynn had explained that the people of the kingdom sent these lanterns off in memory of their lost princess.

Rapunzel had also seen a beautiful mosaic in the town. It showed the King, the Queen and their baby before a wicked woman had stolen her away. *Look at that – I've got green eyes like the baby's mother,* Rapunzel had thought.

"Oh my goodness, Pascal! It's me. I'm the princess!" she suddenly cried out. "It all makes sense: the date of my birthday, the golden emblem..."

Immediately, Rapunzel told Mother Gothel that now she knew everything.

"You're not my mother! You stole me away to make use of my magic hair! You taught me to be afraid of people who might want to steal my power from me. But all the time it was you I should have been afraid of!" Rapunzel was very angry. "I'm leaving! I forgive Flynn. I'm going to ask him to help me!"

"No point, Rapunzel," grunted Mother Gothel. "Flynn can do nothing for you. He didn't abandon you: I had him thrown in prison!"

"Locking people up is a real obsession of yours! But now I'm not a prisoner any more. I can escape from this tower but you depend entirely on the magic of my hair to stay youthful. Well, from now on I refuse to allow you that privilege. You see: the real prisoner is you!"

Having a Ball!

"Ten days until Santa!" the spotted puppies barked, bouncing into one another as they tumbled down the hall.

"Ten days until presents!" Penny barked.

"And ten days until Christmas dinner!" Rolly added.

"Ten days to stay out of trouble!" Pongo said with a smile.

"Do you puppies know what comes before Santa and dinner and presents?" Perdita asked.

"Umm. . . stockings?" Lucky asked.

"No, before that," she said.

Patch wasn't sure. He sat down on the hall rug to think.

"We have to decorate and sing carols," Perdita said, wagging her tail. At that very moment, Roger and Anita threw open the door to the study and invited all the dogs inside.

Patch blinked. He couldn't believe his eyes. "What's a tree doing in the house?"

"Just watch." Perdy gave Patch a quick lick. While the dogs looked on, Roger and Anita began to decorate the tree. They hung lights and angels, snowmen and tinsel. Of all the decorations, Patch liked the glittering glass balls best. Balls were one of his favourite things! He could not take his eyes off them.

When the tree was ready, Anita brought in cocoa and dog biscuits. Munching on a biscuit in front of the fire, Patch didn't think the evening could get any better. Then Roger sat down at the piano, and everyone began to sing.

Patch howled along with the others, but he could not stop looking at the balls on the tree. A large red one was hanging near the floor.

Patch reached over and gave the ball a pat with his front paw. It swung merrily above him. Looking at his reflection, Patch started to laugh. His nose looked huge!

"What are you doing?" Penny stopped singing to see what was so funny. Then Freckles joined them, then Lucky. The puppies took turns knocking the ball and watching it sway, then – *crash!* – it fell to the floor, shattering.

The singing stopped. Poor Patch was sure the special evening was ruined.

"Oh, dear." Anita scooped the puppies out from under the tree. "Careful, now," she said. "Those balls aren't for playing with."

While Roger swept up the glass, Patch cowered. He knew he was in trouble.

"Maybe I should give you all one gift early," Anita said with a grin. Patch couldn't believe his luck. Instead of a firm talking-to, each puppy got to rip open a small package. Patch tore off the paper. Inside was a brand-new red rubber ball!

Look Before You Leap!

Mickey and Goofy were enjoying a game of chess, when something soared through the window and landed in the middle of the chessboard! The two friends looked carefully at something that looked right back at them. It was green. It had webbed feet. It said, "Ribbit, ribbit." It was a frog – a very jumpy frog. Goofy tried to grab it. *PLOP!* The frog leaped out of Goofy's hands and right into the kitchen sink.

"You should look before you leap!" Mickey said to the frog. All of the excitement made Goofy hungry. He decided to make lunch. Just then, the frog took a giant leap right towards Goofy's sandwich! SQUISH!

"Stop!" Mickey cried.

"You really should look before you leap," Goofy said to the frog. "And I should look before I bite!" Goofy carried the frog outside.

"Hold on tight," Mickey said. "He's pretty slippery." Goofy yelped as the frog leaped right towards Daisy's painting! SPLAT!

"You should look before you leap!" Daisy said as the paint splattered everywhere.

"I think we should help our friend the frog find a nice, safe pond," Mickey said. "Then he can leap without causing any trouble."

The frog jumped up and down in agreement. Then he hopped down Main Street with Mickey and Goofy following behind him. He took a great big leap and landed right inside Minnie's goldfish bowl! SPLASH! The big wave made the goldfish fly right out. Minnie gently put the goldfish back into its bowl.

"I don't know if we'll ever find a pond for froggie. We need some help!" Goofy sighed.

"Oh, Toodles!" Mickey called. "The net is the right tool for this job."

They held the frog safely in the net. "He seems sad," Goofy said. Mickey agreed. Then he looked ahead and saw something that made him smile. "I think we've found just the right place!"

The friends walked down the street towards a fountain. Carefully, Mickey placed the net on the ground. The frog hopped out and landed with a SWOOSH! right next to another frog!

"Ribbit, ribbit," he said.

"Ribbit, ribbit," she replied.

"Maybe we didn't find a pond," said Mickey, "but we did find a good place for him to splash and leap. And a friend for him, too."

Later, Mickey and Goofy got back to their game of chess. "C'mon, Mickey," Goofy said, "you haven't made a move in a long time."

"I know, I know," replied Mickey. "I just want to make sure I look carefully before I leap!"

DUMBO
The Show Must Go On

The wind whistled around the Big Top, pulling the canvas tent Dumbo was holding out of reach of his small trunk. "I'll get it," Dumbo's mother said as the tent flapped over their heads.

If the weather hadn't been so terrible, Dumbo thought, he could have flown up to grab the edge of the tent. But the whipping wind was too much, even for Dumbo's wing-like ears.

At last, standing on her back legs, Mrs Jumbo caught the canvas in her trunk. She pulled it taut and let the roustabouts tie it off. But Dumbo noticed several new rips in the fabric.

"Quit your clowning!" the Ringmaster barked at the clowns. He noticed the rips too. He ordered the clowns to sew them up. "The repairs must be finished by showtime!"

Dumbo felt terrible. All the circus performers, animals and roustabouts were working hard in the storm. He had gone and made even more work, by letting the canvas get torn. And now the Ringmaster's mood was as foul as the weather!

Just then Dumbo noticed another blast of cold air whirl the Ringmaster's black top hat off his head.

"That does it!" the Ringmaster shouted. "There will be no show tonight!"

Dumbo could not believe his ears. The announcement was even enough to wake Timothy Q. Mouse from his nap in a nearby bale of hay.

"No show? I can't believe it!" Timothy cried. The rest of the circus folk couldn't believe it either. They silently continued to set up.

"What a fuss over a hat." Timothy shook his head. "The show must go on."

Dumbo nodded. Then something caught his eye. The Ringmaster's hat was caught on the flagpole, high over the Big Top. Perhaps he could get it for him.

Bravely, Dumbo took off. The wind was strong, but he tucked his head down and flapped his ears hard. When the wind calmed for a moment, the small elephant saw his chance. He grabbed the top hat and flew quickly to the ground.

Shyly, Dumbo held out the hat to the Ringmaster.

"Thank you, Dumbo." The Ringmaster took his hat gratefully. He looked around at all the people and animals still hard at work. He looked a little embarrassed. Then, as he placed the hat on his head, he shouted, "The show must go on!"

Everyone cheered.

"What'd I tell ya?" Timothy asked, winking at Dumbo.

Disney · PIXAR
FINDING
NEMO

Old Man Octopus

"You're it!" Nemo tagged Sheldon, who was hiding next to a mollusc.

"Aw, man!" Sheldon swished his tail. "I'm going to get you next time, Nemo."

"Only if you can find me," Nemo teased. Then he called louder, "Ollie, ollie, all swim free!" The rest of the fish who were playing hide-and-seek returned to the giant barnacle they were using as base. When they were all there, Sheldon began to count again.

Nemo swam away, scanning the reef for a good hiding spot. Sheldon would be out to get him for sure. Nemo swam past a large empty abalone shell. "Too easy," he muttered. He darted into an anemone. "Way too obvious." Finally he came to a dark cave in the coral. "Too dark," he shivered, looking into the spooky opening. "It'll be perfect."

Mustering his courage, Nemo swam inside. At first he couldn't see anything. Then, as his eyes adjusted to the dark, Nemo saw a large eye open on the cave wall. What could it be?

Another eye opened. Then the entire wall began to move.

"O-O-Old Man Octopus!" Nemo stammered as eight long arms oozed off the cave wall. Nemo and his friends told stories about Old Man Octopus at sleepovers. In the stories Old Man Octopus sneaked up on little fish and gave them a terrible scare.

"S-sorry to disturb you, sir." Nemo swam towards the cave entrance. Then he noticed something amazing. The octopus's arms were changing colour . . . and texture! Instead of matching the brown bumpy cave wall, now they looked more like the reddish coral at the bottom of the cave.

"You didn't disturb me, boy. Tell me what brings you to this corner of the reef?" The octopus's voice was slow and kind, and Nemo's fear melted away.

"Hide-and-seek, sir," Nemo answered politely. "But I wouldn't need a cave if I could camouflage myself like you!"

Old Man Octopus laughed. "Hide-and-seek, eh? One of my favourites. The camouflage does come in handy, but nothing beats a cloud of ink when you want to make a break for the base!"

"You can shoot ink clouds too?" Nemo was so excited he forgot to be quiet.

"I hear you, Nemo!" Sheldon shouted.

"Are you ready to swim for it?" Old Man Octopus whispered with a wink.

Nemo nodded. He high-fived one of Old Man Octopus's tentacles. Then in a burst of inky blackness he darted out of the cave, past Sheldon, and all the way back to the barnacle base. Safe!

A Family Reunited At Last

Mother Gothel was furious. Rapunzel had discovered the whole truth – that she was the lost Princess, and that Mother Gothel had taken her as a baby. Now Rapunzel was refusing to let Mother Gothel use her magic to stay young.

"I won't sing any more; my hair will never make you youthful again!" Rapunzel declared.

Mother Gothel chained Rapunzel to a chair, but it didn't work – Rapunzel would rather die than obey her!

Just then, Flynn arrived outside the tower. Mother Gothel had had him thrown in prison, but he had escaped from prison and rushed to Rapunzel's aid. Mother Gothel threw down Rapunzel's hair, and fearlessly he hoisted himself up her golden locks. But, when he eventually jumped in through the window, it was Mother Gothel who greeted him... with a stab in the back!

"If you want me to let you sing to heal him," she told Rapunzel. "You must swear to come and live with me in the tower forever. If not, I will leave you gagged and so much the worse for him!"

The young girl promised to do whatever Mother Gothel wanted in order to save Flynn. But Flynn didn't want Rapunzel to sacrifice herself for him. So, as she wouldn't listen to him, he picked up a piece of glass from a mirror that had been broken in the struggle and he cut off Rapunzel's long hair!

Immediately the beautiful shine of Rapunzel's hair faded away, and the golden colour turned to brown. With a roaring yell Mother Gothel began to grow older and older... until she disappeared in pile of dust!

"Rapunzel, you were my new dream," declared the dying Flynn.

Sobbing, Rapunzel tried to sing, but her hair had lost all of its magical power. But suddenly, one of her tears fell onto Flynn's face and began to glow! As they watched, Flynn's wound miraculously healed. There was a drop of magic left inside Rapunzel after all!

Overwhelmed with happiness, the two finally exchanged their first kiss. Then, Flynn didn't waste a moment in taking Rapunzel to the castle, where the King and Queen were overcome with emotion. What joy – their beloved daughter had come home, and their family was reunited at last!

In every corner of the kingdom, the jubilant people celebrated the return of their Princess. They celebrated by launching thousands of lanterns into the sky. Those same lanterns that had helped Rapunzel find her way home.

Cinderella

The Perfect Gifts

The holidays had always been Cinderella's favourite time of the year. Even when she lived in a cold attic room in a house with two mean stepsisters and one truly evil stepmother, Cinderella had loved the cheer and good feeling of the season. She had cooked delicious holiday treats and made small decorations. And she had always managed to set aside time to make some small presents for her mouse friends.

Now that she lived in a beautiful castle, Cinderella found that she enjoyed the holidays even more. She decorated the castle, planned an elaborate holiday menu with the cook, and even threw a holiday ball. But this year Cinderella wanted to give especially wonderful gifts to her mouse friends, who had helped her so much.

First, Cinderella went to the royal kitchen. "My mouse friends like cheese," she told the cook. "Could you make some cheese pudding?" The cook assured her that the cheese pudding would be the best in the world.

Then Cinderella went to the royal tailor. "My mouse friends are each about three inches high. I don't know what size that makes them – maybe extra-extra-extra-extra small," she said. She told him their favourite colours, and he helped her pick out rich, beautiful fabrics. "I will make mouse outfits the likes of which have never

been seen," he said, rubbing his hands together.

Finally, Cinderella went to the royal carpenter. "My mouse friends haven't got any nice furniture. Can you help me?" she asked. The carpenter said he would gladly make tiny beds and chairs and tables for the mice.

The next day, as Cinderella and Prince Charming were having tea, the cook, the carpenter and the tailor arrived to deliver the presents for Cinderella's mouse friends. Cinderella thanked them and sent them each on their way with a kind word. Then she and Prince Charming looked at the gifts for the mice. The pudding was a beautiful colour, the clothes were artfully sewn and the tiny furniture was grand and elegant. But none of it seemed quite right for Cinderella's mouse friends.

"I don't understand," Cinderella said sadly. "The cook and the tailor and the carpenter are the best in all the land. So why don't I like what they made?"

"Well," answered Prince Charming, "You know your mouse friends better than anyone else. Maybe *you* should make their presents."

"You know, that's a wonderful idea." Cinderella was delighted. "I'm going to make my friends the nicest gifts they have ever received."

And she did.

Disney
Winnie the Pooh

Happy Christmas Pooh!

Just a few more hours to go until Christmas! Outside, big snowflakes were falling. Inside it was warm and cosy. Everything seemed ready, but Pooh wasn't satisfied. He was thinking about what he might have forgotten, when there was a knock at the door.

When he opened it, he found himself face to face... with a snowman!

The snowman's voice seemed strangely familiar to Pooh. The creature stood in front of the fire and began to melt....

Then Pooh discovered with surprise that it was his friend Piglet! He had been covered in snow on his walk to Pooh's house.

That was when Pooh realised he had forgotten to get presents for his friends! Piglet seemed a little disappointed, then he went back home to wrap his Christmas presents.

Pooh watched him heading off in the snow. Though Pooh didn't know how to sort out his mistake, he knew someone who would....

Pooh arrived with frozen paws at the house of his friend Christopher Robin. The little boy happily invited him in.

Pooh saw the stockings hanging on the fireplace and, intrigued, asked him, "Are you drying them?"

"No, Pooh... Father Christmas will leave his presents there," the little boy explained.

"Oh! My presents, that's right... I forgot them!" exclaimed Pooh. "And I don't have any stockings either!"

But Christopher Robin was a good friend – he gave Pooh a stocking for each of his friends in the Hundred Acre Wood.

Pooh hurried off to put the stockings outside of his friends' homes, with a little note saying "From Pooh".

When the bear arrived home, he was exhausted. He settled down in his armchair in front of the fire. He was pleased his friends now had stockings, but he still didn't know what he could give them himself. He closed his eyes and fell asleep.

The next morning, Pooh was woken by his friends. Oh no! He still didn't have any presents for them!

Pooh invited his friends in and was preparing to apologize to them... but they all started thanking him!

Each of them had found a special use for the stocking Pooh had left at their house: a vegetable holder for Rabbit, a stone pouch for Gopher, a warm layer for Eeyore and a hat for Piglet. Pooh was happy – he had realized that Christmas really was magical! Happy Christmas, Pooh!

Disney
Mickey's
Christmas Carol

A Merry Christmas

"Merry Christmas!" Ebenezer Scrooge crowed as he watched the Cratchit children open the gifts he'd brought.

"A teddy bear!" Tiny Tim exclaimed. His sister had a new doll, and his brother was busy playing with a new train set.

"And there's another present too," Scrooge said with a twinkle in his eye. "I'll be right back." A moment later, he reappeared, carrying a big package wrapped in red paper and tied with a giant green bow.

The children ripped off the paper and squealed in delight.

"Father, it's a sledge!" they cheered.

"I can see that," Bob Cratchit replied, looking up from the turkey he was carving. Scrooge had brought the turkey over that very morning.

"Can we go sledging? Can we? Can we?" the children chorused.

"Of course," Cratchit replied. "But not until after dinner."

"And dinner is ready right now," Mrs Cratchit said.

"Dinner!" the children shouted as they scrambled to their seats at the table.

Mrs Cratchit sat down at the table. "I can't remember when we've had such a feast, Mr Scrooge," she said happily. "Thank you."

Scrooge raised his glass in the air. "That's what Christmas is all about," he said warmly. "Happiness and goodwill."

Everyone clinked glasses, then got busy eating.

"Now, how about that sledging?" Mr Cratchit said when they had eaten.

Minutes later, everyone was wrapped up. Scrooge pulled the children all through town, singing Christmas carols at the top of his lungs.

"Why is everyone staring at Mr Scrooge?" Tiny Tim whispered to his father.

Mr Cratchit smiled down at his son. "Because they like him," he said.

"I like him too," Tiny Tim said, as Scrooge pulled the sledge to the top of a hill. Everyone climbed off to look at the steep slope.

Scrooge picked up the sledge and walked several paces away from the top of the hill. Then, taking a running start, he jumped onto the sledge and raced to the bottom.

"Whoopeeee!" he cried.

Then Scrooge pulled the sledge back up the hill. "Who's next?" he asked, panting.

"Me!" Tiny Tim shouted. Everyone else got a few turns too.

Later, as he pulled the children back to their house, Scrooge felt warm despite the chill in the air. This was the merriest Christmas he could remember.

A Winter's Tale

One bright, sunny January day, Winnie the Pooh was trudging through the Hundred-Acre Wood on his way to visit his good friend Piglet. Piglet was ill in bed with the sniffles. Overnight it had snowed heavily, and the woods were blanketed in beautiful, fluffy snow.

"Poor Piglet," Pooh said with a sigh. "What a shame he can't come outside to play in this lovely snow." His boots crunched on for a few more steps, and then the bear of very little brain came up with a perfectly wonderful idea. "I know!" he exclaimed. "I will bring some snow to Piglet!" He scooped up a mittenful of snow and formed a snowball. He dropped it into his pocket, and then he made another, and then another. Soon he had three snowballs in each pocket, and another on top of his head, underneath his hat. He hurried on to Piglet's house. When he was nearly there, he passed Tigger, Rabbit, Roo and Eeyore, heading the other way.

"Hello, Pooh!" called Roo. "Come and build a snowman with us!"

"I'm sorry, but I can't," said Pooh wistfully. "You see, I am bringing some snowballs to Piglet, who is sick in bed with the sniffles." He said goodbye and hurried on his way.

Piglet was indeed not well, but he was very happy to see his friend. "Hello, Booh," he said snuffily. "I'b glad you cabe. *Ah-choo!*"

"Poor Piglet," said Pooh. "I'll make tea." He was just putting the kettle on when a large drop of icy water rolled out from underneath his hat and down his nose. This reminded Pooh of something.

"I brought you a present, Piglet!" he cried, snatching off his hat. But there was nothing there. Puzzled, Pooh ran to his jacket, which he had hung on a hook near the door. There were no snowballs in either of the pockets! But there was a sizeable puddle of water on the floor underneath Pooh's coat.

"I don't understand it!" Pooh remarked, scratching his head. "I brought you some snowballs, but they seem to have disappeared."

"Oh d-d-d-dear," Piglet said with a sigh. "Well, thanks for thinkig aboud be. I do wish I could go outside and blay. Could you bull back the curtains so that I can see the snow?"

Pooh hopped up and did what his friend had asked. Both of them gasped when they looked outside.

There, just below Piglet's window, Tigger, Rabbit, Eeyore and Roo had built a beautiful snowman, just for Piglet!

"Oh, friends are wonderbul!" Piglet said happily. "*Ah-choo!*"

New Friends

In South America, Carl was sitting inside his house. He had flown it there with thousands of balloons tied to it. He had promised his wife, Ellie, that he would take her to Paradise Falls one day, but sadly she had passed away. Carl kept his promise but he felt sad. That is, until he looked through Ellie's adventure book. It was full of pictures of their life together. Carl had realized their life had been the true adventure.

A boy named Russell had accidentally come along for the ride. They'd met a strange, big bird called Kevin and a talking dog named Dug. A pack of dogs were trying to catch Kevin. Their leader, the explorer Charles Muntz, wanted to capture the bird. Russell was angry at Carl. Carl had promised to protect Kevin, but he had let the bird go in order to save his house from a fire.

Suddenly, Carl heard something. He hurried outside and saw Russell gripping a bunch of balloons. "I'm gonna help Kevin, even if you won't!" Russell cried.

"No!" Carl shouted. He had to help Russell, but the house wouldn't move. The balloons had lost too much air. He had an idea. He began throwing things out of the house to make it lighter. Carl realized he didn't need the things – Russell was more important!

Carl was on his way, but then he heard a knock at the door. It was Dug. Together they set out to rescue Russell. Then they saw the boy being lowered out of Charles' airship! Carl grabbed the garden hose and, using it like a rope, he swung over to the airship and saved Russell.

Once Russell was safe, Carl and Dug went back for Kevin. They set the bird free, but suddenly Muntz appeared with a sword! Carl fought him and finally escaped. He made it back to the house when *BANG!* The balloons began to pop.

The house plunged downwards and landed on top of Charles' airship. As Carl fell out of the house, Muntz ran inside to grab Kevin. Carl knew he had to save his friends – the house was about to fall off the edge of the airship. Carl told Russell and Dug to hold onto Kevin, then he waved a big bar of chocolate – Kevin loved chocolate. The big bird jumped onto the airship, saving Russell and Dug at the same time. Muntz's foot got caught in some balloons, and he drifted away.

"Sorry about your house," Russell told Carl as they watched it disappear into the clouds.

"You know," said Carl, "it's just a house."

It didn't seem as important to him, now that he had friends. They climbed aboard the airship – it was time to go home.

The Cosiest Carriage

One day O'Malley took Duchess and her kittens down to the junkyard to visit O'Malley's old and dear friend, Scat Cat.

Scat Cat lived in a broken-down carriage that had once been very grand indeed. But the wheels had fallen apart long ago, and the cushions were shredded.

To top it all off, there was an huge hole right in the middle of the worn, tattered roof.

Still, as far as Scat Cat was concerned, his home was perfect. "I feel free here," he told the kittens. "I can come and go as I please. And when I stretch out on the cushions at night, I look up and there are the stars, a-twinklin' and a-winkin' back at me!"

The kittens had a grand time playing with Scat Cat in the junkyard. But they were glad to return to the soft pillows, cosy blankets and warm milk waiting for them back at Madame Bonfamille's mansion.

But a few days later, who should appear at Madame's doorstep but Scat Cat himself. "You'll never believe it," he said. "I went into town to stretch my legs, and when I got back... poof! The carriage was gone!"

"Well, naturally," said Duchess, "you will have to stay with us! I'm sure Madame would be delighted to have you as our guest."

But after only one night, Scat Cat began to feel sad. Everything at Madame Bonfamille's happened according to a schedule. Scat Cat missed doing as he pleased.

"But you know what I miss most?" Scat Cat told O'Malley and the kittens. "My old carriage. What I wouldn't give to be able to look up at the sky and count the twinklin' stars..."

The kittens decided to help Scat Cat. For a while, Madame had been complaining about her old carriage. So, Berlioz climbed into it and began clawing at the old cushions. Toulouse and Marie joined him, and soon, the cushions looked just like the ones in Scat Cat's old carriage!

Finally, Toulouse came crashing down through the carriage roof, making a huge hole. "Oh, my!" exclaimed a voice. The kittens turned, and there was Madame. She surveyed the damage... and smiled! "At last I have an excuse to buy a new carriage," she said. "Let's take this one out to the junkyard at once."

"I don't believe it!" cried Scat Cat, when the kittens led him to his new home, back in the junkyard. "It's purr-fect! How can I ever thank you?" he asked the kittens.

"It was our pleasure," said Berlioz. He flexed his claws. "It's not every day we're thanked for clawing something to pieces!"

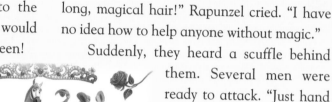

Tangled

Rapunzel and the Crown Jewels

Freed from her tower and Mother Gothel, Rapunzel was travelling back to the kingdom with her friends. Soon she would meet her true parents, the King and Queen!

"I can't believe I'm the lost princess," said Rapunzel.

"You'll be great as a princess," Flynn said. "All you have to do is wear a huge, heavy crown..." he joked.

"Oh, my!" Rapunzel exclaimed.

"Let me start over," Flynn said, feeling bad. "Do you remember that tiara from my satchel? Well, let me tell you a story."

"When I was a kid in the orphanage, I read a book that said a tiara symbolized everything the princess should be."

"White crystals stood for an adventurous spirit; green represented kindness; red stood for courage; and the golden crown stood for leadership. For years I thought of that tiara, and then, I actually met a gal who could wear it. She certainly was adventurous. She also showed kindness, courage and leadership!"

"Flynn, are you talking about... ?" Rapunzel started.

"You!" Flynn exclaimed. "I'm talking about all those amazing things you did when you went in search of the floating lights."

"But I did all those things when I had long, magical hair!" Rapunzel cried. "I have no idea how to help anyone without magic."

Suddenly, they heard a scuffle behind them. Several men were ready to attack. "Just hand over your horse!"

"Rapunzel!" Flynn shouted. "Run away!"

But Rapunzel did not run away. She ran right in to rescue Maximus. When it was over, Rapunzel scolded the bandits.

"It's all my fault," one man replied. "I need your horse to take my son to the doctor."

"Oh, my! Where is he?" Rapunzel asked.

Within minutes, Rapunzel was tending to the boy's injuries. He smiled as he was hoisted onto Maximus for a ride to the kingdom's doctor.

"How can you ever forgive us?" the men asked Rapunzel.

Rapunzel thought of the tiara – adventure, kindness, courage and leadership. Suddenly, she realized she didn't need her magical hair. "Come with me," she said.

At the kingdom, Rapunzel received her princess crown. But as she waved to the crowds, she knew that no one was as supportive as her faithful new friends! And they always would be, too.

the Fox and the Hound

Tod's Homecoming

Tod the fox wanted to show his fox friend Vixey where he grew up. He took her to the top of a hill where they could look down on a beautiful valley.

"I grew up on Widow Tweed's farm," said Tod, pointing with his paw at a farm nestled in the valley. "She took care of me when I was just a cub.

"And that's my best friend Copper," Tod said, pointing to a handsome hound. "Copper lives at Amos Slade's farm. His house is right next door to Mrs Tweed's."

As the two foxes watched, Widow Tweed, Amos Slade, and Amos's cranky old dog, Chief, climbed into an old banger. With a puff of smoke, they drove off.

But Copper was still at home. He was near the fence, snoozing under an old barrel.

"Let's go visit Copper," said Tod.

"Not me!" Vixey declared. "I'm a fox, and I'm not fond of hounds. I'll catch some fish for our dinner. See you later."

Alone, Tod scampered down the hill, excited about seeing his old pal. But, when he got there, he spotted a strange man sneaking into Amos Slade's henhouse.

"Wake up, Copper!" yelled Tod. "A chicken thief is raiding the henhouse!"

Copper woke with a start and leaped into action. But the rope around his neck held him back.

"You'll have to stop that chicken thief yourself!" cried Copper.

"But I can't stop him alone!" Tod replied.

"We'll help," someone chirped. Tod looked up and saw Dinky the Sparrow and Boomer the Woodpecker sitting on the fence.

"Let's go!" said Tod.

Tod burst into the henhouse first. The thief was there, holding a squawking chicken in either hand.

Tod bit the man in the ankle.

"Ouch!" howled the thief.

Boomer flew through the window and pecked at the chicken snatcher's head. The thief dropped the chickens and covered his head.

Meanwhile, Dinky untied the knot that held Copper. Now, Copper was free – and angry too! Barking, he charged at the burglar.

Eggs flying, the chicken snatcher screamed and ran. As he raced down the road, Dinky and Boomer flitted around his head, pecking him until he was out of sight. The fox and the hound trotted back to the farm.

"Good to see you, Tod," said Copper, wagging his tail. "What brings you here?"

"I just stopped by for a quiet visit," Tod replied.

"It was real quiet, all right!" said Copper.

Countdown to Midnight!

"No sleep till midnight!" Lilo and Stitch chanted, bouncing up and down on Lilo's bed. It was New Year's Eve, and Nani had agreed to let them stay up late.

"Okay, okay." Nani held her hands out. "It's only five o'clock now. Don't wear yourselves out. You still have seven hours until the new year."

Lilo and Stitch looked at each other. Wear themselves out? Impossible! "Look, Stitch," Lilo said, looking as serious as possible. "We only have seven hours. What do you want to do first?"

"Surfing!" Stitch cried.

"Sunset surfing it is!" Lilo gave the little alien a high five before turning to Nani. "Okay?" she asked sweetly.

Nani shook her head again. I must be nuts, she thought. "I'll go get my suit." She sighed.

The three surfed until sundown. Then they headed for home.

"So, what's next?" Lilo asked Stitch.

Stitch smacked his lips. "Dinner!"

"Don't worry," Lilo said. "We'll cook."

"And I'll clean," Nani muttered.

When they got home, Nani lay down on the couch with her arm over her eyes. Five hours until bedtime. She switched on the TV and tried to ignore the crashing noises coming from the kitchen.

"Ta-da!" Lilo emerged with a huge plate of something steaming and cheesy.

"What is it?" Nani asked cautiously.

"Pizza, Stitch-style!" Lilo said. "With anchovies, peanut butter and fruit cocktail!"

Nani cringed. "Don't worry, Nani," said Lilo. "We left the toothpaste on the side this time. Plus, there's a milkshake for dessert!"

The three ate the gooey mess while Lilo and Stitch discussed what was next.

"How about that milkshake?" Nani suggested before Lilo could come up with a noisier, messier or more dangerous idea.

Stitch grabbed the blender and dumped the milkshake on his head. Nani shooed the two into the living room and began to tackle the mess in the kitchen.

The washing-up took forever. Nani could not figure out how they'd managed to use so many pots and pans. She was still elbow deep in suds when her eyes grew wide with alarm. Something was wrong. It was too quiet! Nani rushed into the living room. Lilo and Stitch were sound asleep! Nani looked at her watch.

"Five-four-three-two-one," Nani counted down. "Happy New Year," she said softly, as she covered the pair with a blanket.

She smiled as she looked at the clock. It was only 10pm!